THE ESSENTIAL
DR. JEKYLL
& MR. HYDE

THE ESSENTIAL
DR. JEKYLL
& MR. HYDE

Written and Edited by
Leonard Wolf

Including the Complete Novel by
Robert Louis Stevenson

Illustrations by Michael Lark

A Byron Preiss Book

A PLUME BOOK

Special thanks to Keith R.A. DeCandido, Rosemary Ahern, and Arnold Dolin

This edition reproduces the original texts by Robert Louis Stevenson. Any archaic spellings, uses, and/or language have been left intact to preserve fidelity to those texts.

PLUME

Published by the Penguin Group

Penguin Books USA Inc., 375 Hudson Street,
New York, New York 10014, U.S.A.
Penguin Books Ltd, 27 Wrights Lane,
London W8 5TZ, England
Penguin Books Australia Ltd, Ringwood,
Victoria, Australia
Penguin Books Canada Ltd, 10 Alcorn Avenue,
Toronto, Ontario, Canada M4V 3B2
Penguin Books (N.Z.) Ltd, 182–190 Wairau Road,
Auckland 10, New Zealand

Penguin Books Ltd, Registered Offices:
Harmondsworth, Middlesex, England

First published by Plume, an imprint of Dutton Signet, a division of Penguin Books USA Inc.

First Plume Printing, September, 1995
10 9 8 7 6 5 4 3 2 1

ISBN: 0-452-26969-5

Library of Congress Catalog Number: 95-69252

Printed in the United States of America

Acknowledgments

I owe thanks to a great many people who have helped me in the course of making this book. Let me express here my gratitude to them:

Nancy C. Hanger, who, in addition to providing valuable assistance as my research associate, prepared both the Jekyll-Hyde filmography and the list of theatrical productions, and acted as consulting editor for this volume.

Bryan Fernandez for research help and for the arduous labor required to transcribe my tape-recorded notes.

Claudia Murphy for her research help in the preliminary stages of this work.

Glen Montag, who made the two- and three-dimensional drawings of Henry Jekyll's house that enrich this edition.

The physician Dr. Peter Muz, for his help with Jekyll-Hyde's symptoms.

Movies Unlimited, and particularly Irving Slifkin, its catalog editor, who loaned me VCR copies of Jekyll-Hyde movies when I needed them.

The Robert Louis Stevenson Memorial Museum in Monterey, California, and the Silverado Museum in St. Helena, California.

The good people at Henry Holt and Company who sent me Ian Bell's invaluable *Dreams of Exile: Robert Louis Stevenson; A Biography*, as well as Bell's two-volume edition of Stevenson's *The Complete Short Stories*.

The villagers of Le Monastier, France, who continue to cherish Stevenson's name as well as that of Modestine, the donkey with whom he made his famous *Travels with a Donkey*.

As always, I owe a great deal to the librarians in whose libraries I have worked. I want to thank particularly the Beineke Library at Yale University for providing me with a copy of the first edition of *The Strange Case of Dr. Jekyll and Mr. Hyde*. I am grateful, too, to Lois Rebecca Markiewicz at the Kutztown University Library, and the anonymous Samaritans at the New York Public Library, the Columbia University Library, and the University of Alabama Library.

Keith R.A. DeCandido, my patient, encouraging, and kind editor at Byron Preiss Visual Publications, as well as Leigh Grossman, Robert Le-Gault, and Alex Gadd.

Finally, I must add a word of thanks to the Virginia Center for the Creative Arts in Sweet Briar, Virginia, and to William Smart, its director, for providing safe haven, disciplined time, and "leisure to grow wise" to artists and writers from all over the world.

Introduction

Now, I deny that love is a strong passion. Fear is a strong passion; it is with fear that you must trifle, if you wish to taste the intensest joys of living . . . ("The Suicide Club," in *The New Arabian Nights*, in Stevenson, R.L., *The Works*, Vol. 3, p. 23).

> Away with funeral music—
> Set the pipe to powerful lips—
> The cup of life's for him that drinks
> And not for him that sips.

What fun we could have if we were all well. What work we could do, what a happy place we could make it for each other! If I were able to do what I want; but then I am not, and may leave that vein.

Sooner or later, at a film festival, a TV rerun, or in the living room of a friend watching a VCR, we will see a film version of *The Strange Case of Dr. Jekyll and Mr. Hyde*. Curiously enough, even if it is for the first time, the experience will not be new because the story of Jekyll and Hyde has, like those of Dracula and Frankenstein, entered so deeply into our consciousness that, whether we have seen the films or read the books on which they are based, we seem always to have known them. Though they were all born in the nineteenth century, they have, with the advent of movies, become part of our twentieth-century iconography—instantly recognizable images representing psychological states of being.

With Jekyll and Hyde, however, the gap between the print and the film version of the story is even wider than we usually find in film adaptations, because the film industry, in every version of the story from 1920 to the present, has made Jekyll-Hyde's involvement with women an essential part of his image. As first-time readers of the story discover, in Stevenson's 1886 narrative such women characters as do appear have little or nothing to do with the plot. The book is absolutely and only about men.

A quick backward look at some of the more exemplary Jekyll-Hyde films will make the point. In the 1920 silent film, John Barrymore gave a twitching, highly romantic performance of Jekyll-Hyde. His Jekyll is a vaguely Dickensian caricature of Hamlet, while his Hyde, a leering cross between Richard III and Rumpelstiltskin, stumps about doing evil gladly. In 1932, there was Fredric March, whose Jekyll, except when he is under the control of his elixir, is a devoted healer of the poor. As Hyde, he becomes a hoarsely chuckling under-evolved creature, a troglodyte with an appetite for inflicting pain. In 1941, the divisible doctor was played by Spencer Tracy, who, wanting to rely on his own talents in the transformation scene, eschewed the help of the studio's special effects team, with the result that, when Somerset Maugham visited the set, he was perplexed to know whether Tracy, at that moment, was playing Jekyll or Hyde. Finally, there was Jack Palance in a 1968 made-for-TV production. Palance, whose face and undisguisable American manner were constantly at war with the top-hat-and-tails British gentility that seems to be as much a part of Jekyll-Hyde movies as the transformation scene, did his earnest best to convey the moral struggle his character was supposed to be undergoing. One's chief memory of that film, however, is the number of scenes in which window glass, glassware, or bottles are broken.

But in every one of those films, and in scores of others, the Jekyll-Hyde character is involved, for good or ill, with women. Not only that, Jekyll is invariably paired with a "good" woman—that is, a respectable, marriageable woman—while the Hyde figure, exemplifying sexual license, is given a fallen or loose woman to torment. The implicit sexual equation is clear: Jekyll is good, which means he is repressed, while Hyde is evil, and therefore licentious. As Fredric March's Hyde exults after his first transformation, to be Hyde means to be "Free! Free at last!"

None of this should be too surprising, since the plots of the films are derived from Thomas R. Sullivan's stage adaptation of Stevenson's story. Sullivan, shrewdly sensing that Stevenson's tale, which focuses on the lives of half a dozen middle-aged unmarried men, would not have sufficient theatrical tension, complicated Stevenson's plot by adding two women— one virginal and respectable, and the other a whore—to make explicit what in Stevenson's story is unacknowledged: that sexual emotion, and particularly sadistic sexual emotion, drives his plot.

What the filmmakers have retained of Stevenson's story is its central conundrum: to have a divided self is the human condition. Beyond that, and again because it makes for such filmable moments, the movies have imposed on his novel a fake-lore of science fiction at which Stevenson hardly hints. This puts the Jekyll-Hyde movies conveniently into the category of mad scientist films, and is very comforting to people who like a place for everything and everything in its place. As a result, filmgoers can take away with them the pious truism that we risk destruction when we permit science to compete with God. Usually that profundity comes to us in the form of "There are some things mankind was not meant to know." It was, undoubtedly, the formula murmured by Prometheus's neighbors on the morning he was staked to the rock in the Caucasus for stealing fire from the gods.

Category making, however, does not work well with *The Strange Case of Dr. Jekyll and Mr. Hyde,* precisely because it is a great work of fiction— which is to say, Stevenson has created a living text in which too much that happens is inexplicable at the same time that the line of action is understandable; that is, what we see is not necessarily what we get. What we see is the story of a man who has found a way to separate his good from his evil self. What we get is a complex moral and psychological allegory capable of moving readers in any number of ways.

Stevenson himself almost made the mistake of telling the story only as an unambiguous horror fiction. Both Fanny Stevenson, his wife, and her son Lloyd Osbourne have left accounts of what happened.

Osbourne first reminds us that *The Strange Case . . .* was written by a "very sick man. He had horrifying hemorrhages; long spells when he was doomed to lie motionless on his bed lest the slightest movement should re-start the flow . . ." (*Dr. Jekyll and Mr. Hyde Fables*, in Stevenson, R.L., *The Works*, Vol. 10, p. xi).

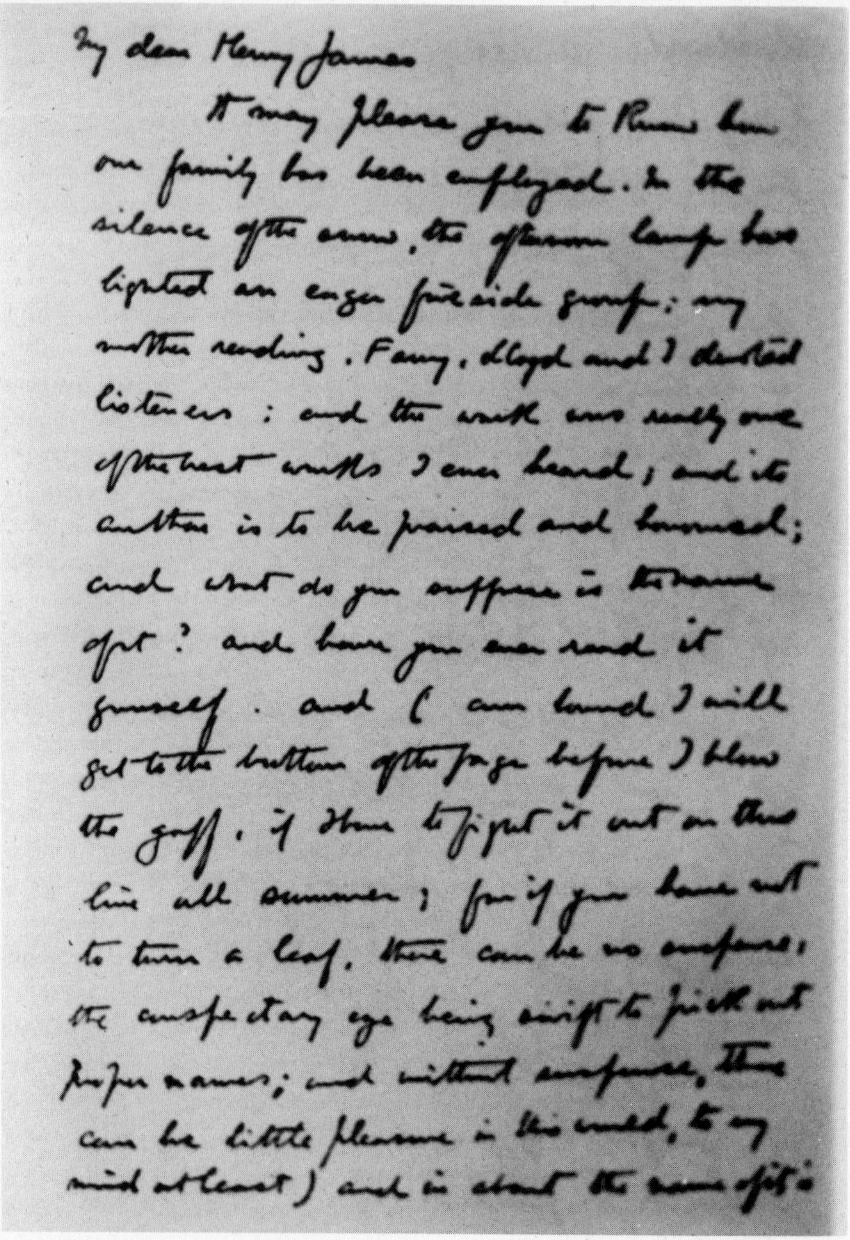

A letter from Stevenson to Henry James

And Fanny Stevenson observes that in 1885, the productive year at Skerryvore, the house in which they lived in Bournemouth, Stevenson, ill though he was, spent a great deal of time with visiting friends. One of them was W.E. Henley, now known, if at all, as the poet who wrote "Invictus," the poem that asserts:

It matters not how strait the gate,
How charged with punishments the scroll,
I am the master of my fate:
I am the captain of my soul.

Stevenson, who had no special feeling for theater, collaborated nevertheless with Henley on several clumsy plays. Henley was not always a friend of Fanny's, and on that account the atmosphere at Skerryvore was sometimes charged. As a result, the sickly Stevenson, one of whose talents was that he could usually drop into a deep sleep at a moment's notice, found himself having restless nights interspersed with horrid dreams. It was from one of these that, when Fanny woke him to still his cries, Stevenson complained that she had waked him just as he "was dreaming a fine bogey tale." That bogey tale, given to him by his unconscious, aspects of which he personalized by calling them his "Brownies," contained the elements of *Jekyll and Hyde*. Not long after that, Stevenson, on going back to his sickroom, announced that he was working on a story and "that he was not to be disturbed even if the house caught fire . . . At the end of three days the mysterious task was finished . . ." (Ibid.).

Fanny Stevenson says that ". . . he was working with feverish activity on the new book. In three days the first draft, containing thirty thousand words was finished . . ." (Ibid., p. xix).

What happened next tells us a great deal about the kind of artist Stevenson was . . . and about Fanny's loyalty and courage. When his three days of driving activity were done, Stevenson came downstairs and, passionately, intensely, read what he had written to Fanny and Lloyd. Lloyd, still a boy, loved what he heard, but Fanny responded only haltingly to the performance. Finally, says Lloyd, "She broke out with criticism. He had missed the point, she said; had missed the allegory; had made it merely a story—a magnificent bit of sensationalism—when it should have been a masterpiece" (Ibid., p. xii).

Not surprisingly, Stevenson was furious. "Never," says Lloyd, "had I seen him so impassioned, so outraged . . ." (Ibid.). There followed a long, interval while the husband, back in his sickroom, and his wife and stepson downstairs lived silently through their emotions. Then Stevenson burst into the room, but not to pour out wrath. Instead, he told Fanny, "You are right! I have absolutely missed the allegory, which, after all, is the whole point of it—the very essence of it" (Ibid.). Having said that, he turned and threw the first draft of *The Strange Case of Dr. Jekyll and Mr. Hyde* into the fire. "Imagine my feelings," writes Lloyd, "my mother's feelings—as we saw it blazing up; as we saw those precious pages wrinkling and blackening and turning into flame" (Ibid.).

It was an amazing gesture, whether of guilt provocation, of anger, of artistic integrity, or of petulance, it is hard to say. But certainly it was as ambiguous as the story he then went back up into his room and rewrote, again in a miraculous three days. That second version, with additions and corrections made over the next six months, became the novel the reader now holds.

It is a curious, but not necessarily a meaningful, coincidence, I think, that three of the nineteenth century's most memorable horror tales are acknowledged by their authors to have been provoked by a dream: Mary Shelley's *Frankenstein* (1816), Stevenson's *The Strange Case of Dr. Jekyll and Mr. Hyde* (1886), and Bram Stoker's *Dracula* (1897). But the dreams merely gave the authors a glimpse of an inchoate shape on the far horizon. The achieved story was the product of an arduous interval in which author sensibility, vision, grasp of form and history, and, finally, hard work, came together.

Though he liked to blame his Brownies for giving him *Jekyll and Hyde*, the extremely literate Stevenson had encountered precursors to his tale long before he put his head to his dream pillow. The fictions most frequently cited as having had an influence on *Jekyll and Hyde* are E.T.A. Hoffman's "The Devil's Elixirs" (1816), Thomas Jefferson Hogg's *The Private Memoirs and Confessions of a Justified Sinner* (1824), Edgar Allan Poe's "William Wilson" (1839), and Théophile Gautier's "Le Chevalier Double" (1840).

Hoffman's "The Devil's Elixirs," like *Jekyll and Hyde*, is a novel in which self-integration is the theme. Its protagonist, Medardus, born of a long line of sinners, is a very close cousin to Matthew Lewis's *The Monk* in the way that Hoffman, like Lewis, exploits sensuality and guilt as a way of intensifying both. Medardus, driven frenziedly and guiltily toward erotic ecstasies, encounters his double in the person of Count Viktorin. Taking advantage of their identical appearance, Medardus gratifies his lust, commits murder, and finally repents, at which point he is absolved by the young Aurelia, whose brother he has stabbed and whose mother he poisoned.

Thomas Jefferson Hogg's *The Private Memoirs and Confessions of a Justified Sinner* is an amazing fiction in which the themes of religious bigotry, the concept of the double, and a surprisingly modern analysis of a disturbed psyche are astutely mixed. The novel's protagonist, Robert Wringhim, has a demonic familiar, Gil Martin, a shape-shifter who, on some occasions, takes the shape of Wringhim himself. Hogg's novel, like Stevenson's, is an allegory, but the moral of *The Private Memoirs* is considerably more blatant than Stevenson's. Hogg tells us that an uncritical belief in the idea that those who have been divinely chosen to be saved cannot possibly do wrong in this life can lead the "elected" to commit monstrous crimes. Though there are scenes in *The Private Memoirs* that are remarkably like some in *Jekyll and Hyde*, Hogg's greatest influence on Stevenson has more to do with form than with content. Both fictions begin, and continue for some time, as third-person narratives, and both end with an explanatory first-person account in the form of a letter.

In Poe's "William Wilson" tale, the profligate young William Wilson has one wicked scheme after another foiled by the appearance, at the climactic moment, of another "William Wilson," who has features identical to himself but whose role is to play the incarnate good angel who nullifies the evil practiced by his wicked other self.

In Gautier's "Le Chevalier Double," we have the story of the young chevalier Oluf, who was born under the influence of a "double star," one aspect of which is as "green as hope" and the other "red as hell"; one favorable, the other disastrous. He was cursed this way because of a widely traveled stranger, a superb singer who carried a gleaming black raven on his shoulder, and whose recitations roused forbidden thoughts in the pregnant, and heretofore innocent, Edwige, the chevalier's mother. In any case, when her son Oluf was born, in the heavens there gleamed the conflicting double star. This explains why Oluf had a double nature and led a tormented life.

In the final scenes of the story, Oluf meets and fights the Knight of the Red Star, his other self, who is "armed in exactly the same way. . . . The only difference was that he wore a red plume on his helmet instead of a green one" (see Appendix B, p. 245). As Oluf wields his sword, he feels its effect on his own body and when, with a furious blow, he strikes his opponent's visor up "It was himself he saw" (Ibid., p. 246).

"Le Chevalier Double" has a happy ending, but Gautier, like Hogg, unwilling for his readers to miss the moral, spells it out: "Young women, never cast your eyes on Bohemian bards who recite intoxicating and diabolical verses. You, young maidens, have faith in no star but the green one. And you, whose misfortune it is to be double, fight bravely though with your own sword you may have to strike at and wound yourself, the interior enemy, the wicked knight" (Ibid., p. 247).

Though Stevenson is said to have asked, "The Chevalier Who?" when Andrew Lang called Gautier's story to his attention, it is hard to take Stevenson's claim of ignorance too seriously. First, we have an 1887 letter of his to Henry James acknowledging that he had seen an essay of James's on Gautier. Second, Stevenson, was from his earliest youth an avid Francophile who lived often in France and spoke and read French fluently. It is unlikely that he would not have known Gautier's *Mademoiselle de Maupin*, that superb novel whose theme is what we nowadays call sex and gender ambiguity.

In Stevenson's own work, one gets intimations of *Jekyll and Hyde* in that bizarre portmanteau fiction "The Suicide Club," which forms part of the loosely linked series of stories he called *The New Arabian Nights* (1882). In "The Suicide Club" we meet a Dr. Noel, who, describing himself, says, "Know, then, although I now make so quiet an appearance—frugal, solitary, addicted to study—when I was younger, my name was once a rallying cry among the most astute and dangerous spirits of London; and while I was outwardly an object for respect and consideration, my true power resided in the most secret, terrible, and criminal relations . . . and I who speak to you, innocent as I appear, was the chieftain of this redoubtable crew" ("The Suicide Club" in *The New Arabian Nights*, in Stevenson R.L., *The Works*, Vol. 3, p. 53). In *Deacon Brodie*, the play he wrote in 1878 in collaboration with W.E. Henley, we have the story of an Edinburgh cabinetmaker who, by day, leads a respectable life, but by night was the leader of a band of burglars.

Aside from the historical facts about Brodie that served Stevenson and Henley, it may be more important to know that there was a cabinet in the Stevenson family home that was reputed to have been made by the famous criminal, and that Stevenson's beloved nurse, Cummie, invented fantastic stories for him in which the piece of furniture played a part.

Robert Louis Stevenson, who died in Samoa in 1894, left as his legacy thirty-two volumes of literary work that included (in the Scribner's South

Seas Edition) novels, short stories, essays, biographies, and, almost best of all, three volumes of his letters. For a man who from the time he was three suffered all of his life from severe and debilitating respiratory illnesses, the sheer quantity of work he got done is astounding. Almost as amazing is the fact that three of his novels and half a dozen of his short stories have become classics. Readers who become acquainted with Stevenson's literary criticism, general essays, and letters will find themselves awed by his wide-ranging curiosity, his travel-writer's sharp eye for landscape and character and, above all, by his supremely balanced and—in the face of so much illness—cheerful view of himself in the world and of the world itself.

David Daiches, knowing that Stevenson is sometimes seen as a popular writer with no great depth to him, puts Stevenson's cheerfulness properly into perspective. He writes: "What looked like optimism was really a wryly pragmatic acceptance of the inexplicable contradictions of life and the inevitability of extinction at death" (Daiches, *Robert Louis Stevenson and His World*, p. xx). What I find admirable is the way that Stevenson, who frequently had to stare death in the face, did not waste his time thinking about the old reaper more than he had to and decided instead to get on with life. Writing to William Archer, Stevenson said,

I should bear false witness if I did not declare life happy . . . To have suffered, nay to suffer, sets a keen edge of what remains of the agreeable. This is a great truth, and has to be learned in the fire . . . the blood on my handkerchiefs are accidents; they do not color my view of life, as you would know, I think, if you had experienced a sickness; they do not exist in my prospect; I would as soon have dragged them under the eyes of my readers as I would mention a pimple I might chance to have (saving your presence) on my posteriors. What does it prove? What does it change? It has not hurt, it has not changed me in any essential part; and I should think myself a trifler and in bad taste if I introduced the world to these unimportant privacies ("The Letters," in Stevenson, R.L. *The Works*, Vol. 2, p. 269).

It is an admirable stoicism which did not keep him from expressing, either in his work or in his letters, his occasional sharp perception, especially in *Jekyll and Hyde*, *The Weir of Hermiston*, and several of his best short stories, that to be human in our world sometimes can require us to walk through dark and dangerous ways.

Stevenson was born on November 13, 1850, in Edinburgh, Scotland, at Number 8, Howard Place, the son of Thomas Stevenson, a lighthouse engineer whose father and grandfather were also lighthouse engineers. It was a prosperous, solid, middle-class Scottish family. His mother, Margaret Stevenson, was the youngest of thirteen children. She was twenty-one when she gave birth to Robert, two years after her marriage. The influence of his mother on Stevenson's life is harder for me to gauge than the more obvious impact on him of his father's mind and will. We have a clue to Margaret's role, however, in a letter that Fanny, Stevenson's wife, wrote to Margaret. "I think," says Fanny, "it must be very sweet to you to have this grown up man of thirty still clinging to you with his child's love."

From boyhood until he was in his middle thirties, Robert Louis was literally dependent on his father. As young Stevenson grew toward manhood, he and his father were at loggerheads over his drifting away from the rigid Scots Presbyterianism that his father espoused. But one thing is clear: Thomas, the father, always cared for his son. When the child was ill, it was Thomas who used to stay up nights to tell him stories to while away the fretful hours. And always, except for one brief lapse, the father continued to support his grown son financially.

Given the religious atmosphere in the family home, one is not entirely surprised to learn that Stevenson's favorite employment as a small boy was the building of toy churches, nor that, when he was three, he is supposed to have said, "See, mother, I have drawed a man. Shall I draw his soul now?" ("Memoirs of Himself," in *Memories and Portraits*, in Stevenson, R.L., *The Works*, Vol. 20, p. 281).

When he was six years old, he dictated a "History of Moses" to his mother, and later a work called the "The Book of Joseph," which he grandly described as "by RLS, the author of a History of Moses."

An influence more powerful on Robert Louis's developing mind and character than his father and mother was undoubtedly that of his nursemaid, Allison Cunningham, whom he called Cummie. Cummie, the fiercest of Covenanters, thought card playing, theaters, and novels were wicked. At the same time, she had her own very vivid sense of language, which she expressed in dramatic readings of Bible texts and especially of *Pilgrim's Progress*, a book that left a deep imprint on the child's imagination. Stevenson, conscious of his debt to her, dedicated *A Child's Garden of Verses* to Cummie. Even as an adult, he continued to send her affectionate letters. "Do not suppose," he said in one of them, "that I shall ever forget those long, bitter nights, when I coughed and coughed and was so unhappy, and you were so patient and loving of the poor sick child. . . . Indeed, I wish I might become a man worth talking of, if it were only that you should not have thrown away your pains" ("The Letters," in Stevenson, R.L., *The Works*, Vol. 1, p. 53).

Ian Bell, in his recent biography of Stevenson, *Dreams of Exile*, adds, "Just as important . . . she gave him a link with the Scots tongue, which was then dying out in the better parts of the city [Edinburgh]" (Bell, p. 26). Bell also makes the astute point that the darling Cummie "might also be accused of having fed the vulnerable, hyperactive imagination of a child prone to nightmares . . . [and] that the nurse was culpable in peopling his terrifying dreams" (Ibid.).

The boy's imagination was nurtured, too, by a series of books called Skelt's *Juvenile Drama*. In the essay "A Penny Plain and Twopence Colored," Stevenson described the theatrical plots that accompanied the books. He tells us that these little books, out of which toy theaters could be constructed, were richly stocked with swords, guns, bandits, pirates, ships at sea, and gypsy-looking dancers—the whole panoply of the sorts of things that move a child.

From the time that Stevenson was two until the age of eleven, he was frequently ill with considerably more than the usual childhood diseases, and as a result had his education frequently interrupted. He was sent for a while to a preparatory school at Canon Mills, but was withdrawn for health reasons. For a time he studied at a day school called The Edinburgh Academy, one of whose founders was Sir Walter Scott. Later, he was sent to a boarding school at Spring Grove, Isleworth, Middlesex, where he was unhappy. Not surprisingly, he became a shy, quiet boy, used to solitude and the sense of himself as living inside a not very reliable body; a boy, too, who was used to trips abroad (especially to France) because of the real or fancied illnesses of his parents.

He grew, nevertheless, into a gangly adolescent who thought of himself as ugly. One of his friends, H.B. Baildon, a fellow pupil, did not exactly disagree with him. Baildon writes:

In body, he was assuredly badly set up. His limbs were long, lean, and spidery, and his chest flat, so as almost to suggest some malnutrition, such sharp corners did his joints make under his clothes. But in his face this was belied. His brow was oval and full, over soft brown eyes that seemed already to have drunk the sunlight under Southern vines. The whole face had a tendency to an oval Madonna-like type. But about the mouth and in the mirthful mocking light of the eyes there lingered ever a ready Autolycus roguery that rather suggested slyly Hermes masquerading as a mortal. . . .

about the mouth there was something a little tricksy and mocking. . . . (Balfour, p. 74).

Stevenson was sixteen when he enrolled at Edinburgh University, ostensibly to study engineering so that he could take his place in the family business. The university turned out to be a fine training ground for the young writer-to-be. He joined the university's Conservative Club and was elected to the Speculative Society. Constrained by a small allowance to low-cost pleasures, he discovered roistering, practical jokes, low life, and atheism. "Twelve pounds a year was my allowance. . . ." he tells us, "hence my acquaintance was of what would be called a very low order. . . I was the companion of seamen, chimney sweeps, and thieves. . . ." And prostitutes, one must add. The companions of what David Daiches has called his "programmatic fornications"—prostitutes with whom, apparently, he was a great favorite and who called him affectionately Velvet Coat.

This was the period of youthful friendships—with Walter Simpson, whose father was the discoverer of chloroform; with James Walter Kerrier, who died early; with his cousin Bob Stevenson, the painter, and with his sister Katharine (later Katharine de Mattos); and with Charles Baxter, a lawyer who was to be a lifelong friend and Stevenson's financial manager.

All this while, the quarrels about religion between Stevenson and his father intensified. The pious Thomas felt betrayed by his son's atheism. Out of a full heart, he spewed scalding guilt at him:

I have worked for you and gone out of my way for you—and the end of it is that I find you in opposition to the Lord Jesus Christ. . . . I would ten times sooner see you lying in your grave than that you should be shaking the faith of other young men and bringing ruin on other houses as you have brought it upon this (Daiches, op. cit., p. 27).

Thomas's language was violent, but his feelings were mixed. "Soon," writes Ian Bell, "father and son began gingerly to resume their walks together, with Louis striving to say nothing that would reopen wounds (Bell, p. 76). On April 8, 1871, Stevenson informed his father that he was giving up his engineering studies. Though Thomas Stevenson was disappointed, he was to some degree mollified when his son offered to read for law so that he could be called to the Scottish bar. Then, in November 1873, as a consequence of Thomas Stevenson's chance meeting on a train with Scotland's chief law officer, Edward Strathearn Gordon, the idea was broached that Robert Louis would go to London to study for the English bar. Stevenson, eager to put distance between himself and his father, was happy to make the move. When he arrived in London, however, his health broke down. Dr. Andrew Clarke, a uniquely insightful physician, prescribed southern France and added the proviso that Stevenson must go alone—without his parents.

By this time, Stevenson had already met and been smitten by Mrs. Fanny Sitwell, who was twelve years his senior. She was a beautiful woman in "reduced circumstances," who lived separated from a husband who may have had a drinking problem, and who supported herself by doing literary translations. She was a woman gifted with a double talent: she inspired passion in younger men at the same time as she kept them skillfully at a proper Victorian distance from the object of their desire.

Young Stevenson, when he wrote about Robert Burns, had the wisdom to know that

> it is hardly safe for a man and woman in the flower of their years to write almost daily, and sometimes in terms almost too ambiguous, sometimes in terms too plain, and generally in terms too warm, for mere acquaintance. ("Some Aspects of Robert Burns," in *Familiar Studies*, in Stevenson, R.L., *The Works*, Vol. 5, p. 61).

However, besotted by love—and by language—he continued for some years to pour out his heart to Fanny in precisely the sort of terms he warned against in his essay on Burns.

Having arrived in France, Stevenson took up residence at Menton on the French Riviera, a favorite recuperation spot for the British. There, in the Hôtel du Pavillon, though his health did not improve at once, he continued an apprenticeship to the craft of writing that he had begun in Scotland by imitating one by one the works of authors whose style intrigued him: "That, like it or not is the way to learn to write; whether I have profited or not, that is the way. It was so Keats learned, and there was never a finer temperament for literature than Keats . . ." (Balfour, p. 120).

At Christmastime in 1873, when his friend Sydney Colvin visited him, he moved to the Hôtel Mirabeau, where he was involved with a couple of sprightly Russian sisters, one the Princess Zassetsky, the other Madame Garschine. Each of the sisters had a child. With the younger of the Russian children, Nelitschka, "a little polyglot button" of only two and a half, who spoke six languages, or fragments of them, Stevenson fell in love as, it is possible, he did with Madame Garschine, whose behavior toward him sorely puzzled him. Writing to Mrs. Sitwell, he says,

> I don't know what Mme. Garschine's little game is with regard to me. Certainly she has either made up her mind to make a fool of me in a somewhat coarse manner, or else she is in train to make a fool of herself . . . I wish you were here to tell me which it is . . . ("The Letters," in Stevenson, R.L., *The Works*, Vol 1, p. 145).

Given his feelings for Mrs. Sitwell, she would seem to be an unsuitable target for that letter, but we are beginning to see how Stevenson could be unconscious of his need to be the focus of a number of women's eyes. There is, for example, a certain amount of preening as he reports Princess Zassetsky's assessment of him: "Monsieur is a young man whom I do not understand. He is not wicked, I know that, but beyond that—shadows, shadows, shadows, nothing but shadows" (Ibid., p. 146).

Meanwhile, Stevenson's self-deception did not interfere with his industry. Both in France, then back in Scotland in the following spring when he resumed his law studies, he kept at his writing, turning out essays for publication. In Edinburgh, too, he met W.E. Henley, the lame poet who was to prove a complex and problematic friend.

In 1875, Stevenson passed the Edinburgh bar and hung out his shingle, though there is no evidence that beyond a couple of briefs he ever actually practiced law. It did not matter. He had made his gesture to his father by passing the bar, and his father acknowledged it with a gift of a thousand pounds, a great deal of money when two hundred pounds a year could feed a family. Now Stevenson could turn his attention fully to a life of literature.

That same year, he went back to France, again for his health's sake. With his cousin Bob, he lived for a while in Fontainebleau, where the so-called Barbizon School of painters had been active. It was, David Daiches writes, "a good life, dining and talking with artists, wandering in the forest, planning essays and stories" (Daiches, op. cit., p. 42).

It was, one needs to say, a masculine good life. When Stevenson, having completed the canoe voyage that resulted in his first little book, *The Inland Voyage*, came back to the Fontainebleau colony in 1876 and learned that women had somehow infiltrated the group living in an annex of the hotel at nearby Grez, he had to take thought about what to do. First, cousin Bob went off to investigate, but he fell victim to the charms of the women and did not come back. Then Walter Simpson, with whom Stevenson had

W.E. Henley, Stevenson's friend and sometime collaborator

made the inland voyage, went but did not return. Finally, Stevenson set off on a rescue mission.

The female intruders were Fanny Osbourne, a thirty-five-year-old American woman, and her seventeen-year-old daughter Isobel. Fanny, separated from her philandering husband in San Francisco, had come to Paris with her daughter, her eight-year-old son, Lloyd, and her five-year-old son, Hervey, to study art. There, Hervey was taken ill and died. The death so broke the mother's health that a Parisian doctor advised a change of place, preferably to the country. And this is why the two women and Lloyd were in Grez.

We have Lloyd Osbourne's romantic version of the meeting with Stevenson:

> Then in the dusk of a summer's day as we all sat at dinner about the long table d'hôte, some sixteen or eighteen people, of whom my mother and sister were the only women and I the only child, there was a startling sound at one of the open windows giving on the street, and in vaulted a young man with a dusty knapsack on his back. The whole company rose in an uproar of delight, mobbing the newcomer (*The Inland Voyage*, in Stevenson, R.L., *The Works*, Vol. 1, p. xii).

Nellie Van de Grift Sanchez, Fanny Stevenson's biographer, wants us to think that Stevenson, coming through the window of the hotel, was so struck by the vision of Fanny in the lamplight that he fell in love with her on the spot. The matter was probably not that simple. For instance, if Fanny was interested in anyone, it was Robert A. Stevenson, not Robert Louis. As for Robert Louis, a few days after that meeting in Grez he went back to Edinburgh. In September, however, he was back at Grez where, little by little, there was an awareness between himself and Fanny and, very soon, there was passion. J.C. Furnas says that the two became lovers in 1877. David Daiches says unequivocally that "Louis and Fanny had been sleeping together in Paris and neither seemed reluctant to let his friends know of their relationship" (Daiches, op. cit., p. 42). By January 1878, the affair was anything but a secret. Even Stevenson's parents knew that their son was involved with a married American woman who was ten years his senior.

Meanwhile, Fanny was still the wife of Samuel Osbourne, a San Francisco court reporter, and it was still the nineteenth century, when complications such as these were even more complicated. Perhaps to seek a divorce

Fanny Van de Grift Stevenson

from Samuel Osbourne, or perhaps, as no one has seemed willing to suggest, to put some space between herself and Stevenson and the uncertainties of her life with him, Fanny returned to the States in August 1878, leaving Stevenson devastated.

Fanny was born Fanny Van de Grift in Indianapolis at a time when the city streets still had no names and when little girls

> wore pantalets, to our ankles, and our dresses were whale-boned down the front, with very long bodices. We had wide flat hats trimmed with wreaths of roses and tied under our chins. We wore low necks and short sleeves summer and winter. I was thin but very tough. . . . I was dark, like my mother, and my complexion was the despair of her life. Beauty of the fair blonde type was in vogue then, so that I was quite out of fashion. It was thought that if one was dark one had a wicked temper. (Sanchez, p. 13–14).

Tough and dark and intense—and extraordinarily courageous—she grew up with all the virtues of a pioneer woman able to ride and shoot and cook. Married at seventeen to Sam Osbourne, a luckless, rootless scapegrace charmer who fathered her three children but was incapable of fidelity or of responsibility, she was the kind of woman who could hold her own in a Virginia City mining camp, in a roomful of British artists and writers, in an upper-class Scottish drawing room, or as the consort of a petty Scottish leader ruling his tiny clan in the wilds of Samoa. She was also often profoundly depressed, haunted by her own interior ghosts and, as she moved deeper into middle age, not always entirely sane.

We do not know precisely what happened to Fanny in San Francisco after she returned in 1878. While she was gone, Stevenson, partly to ease his longing for her and partly to create material for a book, made his way to Le Monastier in France's Cévenol hills, where he bought the tiny donkey, Modestine, whom he immortalized in *Travels with a Donkey*. With Modestine burdened with an enormous sleeping bag concocted for Stevenson out of sheepskins, and with a supply of chocolate squares and tinned bologna, he started off from Le Monastier: "It may sound offensive, but I ate them together, bite by bite, by way of bread and meat. All I had to wash down this revolting mixture was neat brandy . . ." (*Travels with a Donkey*, in Stevenson, R.L., *The Works*, Vol. 1, p. 198). Finally, and for sheer bravado, he carried a pistol in his luggage.

Today, on one wall of Le Monastier's town hall, one can still see the crude map made with a winding rope that indicates the course of the crazy Scotsman's journey: from Le Monastier, to Goudet, to Le Bouchet St. Nicholas, where, thanks to the local innkeeper, he learned to bless the uses of a goad that saved him from having to beat Modestine mercilessly to get her to move. The goad, a simple stick with a nail at its end, though it looked less humane, made sense to Modestine, who accommodated to it at once. From Le Bouchet St. Nicholas donkey and man went on to Pradelles, and from there to Le Cheylard L'Eveque, to which there was no true road. From Cheylard he went to Luc, and from there to Notre-Dame des Neiges (Our Lady of the Snows), where he was terrified by the monastery ("This it is to have a Protestant education," [Ibid., p. 211]). Then to Mirandol, Le Bleymard, Jean Dugard, and finally Le Pont de Montvert, and the twelve-day tramp was done. Surely this was a trip with no purpose but to be the subject of a book. Just the same, it is a lovely little book and shows us Stevenson as marvelously attuned to the way hills and mists and valleys and breezes and rivers and rocks speak to the eye and the heart. Moving through that gorgeous countryside it is as if asking nature to put balm on his heart; and then, having received it in the form of a good night's sleep under a sheltering tree, he leaves money under it as a romantic, and admirably foolish act of gratitude.

Nearly a year later, at the end of July 1879, Stevenson received a telegram from Fanny. No one knows what it said. Whatever it was, Stevenson thought it urgent enough for him to pack hastily and to buy a steamer ticket to New York, for which he sailed on the S.S. *Devonia* on August 7, 1879.

Ever the writer, the events of this urgent trip, too, were destined to be turned into a salable volume that would be called *The Amateur Emigrant*. Though he liked people to think he had traveled in steerage, he acknowledged that he had actually taken a second-class cabin, because in it he could have a table on which to write. On the alert for the kind of copy to be found in other people's lives, he spent many hours among the steerage passengers. "The difference," he tell us, between steerage and second class is that "in the steerage there are males and females; in the second cabin ladies and gentlemen" (*The Amateur Emigrant*, in Stevenson, R.L., *The Works*, Vol. 4, p. 6).

The train trip from New York to San Francisco took a ghastly fourteen days. Stevenson, in a letter to his friend Colvin, says that the second part of *The Amateur Emigrant* describing that journey, "was written in a circle

The Silverado Museum, established in 1969

of hell unknown to Dante—that of the penniless and dying author, for dying I was although now saved" (*The Letters*, in Stevenson, R.L., *The Works*, Vol. 1, p. 392).

When Stevenson arrived in San Francisco, he looked like a walking specter. He was desperately poor and his health, once again, was bad. Inexplicably, Fanny seemed not wildly glad to see him. As Ian Bell puts it, "At any rate, his presence was not convenient. For the first week after his arrival he was . . . utterly miserable" (Bell, p. 135).

There followed several months of physical and psychological turmoil. He left San Francisco on horseback and headed for the Carmel Valley. On the way, his health broke down utterly and he was found unconscious camped in the Coast Range mountains by a goat rancher who spent three weeks nursing him back to health. From there Stevenson moved to Monterey, where he lived until the middle of December. In Monterey, a French restaurateur named Jules Simoneau got several of the locals to collect two dollars a week so that they could create the fiction that Stevenson had earned the money working for the *Monterey Californian*. Finally, in January, it became clear that Fanny was about to get her divorce. There followed another period in which Stevenson was ill and Fanny, as she would for the rest of her life, tended to him. In the midst of their anxieties, Stevenson received a cable from his father that read, "Count on two hundred and fifty pounds annually." It was the bell that saved the boxer, the round, and the match.

On May 8, Stevenson and Fanny were married in Oakland, California, by the Reverend Mr. Scott. On their wedding certificate, Fanny described herself as a widow. Their honeymoon in an abandoned miner's shack near Calistoga is the stuff of which gallant movie comedies are made. Stevenson turned their experience into a book, *The Silverado Squatters*. A charming scale model of the miner's shack that they made habitable is on exhibit in the Silverado Museum at St. Helena, California.

The Stevensons were in the shack for less than three months. At the end of July, they started back to Scotland. This time, however, no longer penniless, Louis and his Fanny traveled first class. In Edinburgh, Fanny endeared herself to her father- and mother-in-law by her devotion to them, but especially by her obvious love for their son.

There followed a period of years during which Stevenson wrote prolifically, no matter how ill he was, and the Stevensons wandered throughout Europe, hoping anxiously to find the one spot where he might enjoy a modicum of health.

For a while they stayed in Edinburgh, but Stevenson's doctor uncle, George Balfour, advised the sanatorium town of Davos, Switzerland, instead. From Davos, where Stevenson was not happy, they went back to Scotland, where they lived with Stevenson's mother at Kinnaird Cottage, Pitlochry in the Vale of Atholl. Here, Stevenson wrote "Thrawn Janet," one of his finest short stories, and began the even better "The Merry Men." "The Body Snatcher," a much thinner story, was also written there (see Appendix A, p. 149ff). Here, too, *The Master of Ballantrae* was conceived.

Once again, following medical advice, the Stevensons moved to Braemar, where, partly to entertain his twelve-year-old stepson, who had responded excitedly to a map Stevenson had drawn, Stevenson began a book for boys he called tentatively *The Sea Cook*. *The Sea Cook*, transmogrified to *Treasure Island*, was to change Stevenson's life forever: when it was published in 1883, it earned him the large sum of three hundred pounds and established him as a working writer.

Their wanderings in search of a healthful environment continued: back to Davos; back to Scotland; then to Hyères on the Côte d'Azur. About Hyères, Stevenson would later write, "I was only happy once, that was in Hyères" ("The Letters," in Stevenson, R.L., *The Works*, Vol. 3, p. 249). But happy or not, his literary output throughout this period continued prodigiously. He worked on *A Child's Garden of Verses*, *Prince Otto*, "Talk and Talkers," and *Familiar Studies of Men and Books*.

Early in 1884, while in Nice, Stevenson had one of his near encounters with death. His doctors told Fanny that there was no hope. He recovered, but later that spring he was stricken again. His symptoms were appalling: he coughed blood, one of his eyes was infected, and one of his hands, because of sciatica, was strapped to his side. In that condition, Stevenson penned a note to comfort Fanny: "Don't be frightened—if this is death it is an easy one" (Bell, p. 158). Stevenson's wife, writing at this period, summarized the medical advice she had been given:

> The doctor says, "Keep him alive till he is forty and then, although he is a winged bird, he may live to be ninety . . . between now and forty he must live as though he were walking on eggs, and for the next two years no matter how well he feels, he must live the life of an invalid" (Sanchez, p. 158).

The invalid and his family returned to England and settled in a cliffside house in Bournemouth, an English watering place. The house was called Skerryvore after a lighthouse designed by Stevenson's uncle, Alan. There, to use his own phrase, Stevenson saw himself as "the pallid brute that lived in Skerryvore like a weevil in a biscuit" ("The Letters," in Stevenson, R.L., *The Works*, Vol. 4, p. 44). It was there, too, that he and Henry James met and forged a most unlikely personal and literary friendship. James, the austere Olympian of prose, and Stevenson, who called himself "a rude, left-handed countryman," nevertheless recognized that each of them was deeply committed to one main thing: the art of fiction.

It was at Skerryvore, too, that Stevenson, driven by the ambitions of his wife and his friend Henley, wasted days and talent writing plays, but in the midst of squandered time and false starts there was also, as I have noted above, the nearly miraculous discovery and execution of *The Strange Case of Dr. Jekyll and Mr. Hyde*.

With the publication of that book in early 1886, Stevenson became simultaneously rich on his own account and very famous. He was also, continually, very sick. So sick that when his father died on May 8, 1887, Stevenson was forbidden to attend the funeral in Edinburgh lest the cold he suffered from turn into something deadly.

"The chief link," writes Graham Balfour, Stevenson's first biographer, "which bound Stevenson to this country [Great Britain] was now broken. . . ." (Balfour, Vol. II, p. 30). Harassed by ill health, but moved perhaps more by what I think was a lifelong yearning to be endlessly elsewhere, Stevenson scanned the horizon. With the three thousand pounds his father had left him, plus the money he was still earning from *Jekyll and Hyde* and *Treasure Island*, he could comfortably choose. Colorado was suggested to him as good for his health. He chose Saranac in upstate New York, which in those years was considered a fine place for tuberculosis sufferers.

Stevenson, Fanny, Maggie Stevenson, Lloyd, and Valentine Roch, an employee, sailed for New York on the *Ludgate Hill* on August 27, 1887. The cargo included horses and monkeys. Among the latter, there was one named Jacko, who attached himself to Stevenson and followed him around the boat.

As a prelude to life on a tropical Pacific island, the winter in Saranac was perfect. Balfour writes:

> It rained, it snowed, it sleeted, it blew, it was thick fog; it froze—the cold was Arctic; it thawed. . . . In December the cold began, and by January the thermometer was sometimes nearly 30 degrees below zero (Ibid., p. 35–36).

An hour after it was placed in the oven to roast, venison still had icicles still in it. The family huddled, wrapped in buffalo hides and other furs. "Fires," wrote Stevenson "do not radiate . . . you burn your hands all the time on what seem to be cold stones" ("The Letters," Stevenson, R.L., *The Works*, Vol. 3, p. 45).

It was in the midst of that cold, with Stevenson already at work on *The Master of Ballantrae*, he was encouraged by the American publisher, Sam McLure, to think about an ocean voyage that would generate a manuscript that McLure would publish. It was an attractive notion for Stevenson, who was always happiest at sea. In March of 1888, Fanny went off to Indiana to visit her family with instructions to go on to San Francisco, where she was to shop for a yacht. Quite an assignment for a faithful wife who hated the sea!

While she was gone, Stevenson received a letter from his soi-disant friend, Henley, that chilled first his blood and then his relationship to the lame poet whom he had helped financially over the years, and with whom he had collaborated on writing the feckless plays that were intended to make them rich. Henley, in an offhand way, told Stevenson that he had seen in *Scribner's* a short story of Fanny's called "The Nixie." Expressing what seems now to be mock amazement, he wrote,

> It's Katharine's; surely it's Katharine's? The situation, the environment, the principal figure—*voyons*! . . . and why there isn't a double signature is what I've not been able to understand (Connell, p. 113–114).

Stevenson rightly read Henley's intent. Henley was accusing Fanny of having plagiarized a story of Stevenson's cousin, Katharine de Mattos.

In fact, Fanny had not plagiarized the story, but what had happened was murky. Katharine de Mattos (to whom, Stevenson dedicated *Jekyll and Hyde*) had indeed written a short story called "The Nixie." When she could not find a publisher for it, she reluctantly let Fanny have it with the understanding (more spoken than felt) that Fanny could do what she liked with it. Fanny rewrote the story and, writes Ian Bell, "the Stevenson name having had its usual magical effect on her husband's publishers," got it accepted by *Scribner's* (Bell, p. 197). To see a story whose germ, and much of whose content, she had created, published over someone else's signature, no doubt galled Katharine de Mattos, but she herself never accused Fanny of plagiarism. It was left to Henley, Stevenson's long-time collaborator and pensioner, to spill this particularly scalding bile. As Stevenson's always loyal friend Charles Baxter pointed out to him, there are no friends quite so resentful as those whom one has helped with money.

In any case, the friendship cooled, though it did not end. And Stevenson, even after "The Nixie" contretemps, continued to help his lame and boozing friend with cash when he needed it. The wound, however, that Henley inflicted was exceedingly painful, and to it, I think, we owe the despairing letter Stevenson sent Baxter in which he writes, "How I wish I had died in Hyères when all was well with me . . ." ("The Quarrel Letters," in Furnas, *Voyage to Windward*, p. 290). Henley, for his part, was not through. He harbored his venom, concentrating it until 1901, when, reviewing Graham Balfour's *Life* of Stevenson, he spewed it all out. Henley's essay in *Pall Mall Magazine* is unseemly, unfair, ungrateful, and cruel as he tries to cut Stevenson's character and achievement down to the trivial size he thought they deserved.

That was years later. Meanwhile, in San Francisco, Fanny had found a yacht. She was the *Casco* and could be chartered for seven hundred fifty dollars a month. A beautiful sailing yacht, ninety-five feet long, weighing seventy tons, she had been built for racing. To Fanny's telegram, Stevenson replied, "Blessed girl, take the yacht and expect us in ten days."

It was a fateful decision. Stevenson, heading westward—far, far westward, beyond San Francisco, beyond Hawaii and into the archipelagoes of the south Pacific—had no way of knowing that he would see neither America nor Great Britain ever again. They boarded the *Casco* on June 26, 1888. There followed nearly three years of Pacific wanderings, first in the *Casco*, then later in the *Janet Nicholl* and the *Equator*. In that period, writes

Balfour, "[Stevenson] visited almost every group of [islands] of importance in the Eastern and Central Pacific" (Balfour, Vol. II, p. 30).

This is the epoch in Stevenson's life which I have the most difficulty understanding. One appreciates his childlike delight in the new world into which he has dropped, but there is a mystery here, a compelled quality to the constant motion, as if the changes of scene, the new breezes, the new smells served to keep his eye focused outward instead of where the maturing writer ought to be looking—endlessly and forever within. As if scenery was easier to describe than insight; as if it was easier to move than to feel.

The movement, in any case, was interrupted at intervals. There was a lengthy stay in Hawaii, in the course of which Stevenson finished *The Master of Ballantrae*. There was a visit, undertaken alone, to the leper colony on the Hawaiian island of Molokai, where Stevenson played croquet with some leper girls.

In December 1889, the Stevensons' Pacific wanderings came to an end when the steamer *Equator* deposited them on the beach at Apia on the Samoan island of Upolu. Six weeks later, Stevenson, who by then had learned the lesson that "civilized" places, such as Honolulu or Sydney, were bad for his health, decided to buy land on Apia and settle there. He bought three hundred fourteen and a half acres

> of beautiful land in the bush behind Apia; when we get the house built, the garden laid, and cattle in the place, it will be something to fall back on for shelter and food. . . . We range from 600 to 1500 feet, have five streams, waterfalls, precipices, profound ravines, rich tablelands, fifty head of cattle on the ground . . . a great view of forest, sea, mountains, the warships in the haven: really a noble place ("The Letters," in Stevenson, R.L., *The Works*, Vol. 3, p. 129).

And so the urban Scotsman became a Scottish laird at last, presiding over an upland domain, the absolute monarch of all he surveyed. Fanny attended to the gardening. His step-daughter, Belle, looked after the household and took Stevenson's dictation; his mother, also there at intervals, was the dowager empress, and there was a staff of native men and women over whom Stevenson exercised rigid (though he believed it to be benign) control.

The miniature empire was called Vailima, meaning Five Waters. The high chief, Stevenson, soon acquired a Samoan name. He was called Tusitala, or the tale-teller; Fanny's title was Tamaitai, meaning madame, more or less, and she was nicknamed Aolele, flying cloud. Isobel, who gave gifts of trinkets to little girls, was called Teuila, the decorator.

Stevenson expanded into the role of a personage. He involved himself in Samoan politics, most often on the side of the native population, and became knowledgeable about the local customs and religions. Vailima, writes his sister-in-law, Nellie Van de Grift Sanchez,

> became the center of social life in the island and was the scene of frequent balls and parties, dinners with twenty-five or thirty guests, Christmas parties with the guests staying for three days, and tennis nearly every day with officers from the men-of-war in the harbor and ladies from the mission (Sanchez, p. 191).

And, in the midst of it all, the laird of the manor was continually at work, turning out pages with the discipline of a sickly writer whose life was visibly bounded by death: "As for my damned literature," he writes, "God knows what a business it is, grinding along with a scrap of inspiration or a note of style. But it has to be ground . . . The treadmill turns; and, with a kind of desperate cheerfulness I mount the idle stair" ("The Letters," in Stevenson, R.L., *The Works*, Vol. 3, p. 250).

Though I am inclined to think, as his friend Sydney Colvin did, that the work done at Vailima shows a considerable decline in Stevenson's powers, one has to except from that judgment the beautifully written *The Weir of Hermiston* in which, finally, Stevenson is clearly ready to tell a love story where both the men and the women characters are fully and complexly conceived. He especially develops the women, who in his fictions tended to be either two-dimensional or stereotypical. On that score, he knew he had a problem. Writing to Colvin, he says,

> I am afraid my touch is a little broad in a love story. I can't mean one thing and write another. As for women, I am no longer in any fear of them; I can do a sort all right; age makes me less afraid of a petticoat, but I am a little afraid of grossness. . . . The difficulty in a love yarn which dwells at all on love, is the dwelling on one string; it is manifold, I grant, but the root fact is there unchanged, and the sentiment being very intense, and very much handled in letters, positively calls for a little pawing and gracing. With a writer of my prosaic literalness and pertinency of point of view, this all shoves toward grossness—positively towards the far more damnable *closeness*. This has kept me off the sentiment hitherto and now I am to try: Lord! ("The Letters," in Stevenson, R.L., *The Works*, Vol. 4, p. 48).

Again he writes, "There was a time when I didn't dare to really draw a woman; but I have no fear now; I shall show a little of what I can do in the two Kristys. . . ." (Ibid.).

There is every evidence in *The Weir of Hermiston* that Stevenson would have kept his promise. Here at last, characterization serves plot, plot serves theme, and all three serve a mature vision. The only thing wrong with *The Weir of Hermiston* is that it remains unfinished.

On Monday, December 3, 1894, toward sunset, Stevenson asked Fanny to help him make a salad for the evening meal. Pope-Hennessy says Stevenson was pouring oil to make a mayonnaise; most other accounts say that he was returning from his wine cellar carrying a bottle of wine. Lloyd Osbourne writes,

Stevenson was lying back in an armchair, unconscious, breathing stertorously and with his unseeing eyes wide open; and on either side of him were my mother and sister, pale and apprehensive. They told me in whispers that he had suddenly cried out, "My head—oh, my head!" and then had fallen insensible ("Weir of Hermiston," in Stevenson, R.L., *The Works*, Vol. 28, p. xv).

A couple of hours later, at ten minutes past eight, he died.

The last words we have of *The Weir of Hermiston* dictated to his stepdaughter Isobel that morning are:

In vain he looked back over the interview [between Archie and Kristie]; he saw not where he had offended. It seemed un-provoked, a willful convulsion of brute nature . . . (Ibid. p. 14).

Indeed it was.

Robert Louis Stevenson

DEDICATION

To

Katharine de Mattos[1]

It's ill to loose the bands that God decreed to bind;
Still will we be the children of the heather and the wind;
Far away from home, O it's still for you and me
That the broom is blowing bonnie in the north countrie.

---

[1] A cousin of Stevenson's with whom he had a particularly close relationship. The dedication is the closing stanza of an entire poem that Stevenson sent Katharine on January 1, 1886 along with a copy of *Dr. Jekyll and Mr. Hyde*. Stevenson wrote,

Dearest Katharine—
   Here, on a very little book and accompanied with lame verses, I have put your name. Our kindness is now getting well on in years: it must be nearly of age; and it gets more valuable to me with every time I see you. It is not possible to express any sentiment, and it is not necessary to try, at least between us. You know very well that I love you dearly, and that I always will. I only wish the verses were better, but at least you like the story; and it is sent to you by the one that loves you—Jekyll, and not Hyde. ("The Letters," in Stevenson, R.L., *The Works,* Vol. 2, p. 274).

The poem's first stanza reads:

   Bells upon the city are ringing in the night;
   High above the gardens are the houses full of light;
   On the heathy Pentlands is the curlew flying free,
   And the broom is blowing bonnie in the north countrie. (Ibid., p. 275)

   The line, "It's ill to loose the bonds that God decreed to bind" is, of course, central to the theme of *Jekyll and Hyde.*

   In 1888, Katharine de Mattos was at the center of a mortifying exchange of letters between Stevenson and his friend, W.E. Henley. Henley, in a letter to Stevenson, who was then living in Saranac, New York, managed to imply that Stevenson's wife, Fanny, had plagiarized a short story of Katharine's. Katharine never made this charge, though Stevenson ended by feeling that she had contributed to the quarrel by not denying the suggestion of plagiarism vigorously enough. See the Introduction to this edition, p. 23–24.

"What's the matter with me? What is this strangeness? Has my face changed?" Those words aren't spoken by Dr. Jekyll or Mr. Hyde in the novel. They are the last words uttered by Robert Louis Stevenson before he died, at age forty four, of a cerebral hemorrhage. But they very well could have been said by Dr. Jekyll when he was transforming into Mr. Hyde.

So who is this "Mr. Hyde"? Is he simply a brilliant literary creation, someone we can read about and shudder, if so inclined, and then dismiss as nothing more than a Victorian "penny dreadful" or "shilling shocker"?

Or is he an accurate and penetrating representation of the beast inside all of us, an embodiment of Doctor Jekyll's—and Stevenson's—darker, baser nature?

Like Frankenstein, Dr. Jekyll and Mr. Hyde is certainly better known because of the movies the novel has inspired. Not very many people read the original today, and I'm not sure I blame them. This is an awkward little book with a rather odd construction that lacks the immediate narrative drive we modern readers seem to demand.

But obviously Stevenson's exploration of the dual nature of humankind is what fascinates and attracts us to the figure of Mr. Hyde. We've seen more recent fictional creations playing upon this theme, including Stephen King's The Dark Half and Richard C. Matheson's Created By, but Stevenson was there first, peeling back the layers and exposing dark, twisted secrets about himself and us.

The basic fear this novel triggers for me is the knowledge that this bloodthirsty, amoral beast is always there, inside you and me, lurking just below the surface like a hungry shark. And it can burst out of us at any moment. The trigger might not be a "magic potion" concocted from impure salts and other chemicals. It might be something like losing our job or lover, or something as simple as getting cut off in traffic.

The real horror of Dr. Jekyll and Mr. Hyde is that we as a species still don't know how to control the beast inside us.

And whenever it slips its leash—God help us!

—Rick Hautala

THE STRANGE CASE OF DR. JEKYLL[2] AND MR. HYDE.[3]

Chapter I

✦

STORY OF THE DOOR[4]

Mr. Utterson[5] the lawyer[6] was a man of a rugged countenance, that was never lighted by a smile; cold, scanty and embarrassed in discourse;

---

[2]   Scholars were long ago curious about the surname Jekyll. W.H. Stevenson, writing in *Notes and Queries*, Series IV (November 9, 1899), summarized the origins and the evolution of the name. He cites its appearance in the *Domesday Book* (1086), where it was written "Ivichelis." W.H. Stevenson suggests that the name was originally French. In its various derivations, the name has elements that can mean "battle" as well as "generous man." Both meanings are apt.

Vladimir Nabokov takes it for granted that Stevenson got both Jekyll's and Hyde's names out of an old book on surnames from which he would have learned that Jekyll is derived from the Danish Jökulle, meaning *icicle* (Nabokov, p. 182).

P.H. Reaney's *A Dictionary of British Surnames* says that Jekyll "was particularly common in Yorkshire and Lincolnshire and in districts where the Breton contingent settled after the Conquest."

[3]   The name "Hyde," according to P.H. Reaney, derives from the word "hide," meaning a measure of land. Nabokov refers it again to the Danish "hide," meaning a harbor or haven. Most obviously, of course, it stands for the hidden aspect of Jekyll. The author himself has Mr. Utterson say later (p. 48): "If he be Mr. Hyde, . . . I shall be Mr. Seek."

The word "hide," as meaning an animal's hide, may also have resonated in Stevenson's mind. When he wrote his youthful *An Inland Voyage*, Stevenson tells us how he was struck by the irony that martial music was made on drums from the stretched hide of donkeys.

backward in sentiment; lean, long, dusty, dreary and yet somehow lovable. At friendly meetings, and when the wine was to his taste, something eminently human beaconed from his eye; something indeed which never found its way into his talk, but which spoke not only in these silent symbols of the after-dinner face, but more often and loudly in the acts of his life. He was austere with himself; drank gin when he was alone, to mortify a taste for vintages;[7] and though he enjoyed the theatre, had not crossed the doors of one for twenty years. But he had an approved tolerance for others; sometimes wondering, almost with envy,[8] at the high pressure of spirits

---

Leaving all this straining for allegorical meaning aside, there is every possibility that Stevenson simply reached for a convenient name and found it in that of London's famous Hyde Park.

By a curious irony, a man named Hyde would, long after the appearance of *Jekyll and Hyde*, impinge on Stevenson's life in a most disturbing fashion. In 1889, three years after the publication of *Jekyll and Hyde*, Stevenson, who had a deep if romanticized admiration of the work Father Damien had done among Hawaiian lepers, was horrified to read of an attack on Damien's life and morals in an Australian church journal by the Reverend Doctor C.M. Hyde. Leaping to Damien's defense, Stevenson wrote an intemperate "open letter" defending the priest.

[4] In his sickly childhood, Stevenson was nursed by the beloved "Cummie," Allison Cunningham, who filled his child's mind with stories from the Bible and especially from Bunyan's *Pilgrim's Progress*. For him, the word "door" teemed with allegorical significance. In Genesis 4:7 we read, "sin lieth at the door," where the point is that the sinner must avoid sin. In the New Testament (John 10:9), Jesus says, "I am the door: by me if any man enters in, he shall be saved." In *Pilgrim's Progress* (p. 42), Stevenson would have been familiar with Evangelist's advice to Christian, "Strive to enter in at the strait gate . . . for strait is the gate that leadeth unto life," echoing the gospel from Luke (Luke 13:24).

Leaving religious references to one side, doors are powerful and mysterious symbols, representing the possibility of things hidden or revealed; of transitional moments or of finality. In 1882, Stevenson published a short story, "The Sire de Maletroit's Door," in which the young Denis de Beaulieu reaps the consequences, first agonizing, then exquisite, of walking through the wrong door.

[5] In P.H. Reaney's *A Dictionary of British Surnames*, the entry for Utterson reads as follows: "**Utterson.** Utter = Otter in Swed. Otter (Northern England) Dweller at the sign of the Otter; descendant of Otthar (terrible, army); dweller at the Otter (otter stream), a river in England."

Given his role as a narrator in the fiction, we may think of him as one who utters. Utterson, we note, is presented to us as paradoxical and complicated. Aloof, dry, and shy, he manages nevertheless to emit geniality. He is the quintessential friendly witness, as well as the quintessential friend.

Though we never see him as "somehow lovable," he is a figure of absolute rectitude who is nevertheless the opposite of cold. His decency is described as being not only passive (as when it shines through his eye), but also active (as when it manifests itself in "the acts of his life"). What he seems to have most is a gift for friendship. We will see that, as regards his treatment of his friend and kinsman, Enfield, he is capable of a certain amount of mean-spirited slyness. On the other hand, as when he acts in concert with Poole, he is capable of direct, vigorous, and decisive action.

[6] Stevenson as a very young man not only studied law in Scotland, he actually passed the bar. Though he never took clients, he once presented himself as a candidate to teach law at Edinburgh University. Perhaps fortunately for Stevenson, his application was rejected.

[7] This touch of fleshly renunciation reflects the impact on Stevenson of his childhood in a strictly Presbyterian home and under the watchful, Calvinist eye of his nurse, the beloved Cummie. In a letter to Adelaide Boodle, Stevenson wrote: " . . . it was what you seemed to set forth as your reasons that fluttered my old Presbyterian spirit—for, mind you, I am a child of the Covenanters—whom I do not love, but they are mine, after all, my father's and my mother's—and they had their merits, too, and their ugly beauties, and their grotesque heroisms, that I love them for, the while I laugh at them" ("The Letters," in Stevenson, R.L., *The Works*, Vol. 3, p. 270).

We note that Utterson, despite his self-punitive rigidities, is capable of admiring sensuality, though it is clear he keeps his own dualities firmly in control.

[8] Here, so early, we have a key passage that helps to define Utterson for us as a friendly—even

32

involved in their misdeeds; and in any extremity inclined to help rather than to reprove. 'I incline to Cain's heresy,'[9] he used to say quaintly: 'I let my brother go to the devil in his own way.' In this character, it was frequently his fortune to be the last reputable acquaintance and the last good influence in the lives of down-going men.[10] And to such as these, so long as they came about his chambers, he never marked a shade of change in his demeanour.

No doubt the feat was easy to Mr. Utterson; for he was undemonstrative at the best, and even his friendships seemed to be founded in a similar catholicity of good-nature. It is the mark of a modest man to accept his friendly circle ready-made from the hands of opportunity; and that was the lawyer's way. His friends were those of his own blood or those whom he had known the longest; his affections, like ivy, were the growth of time, they implied no aptness in the object. Hence, no doubt, the bond that united him to Mr. Richard Enfield,[11] his distant kinsman, the well-known man about town. It was a nut to crack for many, what these two could see in each other, or what subject they could find in common. It was reported by those who encountered them in their Sunday walks, that they said nothing, looked singularly dull, and would hail with obvious relief the appearance of a friend. For all that, the two men put the greatest store by these excursions, counted them the chief jewel of each week, and not only set aside occasions of pleasure, but even resisted the calls of business, that they might enjoy them uninterrupted.[12]

It chanced on one of these rambles that their way led them down a by-street in a busy quarter of London.[13] The street was small and what is

envious—witness of what, for the moment, is diffidently called improper behavior. What the mild-mannered Utterson regards with envy is the energy it takes to commit misdeeds. This will turn out to be Jekyll's bias, as well. As we will see later, misdeeds in their extreme form become evil. But here, Stevenson is signaling an important theme: evil is experienced as vitality, and therefore, can seem attractive.

[9] The full story is in Genesis 3:3–9. When Cain, having slain Abel, was asked by God, "Where is Abel thy brother?" Cain replied, "Am I my brother's keeper?"

[10] This is a provocative thing to say, as if the decent Utterson was himself a sort of door to disaster.

[11] The name "Enfield," William Veeder points out, was the name of the site in Sussex where the Royal Small Arms Factory was located. While Stevenson was a lifelong aficionado of military life and of firearms, I will let the reader decide whether, as Veeder implies, Stevenson's choice of the name has symbolic significance. What is clear is that this young man about town with his wee-hours adventures is nevertheless a close friend of the retiring Utterson. He is clearly meant to be seen as antithetical to his more sedate kinsman Utterson.

[12] Stevenson, in his "Apology for Idlers" wrote: "Perpetual devotion to what a man calls his business, is only to be sustained by perpetual neglect of many other things" (*Virginibus Pueresque*, in Stevenson, R.L., *The Works*, Vol. 2, p. 65).

[13] Stevenson, like the Gothic writers who preceded him, is letting his description of scenery reinforce the theme of duality. The details we are given of this "by-street" deserve careful attention. For one thing, we have no idea where in London the street may be found. It is described as a prosperous

called quiet, but it drove a thriving trade on the week-days. The inhabitants were all doing well, it seemed, and all emulously hoping to do better still, and laying out the surplus of their gains in coquetry; so that the shop fronts stood along that thoroughfare with an air of invitation, like rows of smiling saleswomen.[14] Even on Sunday, when it veiled its more florid charms and lay comparatively empty of passage, the street shone out in contrast to its dingy neighbourhood, like a fire in a forest; and with its freshly painted shutters, well polished brasses, and general cleanliness and gaiety of note, instantly caught and pleased the eye of the passenger.

Two doors from one corner, on the left hand going east, the line was broken by the entry of a court; and just at that point, a certain sinister block of building[15] thrust forward its gable on the street. It was two storeys high; showed no window, nothing but a door on the lower storey and a blind forehead of discoloured wall on the upper; and bore in every feature, the marks of prolonged and sordid negligence. The door, which was equipped with neither bell nor knocker, was blistered and distained. Tramps slouched into the recess and struck matches on the panels; children kept

---

street, whose shopfronts "like rows of smiling saleswomen" have a florid brightness that stands out in contrast to its dingy neighborhood.

And yet two doors from one corner on that same street stands a dreary Gothic pile of a house, which "bore in every feature the marks of prolonged and sordid negligence." As we proceed further in our fiction, Jekyll's house itself will be seen to have an inbuilt duality: congenial, prosperous, respectable, as well as darkly threatening, mysterious, and sinister. And the duality, as Vladimir Nabokov has emphasized in his lecture "Dr. Jekyll and Mr. Hyde," is manifested by each of its two facades: the respectable, Jekyll side of the house stands out in contrast with the down-at-heels seediness of its neighboring structures. The Hyde facade is bleak, neglected, and lowering on a street in which it stands out like a fire in a forest of thriving, well-kept, and prosperous commercial structures (Nabokov, p. 188).

[14] The diction of this passage is notable for the way it suggests street prostitutes ("coquetry . . . air of invitation . . . florid charms . . ."). Readers of *The Strange Case of Dr. Jekyll and Mr. Hyde* who are familiar with any of the film versions in which male-female eroticism play an important part must be struck by the nearly complete absence of effective female characters in this novel. Still, ineffective as most of them are, there are at least half a dozen female persons in the story: the little girl whom Hyde tramples (see below), an unspecified number of her female relatives gathered in the street around her, the housemaid who witnesses the murder of Sir Danvers Carew, a cook and a maid who work for Dr. Jekyll, and finally Hyde's wicked-looking housekeeper.

Stevenson's inability to deal with women in his writing is discussed in the Introduction to this edition, however, an additional comment by Henry James may prove illuminating:

It all comes back to his sympathy with the juvenile and the feeling about life which leads him to regard women as so many superfluous girls in a boys' game. They are almost absent from his pages . . . for they don't like ships and pistols and fights, they encumber the decks and require separate apartments, and almost worst of all, have not the highest literary standard. Why should a person marry when he might be swinging a cutlass or looking for a buried treasure (Maixner, p. 297).

[15] Vladimir Nabokov, in his lecture on *Jekyll and Hyde*, rightly emphasizes the importance of the architecture of the Jekyll-Hyde house. The house, like the body of the man who inhabits it, is a "fortress of identity." But it is a fortress assailed from within rather than from without.

John S. Gibson, in his *Deacon Brodie: Father to Jekyll and Hyde*, suggests that the placing of Jekyll's fine house adjacent to the rundown houses sounds more like an Edinburgh neighborhood than one in London. G.K. Chesterton, too, has urged the Edinburgh-like look of Stevenson's London.

Davos

shop upon the steps; the schoolboy had tried his knife on the mouldings; and for close on a generation, no one had appeared to drive away these random visitors or to repair their ravages.

Mr. Enfield and the lawyer were on the other side of the by-street; but when they came abreast of the entry, the former lifted up his cane and pointed.

'Did you ever remark that door?'[16] he asked; and when his companion had replied in the affirmative, 'It is connected in my mind,' added he, 'with a very odd story.'

'Indeed?' said Mr. Utterson, with a slight change of voice, 'and what was that?'

'Well, it was this way,' returned Mr. Enfield: 'I was coming home from some place at the end of the world, about three o'clock[17] of a black winter morning, and my way lay through a part of town where there was literally nothing to be seen but lamps. Street after street, and all the folks asleep—street after street, all lighted up as if for a procession and all as empty as a church—till at last I got into that state of mind when a man listens and listens and begins to long for the sight of a policeman. All at once, I saw two figures: one a little man[18] who was stumping along eastward

---

[16] This marks the fifth reference to doors in the space of two pages (see note 2).

[17] We don't know where Enfield was, but the lateness of the hour and the darkness of the night are consistent with the perambulations of "a man about town."

[18] "Little" is the very first word we have describing Hyde, and then we are told that he was "stumping along eastward." Not walking or hurrying, but rather moving like one deformed. He is diminished, warped.

at a good walk, and the other a girl[19] of maybe eight or ten who was running as hard as she was able down a cross street. Well, sir, the two ran into one another naturally enough at the corner; and then came the horrible part of the thing; for the man trampled calmly over the child's body and left her screaming on the ground.[20] It sounds nothing to hear, but it was hellish to see. It wasn't like a man; it was like some damned Juggernaut.[21] I gave a view halloa,[22] took to my heels, collared my gentleman, and brought him back to where there was already quite a group about the screaming child. He was perfectly cool and made no resistance, but gave me one look, so ugly that it brought out the sweat on me like running. The people who had turned out were the girl's own family; and pretty soon, the doctor[23] for whom she had been sent, put in his appearance. Well, the child was not much the worse, more frightened, according to the Sawbones; and there you might have supposed would be an end to it. But there was one curious circumstance. I had taken a loathing[24] to my

[19]   Though he had no children of his own, and decided very early never to have any, Stevenson throughout his life was peculiarly sensitive to and concerned about children. His choice of a child to be Hyde's first victim emphasizes the moral awfulness of Hyde's behavior. His friend Sydney Colvin recounted what happened when the very young Stevenson was visiting on Hampstead Hill:

> One morning, while I was attending to my own affairs, I was aware of Stevenson craning intently out of a side window and watching something. Presently he turned with a radiant countenance and the thrill of happiness in his voice to bid me come and watch too. A group of girl children were playing with the skipping-rope a few yards down the lane. Was there ever such heavenly sport? Had I ever seen anything so beautiful? Kids and a skipping-rope—most of all that blessed youngest kid with the broken nose who didn't know how to skip—nothing in the whole wide world had ever made him half so happy in his life before. (in Calder, *Robert L. Stevenson: A Critical Celebration*, p. 29.)

In a letter to Mrs. Sitwell, Stevenson himself described an adventure with a little boy:

> At the most populous place of the city I found a little boy, three years old perhaps, half frantic with terror, and crying to everyone for his "Mammy." I and a good-humored mechanic came up together; and I instantly developed a latent faculty for setting the hearts of children at rest. Master Tommy Murphy (such was his name) soon stopped crying, and allowed me to take him up and carry him. . . . ("The Letters," in Stevenson, R.L., *The Works*, Vol. 2, p. 228).

The child was taken to a police station where, eventually, the story had a happy ending.
In March 1880, Stevenson, then in San Francisco, seriously endangered his own health by staying up nights with his landlady's seriously ill four-year-old son. It was that illness that made him cry out to Sydney Colvin, "O, never, never, any family for me! I am cured of that" (Ibid., p. 388).

[20]   In a remark impossible to overpraise for its astuteness, Gerard Manley Hopkins, defending Stevenson's *Jekyll and Hyde* in a letter to Robert Bridges, writes, "You are certainly wrong about Hyde being overdrawn: my Hyde is worse. The trampling scene is perhaps a convention: he was thinking of something unsuitable for fiction" (Maixner, p. 229).

[21]   Another of the names of Vishnu. The name refers also to the heavy, sixteen-wheeled car drawn by fifty men, used in a Hindu rite. The car was said to contain a bride for Vishnu. His devotees sometimes flung themselves to their deaths under its wheels. The word *juggernaut* now connotes a heavy, inexorably moving force.

[22]   A British fox-hunter's cry when he sees a fox starting from cover. Metaphorically, it is any cry that signals a moment of recognition.

gentleman at first sight. So had the child's family, which was only natural. But the doctor's case was what struck me. He was the usual cut and dry apothecary,[25] of no particular age and colour, with a strong Edinburgh accent, and about as emotional as a bagpipe.[26] Well, sir, he was like the rest of us; every time he looked at my prisoner, I saw that Sawbones turn

---

[23] In a lapse on Stevenson's part, we are told that the child was sent for a doctor, but we are never told who in her family was ill or what happened to the patient after the incident with Hyde. Or why, since clearly the child's father is perfectly able-bodied (since later he accompanies Enfield and Hyde to Enfield's rooms) the father did not himself go for the doctor instead of sending an eight-year-old girl out into the night at three o'clock in the morning. Finally, there is this mystery: Why, since Enfield, the doctor, and the child's family all joined in loathing the heartless Hyde, who had just committed battery, it seems not to have occurred to anyone to call for a policeman. Instead, the father, the doctor, and Enfield, by one accord, join in a conspiracy to blackmail Hyde.

The mention of a doctor stresses the importance of Stevenson's decision to make Jekyll, his protagonist, a physician. This fact bolsters critics who insist on seeing this story as science fiction in which, once again, wicked science is the villain. I would suggest that for a sickly Stevenson, who spent much of his life under the care of physicians, a doctor is primarily a figure of trust. Writing to Dr. W. Bamford (a name, Stevenson said, "the muse repels") he said, "You doctors have a serious responsibility. You recall a man from the gates of death, you give him health and the strength once more to use or to abuse. But for your kindest skill, this would have been my last book, and now I am in hopes that it will be neither my last nor my best" (Balfour, Vol. I, p. 199).

Stevenson turned the word "doctor" into a symbol of death in a short story "Will of the Mill" (1878), in which Stevenson's protagonist, Will, meets a man whom he addresses: " 'You are a doctor?' quavered Will. 'The best that ever was,' replied the other; 'for I cure both mind and body with the same prescription. I take away all pain and I forgive all sins; and where my patients have gone wrong in life, I smooth out all complications and set them free again upon their feet" (The Merry Men, in Stevenson R.L., The Works, Vol. 12, p. 98).

[24] Hyde inspires loathing because, we are asked to believe, he is a personification of pure evil.

[25] Though in America the word refers to a pharmacist, in Britain after 1700 the word apothecary could, as here, also mean a general medical practitioner.

In an early charming and satirical poem called "Robin and Ben: or, The Pirate and the Apothecary," Stevenson compared the lives of two friends, Robin, the pirate, and the apothecary, Ben. Robin is a candid pirate, Ben a moralizing hypocrite who compounds useless drugs and says, "Here is the key to right and wrong/Steal little but steal all day long." When Robin learns that the apothecary has sold tap water as a life-saving drug and that the patient died, "Out flashed the cutlass, down went Ben/ Dead and rotten, there and then" ("Poems," in Stevenson, R.L., The Works, Vol. 2, p. 235).

[26] This slur by a Scotsman against a musical instrument so closely identified with his native land is surely a bit of sly humor on Stevenson's part. Stevenson, a lifelong aficionado of military strategy, and who, along with his stepson Lloyd, spent endless hours playing with toy soldiers, was familiar with the use of Scottish pipers to lead soldiers into battle.

Stevenson invoked the pipes again in his poem "Ticonderoga," in which a Cameron clansman is required to avenge the murder of his brother by a Stewart. In that poem, we read that all

That loved their father's tartan
    And the ancient game of war.
Down the watery valley
    And up the windy hill,
Once more, as in the olden,
    The pipes were sounding shrill;
Again in highland sunshine
    The naked steel was bright;
And the lads, once more in tartan
    Went forth again to fight.
("Poems," in Stevenson R.L., The Works, Vol. 2, p. 64.)

sick and white with the desire to kill him. I knew what was in his mind, just as he knew what was in mine; and killing being out of the question, we did the next best. We told the man we could and would make such a scandal out of this, as should make his name stink from one end of London to the other. If he had any friends or any credit, we undertook that he should lose them. And all the time, as we were pitching it in red hot, we were keeping the women off him as best we could, for they were as wild as harpies.[27] I never saw a circle of such hateful faces; and there was the man in the middle, with a kind of black, sneering coolness—frightened too, I could see that—but carrying it off, sir, really like Satan.[28] "If you choose to make capital out of this accident," said he, "I am naturally helpless. No gentleman but wishes to avoid a scene," says he. "Name your figure." Well, we screwed him up to a hundred pounds for the child's family; he would have clearly liked to stick out; but there was something about the lot of us that meant mischief, and at last he struck.[29] The next thing was to get the money; and where do you think he carried us[30] but to that place with the door?—whipped out a key, went in, and presently came back with the matter of ten pounds in gold[31] and a cheque for the balance on Coutts's,[32] drawn payable to bearer and signed with a name that I

---

[27] Monsters in classical literature who are the instruments of divine vengeance. They had the form of vultures with the head and breasts of a woman. Samuel Johnson's *Dictionary* says that they are "filthy creatures; which when the table was furnished for Phineus, came flying in, and devouring or carrying away the greater part of the victuals, did so defile the rest that they could not be endured." Phineus was punished by the gods with blindness and torment by the harpies because he had blinded and imprisoned the children of his wife Idaea.

[28] The early reference to Satan, coupled with the remark Hyde makes several lines later, "No gentleman but wishes to avoid a scene," is the first hint we have of a theme that will be developed later: Hyde as an ally, or a manifestation, of the devil. Stevenson, of course, is playing on Percy Bysshe Shelley's remark in *Peter Bell the Third*: "The devil is a gentleman."

Speaking of the devil, we have a charming bit of autobiographical confession in "Reminiscences of Colinton Manse," cited in Balfour's *Life*. Stevenson writes, "I may even confess, since the laws against sorcery have been for some time in abeyance, that I essayed at divers times to bring up the Devil, founding my incantations on no more abstruse a guide than Skelt's *Juvenile Drama of Der Freischütz*" (Balfour, p. 52).

One other point needs to be made. Hyde's assertion that he is a gentleman (especially in the light of his behavior), with all the class implications the word had (and has) for the British is one more gauge by which to measure the degree of irony implicit in the way Stevenson uses the word.

[29] Yielded, as in striking one's colors.

[30] "Led us . . ."

[31] Gold coins to the value of ten pounds. In 1886, the British pound was worth five American dollars.

[32] A famous bank in London. The name of the bank is well known to fans of Gilbert and Sullivan, who will remember the song in *The Gondoliers* that includes the lines:

The Chancellor in his peruke—
The Earl, the Marquis and the Duke,
The Groom, the Butler and the Cook—
    They all shall equal be.
The Aristocrat who banks with Coutts,
The Aristocrat who cleans our boots . . . (Gilbert, p. 549.)

can't mention, though it's one of the points of my story, but it was a name at least very well known and often printed. The figure was stiff; but the signature was good for more than that, if it was only genuine. I took the liberty of pointing out to my gentleman that the whole business looked apocryphal,[33] and that a man does not, in real life, walk into a cellar door[34] at four in the morning and come out of it with another man's cheque for close upon a hundred pounds. But *he* was quite easy and sneering. "Set your mind at rest," says he, "I will stay with you till the banks open and cash the cheque myself." So we all set off, the doctor, and the child's father, and our friend and myself, and passed the rest of the night in my chambers;[35] and next day, when we had breakfasted, went in a body to the bank.[36] I gave in the cheque myself, and said I had every reason to believe it was a forgery. Not a bit of it. The cheque was genuine.'

'Tut-tut,' said Mr. Utterson.

'I see you feel as I do,' said Mr. Enfield. 'Yes, it's a bad story. For my man was a fellow that nobody could have to do with, a really damnable man; and the person that drew the cheque is the very pink[37] of the proprieties, celebrated too, and (what makes it worse) one of your fellows who do what they call good.[38] Black mail, I suppose; an honest man paying through the nose for some of the capers of his youth.[39] Black Mail House

---

[33]   Of questionable authenticity. The Apocrypha is the name given to the fourteen books of the Septuagint which some Protestants do not regard as canonical. Eleven of the books are included in the Douay Bible, used by Roman Catholics.

[34]   Here is another of Stevenson's oversights. The door through which Hyde enters the house cannot be a cellar door. In Chapter VIII, "The Last Night," we learn that the cellar door in this part of the house had been sealed for years by "a perfect mat of cobwebs."

[35]   This is very strange. One tries to imagine how Enfield, the child's father, and the doctor, all of whom by then detested Hyde, whiled away the wee hours of the night with him as they waited for the bank to open. And what was the breakfast table conversation like?

[36]   Bank hours in Stevenson's day were from 9:00 A.M. to 3:30 P.M. Banks closed at noon on Saturdays.

[37]   The very height of . . .

[38]   This is not a throwaway phrase. The ironic emphasis is on the word "call." Enfield, the man about town, has some reservations about do-gooders. Though Stevenson is conveniently vague about just what kind of good Jekyll does, we will do well to remember that much of the evil Robert Wringhim does in Hogg's *Confessions of a Justified Sinner* derives from Wringhim's lust for the power to do good.

In 1882, in an essay on Thoreau, Stevenson approvingly quoted Thoreau's remark, "As for doing good, that is one of the professions that are full. Moreover, I have tried it fairly, and, strange as it may seem, am satisfied that it does not agree with my constitution" (*Familiar Studies*, in Stevenson, R.L., *The Works*, Vol. 5, p. 144).

And in "Pulvis et Umbra" (1888), Stevenson wrote:

It is not strange if we are tempted to despair of good. We ask too much. Our religions and moralities have been trimmed to flatter us, till they are all emasculate and sentimentalized, and only please and weaken. Truth is of a rougher strain. . . . (*Memories and Portraits*, in Stevenson, R.L., *The Works*, Vol. 13, p. 104).

[39]   Throughout this opening chapter, there have been tight-lipped suggestions of erotic misbehavior. Now, though we have not yet met Jekyll, an obvious suspicion is being sown.

is what I call that place with the door, in consequence. Though even that, you know, is far from explaining all,' he added, and with the words fell into a vein of musing.

From this he was recalled by Mr. Utterson asking rather suddenly: 'And you don't know if the drawer of the cheque lives there?'

'A likely place, isn't it?' returned Mr. Enfield. 'But I happen to have noticed his address; he lives in some square or other.'[40]

'And you never asked about the—place with the door?' said Mr. Utterson.

'No, sir: I had a delicacy,' was the reply. 'I feel very strongly about putting questions; it partakes too much of the style of the day of judgment. You start a question, and it's like starting a stone. You sit quietly on the top of a hill; and away the stone goes, starting others; and presently some bland old bird[41] (the last you would have thought of) is knocked on the head in his own back garden and the family have to change their name. No, sir, I make it a rule of mine: the more it looks like Queer Street,[42] the less I ask.'

'A very good rule, too,' said the lawyer.

'But I have studied the place for myself,' continued Mr. Enfield. 'It seems scarcely a house. There is no other door, and nobody goes in or out of that one but, once in a great while, the gentleman of my adventure. There are three windows looking on the court on the first floor;[43] none below; the windows are always shut but they're clean. And then there is a chimney which is generally smoking; so somebody must live there. And yet it's not so sure; for the buildings are so packed together about that court, that it's hard to say where one ends and another begins.'[44]

The pair walked on again for a while in silence; and then 'Enfield,' said Mr. Utterson, 'that's a good rule of yours.'[45]

'Yes, I think it is,' returned Enfield.

---

[40]   Here is another puzzle. The drawer of the check is Dr. Jekyll, a fact that Utterson already knows. He knows, too, where Jekyll lives. Why then does he not now clear up the mystery of "in some square or other" and the name of the man who drew the check?
   Stevenson evidently recognized his error, because he rather lamely corrects it at the beginning of Chapter VII, "Incident at the Window."

[41]   Enfield's remark is clearly meant to foreshadow an event still to come. See the account of the death of Sir Danvers Carew, pages 62–63.

[42]   A Britishism that refers to financial problems.

[43]   In Britain, that would be the second story.

[44]   See note 2 of Chapter VII, "Incident at the Window," page 85, where it is clear that Utterson knows precisely which home is which.

[45]   See note 9 on page 33. Utterson restates what we have already learned: he is prepared to let his brother go to the devil in his own way.

40

'But for all that,' continued the lawyer, 'there's one point I want to ask: I want to ask the name of that man who walked over the child.'

'Well,' said Mr. Enfield, 'I can't see what harm it would do. It was a man of the name of Hyde.'

'Hm,' said Mr. Utterson. 'What sort of a man is he to see?'

'He is not easy to describe. There is something wrong with his appearance; something displeasing, something downright detestable. I never saw a man I so disliked, and yet I scarce know why. He must be deformed somewhere;[46] he gives a strong feeling of deformity, although I couldn't specify the point. He's an extraordinary looking man, and yet I really can name nothing out of the way. No, sir; I can make no hand of it; I can't describe him. And it's not want of memory; for I declare I can see him this moment.'

Mr. Utterson again walked some way in silence and obviously under a weight of consideration. 'You are sure he used a key?' he inquired at last.

'My dear sir . . .'[47] began Enfield, surprised out of himself.

'Yes, I know,' said Utterson; 'I know it must seem strange. The fact is, if I do not ask you the name of the other party, it is because I know it already. You see, Richard, your tale has gone home. If you have been inexact in any point, you had better correct it.'

'I think you might have warned me,' returned the other with a touch of sullenness. 'But I have been pedantically exact, as you call it. The fellow had a key; and what's more, he has it still. I saw him use it, not a week ago.'

Mr. Utterson sighed deeply but said never a word; and the young man presently resumed. 'Here is another lesson to say nothing,' said he. 'I am ashamed of my long tongue. Let us make a bargain never to refer to this again.'

'With all my heart,' said the lawyer. 'I shake hands on that, Richard.'

---

[46] Unspecific as this description is here, it will be amplified and repeated at intervals. Hyde's physical loathsomeness fits the notion advanced by Cesare Lombroso in the late nineteenth century that criminals had distinct physical and mental characteristics. According to Lombroso, the criminal type had a low cranial capacity, a retreating forehead, and a thick-boned skull. He was inordinately sensual, lazy, impulsive, and vain.

[47] There is a petulance to this exchange. Enfield is properly irritated to have been entrapped, as it were, by Utterson.

When I was six or seven my best pal Danny had a brother Jimmy who was maybe a hundred years old because he went to high school and could buy all those lurid horror comics. This was not approved reading, especially for Danny and me. So we'd sneak into Jimmy's room and steal the comics he'd hidden under his bed, read them in Danny's room, and afterward Danny had nightmares and I would write and draw horror comics.

Thus I first encountered Dr. Jekyll and Mr. Hyde. I still have a vivid memory of pulling the comic book out of the stack: Dr. Jekyll and Mr. Hyde *was a 1950 Fox publication, with one of their typical headlight covers (terrified dame in net hose showing lots of leg). Being many years away from puberty, this did not impress me: girls were sissies, but monsters were cool. If I just had the right potion, I could be huge and strong and bash in school bullies' heads, and no one would ever know it was me.*

I began to experiment with potions. My oldest brother had a chemistry set, so I stole various bottles from it and pursued secret research. Next and even better, my mother had a large spice cabinet, filled with strange smelling powders and food colors. Curry powder, chili powder, red and green food color, ginger. . . . I was soon forbidden to continue my experiments. This was a scientific tragedy, as I'm certain that one of my potions made my experimental watermelon the largest in the patch.

I was considered a very strange child in the 1950s.

Years passed. I saw a few dozen film versions of Jekyll and Hyde, and read the book. Even became a doctor. In treating psychotic patients, I often wondered whether the medications I gave them were not some reverse form of Dr. Jekyll's experiments. Then there was all the acid my friends and I took during the 1960s. And friends who had one drink too many and suddenly were abusive, belligerent strangers. The hidden self unleashed?

The brain functions through chemical and electrical interactions. Alter these, and we can bring out the good or the evil in ourselves. Or we can create a monster.

—Karl Edward Wagner

Chapter II

Search for Mr. Hyde

That evening, Mr. Utterson came home to his bachelor[1] house in sombre spirits and sat down to dinner without relish. It was his custom of a Sunday, when this meal was over, to sit close by the fire, a volume of some dry divinity[2] on his reading desk, until the clock of the neighbouring church rang out the hour of twelve, when he would go soberly and gratefully to bed. On this night, however, as soon as the cloth was taken away, he took up a candle and went into his business room. There he opened his safe, took from the most private part of it a document endorsed on the envelope as Dr. Jekyll's Will, and sat down with a clouded brow to study its contents. The will was holograph, for Mr. Utterson, though he took

---

[1]   It is notable that *all* of the central figures in this fiction are both male and bachelors. All of them, with the exception of Hyde, who is described as being young, are middle-aged. Stevenson was himself a bachelor until his thirtieth year. At the time Stevenson was writing *Jekyll and Hyde*, he was thirty-six, but after thirty he often spoke of himself as aging.

[2]   Shrewdly, Stevenson does not insist on the religious implications of his allegory, but even this early in the fiction, a reader will have noticed the tangential religious references (the near presence of church bells in Utterson's life, for instance, and the naming of Satan in the previous chapter).

The "volume of dry divinity" undoubtedly comes from a memory Stevenson had of his maternal grandfather, Lewis Balfour, of whom Stevenson, in an essay called "The Manse," wrote: "But his strictness and distance, the effect, I now fancy, of old age and settled habit, oppressed us with a kind of terror. When not abroad he sat much alone, writing sermons or letters to his scattered family in a dark and cold room with a library of bloodless books. . . ." (Ibid., p. 60–61).

charge of it now that it was made, had refused to lend the least assistance in the making of it; it provided not only that, in case of the decease of Henry Jekyll, M.D., D.C.L., LL.D., F.R.S.,[3] &c., all his possessions were to pass into the hands of his 'friend and benefactor Edward Hyde,' but that in case of Dr. Jekyll's 'disappearance[4] or unexplained absence for any period exceeding three calendar months,' the said Edward Hyde should step into the said Henry Jekyll's shoes without further delay and free from any burthen[5] or obligation, beyond the payment of a few small sums to the members of the doctor's household. This document had long been the lawyer's eyesore. It offended him both as a lawyer and as a lover of the sane and customary sides of life, to whom the fanciful was the immodest.[6] And hitherto it was his ignorance of Mr. Hyde that had swelled his indigna- tion; now, by a sudden turn, it was his knowledge. It was already bad enough when the name was but a name of which he could learn no more. It was worse when it began to be clothed upon with detestable attributes; and out of the shifting, insubstantial mists that had so long baffled his eye, there leaped up the sudden, definite presentment of a fiend.[7]

'I thought it was madness,' he said, as he replaced the obnoxious paper in the safe, 'and now I begin to fear it is disgrace.'

With that he blew out his candle, put on a great coat and set forth in the direction of Cavendish Square,[8] that citadel of medicine, where his friend, the great Dr. Lanyon,[9] had his house and received his crowding patients. 'If anyone knows, it will be Lanyon,' he had thought.

The solemn butler knew and welcomed him; he was subjected to no stage of delay, but ushered direct from the door to the dining-room where Dr. Lanyon sat alone over his wine.[10] This was a hearty, healthy, dapper,

---

[3]   Doctor of Medicine, Doctor of Civil Law, Doctor of Laws, Fellow of the Royal Society.

[4]   In an early unsigned review of *The Strange Case of Dr. Jekyll and Mr. Hyde*, E.T. Cook called attention to the improbability of this clause in a will. Writing in *The Athenaeum* on January 16, 1886, Cook pointed out: "Mr. Stevenson has overlooked the fact that a man's will does not come into force until he is dead, and that the fact that he has not been heard of for three months would not enable his executor to carry out his testamentary directions." (Maixner, p. 202–203)

[5]   Burden

[6]   Utterson, the dry lawyer, seems threatened by the disorder implicit in what he regards as "fanciful." The word "immodest," immediately following, recalls the bystreet in Chapter I, where the language describing the shops included "coquetry . . . invitation, like rows of smiling saleswomen . . . florid charms . . ."

[7]   We have not yet actually met Hyde, but his link to the demonic has already been well established. See Chapter I page 38, note 28.

[8]   A square just north of Oxford Street in the St. Marylebone district of London surrounded by late eighteenth- and nineteenth-century houses. Harley Street, which runs along the west side of the square, was and is famous as the place where prestigious physicians have their offices. Baker Street, where the fictional Sherlock Holmes lived, is nearby.

[9]   The name may mean "dweller near John's church" or "church of St. Jona."

red-faced gentleman, with a shock of hair prematurely white, and a boisterous and decided manner. At sight of Mr. Utterson, he sprang up from his
chair and welcomed him with both hands. The geniality, as was the way
of the man, was somewhat theatrical to the eye; but it reposed on genuine
feeling. For these two were old friends, old mates both at school and
college, both thorough respecters of themselves and of each other, and,
what does not always follow, men who thoroughly enjoyed each other's
company.[11]

After a little rambling talk, the lawyer led up to the subject which so
disagreeably preoccupied his mind.

'I suppose, Lanyon,' said he, 'you and I must be the two oldest friends
that Henry Jekyll has?'

'I wish the friends were younger,' chuckled Dr. Lanyon. 'But I suppose we are. And what of that? I see little of him now.'

'Indeed?' said Utterson. 'I thought you had a bond of common
interest.'

'We had,' was the reply. 'But it is more than ten years since Henry
Jekyll became too fanciful[12] for me. He began to go wrong, wrong in mind;
and though of course I continue to take an interest in him for old sake's
sake as they say, I see and I have seen devilish little of the man. Such
unscientific balderdash,' added the doctor, flushing suddenly purple, 'would
have estranged Damon and Pythias.'[13]

This little spirt of temper was somewhat of a relief to Mr. Utterson.
'They have only differed on some point of science,' he thought; and being a

---

[10]   One and all, the bachelors are not only wine-bibbers, but also wine connoisseurs. Vladimir Nabokov
has commented, "There is a delightful winey taste about this book; in fact, a good deal of old mellow
wine is drunk in the story . . ." (Nabokov, p. 180).

    All his life, Stevenson cultivated his taste for wine, so that, even in Samoa, he was constantly
supplied with it. Complaining about Thoreau, Stevenson wrote, "his palate [was] so unsophisticated
that, like a child, he disliked the taste of wine—or perhaps, living in America, had never tasted any
that was good . . ." (Balfour, p. 119).

[11]   We have had this said of Utterson and Enfield. Now Lanyon and Utterson are similarly described.
What's fascinating is that though it is Utterson who is said to have this talent for friendship, we get
very little demonstration of it.

[12]   Now Jekyll is the one who is "fanciful," a code, as we have seen, for the disorderly, the instinctive.
Lanyon, however, forbears to describe Jekyll's "unscientific balderdash."

[13]   Classical Greek models of friendship between men. They are as famous as David and Jonathan are
in the Judeo-Christian tradition.

    The story has it that Dionysus, the tyrant of Syracuse, had condemned Pythias to death for having
plotted against him. Pythias then asked for time to get his family affairs in order and offered his friend
Damon as a willing hostage to guarantee his (Pythias') return. Dionysus, amazed at this gesture of
friendship, accepted the offer. What followed is a cliff-hanging scene in the story when, at the end of
the time allowed him, Pythias, delayed by various obstacles, all but failed to return at the time promised.
Pythias, however, showed up in the knick of time, and Dionysus not only pardoned him, but he pleaded
with the loyal pair to let him share their friendship.

man of no scientific passions (except in the matter of conveyancing)[14] he even added: 'It is nothing worse than that!' He gave his friend a few seconds to recover his composure, and then approached the question he had come to put. 'Did you ever come across a protégé of his—one Hyde?' he asked.

'Hyde?' repeated Lanyon. 'No. Never heard of him. Since my time.'

That was the amount of information that the lawyer carried back with him to the great, dark bed on which he tossed to and fro, until the small hours of the morning began to grow large. It was a night of little ease to his toiling mind, toiling in mere darkness and besieged by questions.

Six o'clock struck on the bells[15] of the church that was so conveniently near to Mr. Utterson's dwelling, and still he was digging at the problem. Hitherto it had touched him on the intellectual side alone; but now his imagination[16] also was engaged or rather enslaved; and as he lay and tossed in the gross darkness of the night and the curtained room, Mr. Enfield's tale went by before his mind in a scroll of lighted pictures.[17] He would be aware of the great field of lamps[18] of a nocturnal city; then of the figure of a man walking swiftly; then of a child running from the doctor's; and then these met, and that human Juggernaut trod the child down and passed on regardless of her screams. Or else he would see a room in a rich house, where his friend lay asleep, dreaming and smiling at his dreams;[19] and then the door of that room would be opened, the curtains of the bed plucked apart, the sleeper recalled, and lo! there would stand by his side a figure to whom power was given, and even at that dead hour, he must rise and do its bidding. The figure in these two phases[20] haunted the lawyer all night; and if at any time he dozed over, it was but to see it glide more stealthily through sleeping houses, or move the more swiftly and still the more swiftly,[21] even to dizziness, through wider labyrinths of lamplighted

---

[14] Drawing up deeds or leases; the preparation of documents required to transfer property. Graham Balfour, in his *Life of Robert Louis Stevenson*, said that in 1872 and 1873, Stevenson worked in the law offices of Skene, Edwards and Bilton in order to learn conveyancing (Balfour, Vol. I, p. 125). In 1874, Stevenson attended lectures at Edinburgh University on the same subject.

[15] It is six A.M., and in London in late October, it is still dark.

In light of Stevenson's feelings about bells, these tolling at a nearby church must be considered ominous. In *The Inland Voyage*, Stevenson writes of bells that "there is often a threatening note, something blatant and metallic, in the voice of bells, that I believe we have fully more pain than pleasure from hearing them" (*The Inland Voyage*, in Stevenson, R.L., *The Works*, Vol. 1, p. 60).

[16] Utterson's dichotomies, we have seen, are cold, dry reason versus the more dangerous, but secretly admirable, acts of the imagination. Stevenson's addition of the word "enslaved" suggests, again, that imagination is, in the context of this fiction, a negative idea.

[17] Does Utterson have a zoetrope in mind? The zoetrope was a nineteenth-century device in which images on the inside of a revolving cylinder appeared to be moving when they were seen through slits in its outer circumference. Or, he may be thinking of a diorama, in which, says *Webster's Third New International Dictionary*, there "is a scenic representation (as of a theatrical stage) in which sculptured figures and lifelike details are displayed . . . so as to blend with a realistic painted background."

city, and at every street corner crush a child and leave her screaming. And still the figure had no face by which he might know it; even in his dreams, it had no face, or one that baffled him and melted before his eyes; and thus it was that there sprang up and grew apace in the lawyer's mind a singularly strong, almost an inordinate, curiosity to behold the features of the real Mr. Hyde. If he could but once set eyes on him, he thought the mystery would lighten and perhaps roll altogether away, as was the habit of mysterious things when well examined. He might see a reason for his friend's strange preference or bondage[22] (call it which you please) and even for the startling clause of the will. At least it would be a face worth seeing; the face of a man who was without bowels of mercy:[23] a face which had but to show itself to raise up, in the mind of the unimpressionable Enfield, a spirit of enduring hatred.

---

[18] See page 35, where Enfield says that "there was literally nothing to be seen but lamps." Beyond this touch of the surreal, it is fascinating to discover the hold that lamps had on Stevenson's imagination. The most obvious example of course is to be found in his poem "The Lamplighter," in which the child who is the voice of the poem expresses the wish to grow up to be a lamplighter. But the poem is slight in comparison with the more moving account he gives involving lanterns in an essay called "The Lantern-Bearers." In that essay, he tells us how, in a fishing village at the end of summer, he and his boy contemporaries carried darkened bull's-eye lanterns under their coats: "The essence of this bliss was to walk by yourself in the black night; the slide shut, the top-coat buttoned; not a ray escaping, whether to conduct your footsteps or to make your glory public; a mere pillar of darkness in the dark; and deep down in the privacy of your fool's heart, to know you had a bull's-eye at your belt, and to exult and sing over the knowledge."

For Stevenson, it was the knowledge of that hidden light that made him sing, and he ends the essay exultantly: "And the true realism, always and everywhere, is that of the poets to find out where joy resides, and give it a voice far beyond singing . . . for no man lives in the external truth, among salts and acids, but in the warm, phantasmagoric chambers of his brain, with the painted windows and the storied walls . . ." (Memories and Portraits, Stevenson, R.L., The Works, Vol. 13, p. 185–186). The above reference to "salts and acids" will illuminate, "Dr. Lanyon's Narrative." See especially page 108.

[19] In an important essay, "A Chapter on Dreams," published in Scribner's Magazine a couple of years after Jekyll and Hyde, Stevenson described dreams as taking place on "that small theatre of the brain which we keep brightly lighted all night long, after the jets are down, and darkness and sleep reign undisturbed in the remainder of the body." He acknowledged that he used his own dreams as a source of plot ideas and described the contribution of his dreams to the development of the Jekyll and Hyde story. He spoke, too, about the power of nightmare and gave several vivid examples.

The essay is remarkable for its surprisingly modern point of view about the role of the unconscious in the creative process. Stevenson divided the responsibility for creative work equally between the contribution of the unconscious (which he called his busy Brownies) and the work of his conscious mind as it attended to the details of writing—organization, editing, diction. Astutely, he suggested that the Brownies might even be affecting his conscious labors.

[20] In the first "phase," the action is out of doors; in the second, the scene is indoors.

[21] The facelessness or the amorphous quality of the figure and the reiterated whirling images of nightmarish detail are remarkably cinematographic, yet no film has yet exploited this passage.

[22] Since Utterson never tells us what he suspects in the relationship between Jekyll and Hyde, this phrase stands out. Blackmail has already been suggested. Now we might guess that Utterson is guessing at homosexuality—the love that knows no name.

[23] Biblical texts often associate the bowels with the heart. The bowels, therefore, have been seen as the seat of compassion and mercy. In the King James Version of Philippians 2:1–2, we read, "If there be therefore any consolation in Christ, if any comfort of love, if any fellowship of the Spirit, if any bowels and mercies, Fulfill ye my joy . . ."

From that time forward, Mr. Utterson began to haunt the door in the bystreet of shops. In the morning before office hours, at noon when business was plenty, and time scarce, at night under the face of the fogged city moon, by all lights and at all hours of solitude or concourse, the lawyer was to be found on his chosen post.

'If he be Mr. Hyde,' he had thought, 'I shall be Mr. Seek.'

And at last his patience was rewarded. It was a fine dry night; frost in the air;[24] the streets as clean as a ballroom floor; the lamps, unshaken by any wind, drawing a regular pattern of light and shadow. By ten o'clock, when the shops were closed, the bystreet was very solitary and, in spite of the low growl of London from all round, very silent. Small sounds carried far; domestic sounds out of the houses were clearly audible on either side of the roadway; and the rumour[25] of the approach of any passenger preceded him by a long time. Mr. Utterson had been some minutes at his post, when he was aware of an odd, light footstep drawing near. In the course of his nightly patrols, he had long grown accustomed to the quaint effect with which the footfalls of a single person, while he is still a great way off, suddenly spring out distinct from the vast hum and clatter of the city. Yet his attention had never before been so sharply and decisively arrested; and it was with a strong, superstitious prevision of success that he withdrew into the entry of the court.[26]

The steps drew swiftly nearer, and swelled out suddenly louder as they turned the end of the street. The lawyer, looking forth from the entry, could soon see what manner of man he had to deal with. He was small and very plainly dressed, and the look of him, even at that distance, went somehow strongly against the watcher's inclination.[27] But he made straight for the door, crossing the roadway to save time; and as he came, he drew a key[28] from his pocket like one approaching home.

Mr. Utterson stepped out and touched him on the shoulder as he passed. 'Mr. Hyde, I think?'

Mr. Hyde shrank back with a hissing intake of the breath.[29] But his

---

[24] It is late October. See note 15 on page 46.

[25] Sounds.

[26] The courtyard, we remember, is two doors down from the corner of the street. Hyde's footsteps ring louder as he turns the corner and starts toward this court.

[27] Hyde's negative qualities, which are often asserted, are never attached to any nameable detail. We are meant to think that decent people instinctively know that there is something morally wrong with him.

[28] The significance of the conversation between Utterson and Enfield about the key is now clearer. It signifies a familial right on Hyde's part.

[29] Hyde has already been linked to Satan, one of whose forms is that of a serpent. Stevenson is not especially subtle in the way he makes Hyde seem to be less than a fully evolved human, more akin to animals than the rest of mankind.

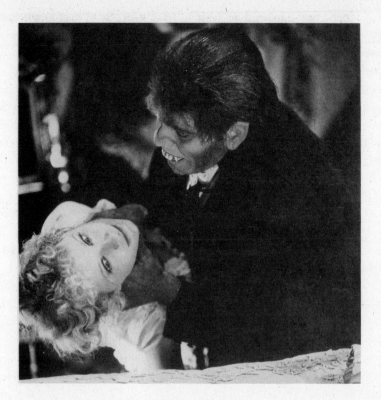

Scene from *Dr. Jekyll and Mr. Hyde* (1932)

fear was only momentary; and though he did not look the lawyer in the face, he answered coolly enough: 'That is my name. What do you want?'

'I see you are going in,' returned the lawyer. 'I am an old friend of Dr. Jekyll's—Mr. Utterson of Gaunt Street[30]—you must have heard my name; and meeting you so conveniently, I thought you might admit me.'

'You will not find Dr. Jekyll; he is from home,' replied Mr. Hyde, blowing in the key. And then suddenly, but still without looking up, 'How did you know me?' he asked.[31]

'On your side,' said Mr. Utterson, 'will you do me a favour?'

'With pleasure,'[32] replied the other. 'What shall it be?'

'Will you let me see your face?' asked the lawyer.

---

[30]   We note that Lanyon and Hyde live comparatively near each other. Utterson, on the other hand is "a long way off (near the Elephant and Castle) . . ." (Noble, p. 56).

[31]   We note that Utterson does not immediately answer the question.

[32]   Given the emphasis Stevenson has already given to Hyde's brutal nature, Hyde's behavior here is extremely civil, and therefore a matter for considerable wonder.

Mr. Hyde appeared to hesitate, and then, as if upon some sudden reflection, fronted about with an air of defiance; and the pair stared at each other pretty fixedly for a few seconds. 'Now I shall know you again,' said Mr. Utterson. 'It may be useful.'

'Yes,' returned Mr. Hyde, 'it is as well we have met;[33] and à propos, you should have my address.'[34] And he gave a number of a street in Soho.

'Good God!' thought Mr. Utterson, 'can he, too, have been thinking of the will?' But he kept his feelings to himself and only grunted in acknowledgment of the address.

'And now,' said the other, 'how did you know me?'

'By description,' was the reply.

'Whose description?'

'We have common friends,' said Mr. Utterson.

'Common friends?' echoed Mr. Hyde, a little hoarsely. 'Who are they?'

'Jekyll, for instance,' said the lawyer.

'He never told you,' cried Mr. Hyde, with a flush of anger. 'I did not think you would have lied.'

'Come,' said Mr. Utterson, 'that is not fitting language.'

The other snarled aloud into a savage laugh; and the next moment, with extraordinary quickness, he had unlocked the door and disappeared into the house.[35]

The lawyer stood awhile when Mr. Hyde had left him, the picture of disquietude. Then he began slowly to mount the street, pausing every step or two and putting his hand to his brow like a man in mental perplexity. The problem he was thus debating as he walked, was one of a class that is rarely solved. Mr. Hyde was pale and dwarfish, he gave an impression of deformity without any nameable malformation, he had a displeasing smile, he had borne himself to the lawyer with a sort of murderous mixture of timidity and boldness, and he spoke with a husky, whispering and somewhat

[33] Hyde's response seems to imply a recognition on his part that Utterson is an antagonist. Why this is so is a mystery, since at this point neither Hyde nor his other self, Jekyll, could have any notion of what prompted Utterson's interest in Hyde.

[34] Everything about this brief conversation between Utterson and Hyde is strange. Two men, strangers to each other, meet one night. One of them asserts he is a friend of a friend and asks to look at the other man's face. The other man, "with an air of defiance," gives the first man his address but does not ask for his interlocutor's address in return. Utterson's suspicion that Hyde is thinking about the will is a possible explanation, but a rather weak one.

[35] Shortly after Hyde leaves Utterson in the courtyard, Stevenson again emphasizes Hyde's animality. Utterson then thinks about Hyde as he walks away: "pale and dwarfish . . . deformity . . . murderous . . . husky . . ." Again, though we are told that Hyde inspires "disgust and loathing and fear," we are never told precisely how.

broken voice; all these were points against him, but not all of these together could explain the hitherto unknown disgust, loathing and fear with which Mr. Utterson regarded him. 'There must be something else,' said the perplexed gentleman. 'There *is* something more, if I could find a name for it. God bless me, the man seems hardly human! Something troglodytic,[36] shall we say? or can it be the old story of Dr. Fell?[37] or is it the mere radiance of a foul soul that thus transpires through, and transfigures, its clay continent?[38] The last, I think; for O my poor old Harry Jekyll, if ever I read Satan's signature upon a face,[39] it is on that of your new friend.'

Round the corner from the bystreet, there was a square of ancient, handsome houses, now for the most part decayed from their high estate and let in flats and chambers to all sorts and conditions of men: map-engravers, architects, shady lawyers and the agents of obscure enterprises. One house, however, second from the corner,[40] was still occupied entire; and at the door of this, which wore a great air of wealth and comfort,[41] though it was now plunged in darkness except for the fanlight, Mr. Utterson stopped and knocked. A well-dressed, elderly servant opened the door.

'Is Dr. Jekyll at home, Poole?'[42] asked the lawyer.

---

[36] Like a prehistoric cave dweller. The emphasis continues to be on Hyde's unevolved state.

[37] The verse about Dr. Fell is:

I do not love thee, Dr. Fell.
The reason why I cannot tell,
But this I know, I know full well,
I do not love thee, Dr. Fell.

The author of the verse is reputed to be Thomas Brown (1663–1704), a considerable scholar who was instrumental in the founding of Oxford University Press. The verses were written against Dr. Fell, Dean of Christchurch, Oxford (1625–1686), who expelled the author but promised to rescind the expulsion if he would translate the thirty-third Epigram of Martial: "*Non amo te, Zabidi, non posso dicere quaere; Hoac tanto possum dicere, non amo te.*"

[38] That which contains. A container. The *Oxford English Dictionary* says this is now a rare use of the word. We note that Stevenson is ironically using the language of spiritual transfiguration to describe possession of the body by a satanic soul.

[39] See Chapter I, note 47, page 41. There, Hyde's ill-featured appearance is simply a sign of what we may think of as secular evil (criminality). Here, he has the mark of Satan on him.

[40] Hyde's courtyard is second from the corner of the bystreet. Jekyll's, we now see, is second from the corner on the main street. We conclude that Hyde's house is L-shaped. His front entrance is on the main street. The courtyard leading to what was formerly the dissecting room is second from the corner on the bystreet. (See Appendix C, p. 249.)

It should now be clear that Utterson knew from the beginning whose house it was into which Hyde disappeared.

[41] Given the tawdry quality of the neighborhood, there is every reason to wonder why the prosperous Dr. Jekyll is still living in such a declassé place. The answer may be that it reflects the insecure hold Jekyll had on decency and respectability even before he meddled with his potion.

[42] In Britain, in numerous forms that include Polle, Powell, Powles, and Powel, the name *Poole* can be traced as far back as the eleventh century. It appears to be derived from the Latin *paulus*, meaning "small" (P.H. Reaney, *A Dictionary of British Surnames* [London: Rutledge, Kegan & Paul], 1976).

51

'I will see, Mr. Utterson,' said Poole, admitting the visitor, as he spoke, into a large, low-roofed, comfortable hall, paved with flags, warmed (after the fashion of a country house) by a bright, open fire, and furnished with costly cabinets of oak. 'Will you wait here by the fire, sir? or shall I give you a light in the dining-room?'

'Here, thank you,' said the lawyer, and he drew near and leaned on the tall fender.[43] This hall, in which he was now left alone, was a pet fancy of his friend the doctor's; and Utterson himself was wont to speak of it as the pleasantest room in London. But to-night there was a shudder in his blood; the face of Hyde sat heavy on his memory; he felt (what was rare with him) a nausea and distaste of life; and in the gloom of his spirits, he seemed to read a menace in the flickering of the firelight[44] on the polished cabinets and the uneasy starting of the shadow on the roof. He was ashamed of his relief, when Poole presently returned to announce that Dr. Jekyll was gone out.

'I saw Mr. Hyde go in by the old dissecting room door,[45] Poole,' he said. 'Is that right, when Dr. Jekyll is from home?'

'Quite right, Mr. Utterson, sir,' replied the servant. 'Mr. Hyde has a key.'

'Your master seems to repose a great deal of trust in that young man, Poole,' resumed the other musingly.

'Yes, sir, he do indeed,' said Poole. 'We have all orders to obey him.'

'I do not think I ever met Mr. Hyde?'[46] asked Utterson.

'O, dear no, sir. He never *dines* here,' replied the butler. 'Indeed we see very little of him on this side of the house; he mostly comes and goes by the laboratory.'[47]

'Well, good night, Poole.'

'Good night, Mr. Utterson.'

And the lawyer set out homeward with a very heavy heart. 'Poor Harry Jekyll,' he thought, 'my mind misgives me he is in deep waters! He was wild when he was young;[48] a long while ago to be sure; but in the

---

[43] A metal guard in front of a fireplace to keep sparks and live coals from falling into the room. This one must be exceptionally tall if Utterson could lean against it.

[44] A menace as it brings a premonition of the fires of hell.

[45] That is, the one that opens onto the courtyard that faces the bystreet.

[46] Since we know that Utterson has just come from meeting Mr. Hyde, the remark here simply means that Utterson has never been formally introduced to him. This conjecture is confirmed for us by Poole's reply, "He never *dines* here." That is, he has no recognizable social position in the household.

[47] The physical layout of Dr. Jekyll's home is becoming clearer. See page 71, where the description is more fully developed and where we learn that the dissecting room and the laboratory are one and the same.

[48] Utterson's speculations, not for the first time, drift comfortably to a worst-case scenario.

law of God, there is no statute of limitations. Ay, it must be that; the ghost of some old sin, the cancer of some concealed disgrace: punishment coming, *pede clando*,[49] years after memory has forgotten and self-love condoned the fault.' And the lawyer, scared by the thought, brooded awhile on his own past, groping in all the corners of memory, lest by chance some Jack-in-the-Box of an old iniquity should leap to light there.[50] His past was fairly blameless; few men could read the rolls of their life with less apprehension; yet he was humbled to the dust by the many ill things he had done, and raised up again into a sober and fearful gratitude by the many that he had come so near to doing, yet avoided. And then by a return on his former subject, he conceived a spark of hope.[51] 'This Master Hyde, if he were studied,' thought he, 'must have secrets of his own; black secrets, by the look of him; secrets compared to which poor Jekyll's worst would be like sunshine. Things cannot continue as they are. It turns me cold to think of this creature stealing like a thief to Harry's bedside;[52] poor Harry, what a wakening! And the danger of it; for if this Hyde suspects the existence of the will, he may grow impatient to inherit. Ay, I must put my shoulder to the wheel—if Jekyll will but let me,' he added, 'if Jekyll will only let me.' For once more he saw before his mind's eye, as clear as a transparency, the strange clauses of the will.

---

[49] One who walks club-footed, or whose feet are clumsy.

[50] It is shrewd of Stevenson to have his dry-as-dust narrator, from whose point of view the Jekyll problem is first put before us, wonder about the degree to which he is himself capable of iniquities. The allegory has universal application if Utterson, a man of "fairly blameless" life, is "humbled to the dust by the many ill things" he had done.

[51] It is hard to find where, in the next eight or ten lines, there is anything on which to build one's hopes, unless the train of thought is meant to suggest that Hyde's sins, being so much blacker than Jekyll's, might control Jekyll by a threat of blackmail.

[52] The idea that Hyde steals to Jekyll's bedside appears first in the account we have of Utterson's sleepless or fitful night (see page 46). Utterson reimagines it here and inevitably makes us wonder once again whether Hyde's "black secrets," as well as Jekyll's, do not also include homosexuality.

The image, reiterated twice, of a monstrous being appearing at Jekyll's bedside, is powerfully suggestive of Fuselli's famous painting "The Nightmare," in which a horse with pupilless eyes stares at a sleeper on whose chest some apelike creature squats.

This novel is about doors, and the interiors that doors preserve. Doors protect secrets, but they also betray them. It is the nature of doors to allow entry as well as forbid it.

Sometimes I visit the house in Monterey, California, where Stevenson lived for a few months during his travels. The house is open to the public, and there are hourly tours. It's a large house, stately, adobe under a coat of plaster and whitewash. The windows are deep-set, the walls thick. The interior is peaceful, and the window glass is old, panes that have warped with time and gently distort the view.

My favorite visits are to the garden outside the house, a garden which I doubt Stevenson ever saw in its present form. Cats sleep in the garden, among the sage. It's in the garden—outdoors—that I feel closest to Stevenson. When we see a thing we have lost it to the imagination. The rooms, the furniture, become merely real. But when we draw close to a locked door we feel enthralled by what is forbidden to us, enchanted by the necessity of imagining what lies within.

I wonder if to Stevenson a book itself is a kind of door, one that opens at a touch, to transform us from a merely real person to a creature much more alive.

—*Michael Cadnum*

Chapter III

>≫€≪

DR. JEKYLL WAS QUITE AT EASE

A fortnight later, by excellent good fortune, the doctor gave one of his pleasant dinners to some five or six old cronies, all intelligent, reputable men and all judges of good wine;[1] and Mr. Utterson so contrived that he remained behind after the others had departed. This was no new arrangement, but a thing that had befallen many scores of times. Where Utterson was liked, he was liked well.[2] Hosts loved to detain the dry lawyer, when the light-hearted and the loose-tongued had already their foot on the threshold; they liked to sit awhile in his unobtrusive company, practising for solitude, sobering their minds in the man's rich silence after the expense and strain of gaiety.[3] To this rule, Dr. Jekyll was no exception; and as he now sat on the opposite side of the fire—a large, well-made,

---

[1] This is one of those "friendly meetings . . . when the wine was to his taste" at which Utterson turns "eminently human," as on page 32.

One notes that wine is frequently alluded to in this story. Balfour described how, on one occasion, Stevenson and his white friends in Samoa spent an entire morning decanting and bottling a hogshead of wine because "Stevenson feared the effect of the fumes even of the light wine upon the natives . . ." (Balfour, Vol. II, p. 174).

We remember, too, that Utterson "mortifies" a taste for good wine by drinking gin (see page 32). We will see later that Hyde, too, is a wine drinker.

[2] Unlike Hyde, who inspires universal disgust. In neither case are we given details to explain why they affect others the way they do.

smooth-faced man of fifty,[4] with something of a slyish cast[5] perhaps, but every mark of capacity and kindness—you could see by his looks that he cherished for Mr. Utterson a sincere and warm affection.

'I have been wanting to speak to you, Jekyll,' began the latter. 'You know that will of yours?'

A close observer might have gathered that the topic was distasteful; but the doctor carried it off gaily. 'My poor Utterson,' said he, 'you are unfortunate in such a client. I never saw a man so distressed as you were by my will; unless it were that hide-bound pedant, Lanyon, at what he called my scientific heresies. O, I know he's a good fellow—you needn't frown—an excellent fellow, and I always mean to see more of him; but a hide-bound pedant for all that; an ignorant, blatant pedant.[6] I was never more disappointed in any man than Lanyon.'

'You know I never approved of it,' pursued Utterson, ruthlessly disregarding the fresh topic.

'My will? Yes, certainly, I know that,' said the doctor, a trifle sharply. 'You have told me so.'

'Well, I tell you so again,' continued the lawyer, 'I have been learning something of young Hyde.'[7]

---

[3] See page 115 where, again, "gaiety" is given a pejorative emphasis.

As a young bachelor, Stevenson had been, in W.E. Henley's words, "my old, riotous, intrepid, scornful Stevenson," who used to frequent the whorehouses and low-class dives in Edinburgh.

Jenni Calder wrote:

He walked about the city, long-haired, dressed in black shirt and neckerchief and velvet jacket, standard bohemian garb of the time but not common in Edinburgh, avidly interested in the underside of the city's life. . . . He frequented the taverns and brothels that most New Town residents preferred not to think about (Calder, p. 11).

David Daiches wrote:

He really did seek out publicans and harlots, and later reproached himself for having cut off communication with a prostitute whose repeated letters he left unanswered so that they might cease (Daiches, op. cit., p. 24).

We have further evidence of Stevenson's youthful "gaiety" in the spurious or contradictory business proposals that Stevenson and Baxter sent to reputable Edinburgh merchants. Delancey Ferguson and Marshall Waingrow wrote that, "Stevenson was so mercurial that in his earlier years his gaiety sometimes reached the pitch of actual hysteria . . ." (Ferguson and Waingrow, p. viii, x–xi).

[4] None of the films based on Stevenson's fiction has depicted Jekyll as a man in middle life.

[5] As with Hyde, Jekyll's hypocritical character has left its mark on his features.

[6] Compare Jekyll's description of Lanyon with Lanyon's view of Jekyll on page 45. William Veeder, in his essay "Children of the Night," notes the pun (Hyde = hide-bound) buried in this phrase which, says Veeder, links Lanyon to Hyde.

[7] Here, for the first time, we learn that Hyde is younger than Jekyll. How much younger, we will never know.

The large handsome face of Dr. Jekyll grew pale to the very lips, and there came a blackness about his eyes. 'I do not care to hear more,' said he. 'This is a matter I thought we had agreed to drop.'

'What I heard was abominable,' said Utterson.

'It can make no change. You do not understand my position,' returned the doctor, with a certain incoherency of manner. 'I am painfully situated, Utterson; my position is a very strange—a very strange one. It is one of those affairs that cannot be mended by talking.'

'Jekyll,' said Utterson, 'you know me: I am a man to be trusted. Make a clean breast of this in confidence; and I make no doubt I can get you out of it.'

'My good Utterson,' said the doctor, 'this is very good of you, this is downright good of you, and I cannot find words to thank you in. I believe you fully; I would trust you before any man alive, ay, before myself, if I could make the choice; but indeed it isn't what you fancy; it is not so bad as that;[8] and just to put your good heart at rest, I will tell you one thing: the moment I choose, I can be rid of Mr. Hyde.[9] I give you my hand upon that; and I thank you again and again; and I will just add one little word, Utterson, that I'm sure you'll take in good part: this is a private matter, and I beg of you to let it sleep.'

Utterson reflected a little looking in the fire.

'I have no doubt you are perfectly right,' he said at last, getting to his feet.

'Well, but since we have touched upon this business, and for the last time I hope,' continued the doctor, 'there is one point I should like you to understand. I have really a very great interest in poor Hyde.[10] I know you have seen him; he told me so; and I fear he was rude. But I do sincerely take a great, a very great interest in that young man; and if I am taken away, Utterson, I wish you to promise me that you will bear with him and get his rights for him. I think you would, if you knew all; and it would be a weight off my mind if you would promise.'

'I can't pretend that I shall ever like him,' said the lawyer.

---

[8] Without being told, Jekyll intuits what Utterson has been thinking: blackmail, crimes, sins, or sexual scandal.

[9] This is a commonly held view of addictive personalities, who are always convinced that they can stop drinking or using drugs whenever they like. It will be seen that Jekyll's need to be Hyde is frequently described in terms of addiction. See especially Chapter X, "Henry Jekyll's Full Statement of the Case."

[10] At this point in the fiction, it is hard to know why Jekyll speaks pityingly of Hyde. But see page 135.

'I don't ask that,' pleaded Jekyll, laying his hand upon the other's arm; 'I only ask for justice; I only ask you to help him[11] for my sake, when I am no longer here.'[12]

Utterson heaved an irrepressible sigh. 'Well,' said he. 'I promise.'

---

[11] In a particularly ironic way, Utterson will keep his promise (see page 98).
[12] Jekyll's language throughout this scene can hardly reassure Utterson, who has already been thinking the worst. What relationship, if not criminal or perverse, can Utterson possibly imagine exists between Jekyll and Hyde?

This story of Dr. Jekyll and his evil alter ego is a mystery tale, a detective yarn, a fantasy, and a horror story. A horror story in the classic tradition, that is; not the garbage-language gore that has given such writing a bad reputation of late.

It is also a social document that perhaps ought to be required reading for today's young people because, in a sense, it is more meaningful today, with drugs and violence eroding the fabric of our world, than when it was first published in 1886.

In the beginning, Dr. Jekyll is a thoroughly good man, admired by all. Why, then, does he use the potion that changes him into a monster? Why do so many of today's good young people use drugs when they know the drugs will change their personalities for the worse and eventually destroy them?

In the end, Jekyll doesn't need the magic potion; he becomes the evil Mr. Hyde without it. In fact, he is unable to stop becoming his monstrous other self and finds that he can't consume enough of the antidote, or can't obtain enough of it, for his usual return to normal. Once hooked, forever lost.

So, then, this Stevenson "thriller" is really a morality tale of real significance in today's world. And because its author was one of the finest writers of his or any other time, it is delivered with tremendous power and clarity—a story loaded with suspense and excitement.

No murky prose here. None of the deliberate obscurity so favored by too many writers and editors today. You know exactly what this story is about and what it means.

I often wonder how many hours Robert Louis devoted to its creation, and whether he himself thought of it as anything more than "just another macabre tale."

—Hugh B. Cave

Chapter IV

※

The Carew[1] Murder Case

Nearly a year later,[2] in the month of October, 18—, London was startled by a crime of singular ferocity and rendered all the more notable by the high position of the victim. The details were few and startling. A maid servant[3] living alone in a house not far from the river, had gone up

---

[1] Without minimizing Hyde's monstrosity, it is notable that in a story as famous for horror as *Jekyll and Hyde* there are in fact only two identifiable victims of Hyde's brutality: the young girl, over whom he tramples, and Sir Danvers Carew, whom he murders. (See also note 17 in this chapter, page 64.)

[2] Our story, then, at its beginning was set in the fall; Utterson's meeting with Jekyll, in the previous chapter, took place in October, as noted.

[3] Stevenson surely meant that she was alone on the night in question. She cannot be said to be living alone, since she works for an unnamed employer, the location of whose house is not specified.

This maid servant is the only adult female character in the story who plays any significant part in the action. Though she appears only briefly, we do have a sense of her character: she is romantically inclined, attentive, observant, and sensitive. Like everyone else who has seen Hyde, the sight of him fills her with repugnance.

Stevenson had a warm spot in his heart for housemaids. In an essay called "Old Mortality," he recounts how, when he was young and given to mooning about fame and death in a graveyard, a beautiful housemaid employed at the hotel where he was staying distracted him: ". . . and when the housemaid, broom in hand, smiled and beckoned from the open window, the fame of that bewigged philosopher [David Hume] melted like a raindrop in the sea" ("Old Mortality," in *Memories and Portraits*, in Stevenson, R.L., *The Works*, Vol. 13, p. 51).

This entire scene is structurally very like one in Thomas Jefferson Hogg's *Confessions of a Justified Sinner*. In that scene, Mrs. Arabella Calvert recounts how she witnessed, from a window in a bordello, the murder of George Cowan by his brother Robert Wringhim, and his alter ego, the demonic Gil Martin. There, too, a full moon illuminates the scene.

stairs to bed about eleven. Although a fog[4] rolled over the city in the small hours, the early part of the night was cloudless, and the lane, which the maid's window overlooked, was brilliantly lit by the full moon.[5] It seems she was romantically given, for she sat down upon her box, which stood immediately under the window, and fell into a dream of musing. Never (she used to say, with streaming tears, when she narrated that experience), never had she felt more at peace with all men or thought more kindly of the world. And as she so sat she became aware of an aged and beautiful gentleman with white hair,[6] drawing near along the lane; and advancing to meet him, another and very small gentleman, to whom at first she paid less attention. When they had come within speech (which was just under the maid's eyes) the older man bowed and accosted the other with a very pretty manner of politeness. It did not seem as if the subject of his address were of great importance; indeed, from his pointing, it sometimes appeared as if he were only inquiring his way; but the moon shone on his face as he spoke, and the girl was pleased to watch it, it seemed to breathe such an innocent and old-world kindness of disposition, yet with something high too, as of a well-founded self-content. Presently her eye wandered to the other, and she was surprised to recognise in him a certain Mr. Hyde, who had once visited her master and for whom she had conceived a dislike. He had in his hand a heavy cane[7] with which he was trifling; but he answered

---

[4] London in the 1880s was famous for its "fogs," which were caused by the heavy use of sulfur-laden coal for heating, transportation, and manufacturing. In modern times, we would call this form of pollution "smog."

[5] In classical lore, the full moon is Selene, or Luna, who loved the sleeping Endymion.

  If this scene were only set on January 21, the maid servant might be suspected of gazing out at the night hoping to catch a glimpse of her own true love, as the beautiful Madeleine does in Keats' "Eve of St. Agnes." Wrong though the date is, the description of the maid servant looking out over the moonlit scene and seduced by it into a "dream of musing" has some of the soft loveliness Keats put into his description of the breathless Madeleine.

  There is a more prosaic reason for thinking the maid was in that sort of romantic mood. In 1879, in a letter to his friend Edmund Gosse, Stevenson writes that he went to lunch at the Royal Hotel in Bathgate, where he observed a maid servant looking out of a window. "On being asked what she was after," Stevenson writes, " 'I'm looking' for my lad,' says she. 'Is that him?' 'Weel, I've been lookin' for him a' my life and I've never seen him yet,' was the response" ("The Letters," in Stevenson, R.L., *The Works*, Vol. 1, p. 343).

[6] In an essay entitled "The Manse," Stevenson describes his maternal grandfather, Lewis Balfour, as "a man of singular simplicity of nature . . . standing contented on the old ways; a lover of his life and innocent habits to the end. . . . We children admired him: partly for his beautiful face and silver hair . . ." (*Memories and Portraits*, in Stevenson, R.L., *The Works*, Vol. 13, p. 60).

  In the story "The Rajah's Diamond," there is another "beautiful old man," but there he is the brilliant but villainous General Vandeleur.

[7] Stevenson himself affected a cane just like this one. In an essay entitled, "Stevenson at Twenty-Eight," Stevenson's stepson, Lloyd Osbourne, wrote that when he [Osbourne] was ten years old he ". . . was greatly fascinated by the cane he [Stevenson] carried. In appearance it was just an ordinary and rather slender walking stick, but on lifting it one discovered that it was a steel bludgeon of considerable weight. R.L.S. said it was the finest weapon a man could carry, for it could not go off

never a word, and seemed to listen with an ill-contained impatience. And then all of a sudden he broke out in a great flame of anger,[8] stamping with his foot, brandishing the cane, and carrying on (as the maid described it) like a madman. The old gentleman took a step back, with the air of one very much surprised and a trifle hurt; and at that Mr. Hyde broke out of all bounds and clubbed him to the earth. And next moment, with ape-like fury,[9] he was trampling his victim under foot and hailing down a storm of blows, under which the bones were audibly shattered and the body jumped upon the roadway. At the horror of these sights and sounds, the maid fainted.[10]

It was two o'clock[11] when she came to herself and called for the police. The murderer was gone long ago; but there lay his victim in the middle of the lane, incredibly mangled. The stick with which the deed had been done, although it was of some rare and very tough and heavy wood, had broken in the middle under the stress of this insensate cruelty; and one splintered half had rolled in the neighbouring gutter—the other, without doubt, had been carried away by the murderer. A purse and a gold watch were found upon the victim: but no cards or papers,[12] except a sealed and

---

of itself like a pistol, nor was it so hard to get into action as a sword-cane. He said that in a tight place there was nothing to equal it.'' (*New Arabian Nights*, in Stevenson, R.L., *The Works*, Vol. 3, p. x).

Stevenson's attachment to such a weapon goes back to his childhood readings in *Skelt's Juvenile Drama*, whose swashbuckling tales prompted Stevenson, when he was fourteen, to buy ''a certain cudgel, got a friend to load it, and thenceforward walked the tame ways of the earth my own ideal, radiating pure romance—still I was but a puppet in the hand of Skelt'' (''A Penny Plain, Twopence Colored,'' in *Memories and Portraits*, in Stevenson, R.L., *The Works*, Vol. 13, p. 120).

[8] Stevenson's familiarity with such behavior is not abstract. In adult life, he often signed his letters with the name ''The Old Man Virulent,'' which his friend, Sidney Colvin, who edited Stevenson's letters, explained as follows: ''The signature . . . alludes to the fits of uncontrollable anger to which he was often in youth . . . subject: fits occasioned sometimes by instances of official stolidity or impertinence or what he took for such . . .'' (''The Letters,'' in Stevenson, R.L., *The Works*, Vol. 3, p. 71).

[9] See page 51, where Utterson, at the sight of Hyde, thinks, ''God bless me, the man seems hardly human!''

Hyde's animality has been urged on the reader from the beginning of the story: his lightness of foot, his speed, his ability to glide stealthily, his husky, hissing voice.

[10] This long opening paragraph is a striking example of Stevenson's narrative skill. In the foreground, we have the ghastly murder seen from the maid's point of view. In the background—or, better, underlying the description of the murder—is the intensely lyric prose recounting the setting: the soft, clear quiet night, the full moon, the maid's peaceful musings, and the sweet loveliness of the white-haired gentle old man whose face ''seemed to breathe such an innocent and old-world kindness of disposition.'' And all of this is seamlessly interwoven with the description of the irritable small man with the heavy cane and the brutal murder he commits.

[11] The murder was committed at or about eleven o'clock in the evening. The maid has been unconscious for nearly three hours.

[12] Everything about Sir Danvers Carew is suspicious. He is out late at night. He accosts a stranger. He carries a watch and a purse full of money but no identification. Had he mailed the stamped letter he was carrying, there would have been no immediate way to identify him. See the Afterword to this volume for a further discussion of this matter.

stamped envelope, which he had been probably carrying to the post,[13] and which bore the name and address of Mr. Utterson.[14]

This was brought to the lawyer the next morning, before he was out of bed; and he had no sooner seen it, and been told the circumstances, than he shot out a solemn lip. 'I shall say nothing till I have seen the body,' said he; 'this may be very serious. Have the kindness to wait while I dress.'[15] And with the same grave countenance he hurried through his breakfast and drove to the police station, whither the body had been carried. As soon as he came into the cell,[16] he nodded.

'Yes,' said he, 'I recognise him.[17] I am sorry to say that this is Sir Danvers Carew.'[18]

'Good God, sir,' exclaimed the officer, 'is it possible?' And the next moment his eye lighted up with professional ambition. 'This will make a deal of noise,' he said. 'And perhaps you can help us to the man.' And he briefly narrated what the maid had seen, and showed the broken stick.

Mr. Utterson had already quailed at the name of Hyde; but when the stick was laid before him, he could doubt no longer; broken and battered as it was, he recognized it for one that he had himself presented many years before to Henry Jekyll.

'Is this Mr. Hyde a person of small stature?' he inquired.

'Particularly small and particularly wicked-looking, is what the maid calls him,' said the officer.

---

[13] British gentlemen, we must deduce, are given to late-night walks. We have seen that Enfield was out walking at three A.M. (page 35), and now Sir Danvers Carew was evidently looking for a mailbox at eleven o'clock at night.

[14] Here we have another of Stevenson's lapses. We never learn how or to what degree Utterson and Carew have known each other, or discover the contents of the letter. Indeed, the letter is never mentioned again.

[15] Utterson is apparently speaking to someone who has been sent, in all likelihood, from the police. The message-bringer is standing at Utterson's bedside. What follows then is curious. Utterson, who has been told that a murder has been committed, instead of only dressing, as he said he will do, also takes time out for a quick breakfast. Utterson's comment on being shown Carew's letter seems inappropriate, especially the remark, "This may be very serious," which is downright ludicrous if one considers that he has just been told that someone who may be a friend or a client (or both) has been murdered.

[16] One would suppose that the body would be in the morgue rather than in a cell.

[17] Note that Utterson has said he would say nothing until he had seen the body. Now, having seen it, he merely identifies it without saying anything further.

[18] The name "Danvers" derives from the French, "D'Anvers" meaning "from Antwerp." A likely source of the name can be found in a book written by a Scotsman with an avid interest in his country's history, Henry Danvers, one of the English conspirators living in Amsterdam who hatched the plot that led to the Duke of Argyll's ill-fated military venture against King James II.

Given the ambiguities that surround the character of Sir Danvers Carew, I like to believe that Stevenson, always a sly prankster, gave Hyde's victim the surname of the poet, Thomas Carew (pronounced Carey). Carew, a disciple of Ben Jonson, was the author of a number of exquisite love poems, notably "The Rapture," which The Oxford Companion to English Literature (Fourth Edition) calls a "fine but licentious amatory poem."

Skerryvore

Mr. Utterson reflected; and then, raising his head, 'if you will come with me in my cab,' he said, 'I think I can take you to his house.'[19]

It was by this time about nine in the morning, and the first fog of the season. A great chocolate-coloured pall[20] lowered over heaven, but the wind was continually charging and routing these embattled vapours; so that as the cab crawled from street to street, Mr. Utterson beheld a marvellous number of degrees and hues of twilight; for here it would be dark like the back-end of evening; and there would be a glow of a rich, lurid brown, like the light of some strange conflagration; and here, for a moment, the fog would be quite broken up, and a haggard shaft of daylight would glance

---

[19] Here one has to wonder again what prompted Hyde to give Utterson, an intrusive stranger, his address (see page 50).

[20] The fog (or, rather, "smog," as described in the following lines) rolled in during the "small" hours of the morning (see page 62).

Stevenson's choice of the word "chocolate-coloured" has special significance if we know that he had powerful feelings about the color brown which appeared to him often during his childhood nightmares. In "A Chapter on Dreams," he writes that he "would be haunted, for instance, by nothing more definite than a certain hue of brown, which he did not mind in the least while he was awake, but feared and loathed while he was dreaming . . ." (*Memories and Portraits*, in Stevenson, R.L., *The Works*, Vol. 13, p. 162). In that same essay Stevenson describes another dream in which a devilish brown dog catches a fly "in his open palm . . . carried it to his mouth like an ape, and looking suddenly up at the dreamer in the window, winked at him with one eye" (Ibid., p. 165).

in between the swirling wreaths. The dismal quarter of Soho seen under these changing glimpses, with its muddy ways, and slatternly passengers, and its lamps,[21] which had never been extinguished or had been kindled afresh to combat this mournful reinvasion of darkness, seemed, in the lawyer's eyes, like a district of some city in a nightmare. The thoughts of his mind, besides, were of the gloomiest dye; and when he glanced at the companion of his drive, he was conscious of some touch of that terror of the law and the law's officers, which may at times assail the most honest.

As the cab drew up before the address indicated, the fog lifted a little and showed him a dingy street, a gin palace,[22] a low French eating house, a shop for the retail of penny numbers and twopenny salads, many ragged children huddled in the doorways, and many women of many different nationalities passing out, key in hand, to have a morning glass; and the next moment the fog settled down again upon that part, as brown as umber, and cut him off from his blackguardly surroundings. This was the home of Henry Jekyll's favourite,[23] of a man who was heir to quarter of a million sterling.[24]

An ivory-faced and silvery-haired old woman opened the door. She had an evil face,[25] smoothed by hypocrisy;[26] but her manners were excellent. Yes, she said, this was Mr. Hyde's, but he was not at home; he had been in that night very late, but had gone away again in less than an hour; there was nothing strange in that; his habits were very irregular, and he was often absent; for instance, it was nearly two months since she had seen him till yesterday.

'Very well, then, we wish to see his rooms,' said the lawyer; and when the woman began to declare it was impossible, 'I had better tell you who this person is,' he added. 'This is Inspector Newcomen of Scotland Yard.'[27]

---

[21] See page 35, where the surreal effect of streetlamps is first suggested.

[22] Heavy drinking was endemic in Victorian Britain. "Gin was mother's milk to her," wrote George Bernard Shaw. Though Stevenson says that women of "different nationalities" were going out for their morning glass, this sort of early drinking was not confined to women of foreign extraction. Between 1879 and 1900, a series of laws known as the "Inebriate Acts" was passed to deal with the problem. The acts established therapeutic centers for alcoholics throughout Britain.

[23] The possibility that Jekyll and Hyde have a clandestine erotic relationship continues to be hinted at.

[24] In 1886, that would have amounted to $1,250,000 (American).

[25] The slightly yellow cast to her features is the only clue we have that this well-mannered woman deserves to be described as having "an evil face." We note again with what economy Stevenson characterizes his personages.

[26] Hypocrisy, as we will see, is Jekyll's problem. (See Maixner, p. 139–140.)

[27] The name "Newcomen" (a variant of Newcombe or Newcome) appears in texts as early as the twelfth century. P.H. Reaney, the editor of A Dictionary of British Surnames, says that it means "a newly arrived stranger," which seems to fit the name for the use to which Stevenson puts it. Harder to explain is whether Newcomen was the messenger who came to Utterson's bedside with the letter found on Sir Danvers Carew's body. And was it still (as I suppose) Newcomen who rode with Utterson to

A flash of odious joy appeared upon the woman's face. 'Ah!' said she, 'he is in trouble! What has he done?'

Mr. Utterson and the inspector exchanged glances. 'He don't[28] seem a very popular character,' observed the latter. 'And now, my good woman, just let me and this gentleman have a look about us.'

In the whole extent of the house, which but for the old woman remained otherwise empty, Mr. Hyde had only used a couple of rooms; but these were furnished with luxury and good taste.[29] A closet was filled with wine; the plate was of silver, the napery elegant; a good picture hung upon the walls, a gift (as Utterson supposed) from Henry Jekyll,[30] who was much of a connoisseur; and the carpets were of many plies and agreeable in colour. At this moment, however, the rooms bore every mark of having been recently and hurriedly ransacked; clothes lay about the floor, with their pockets inside out; lockfast drawers[31] stood open; and on the hearth there lay a pile of gray ashes, as though many papers had been burned. From these embers the inspector disinterred the butt end of a green cheque book, which had resisted the action of the fire; the other half of the stick was found behind the door; and as this clinched his suspicions, the officer declared himself delighted. A visit to the bank, where several thousand pounds were found to be lying to the murderer's credit, completed his gratification.

'You may depend upon it, sir,' he told Mr. Utterson: 'I have him in my hand. He must have lost his head, or he never would have left the stick or, above all, burned the cheque book. Why, money's life to the man. We have nothing to do but wait for him at the bank, and get out the handbills.'

This last, however, was not so easy of accomplishment; for Mr. Hyde had numbered few familiars—even the master of the servant maid had only

---

the police station and then later to Soho?

Scotland Yard was the name of the original building at 4 Whitehall Place in which the London Metropolitan Police force was housed at its founding in 1829. The building, originally a thirteenth-century medieval palace, was used to house visiting Scottish royalty, hence the name. New Scotland Yard was founded in 1890.

[28] The policeman, like the butler, Poole (see page 52), neither of whom is a gentleman, speaks ungrammatically.

[29] Since Hyde is frequently presented to us as an atavism, an unevolved creature, or as animal-like, one supposes that the fine furnishings are an expression of Jekyll's tastes.

[30] Utterson's conjecture that the picture was a gift from Jekyll to Hyde is in keeping with his previous suspicions about the relationship between the two men.

[31] Drawers that lock when they are closed, often seen in nineteenth-century medical or scientific cabinets.

seen him twice;[32] his family could nowhere be traced; he had never been photographed; and the few who could describe him differed widely, as common observers will. Only on one point, were they agreed; and that was the haunting sense of unexpressed deformity with which the fugitive impressed his beholders.

---

[32] See page 62, where the maid is said to have seen Hyde when he "once visited her master." Her master, on the other hand, has seen him twice.

The Strange Case of Dr. Jekyll and Mr. Hyde *is about doubles, two men who are one man. However, the doubling—the duplicity—goes astonishingly far beyond the title character. The praiseworthy Utterson takes vicarious pleasure from friendship with "downgoing men," his own Mr. Hydes. Every major scene in the story features two contrasting men. Duplicity invades the inanimate: the sinister Hyde-door has its counterpart in the respectable Jekyll-door; the white salt exists in two states, the harmless pure form and the sinister tainted form. Stevenson even doubles his work with that of other writers. The opening of Dickens's* Bleak House *is reflected in Utterson's and Newcomen's journey through the fog in quest of Hyde; the opening description of Utterson echoes that of Ebenezer Scrooge; Utterson's dream of Hyde; the opening description of Utterson echoes that of Ebeneezer Scrooge; Utterson's dream of Hyde parting Jekyll's bed curtains mirrors the central dream-born scene of Mary Shelley's* Frankenstein.

The doubling continues outside the book's covers. The tale grew from two dreams. Stevenson wrote the book twice, *burning the first draft.* Two *eyewitness accounts of the burning differ in detail.* Two *partial manuscripts of the revised version survive. Twos multiply twos into infinity, finally resulting in what Jekyll feared, "mere polity" and dissolution. That has happened with differing interpretations of the story. Approaches vary from the feminist to the deconstructionist, from Marxist to New Critical. A strange case, indeed, that such a short work can support the heavy weight of such multifarious interpretation. A fortunate case that, following all the critical evaluations and reassessments, the story remains untouched to trouble (and double) our nightmares.*

—Brad Strickland

Chapter V

❧❧❧

INCIDENT OF THE LETTER

It was late in the afternoon[1] when Mr. Utterson found his way to Dr. Jekyll's door, where he was at once admitted by Poole, and carried down[2] by the kitchen offices[3] and across a yard which had once been a garden,[4] to the building which was indifferently known as the laboratory or the dissecting rooms.[5] The doctor had bought the house from the heirs of a celebrated surgeon; and his own tastes being rather chemical than anatomical, had changed the destination[6] of the block at the bottom of the garden. It was the first time that the lawyer had been received in that part of his friend's quarters: and he eyed the dingy windowless structure[7] with

---

[1] This refers to the day after the murder of Sir Danvers Carew. Utterson was waited upon early in the morning by a policeman (perhaps Newcomen), who brought him Sir Danvers Carew's letter. It was nine o'clock when Utterson and the officer took a cab to Soho. After that, there is a considerable gap in time. One would like to know what Utterson did between that morning visit and "late in the afternoon," when he went to visit Dr. Jekyll.

[2] Led down through.

[3] Kitchen rooms.

[4] See the architect's sketch of the Jekyll-Hyde house, Appendix C, page 249.

[5] Here is a brilliant piece of plotting that serves Stevenson's theme. Though Jekyll's "own tastes [were] rather chemical than anatomical" he is, nevertheless, like the departed Dr. Denman, engaged in dissection, teasing apart the moral elements of the soul.

[6] Americans would say "purpose."

[7] It is the medical theater on the ground floor that is windowless (see note 13 page 72).

curiosity, and gazed round with a distasteful sense of strangeness as he crossed the theatre, once crowded with eager students and now lying gaunt and silent, the tables laden with chemical apparatus, the floor strewn with crates and littered with packing straw, and the light falling dimly through the foggy cupola.[8] At the further end, a flight of stairs mounted to a door covered with red baize;[9] and through this, Mr. Utterson was at last received into the doctor's cabinet.[10] It was a large room, fitted round with glass presses,[11] furnished, among other things, with a cheval-glass[12] and a business table, and looking out upon the court by three dusty windows[13] barred with iron. The fire burned in the grate; a lamp was set lighted on the chimney shelf, for even in the houses the fog began to lie thickly; and there, close up to the warmth, sat Dr. Jekyll, looking deadly sick. He did not rise to meet his visitor, but held out a cold hand and bade him welcome in a changed voice.

'And now,' said Mr. Utterson, as soon as Poole had left them, 'you have heard the news?'

The doctor shuddered. 'They were crying it in the square,'[14] he said. 'I heard them in my dining room.'

'One word,' said the lawyer. 'Carew was my client, but so are you, and I want to know what I am doing. You have not been mad enough to hide this fellow?'

'Utterson, I swear to God,' cried the doctor, 'I swear to God I will never set eyes on him again. I bind my honour to you that I am done with him in this world.[15] It is all at an end. And indeed he does not want my help; you do not know him as I do; he is safe, he is quite safe; mark my words, he will never more be heard of.'

The lawyer listened gloomily; he did not like his friend's feverish man-

---

8   A small windowed structure built on top of a roof.
9   Baize is a long-napped woven woolen fabric, used during that time for upholstery and curtains.
10   A small room or office. As in *The Cabinet of Dr. Caligari.*
There are scholars who have seen in Stevenson's use of this word, with its French etymology, a reference to the piece of furniture made by the notorious Deacon Brodie, who served as a model for the Henley-Stevenson play with that name. Brodie, a respected cabinetmaker by day, was the ringleader of a gang of burglars, gamblers, and thieves by night (see the Introduction to this edition).
11   *The Oxford English Dictionary* (1971) cites a Scots use of the word *press* as a recess in a wall "for holding victuals, plates, dishes. . . ."
12   A full-length mirror whose frame can be tilted.
13   On page 40, we are told that these windows, seen from the outside, "are always shut but they're clean." However, if we keep in mind that Enfield made that remark more than a year ago, their condition now is in keeping with the change in Dr. Jekyll's fortunes vis-à-vis Hyde.
14   Newsboys, shouting the headlines (see page 74).
15   This is an apt, if provocative, vow for the good Christian Jekyll to make, suggesting that he knows he might well be held accountable for Hyde's sins in God's Judgment Book. See pages 52–53, where Utterson muses that "in the law of God, there is no statute of limitations."

ner. 'You seem pretty sure of him,' said he; 'and for your sake, I hope you might be right. If it came to a trial, your name might appear.'

'I am quite sure of him,' replied Jekyll; 'I have grounds for certainty that I cannot share with anyone. But there is one thing on which you may advise me. I have—I have received a letter,[16] and I am at a loss whether I should show it to the police. I should like to leave it in your hands, Utterson; you would judge wisely I am sure; I have so great a trust in you.'

'You fear, I suppose, that it might lead to his detection?' asked the lawyer.

'No,' said the other. 'I cannot say that I care what becomes of Hyde; I am quite done with him. I was thinking of my own character, which this hateful business has rather exposed.'

Utterson ruminated awhile; he was surprised at his friend's selfishness,[17] and yet relieved by it. 'Well,' said he, at last, 'let me see the letter.'

The letter was written in an odd, upright hand and signed 'Edward Hyde': and it signified, briefly enough, that the writer's benefactor, Dr. Jekyll, whom he had long so unworthily repaid for a thousand generosities, need labour under no alarm for his safety as he had means of escape on which he placed a sure dependence. The lawyer liked this letter well enough; it put a better colour on the intimacy than he had looked for; and he blamed himself for some of his past suspicions.[18]

'Have you the envelope?' he asked.

'I burned it,' replied Jekyll, 'before I thought what I was about. But it bore no postmark. The note was handed in.'

'Shall I keep this and sleep upon it?' asked Utterson.

'I wish you to judge for me entirely,' was the reply. 'I have lost confidence in myself.'

'Well, I shall consider,' returned the lawyer. 'And now one word more: it was Hyde who dictated the terms in your will about that disappearance?'

The doctor seemed seized with a qualm of faintness; he shut his mouth tight and nodded.

---

[16] This is a significant hesitation on Jekyll's part (see page 76).

   This entire episode of the letter gives us a glimpse of Jekyll's shabbiness well before we discover his real situation.

[17] Utterson might well be surprised. On page 57, Jekyll, speaking of Hyde, said: "I have really a very great interest in poor Hyde. . . . I do sincerely take a great, a very great interest in that young man."

[18] For an astute lawyer, Utterson seems readily taken in by this spurious letter.

'I knew it,' said Utterson. 'He meant to murder you. You have had a fine escape.'

'I have had what is far more to the purpose,' returned the doctor solemnly: 'I have had a lesson—O God, Utterson, what a lesson I have had!' And he covered his face for a moment with his hands.

On his way out, the lawyer stopped and had a word or two with Poole. 'By the by,' said he, 'there was a letter handed in to-day: what was the messenger like?' But Poole was positive nothing had come except by post; 'and only circulars by that,' he added.

This news sent off the visitor with his fears renewed. Plainly the letter had come by the laboratory door; possibly, indeed, it had been written in the cabinet; and if that were so, it must be differently judged, and handled with the more caution.[19] The newsboys, as he went, were crying themselves hoarse along the footways: 'Special edition. Shocking murder of an M. P.' That was the funeral oration of one friend and client; and he could not help a certain apprehension lest the good name of another should be sucked down in the eddy of the scandal. It was, at least, a ticklish decision that he had to make; and self-reliant as he was by habit, he began to cherish a longing for advice. It was not to be had directly; but perhaps, he thought, it might be fished for.

Presently after,[20] he sat on one side of his own hearth, with Mr. Guest,[21] his head clerk, upon the other, and midway between, at a nicely calculated distance from the fire, a bottle of a particular old wine that had long dwelt unsunned in the foundations of his house. The fog still slept on the wing[22] above the drowned city, where the lamps glimmered like carbuncles; and through the muffle and smother of those fallen clouds, the procession of the town's life was still rolling in through the great arteries with a sound as of a mighty wind.[23] But the room was gay with firelight. In the bottle the acids were long ago resolved; the imperial dye had softened with time,

---

[19] Because the letter, then, would have been written by Hyde in collusion with Jekyll. Utterson, we see, is thrown back on his previous suspicions.

[20] "Soon after." The chronology here is important. Sir Danvers Carew was murdered yesterday. Today Utterson has received news of the death, been to the police station and, now, come to call on Dr. Jekyll.

[21] Brief as his appearance is in this book, Mr. Guest, chief clerk and handwriting expert, is a keen observer, shrewder—despite the warming effects of the fine bottle of wine that Utterson has caused to be opened—than his employer.

[22] The metaphor is taken from the notion of a bird asleep in flight.

[23] This is another example of the skill with which Stevenson creates atmosphere without giving precise detail. At intervals throughout this story, we are made aware of the urban backgrounds to the foreground action we are watching. Here, "the town's life is rolling in." In Chapter II, "the bystreet was very solitary and, in spite of the low growl of London from all round, very silent."

as the colour grows richer in stained windows; and the glow of hot autumn afternoons on hillside vineyards, was ready to be set free and to disperse the fogs of London.[24] Insensibly the lawyer melted. There was no man from whom he kept fewer secrets than Mr. Guest; and he was not always sure that he kept as many as he meant. Guest had often been on business to the doctor's; he knew Poole; he could scarce have failed to hear of Mr. Hyde's familiarity about the house, he might draw conclusions: was it not as well, then, that he should see a letter which put that mystery to rights? and above all since Guest, being a great student and critic of handwriting,[25] would consider the step natural and obliging? The clerk, besides, was a man of counsel;[26] he would scarce read so strange a document without dropping a remark; and by that remark Mr. Utterson might shape his future course.

'This is a sad business about Sir Danvers,' he said.

'Yes, sir, indeed. It has elicited a great deal of public feeling,' returned Guest. 'The man, of course, was mad.'

'I should like to hear your views on that,' replied Utterson. 'I have a document here in his handwriting; it is between ourselves, for I scarce know what to do about it; it is an ugly business at the best. But there it is; quite in your way:[27] a murderer's autograph.'

Guest's eyes brightened, and he sat down at once and studied it with passion. 'No, sir,' he said: 'not mad; but it is an odd hand.'

'And by all accounts a very odd writer,' added the lawyer.

Just then the servant entered with a note.

'Is that from Doctor Jekyll, sir?' inquired the clerk. 'I thought I knew the writing. Anything private, Mr. Utterson?'

'Only an invitation to dinner.[28] Why? do you want to see it?'

---

[24] Lines from Keats' "Ode to a Nightingale" are echoing in Stevenson's ear:

O, for a draught of vintage! that hath been
Cooled a long age in the deep-delvèd earth,
Tasting of Flora and the country green,
Dance, and Provencal song, and sunburnt mirth!
O for a beaker full of the warm South,
Full of the true, the blushful Hippocrene,
With beaded bubbles winking at the brim,
And purple-stainèd mouth . . .

[25] Though the handwriting problem presented here seems primitive enough to be solved by the rankest amateur.

[26] To be counted on for good advice.

[27] Of special interest to you; "right up your alley."

[28] This is very surprising. Jekyll, on the day after Sir Danvers Carew's murder, and only hours after his conversation with Utterson about Hyde's guilt, sends out an invitation to Utterson for dinner. Since

'One moment. I thank you, sir;' and the clerk laid the two sheets of paper alongside and seduously compared their contents. 'Thank you, sir,' he said at last, returning both; 'it's a very interesting autograph.'

There was a pause, during which Mr. Utterson struggled with himself. 'Why did you compare them, Guest?' he inquired suddenly.

'Well, sir,' returned the clerk, 'there's a rather singular resemblance; the two hands are in many points identical:[29] only differently sloped.'

'Rather quaint,' said Utterson.

'It is, as you say, rather quaint,' returned Guest.

'I wouldn't speak of this note, you know,' said the master.

'No, sir,' said the clerk. 'I understand.'

But no sooner was Mr. Utterson alone that night, than he locked the note into his safe, where it reposed from that time forward. 'What!' he thought. 'Henry Jekyll forge for a murderer!' And his blood ran cold in his veins.

---

we will not get to hear more about this dinner, we must suppose that this is Stevenson's heavy-handed way of giving Guest a chance to compare Jekyll's and Hyde's handwriting.

[29] William Henry Meyers, in a long letter dated February 21, 1886, gave Stevenson the benefit of his "psychological" reading of Stevenson's successes and failures in The Strange Case of Dr. Jekyll and Mr. Hyde. Among his other observations, we find the following comment on the handwriting question:

Here [as regards the matter of the handwriting] I think you miss a point for want of familiarity with recent psycho-physical discussions. Handwriting in cases of double personality (spontaneous . . . or induced, as in hypnotic cases) is not and cannot be the same in the two personalities. Hyde's writing might look like Jekyll's done with the left hand, or done when partly drunk or ill: that is the kind of resemblance there might be. Your imagination can make a good point of this (Maixner, p. 215).

Since my mother always wanted me to be a doctor, my model was to be Dr. Jekyll. But then I wasn't certain if he was the good guy or the bad guy. After I saw the movie of The Picture of Dorian Gray, *I decided he was the guy whose portrait got older while he remained the same age. I guess I wasn't sufficiently frightened by the story; but since the terrors of life in Lakewood, Ohio, a suburb of Cleveland, occupied all the room for horror in my psyche, I still don't have my medical degree and my face grows ever older while the portraits in the attic remain the same age.*

—Herbert Gold

Chapter VI

֎

REMARKABLE INCIDENT OF DOCTOR LANYON

Time ran on; thousands of pounds were offered in reward, for the death of Sir Danvers was resented as a public injury; but Mr. Hyde had disappeared out of the ken of the police as though he had never existed. Much of his past was unearthed, indeed, and all disreputable: tales came out of the man's cruelty, at once so callous and violent, of his vile life, of his strange associates, of the hatred that seemed to have surrounded his career;[1] but of his present whereabouts, not a whisper. From the time he had left the house in Soho on the morning of the murder, he was simply blotted out; and gradually, as time drew on, Mr. Utterson began to recover from the hotness of his alarm, and to grow more at quiet with himself. The death of Sir Danvers was, to his way of thinking, more than paid for[2] by the disappearance of Mr. Hyde. Now that that evil influence had been withdrawn, a new life began for Dr. Jekyll. He came out of his seclusion, renewed relations with his friends, became once more their familiar guest and entertainer,[3] and whilst he had always been known for charities, he

---

[1] Here, as almost everywhere in this fiction, Stevenson contents himself with little or no detail. What, besides the trampling of the little girl and the murder of Sir Danvers Carew, constituted Hyde's career of violence? And what was in the "tales of cruelty?"

[2] Utterson's moral bookkeeping is very suspicious. As he seems to see it, the murder of an innocent man is a small price to pay for the "new life" his friend Dr. Jekyll leads after Hyde's disappearance.

was now no less distinguished for religion. He was busy, he was much in the open air, he did good;[4] his face seemed to open and brighten, as if with an inward consciousness of service; and for more than two months; the doctor was at peace.

On the 8th of January[5] Utterson had dined at the doctor's with a small party; Lanyon had been there; and the face of the host had looked from one to the other as in the old days when the trio were inseparable friends. On the 12th, and again on the 14th, the door was shut against the lawyer. 'The doctor was confined to the house,' Poole said, 'and saw no one.' On the 15th, he tried again, and was again refused; and having now been used for the last two months to see his friend almost daily, he found this return of solitude to weigh upon his spirits. The fifth night, he had in Guest to dine with him; and the sixth he betook himself to Doctor Lanyon's.

There at least he was not denied admittance; but when he came in, he was shocked at the change which had taken place in the doctor's appearance. He had his death-warrant written legibly upon his face. The rosy man had grown pale; his flesh had fallen away; he was visibly balder and older; and yet it was not so much these tokens of a swift physical decay that arrested the lawyer's notice, as a look in the eye and quality of manner that seemed to testify to some deep-seated terror of the mind. It was unlikely that the doctor should fear death; and yet that was what Utterson was tempted to suspect. 'Yes,' he thought; 'he is a doctor, he must know his own state and that his days are counted; and the knowledge is more than he can bear.' And yet when Utterson remarked on his ill-looks, it was with an air of great firmness that Lanyon declared himself a doomed man.

'I have had a shock,' he said, 'and I shall never recover. It is a question of weeks. Well, life has been pleasant;[6] I liked it; yes, sir, I

---

[3] Here, by stretching a point, we might justify the dinner invitation noted in the previous chapter. At that time, Dr. Jekyll was not entirely free from his enslavement to Hyde. Talking with Utterson, Jekyll was feverish and looked "deadly sick." Here, he is presented as a fully recovered man.

[4] See Chapter I, note 38, page 39.

[5] The mention of this date provides an editor with the opportunity to create a reasonable, though not precise, calendar of events. See the calendar in Appendix D, p. 253.

[6] Stevenson, gravely ill at intervals throughout his life, often had such summing-up feelings. In the spring of 1891, three years before he died, he wrote to H.D. Baildon, "Sick and well, I have had a splendid life of it, grudge nothing, regret very little—and then only some little corners of misconduct for which I deserve hanging, and must infallibly be damned" ("The Letters," in Stevenson, R.L., *The Works*, Vol. 3, p. 245).

A year later, in some extracts from his journal that he sent to Sidney Colvin, he wrote: ". . . I have endured some forty-two years without public shame, and had a good time as I did it." He then added, "If only I could secure a violent death, what a fine success! I wish to die in my boots. . . . To be drowned, to be shot, to be thrown from a horse—aye to be hanged, rather than pass again through that slow dissolution" (Ibid., Vol. 4, p. 51).

used to like it. I sometimes think if we knew all, we should be more glad to get away.'

'Jekyll is ill, too,' observed Utterson. 'Have you seen him?'

But Lanyon's face changed, and he held up a trembling hand. 'I wish to see or hear no more of Doctor Jekyll,' he said in a loud, unsteady voice. 'I am quite done with that person; and I beg that you will spare me any allusion to one whom I regard as dead.'

'Tut-tut,' said Mr. Utterson; and then after a considerable pause, 'Can't I do anything?' he inquired. 'We are three very old friends, Lanyon; we shall not live to make others.'

'Nothing can be done,' returned Lanyon; 'ask himself.'

'He will not see me,' said the lawyer.

'I am not surprised at that,' was the reply. 'Some day, Utterson, after I am dead, you may perhaps come to learn the right and wrong of this. I cannot tell you. And in the meantime, if you can sit and talk with me of other things, for God's sake, stay and do so; but if you cannot keep clear of this accursed topic, then, in God's name, go, for I cannot bear it.'

As soon as he got home, Utterson sat down and wrote to Jekyll, complaining of his exclusion from the house, and asking the cause of this unhappy break with Lanyon; and the next day[7] brought him a long answer, often very pathetically worded, and sometimes darkly mysterious in drift. The quarrel with Lanyon was incurable. 'I do not blame our old friend,' Jekyll wrote, 'but I share his view that we must never meet. I mean from henceforth to lead a life of extreme seclusion; you must not be surprised, nor must you doubt my friendship, if my door is often shut even to you. You must suffer me to go my own dark way. I have brought on myself a punishment and a danger that I cannot name. If I am the chief of sinners,[8] I am the chief of sufferers also. I could not think that this earth contained a place for sufferings and terrors so unmanning; and you can do but one thing, Utterson, to lighten this destiny, and that is to respect my silence.' Utterson was amazed; the dark influence of Hyde had been withdrawn, the doctor had returned to his old tasks and amities; a week ago, the prospect had smiled with every promise of a cheerful and an honoured age; and now in a moment, friendship, and peace of mind and the whole tenor of his life were wrecked. So great and unprepared a change pointed to madness; but in view of Lanyon's manner and words, there must lie for it[9] some deeper ground.

---

7   January 18.
8   This phrase is from The General Confession, Church of Scotland rite.
9   Under it.

A week afterwards[10] Dr. Lanyon took to his bed, and in something less than a fortnight[11] he was dead. The night after the funeral, at which he had been sadly affected, Utterson locked the door of his business room, and sitting there by the light of a melancholy candle, drew out and set before him an envelope addressed by the hand and sealed with the seal of his dead friend. 'PRIVATE: for the hands of J. G. Utterson ALONE and in case of his predecease *to be destroyed unread*,' so it was emphatically superscribed; and the lawyer dreaded to behold the contents. 'I have buried one friend to-day,' he thought: 'what if this should cost me another?' And then he condemned the fear as a disloyalty, and broke the seal. Within there was another enclosure, likewise sealed, and marked upon the cover as 'not to be opened till the death or disappearance of Dr. Henry Jekyll.' Utterson could not trust his eyes. Yes, it was disappearance; here again, as in the mad will[12] which he had long ago restored to its author, here again were the idea of a disappearance and the name of Henry Jekyll bracketted. But in the will, that idea had sprung from the sinister suggestion of the man Hyde; it was set there with a purpose all too plain and horrible. Written by the hand of Lanyon, what should it mean? A great curiosity came on the trustee, to disregard the prohibition and dive at once to the bottom of these mysteries; but professional honour and faith to his dead friend were stringent obligations; and the packet slept in the inmost corner of his private safe.

It is one thing to mortify[13] curiosity, another to conquer it; and it may be doubted, if, from that day forth, Utterson desired the society of his surviving friend with the same eagerness. He thought of him kindly; but his thoughts were disquieted and fearful. He went to call indeed; but he was perhaps relieved to be denied admittance; perhaps, in his heart, he preferred to speak with Poole upon the doorstep and surrounded by the air and sounds of the open city, rather than to be admitted into that house of voluntary bondage,[14] and to sit and speak with its inscrutable recluse. Poole had, indeed, no very pleasant news to communicate. The doctor, it appeared, now more than ever confined himself to the cabinet over the laboratory, where he would sometimes even sleep; he was out of

---

[10]   January 25.
[11]   On or about February 7.
[12]   See page 44.
[13]   See page 32, where Utterson is said to "mortify" a taste for vintages. Here, as before, it is meant "to subdue."
[14]   See page 47, where *bondage* is used to describe Jekyll's relationship with Hyde.

spirits, he had grown very silent, he did not read; it seemed as if he had something on his mind. Utterson became so used to the unvarying character of these reports, that he fell off little by little in the frequency of his visits.

Sometimes a reading experience affects you for life. I first absorbed The Strange Case of Dr. Jekyll and Mr. Hyde *when I was in ninth grade. I found it in the high school library in their spoken-arts section: three phonograph albums containing an unabridged reading of the short novel. Of course nobody else in school wanted to listen to three albums of someone reading a book, but I checked out the old relics and brought them home. . . . and promptly fell very ill with the flu. I remember lying in my bed in the dark, shivering with fever, and listening to the deep-voiced reader telling the gruesome tale at 16 RPM. That made Henry Jekyll's predicament all the more real. It was absolutely the most perfect way to experience the story of Jekyll and Hyde. Other readers, however, may not think acquiring the flu is an essential part of enjoying the book . . .*

—Kevin J. Anderson

Chapter VII

◆➤◆

INCIDENT AT THE WINDOW

It chanced on Sunday,[1] when Mr. Utterson was on his usual walk with Mr. Enfield, that their way lay once again through the bystreet; and that when they came in front of the door,[2] both stopped to gaze on it.

'Well,' said Enfield, 'that story's at an end at least. We shall never see more of Mr. Hyde.'

---

[1] It is now a year and a quarter since the beginning of this story.

[2] It should be possible now to position this door with some accuracy. On page 34, with Utterson and Enfield walking from west to east, the door is described as being just to the right of a court and set into the first story of a certain "sinister block of building." On page 39, Enfield says that Hyde went into "a cellar door." Around the corner from that "sinister block of building" is Dr. Jekyll's main house. On page 71, we are told that from the kitchen of that house, one crosses a yard that was once a garden in order to get to the block of building that houses the "laboratory or dissecting rooms." From the "theatre" there is a flight of stairs that leads to the red baize door of Dr. Jekyll's office in that same building. On page 100, we learn that there is indeed a "spacious cellar" filled with "crazy lumber," but "a perfect mat of cobweb" at its entrance makes it clear that no one has been in it for years. Enfield then must simply have been wrong when he spoke of a cellar door (or else Stevenson, having put the words in his mouth, forgot to change them).

On page 48, we learn that Utterson, hoping to see Hyde, lurks in the entryway to the court and sees him crossing the roadway straight for the door into which, after his meeting with Utterson, he disappears into the house. On page 52, we learn that the door leads into the dissecting room. On page 100, we learn three things: the "cabinet" looks out upon the court; there is a corridor that leads from the theater to the bystreet; and there is a separate stairway leading from the cabinet to that corridor. With all this before us it is now possible to sketch the layout of Dr. Jekyll's house and its relationship to the laboratory. See drawing, Appendix C, page 249.

'I hope not,' said Utterson. 'Did I ever tell you that I once saw him, and shared your feeling of repulsion?'

'It was impossible to do the one without the other,' returned Enfield. 'And by the way, what an ass you must have thought me, not to know that this was a back way to Dr. Jekyll's! It was partly your own fault that I found it out,[3] even when I did.'

'So you found it out, did you?' said Utterson. 'But if that be so, we may step into the court and take a look at the windows. To tell you the truth, I am uneasy about poor Jckyll; and even outside, I feel as if the presence of a friend might do him good.'

The court was very cool and a little damp, and full of premature twilight, although the sky, high up overhead, was still bright with sunset. The middle one of the three windows was half way open; and sitting close beside it, taking the air with an infinite sadness of mien, like some disconsolate prisoner,[4] Utterson saw Dr. Jekyll.

'What! Jekyll!' he cried. 'I trust you are better.'

'I am very low, Utterson,' replied the doctor drearily, 'very low. It will not last long, thank God.'

'You stay too much indoors,' said the lawyer. 'You should be out, whipping up the circulation like Mr. Enfield and me. (This is my cousin— Mr. Enfield—Dr. Jekyll.) Come now; get your hat and take a quick turn with us.'

'You are very good,' sighed the other. 'I should like to very much; but no, no, no, it is quite impossible; I dare not. But indeed, Utterson, I am very glad to see you; this is really a great pleasure; I would ask you and Mr. Enfield up, but the place is really not fit.'

'Why then,' said the lawyer, good-naturedly, 'the best thing we can do is to stay down here and speak with you from where we are.'

'That is just what I was about to venture to propose,' returned the doctor with a smile. But the words were hardly uttered, before the smile was struck out of his face and succeeded by an expression of such abject terror and despair, as froze the very blood of the two gentlemen below. They saw it but for a glimpse, for the window was instantly thrust down; but that glimpse had been sufficient, and they turned and left the court without a word. In silence, too, they traversed the bystreet; and it was not until they had come into a neighbouring thoroughfare, where even upon

---

[3] We never learn how Enfield "found it out," and Utterson does not pursue the matter.

[4] See page 40, where the windows are described as clean, and page 72, where they are dusty and barred with iron. Here, of course, it is the bars on the windows that create the prison effect.

a Sunday there were still some stirrings of life, that Mr. Utterson at last turned and looked at his companion. They were both pale; and there was an answering horror in their eyes.

'God forgive us, God forgive us,' said Mr. Utterson.

But Mr. Enfield only nodded his head very seriously,[5] and walked on once more in silence.

---

[5] With this serious nod, Enfield—who introduced us in the first chapter to the mystery of Edward Hyde—now disappears completely from the story.

It is problematical if Frankenstein, Dracula, or Dr. Jekyll and Mr. Hyde holds the world record for greatest number of motion picture remakes and spinoffs and it is not worth the research for these brief remarks about the good doctor (and his badder half) but J&H holds at least two records, one for being the first version, 1908 (again in 1909, 12, 13—twice!— 14, 15, 20—three times!!!—and the 1932 version which garnered an Academy Award). Such distinguished actors have portrayed the anguished doctor (before he was extinguished) as John Barrymore, Fredric March, Spencer Tracy, Boris Karloff (Abbott & Costello comedy), Mel Ferrer (cameo), Martine Beswicke (Sister Hyde), Christopher Lee, Jerry Lewis (!—comedy), Jack Palance, and Kirk Douglas (TV musical version!). I don't know whether it is known if the author had a preferred pronunciation in mind for Jekyll but in the definitive version of 1932 he was called (fittingly) Gee-kill.

—Forrest J. (Jekyll) Ackerman

Chapter VIII

> ❦

THE LAST NIGHT

Mr. Utterson was sitting by his fireside one evening after dinner, when he was surprised to receive a visit from Poole.

'Bless me, Poole, what brings you here?' he cried; and then taking a second look at him. 'What ails you?' he added, 'is the doctor ill?'

'Mr. Utterson,' said the man, 'there is something wrong.'

'Take a seat, and here is a glass of wine for you,' said the lawyer. 'Now, take your time, and tell me plainly what you want.'

'You know the doctor's ways, sir,' replied Poole, 'and how he shuts himself up. Well, he's shut up again in the cabinet; and I don't like it, sir—I wish I may die if I like it. Mr. Utterson, sir, I'm afraid.'

'Now, my good man,' said the lawyer, 'be explicit. What are you afraid of?'

'I've been afraid for about a week,'[1] returned Poole, doggedly disregarding the question, 'and I can bear it no more.'

The man's appearance amply bore out his words; his manner was altered for the worse; and except for the moment when he had first announced his terror, he had not once looked the lawyer in the face. Even now, he

---

[1] It is about March now. A week or so has gone by since Enfield and Utterson spoke with Dr. Jekyll at his window and caught a glimpse of him in the grip of a seizure.

89

sat with the glass of wine untasted[2] on his knee, and his eyes directed to a corner of the floor. 'I can bear it no more,' he repeated.

'Come,' said the lawyer, 'I see you have some good reason, Poole; I see there is something seriously amiss. Try to tell me what it is.'

'I think there's been foul play,' said Poole, hoarsely.

'Foul play!' cried the lawyer, a good deal frightened and rather inclined to be irritated in consequence. 'What foul play? What does the man mean?'

'I daren't say, sir,' was the answer; 'but will you come along with me and see for yourself?'

Mr. Utterson's only answer was to rise and get his hat and great coat; but he observed with wonder the greatness of the relief that appeared upon the butler's face, and perhaps with no less, that the wine was still untasted when he set it down to follow.

It was a wild, cold, seasonable night of March, with a pale moon, lying on her back[3] as though the wind had tilted her, and a flying wrack[4] of the most diaphanous and lawny texture. The wind made talking difficult, and flecked the blood into the face. It seemed to have swept the streets unusually bare of passengers, besides; for Mr. Utterson thought he had never seen that part of London so deserted. He could have wished it otherwise; never in his life had he been conscious of so sharp a wish to see and touch his fellow-creatures;[5] for struggle as he might, there was borne in upon his mind a crushing anticipation of calamity.[6] The square, when they got there, was all full of wind and dust, and the thin trees in the garden were lashing themselves along the railing. Poole, who had kept all the way a pace or two ahead, now pulled up in the middle of the pavement, and in spite of the biting weather, took off his hat and mopped his brow with a red pocket-handkerchief.[7] But for all the hurry of his coming, these were not the dews of exertion that he wiped away, but the moisture of some strangling anguish; for his face was white and his voice, when he spoke, harsh and broken.

---

[2] In the home of a wine connoisseur, this is clearly a signal of bad things to come.

[3] Dr. Suzanne Chippendale, astronomy writer and producer at the American Museum of Natural History, says that Stevenson must have had a waxing crescent in mind. In March 1885, the moon was in that phase between March 18 and March 23.

[4] Vestiges of clouds that are being blown about.

[5] See page 35, where Enfield, on a similar night, yearns for the sight of a policeman.

[6] Much as Stevenson has insisted upon Utterson's dry rationality, he is the one who has what we would call extrasensory perceptions (see pages 44, 48, and 52).

[7] This may be meant to be a comic touch, though comedy seems inappropriate at this moment. Otherwise, why would Poole, an impeccable butler, carry a red pocket handkerchief? Poole's handkerchief is red, and so is the baize-covered door that opens into Dr. Jekyll's study.

'Well, sir,' he said, 'here we are, and God grant there be nothing wrong.'

'Amen, Poole,' said the lawyer.

Thereupon the servant knocked in a very guarded manner; the door was opened on the chain; and a voice asked from within, 'Is that you, Poole?'

'It's all right,' said Poole. 'Open the door.'

The hall, when they entered it, was brightly lighted up; the fire was built high; and about the hearth the whole of the servants, men and women,[8] stood huddled together like a flock of sheep. At the sight of Mr. Utterson, the housemaid broke into hysterical whimpering; and the cook, crying out 'Bless God! it's Mr. Utterson,' ran forward as if to take him in her arms.

'What, what? Are you all here?' said the lawyer peevishly. 'Very irregular, very unseemly; your master would be far from pleased.'

'They're all afraid,' said Poole.

Blank silence followed, no one protesting; only the maid lifted up her voice and now wept loudly.

'Hold your tongue!' Poole said to her, with a ferocity of accent that testified to his own jangled nerves; and indeed, when the girl had so suddenly raised the note of her lamentation, they had all started and turned towards the inner door with faces of dreadful expectation. 'And now,' continued the butler, addressing the knife-boy,[9] 'reach me a candle, and we'll get this through hands at once.'[10] And then he begged Mr. Utterson to follow him, and led the way to the back garden.[11]

'Now, sir,' said he, 'you come as gently as you can. I want you to hear, and I don't want you to be heard. And see here, sir, if by any chance he was to ask you in, don't go.'

Mr. Utterson's nerves, at this unlooked for termination, gave a jerk that nearly threw him from his balance; but he recollected his courage and

---

[8] With the introduction of the housemaid and the cook, we now have a total of five female characters in the novel: the little girl who was trampled, the maid who witnessed the murder of Sir Danvers Carew, Hyde's evil landlady, and Doctor Jekyll's maid and cook. Their roles, as we have seen, are absolutely minimal.

[9] In addition to looking after the knives, the knife-boy in a well-managed British household served also as an errand boy.

[10] A Britishism for getting the job done.

[11] This is the area between the main house and the "sinister block," in which the lecture or dissecting room is to be found. Earlier, we were told it was a "yard which had once been a garden . . ." (page 71).

This may be a good place to notice that many of the amenities of Jekyll's house are to be found in Stevenson's suggestions for what to include in an "Ideal House" (*Miscellanea*, 1898). A garden, and especially a deliberately untended garden, is one of the features of that description.

followed the butler into the laboratory building and through the surgical theatre,[12] with its lumber of crates and bottles, to the foot of the stair. Here Poole motioned him to stand on one side and listen; while he himself, setting down the candle and making a great and obvious call on his resolution, mounted the steps and knocked with a somewhat uncertain hand on the red baize of the cabinet door.

'Mr. Utterson, sir, asking to see you,' he called; and even as he did so, once more violently signed to the lawyer to give ear.

A voice answered from within: 'Tell him I cannot see anyone,' it said complainingly.

'Thank you, sir,' said Poole, with a note of something like triumph in his voice: and taking up his candle, he led Mr. Utterson back across the yard and into the great kitchen, where the fire was out and the beetles were leaping on the floor.[13]

'Sir,' he said, looking Mr. Utterson in the eyes, 'was that my master's voice?'

'It seems much changed,' replied the lawyer, very pale, but giving look for look.

'Changed? Well, yes, I think so,' said the butler. 'Have I been twenty years in this man's house, to be deceived about his voice? No, sir; master's made away with; he was made away with, eight days ago, when we heard him cry out upon the name of God;[14] and *who's* in there instead of him, and *why* it stays there, is a thing that cries to Heaven, Mr. Utterson!'

'This is a very strange tale, Poole; this is rather a wild tale, my man,' said Mr. Utterson, biting his finger. 'Suppose it were as you suppose, supposing Dr. Jekyll to have been—well, murdered, what could induce the murderer to stay? That won't hold water; it doesn't commend itself to reason.'

'Well, Mr. Utterson, you are a hard man to satisfy, but I'll do it yet,'

---

12   Among the nightmares Stevenson describes in his "Chapter on Dreams" (*Memories and Portraits*, in Stevenson, R.L., *The Works*, Vol. 13, p.164) is one in which he dreams that he is a medical student who spends his days in a surgical theater, "with his heart in his mouth, his teeth on edge seeing monstrous malformations and the abhorred dexterity of surgeons" and his nights climbing an endless stairway brushing by "beggarly women of the street, great, weary, muddy laborers, poor scarecrows of men, pale parodies of women . . ." until dawn, when he trudges back to the surgical theater and "another day of monstrosities and operations."
13   Stevenson most likely means cockroaches. E. Cobham Brewer, in *The Dictionary of Phrase and Fable*, writes; "Those who know London know how it is overrun with cockroaches, wrongly called blackbeetles" (Brewer, p. 116).
14   Certainly this refers to the moment on page 86, when Dr. Jekyll starts back from the window with "an expression of such abject terror and despair as froze the blood of the two gentlemen below [Enfield and Utterson]."

said Poole. 'All this last week (you must know) him, or it, or whatever it is that lives in that cabinet, has been crying night and day for some sort of medicine and cannot get it to his mind.[15] It was sometimes his way— the master's, that is—to write his orders on a sheet of paper and throw it on the stair. We've had nothing else this week back; nothing but papers, and a closed door, and the very meals left there to be smuggled in when nobody was looking. Well, sir, every day, ay, and twice and thrice in the same day, there have been orders and complaints, and I have been sent flying to all the wholesale chemists[16] in town. Everytime I brought the stuff back, there would be another paper telling me to return it, because it was not pure, and another order to a different firm. This drug is wanted bitter bad, sir, whatever for.'

'Have you any of these papers?' asked Mr. Utterson.

Poole felt in his pocket and handed out a crumpled note, which the lawyer, bending nearer to the candle, carefully examined. Its contents ran thus: 'Dr. Jekyll presents his compliments to Messrs. Maw. He assures them that their last sample is impure and quite useless for his present purpose. In the year 18—, Dr. J. purchased a somewhat large quantity from Messrs. M. He now begs them to search with the most sedulous care, and should any of the same quality be left, to forward it to him at once. Expense is no consideration. The importance of this to Dr. J. can hardly be exaggerated.' So far the letter had run composedly enough, but here with a sudden splutter of the pen, the writer's emotion had broken loose. 'For God's sake,' he had added, 'find me some of the old.'

'This is a strange note,' said Mr. Utterson; and then sharply, 'How do you come to have it open?'

'The man at Maw's was main angry, sir, and he threw it back to me like so much dirt,' returned Poole.

'This is unquestionably the doctor's hand, do you know?' resumed the lawyer.

'I thought it looked like it,' said the servant rather sulkily; and then, with another voice, 'But what matters hand of write,' he said. 'I've seen him!'

'Seen him?' repeated Mr. Utterson. 'Well?'

'That's it!' said Poole. 'It was this way. I came suddenly into the theatre from the garden. It seems he had slipped out to look for this drug or whatever it is; for the cabinet door was open, and there he was at the far end of the room digging among the crates. He looked up when I came in, gave

---

[15] To suit him.
[16] Pharmacies, in Britain.

93

a kind of cry, and whipped upstairs into the cabinet. It was but for one minute that I saw him, but the hair stood upon my head like quills. Sir, if that was my master, why had he a mask upon his face? If it was my master, why did he cry out like a rat, and run from me? I have served him long enough. And then . . .' the man paused and passed his hand over his face.

'These are all very strange circumstances,' said Mr. Utterson, 'but I think I begin to see daylight. Your master, Poole, is plainly seized with one of those maladies that both torture and deform the sufferer;[17] hence, for aught I know, the alteration of his voice; hence the mask and the avoidance of his friends; hence his eagerness to find this drug, by means of which the poor soul retains some hope of ultimate recovery—God grant that he be not deceived! There is my explanation; it is sad enough, Poole, ay, and appalling to consider; but it is plain and natural, hangs well together and delivers us from all exorbitant alarms.'

'Sir,' said the butler, turning to a sort of mottled pallor, 'that thing was not my master, and there's the truth. My master'—here he looked round him and began to whisper—'is a tall fine build of a man, and this was more of a dwarf.' Utterson attempted to protest. 'O, sir,' cried Poole, 'do you think I do not know my master after twenty years? do you think I do not know where his head comes to in the cabinet door, where I saw him every morning of my life? No, sir, that thing in the mask was never Doctor Jekyll—God knows what it was, but it was never Doctor Jekyll; and it is the belief of my heart that there was murder done.'

'Poole,' replied the lawyer, 'if you say that, it will become my duty to make certain. Much as I desire to spare your master's feelings, much as I am puzzled by this note which seems to prove him to be still alive, I shall consider it my duty to break in that door.'

'Ah, Mr. Utterson, that's talking!' cried the butler.

'And now comes the second question,' resumed Utterson: 'Who is going to do it?'

'Why, you and me,' was the undaunted reply.

'That's very well said,' returned the lawyer; 'and whatever comes of it, I shall make it my business to see you are no loser.'[18]

---

[17] I am indebted to Dr. Peter Muz, who has helped me to identify various possible illnesses that might fit Utterson's speculation: 1. P.A.N., or Polyarticulitis nodosa, which affects the skin and joints. 2. Neurological diseases that produce tics or spasms. 3. Infectious diseases like leprosy, which cause disfiguration.

[18] Utterson is being sensitive to the particular danger that Poole, as a servant, will run if he breaks or helps to break down the door. Utterson, as a gentleman and an attorney, has less to fear. See page 97, where Utterson says that his "shoulders are broad enough" to bear the blame.

'There is an axe in the theatre,' continued Poole; 'and you might take the kitchen poker for yourself.'

The lawyer took that rude but weighty instrument into his hand, and balanced it. 'Do you know, Poole,' he said, looking up, 'that you and I are about to place ourselves in a position of some peril?'[19]

'You may say so, sir, indeed,' returned the butler.

'It is well, then, that we should be frank,' said the other. 'We both think more than we have said; let us make a clean breast. This masked figure that you saw, did you recognise it?'

'Well, sir, it went so quick, and the creature was so doubled up, that I could hardly swear to that,' was the answer. 'But if you mean, was it Mr. Hyde?—why, yes, I think it was! You see, it was much of the same bigness; and it had the same quick light way with it; and then who else could have got in by the laboratory door? You have not forgot, sir, that at the time of the murder he had still the key[20] with him? But that's not all. I don't know, Mr. Utterson, if ever you met this Mr. Hyde?'

'Yes,' said the lawyer, 'I once spoke with him.'

'Then you must know as well as the rest of us that there was something queer about that gentleman—something that gave a man a turn—I don't know rightly how to say it, sir, beyond this: that you felt it in your marrow kind of cold and thin.'

'I own I felt something of what you describe,' said Mr. Utterson.

"Quite so, sir,' returned Poole. 'Well, when that masked thing like a monkey[21] jumped from among the chemicals and whipped into the cabinet,

---

[19] Poole and Utterson face two dangers. The first is that they may be arrested for breaking down the door; the second, that whoever or whatever is inside the room may harm them.

[20] The importance of this key has been emphasized from the first (see pages 38, 41, 48, and 100). Hyde, in fact holds the key to the mystery at hand.

   One does not need to look far for the symbolic significance of a key. It represents power, authority: see Isaiah 22:22, "And the key of the house of David will I lay upon his [Eliakim's] shoulder; so he shall open, and none shall shut; and he shall shut, and none shall open." See also Matthew 16:19, where Jesus says to Peter, "And I will give unto thee the keys of the kingdom of heaven: and whatsoever thou shalt bind on earth shall be bound in heaven: and whatsoever thou shalt loose on earth shall be loosed in heaven." And in Revelation 1:18, Jesus says, "I am he that liveth, and was dead; and, behold, I am alive for evermore, Amen; and have the keys of hell and of death."

   In the context of this fiction, of course, the key bestows satanic (therefore doomed and damned) power.

[21] See page 63, note 9. If one is tempted to think of Hyde as revealing aspects of Stevenson's own character, the following early poem of his makes curious reading.

   A Portrait
I am a kind of farthing dip[1]
   Unfriendly to the nose and eyes;
A blue-behinded ape, I skip
   Upon the trees of Paradise.

95

it went down my spine like ice. O, I know it's not evidence, Mr. Utterson; I'm book-learned enough for that; but a man has his feelings, and I give you my bible-word[22] it was Mr. Hyde!'

'Ay, ay,' said the lawyer. 'My fears incline to the same point. Evil, I fear, founded—evil was sure to come—of that connection. Ay, truly, I believe you; I believe poor Harry is killed; and I believe his murderer (for

---

At mankind's feast I take my place
    In solemn, sanctimonious state,
And have the air of saying grace
    While I defile the dinner plate.
I am "the smiler with the knife,"[2]
    The batterer upon garbage, I—
Dear Heaven, with such a rancid life,
Were it not better far to die?

Yet still, about the human pale,
    I love to scamper, love to race,
To swing by my irreverent tail
All over the most holy place;

And when at length, some golden day,
    The unfailing sportsman, aiming at,
Shall bag me—all the world shall say:
    Thank God, and there's an end of that!
("Poems," in Stevenson, R.L., *The Works*, Vol. 1, p. 95–96.)

1. A cheap candle that sputters and smokes.
2. The image is from Chaucer's "The Knight's Tale," describing the hypocritical murderer.

Mrs. Stevenson gives us an unperplexed explanation of how Stevenson came to write this poem:

The verses entitled 'A Portrait,' so unlike anything else my husband ever wrote, do not explain themselves, and must have puzzled many of his readers. He had just finished, with wondering disgust, a book of poems in the most musical English, but excessively morbid and unpleasant in sentiment. His criticisms were generally sympathetic and kind; but this 'batterer upon garbage' with his 'air of saying grace' was more than my husband could endure, and in the first heat of his indignation he wrote 'A Portrait' (Ibid., p. 59–60).

Sidney Colvin, however, described the incident that provoked this poem as taking place at the Saville Club, of which Stevenson was a member:

A certain newly elected member of some social and literary standing, but unacquainted with the spirit of the place, sat lunching alone. Stevenson, desiring to welcome him and make him feel at home, went over and opened talk in his most gracious manner. His advance was received with cold rebuff and implied intimation that the stranger desired no company but his own. Stevenson came away furious, and presently relieved his wrath with the lampoon which is included in his published works and begins . . . 'I am a kind of farthing dip. . . .' (Calder, *Robert L. Stevenson: A Critical Celebration*, p. 28).

Mrs. Stevenson's version is that of a widow intent on idealizing her husband. We, reading the lines in a later, harsher critical climate, can hardly avoid thinking that "A Portrait" is an ironic exercise in self-caricature, just as Stevenson's creation of the apelike Hyde seems to indicate a certain self-awareness.
22 Not many minutes ago, Poole "could hardly swear" to the identity of the masked figure (see page 95). Now, he is willing to give his "bible-word" that it was Hyde.

what purpose, God alone can tell) is still lurking in his victim's room. Well, let our name be vengeance.[23] Call Bradshaw.'

The footman[24] came at the summons, very white and nervous.

'Pull yourself together, Bradshaw,' said the lawyer. 'This suspense, I know, is telling upon all of you; but it is now our intention to make an end of it. Poole, here, and I are going to force our way into the cabinet. If all is well, my shoulders are broad enough to bear the blame. Meanwhile, lest anything should really be amiss, or any malefactor seek to escape by the back, you and the boy[25] must go round the corner with a pair of good sticks, and take your post at the laboratory door.[26] We give you ten minutes,[27] to get to your stations.'

As Bradshaw left, the lawyer looked at his watch. 'And now, Poole, let us get to ours.' he said; and taking the poker under his arm, led the way into the yard. The scud[28] had banked over the moon, and it was now quite dark. The wind, which only broke in puffs and draughts into that deep well of building,[29] tossed the light of the candle to and fro about their steps, until they came into the shelter of the theatre, where they sat down[30]

---

[23] For good Christians, this is a prideful assertion, since, as we read in Psalms 94, "O Lord God, to whom vengeance belongeth; O God, to whom vengeance belongeth, shew thyself." And, in Romans 12:19, we read: "Dearly beloved, avenge not yourselves, but rather give place unto wrath; for it is written, Vengeance is mine; I will repay, saith the Lord."

[24] *Webster's Third New International Dictionary* says that a footman is "a house servant who assists the butler in serving at table, tending the door, carrying luggage and parcels, running errands."

[25] This is the knife-boy (see page 91).

[26] If we consider that the possibility of murder hovers over this scene, then Stevenson makes considerable demands on our capacity for a willing suspension of disbelief. On page 95, Utterson says to Poole, "Do you know, Poole . . . that you and I are about to place ourselves in a position of some peril?" Now Utterson, who is not the master of the house, orders a low-paid and frightened footman and an even lower-paid boy, armed only with sticks, to risk their lives in a possible encounter with a malefactor fleeing through the laboratory door. One would suppose that they should have called the police.

[27] This seems a long time. There are two routes Bradshaw and the boy could take to make their way to Hyde's door. We will recall that Poole and Utterson had their conversation in the kitchen, where Bradford and the boy received their instructions. To get to Hyde's door, they must go through the area that was once a garden, then into the theater. Since Utterson will be armed with an ax from the dissection theater, where there is all kinds of lumber, we may suppose that the footman and the boy would search for their sticks there. Then they would go through the corridor that leads to Hyde's door (see architect's drawing in Appendix C). This would be the most direct route.

On the other hand, there is the longer route: they might leave the kitchen to go back through Jekyll's residence, then out the front entrance and from there around the corner to Hyde's door.

The time allowed may not be excessive if we suppose that Bradford and his helper had to spend some time searching for the sticks with which to arm themselves.

[28] Fragments of clouds driven by the wind.

[29] The yard (formerly the garden) is enclosed on all sides.

[30] Where are they sitting? On page 92, we were told that there were steps leading up from the surgical theater to Jekyll's cabinet, but no steps are mentioned in the present scene. Since they can hear the footsteps in Dr. Jekyll's cabinet, they may be sitting just below it, in the theater, or just outside it on the second floor.

silently to wait. London hummed solemnly all around; but nearer at hand, the stillness was only broken by the sounds of a footfall moving to and fro along the cabinet floor.

'So it will walk all day, sir,' whispered Poole; 'ay, and the better part of the night. Only when a new sample comes from the chemist, there's a bit of a break. Ah, it's an ill-conscience that's such an enemy to rest! Ah, sir, there's blood foully shed in every step of it! But hark again, a little closer—put your heart in your ears. Mr. Utterson, and tell me, is that the doctor's foot?'[31]

The steps fell lightly and oddly, with a certain swing, for all they went so slowly; it was different indeed from the heavy creaking tread of Henry Jekyll. Utterson sighed. 'Is there never anything else?' he asked.

Poole nodded. 'Once,' he said. 'Once I heard it weeping!'

'Weeping? how that?' said the lawyer, conscious of a sudden chill of horror.

'Weeping like a woman or a lost soul,' said the butler. 'I came away with that upon my heart, that I could have wept too.'

But now the ten minutes drew to an end.[32] Poole disinterred the axe from under a stack of packing straw; the candle was set upon the nearest table to light them to the attack; and they drew near with bated breath to where that patient foot[33] was still going up and down, up and down, in the quiet of the night.

'Jekyll,' cried Utterson, with a loud voice, 'I demand to see you.' He paused a moment, but there came no reply. 'I give you fair warning, our suspicions are aroused, and I must and shall see you,' he resumed; 'if not by fair means, then by foul—if not of your consent, then by brute force!'

'Utterson,' said the voice, 'for God's sake, have mercy!'

'Ah, that's not Jekyll's voice—it's Hyde's!' cried Utterson. 'Down with the door, Poole.'

Poole swung the axe over his shoulder; the blow shook the building, and the red baize door leaped against the lock and hinges. A dismal screech, as of mere animal terror, rang from the cabinet. Up went the axe again, and again the panels crashed and the frame bounded; four times the blow fell; but the wood was tough and the fittings were of excellent workman-

---

[31]   Very early on, Stevenson attributed animal light-footedness to Hyde (see page 48).

[32]   This is the time Utterson allowed for Bradshaw and the knife-boy to get to their posts outside of Hyde's door.

[33]   When the "steps fell lightly and oddly" (above), the implication was that these were Hyde's footsteps. The expression "the patient foot" would be more in keeping with "the heavy, creaky tread of Henry Jekyll."

Scene from *Dr. Jekyll and Mr. Hyde* (1920)

ship; and it was not until the fifth, that the lock burst in sunder and the wreck of the door fell inwards on the carpet.

The besiegers appalled by their own riot[34] and the stillness that had succeeded, stood back a little and peered in. There lay the cabinet before their eyes in the quiet lamplight, a good fire glowing and chattering on the hearth,[35] the kettle singing its thin strain, a drawer or two open, papers neatly set forth on the business table, and nearer the fire, the things laid out for tea: the quietest room, you would have said, and, but for the glazed presses full of chemicals, the most commonplace that night in London.

Right in the midst there lay the body of a man sorely contorted and

---

[34] Throughout this fiction, Stevenson has made use of the tension between order and disorder. Utterson is the supremely orderly fellow. Jekyll, the hypocrite, maintains a facade of order. Now here, Utterson (with the help of his accomplice, the equally orderly Poole), has briefly entered the domain of chaos. No wonder they are appalled.

[35] Opposite aspects of a single self though they may be, Jekyll and Hyde have one thing in common: they both like civilized comforts. Presumably this is not so surprising in the case of Dr. Jekyll, whose facade is civility and middle-class respectability. Hyde, on the other hand, to whom animal characteristics are frequently attributed, ought not to need—or want—silver plate, a fine tea service, or a comfortable fire.

The most obvious explanation for what might otherwise seem contradictory is that the person behind the red baize door is, and has been for some time, a continually metamorphosing creature who is alternately Jekyll and then Hyde.

still twitching. They drew near on tiptoe, turned it on its back and beheld the face of Edward Hyde. He was dressed in clothes far too large for him,[36] clothes of the doctor's bigness; the cords of his face still moved with a semblance of life, but life was quite gone: and by the crushed phial in the hand and the strong smell of kernels [37] that hung upon the air, Utterson knew that he was looking on the body of a self-destroyer.

'We have come too late,' he said sternly, 'whether to save or punish. Hyde is gone to his account; and it only remains for us to find the body of your master.'

The far greater proportion of the building was occupied by the theatre, which filled almost the whole ground story and was lighted from above, and by the cabinet, which formed an upper story at one end and looked upon the court. A corridor joined the theatre to the door on the bystreet; and with this the cabinet communicated separately by a second flight of stairs.[38] There were besides a few dark closets and a spacious cellar. All these they now thoroughly examined. Each closet needed but a glance, for all were empty, and all, by the dust that fell from their doors, had stood long unopened. The cellar, indeed, was filled with crazy lumber,[39] mostly dating from the times of the surgeon who was Jekyll's predecessor; but even as they opened the door they were advertised of the uselessness of further search, by the fall of a perfect mat of cobweb[40] which had for years sealed up the entrance. Nowhere was there any trace of Henry Jekyll, dead or alive.

Poole stamped on the flags of the corridor.[41] 'He must be buried here,' he said, hearkening to the sound.

'Or he may have fled,' said Utterson, and he turned to examine the door in the bystreet. It was locked; and lying near by on the flags, they found the key, already stained with rust.[42]

---

[36] This is an important detail. Neither in the single glimpse of Hyde on page 48, nor in any of the other accounts of his appearance, have we been told that he was wearing someone else's clothes.

[37] The characteristic smell of cyanide.

[38] See architect's drawing in Appendix C, p. 249.

[39] Discarded furniture.

[40] See Chapter I, note 34, page 39, for the significance of these cobwebs.

[41] On the flagstones, to check whether there was a hollow sound.

[42] The condition of the key and Poole's further comments on it encapsulate a complete little scenario. Stevenson here lets us know that Jekyll, when he returned home on the morning after Sir Danvers Carew's murder, stamped on the key, breaking it, and then, presumably, vowed never to be Hyde again. We know that for better than two months he was able to keep his vow. Then, sometime after the January 8, but before January 12, he was repossessed by Hyde.

   This poses a perplexing question: why would a triumphant, vibrant, and wicked Hyde be desperate to recreate the potion that would turn him back to a dreary Jekyll? The only answer that makes sense

'This does not look like use,' observed the lawyer.

'Use!' echoed Poole. 'Do you not see, sir, it is broken? much as if a man had stamped on it.'

'Ay,' continued Utterson, 'and the fractures, too, are rusty. The two men looked at each other with a scare. 'This is beyond me, Poole,' said the lawyer. 'Let us go back to the cabinet.'

They mounted the stair in silence, and still with an occasional awestruck glance at the dead body,[43] proceeded more thoroughly to examine the contents of the cabinet. At one table, there were traces of chemical work, various measured heaps of some white salt[44] being laid on glass saucers, as though for an experiment in which the unhappy man had been prevented.

'That is the same drug that I was always bringing him,' said Poole; and even as he spoke, the kettle with a startling noise boiled over.[45]

This brought them to the fireside, where the easy chair was drawn cosily up, and the tea things stood ready to the sitter's elbow, the very sugar in the cup. There were several books on a shelf; one lay beside the tea things open, and Utterson was amazed to find it a copy of a pious work,[46] for which Jekyll had several times expressed a great esteem, annotated, in his own hand, with startling blasphemies.[47]

Next, in the course of their review of the chamber, the searchers came to the cheval glass, into whose depths they looked with an involuntary horror. But it was so turned as to show them nothing but the rosy glow playing on the roof, the fire sparkling in a hundred repetitions along the

---

is the one suggested above in note 35, page 99: from January 9 or so to the present moment, Jekyll and Hyde were equally unstable and transitory presences, each of whom needed to find the potion in order to be finally in possession of the body they inhabited. This explanation also accounts for Hyde being found wearing Jekyll's clothes.

[43]   Convinced, as Poole and Utterson now are, that Jekyll has been murdered, one has to wonder once again why they have not called the police.

[44]   In this context, the word "salt" refers to a chemical compound formed by the neutralization of an acid by a base.

[45]   The boiling tea kettle, along with the other details of solid comfort in the room, show Stevenson at his theatrical and narrative best. At stage center is Hyde's corpse stiffening. At stage left and right, we see nothing that is not innocent, friendly, and warm: the tea things, the fire, the glass fronts of the presses glistening in the cheval glass, and the "rosy glow playing on the roof."

[46]   Utterson was also given to such reading (see page 43).

[47]   In the essay "Memoires of Himself" in Memories and Portraits, Stevenson tells us of a stage in his life when it was fashionable for young men to speak blasphemy. He writes:

[Kingdon] Clifford was then in the hot fit of the most noisy atheism. . . . It was indeed the fashion of the hour . . . the humblest pleasantry was welcome if it were winged against God Almighty or the Christian Church. It was my own proficiency in such remarks that gained me most credit; and my great social success of that period . . . was gained by outdoing poor Clifford in a contest of schoolboy blasphemy. . . . (Memories and Portraits, in Stevenson, R.L., The Works, Vol. 13, p.242).

glazed front of the presses, and their own pale and fearful countenances stooping to look in.

'This glass have seen some strange things, sir,' whispered Poole.

'And surely none stranger than itself,' echoed the lawyer in the same tones. 'For what did Jekyll'—he caught himself up at the word with a start,[48] and then conquering the weakness: 'what could Jekyll want with it?'[49] he said.

'You may say that!' said Poole.

Next they turned to the business table. On the desk among the neat array of papers, a large envelope was uppermost, and bore, in the doctor's hand, the name of Mr. Utterson. The lawyer unsealed it, and several enclosures fell to the floor. The first was a will, drawn in the same eccentric terms as the one which he had returned six months before, to serve as a testament in case of death and as a deed of gift in case of disappearance; but in place of the name of Edward Hyde, the lawyer, with indescribable amazement, read the name of Gabriel John Utterson.[50] He looked at Poole, and then back at the paper, and last of all at the dead malefactor stretched upon the carpet.

'My head goes round,' he said. 'He has been all these days in possession; he had no cause to like me;[51] he must have raged to see himself displaced; and he has not destroyed this document.'

He caught up the next paper; it was a brief note in the doctor's hand and dated at the top. 'O Poole!' the lawyer cried, 'he was alive and here

---

[48]   What makes Utterson pause is his inadvertent use of the past tense, "What *did* Jekyll want with it?" Then, confronting the fact that his friend is dead, he conquers his weakness and goes on, "What could . . ."

[49]   To watch the transformations between Jekyll and Hyde, which must have been fascinating. As fascinating as the film industry has always found these transformations, most of the actors who played the role made use of complicated makeup to achieve their transformations. Spencer Tracy relied solely on his ability to distort his own features (see Filmography, Appendix F, p. 283).

[50]   Now that we have Utterson's full name, we can elaborate our speculations on the significance of it.

Stevenson's choice of Gabriel for a first name is most interesting. Gabriel is one of the four archangels, usually given the role of a divine messenger. In Luke 1:19, we read that Gabriel was the angel who predicted that Elisabeth, Zachariah's wife, would give birth to John. Gabriel says of himself, "I am Gabriel that stands in the presence of God." In Luke 1:26 we learn that it is Gabriel who is responsible for the annunciation to Mary that she is to be the mother of Jesus. In Daniel 8:16, Gabriel is the angel who appears to clarify the meaning of Daniel's vision. In Daniel 9:22, Gabriel says of himself, 'O Daniel, I am now come forth to give thee skill and understanding."

John, Utterson's middle name, is shared by several important New Testament figures: John the Baptist who sent the Apostle John (author of the fourth gospel) to Jesus; John, who wrote the three epistles; and, finally, there is John, who wrote the Revelation.

The point for us is that both of Utterson's names, Gabriel and John, allude to men who were revealers or explainers of the truth—which is Utterson's task in this fiction.

[51]   Nor to dislike him, either. Utterson's entire acquaintance with Hyde has been very brief (see pages 48–49). Their one meeting was conducted, on both sides, with considerable courtesy. Hyde, it will be remembered, ended the interview by giving Utterson his address.

this day. He cannot have been disposed of in so short a space, he must be still alive, he must have fled! And then, why fled? and how? and in that case, can we venture to declare this suicide?[52] O, we must be careful.[53] I foresee that we may yet involve your master in some dire catastrophe.'

'Why don't you read it, sir?' asked Poole.

'Because I fear,' replied the lawyer solemnly, 'God grant I have no cause for it!' And with that he brought the paper to his eyes and read as follows:

'My dear Utterson,—When this shall fall into your hands, I shall have disappeared, under what circumstances I have not the penetration to foresee, but my instinct and all the circumstances of my nameless situation tell me that the end is sure and must be early. Go then, and first read the narrative which Lanyon warned me he was to place in your hands; and if you care to hear more, turn to the confession of

'Your unworthy and unhappy friend,

'HENRY JEKYLL.'

'There was a third enclosure?' asked Utterson.

'Here, sir,' said Poole, and gave into his hands a considerable packet sealed in several places.

The lawyer put it in his pocket. 'I would say nothing of this paper. If your master has fled or is dead, we may at least save his credit.[54] It is now ten; I must go home and read these documents in quiet; but I shall be back before midnight, when we shall send for the police.'[55]

They went out, locking the door of the theatre behind them; and Utterson, once more leaving the servants gathered about the fire in the hall, trudged back to his office to read the two narratives in which this mystery was now to be explained.

---

[52] We have seen that Utterson is given to worst-case scenarios. Now he suspects Jekyll of having murdered Hyde.

[53] About what? One can hardly imagine a catastrophe more dire than the one in the midst of which this dialogue is taking place. I think that what is behind these words is Utterson's anxiety about his friend's good name (see note 54, below).

[54] His reputation. Enfield threatened Hyde with a loss of credit on page 38. Here, the loyal Utterson, not yet sure whether his friend is a criminal or dead, prepares to defend Jekyll's good name. It is a loyalty we may wonder at if we recall the glib lies Jekyll told his trusting friend.

[55] At last a citizen's simple duty is mentioned. But note the cavalier way in which Utterson puts off calling the police. He is going home, leaving behind a houseful of frightened servants to cower for two hours in a home with a corpse.

Though melodramatic in conception, The Strange Case of Dr. Jekyll and Mr. Hyde is not melodramatic in execution since virtually all its scenes are narrated and summarized after the fact. There is no ironic ambiguity, no Wildean subtlety, in the doomed Dr. Jekyll's confession: he presents himself to the reader as a congenital "double dealer" who has nonetheless "an almost morbid sense of shame" and who, in typically Victorian middle-class fashion, must act to dissociate "himself" (i.e., his reputation as a highly regarded physician) from his baser instincts. He can no longer bear to suppress them and it is impossible to eradicate them. His discovery that "Man is not truly one, but two" is seen to be a scientific fact, not a cause for despair.

Thus Dr. Jekyll's uncivilized self, to which he gives the symbolic name Hyde, is at once the consequence of a scientific experiment and a shameless indulgence of appetites that cannot be assimilated into the propriety of everyday Victorian life. There is a sense in which Hyde, for all his monstrosity, is but an addiction like alcohol, nicotine, drugs: "The moment I choose," Dr. Jekyll says, "I can be rid of him." Hyde must be hidden not simply because he is wicked but because Dr. Jekyll is a willfully good man—an example to others, like the much-admired lawyer Mr. Utterson who is "lean, long, dusty, dreary and yet somehow [improbably?] lovable." Had the Victorian ideal been less hypocritically ideal or had Dr. Jekyll been content with a less perfect public reputation his tragedy would not have occurred.

—Joyce Carol Oates

Chapter IX

DOCTOR LANYON'S NARRATIVE

On the ninth of January, now four days ago,[1] I received by the evening delivery a registered envelope, addressed in the hand of my colleague and old school-companion, Henry Jekyll. I was a good deal surprised by this; for we were by no means in the habit of correspondence; I had seen the man, dined with him, indeed, the night before;[2] and I could imagine nothing in our intercourse that should justify formality of registration. The contents increased my wonder; for this is how the letter ran:

'10th December, 18—[3]

'Dear Lanyon,—You are one of my oldest friends; and although we may have differed at times on scientific questions, I cannot remember, at

---

[1] The date of this letter, then, is January 13.

[2] That was on the eighth of January (see page 80).

[3] The date of this letter must be wrong. Lanyon says that he received Jekyll's letter on January 9, a day after having dined with him. But the urgency of the letter ("If you fail me tonight, I am lost . . .") make the December 10 date, more than three weeks ago, impossible.

We have further evidence that the date is wrong because we know Jekyll withdrew abruptly from contact with his friends immediately after his dinner on January 8. The date of Lanyon's document, January 9, must be the day on which Jekyll's catastrophic reversion to Hyde took place.

least on my side, any break in our affection. There was never a day when, if you had said to me, "Jekyll, my life, my honour, my reason, depend upon you," I would not have sacrificed my left hand[4] to help you. Lanyon, my life, my honour, my reason, are all at your mercy; if you fail me to-night, I am lost. You might suppose, after this preface, that I am going to ask you for something dishonourable to grant. Judge for yourself.

'I want you to postpone all other engagements for to-night—ay, even if you were summoned to the bedside of an emperor; to take a cab, unless your carriage should be actually at the door; and with this letter in your hand for consultation, to drive straight to my house. Poole, my butler, has his orders; you will find him waiting your arrival with a locksmith. The door of my cabinet is then to be forced: and you are to go in alone; to open the glazed press[5] (letter E) on the left hand, breaking the lock if it be shut; and to draw out, *with all its contents as they stand*, the fourth drawer from the top or (which is the same thing) the third from the bottom.[6] In my extreme distress of mind, I have a morbid fear of misdirecting you; but even if I am in error, you may know the right drawer by its contents: some powders, a phial and a paper book.[7] This drawer I beg of you to carry back with you to Cavendish Square[8] exactly as it stands.

'That is the first part of the service: now for the second. You should be back, if you set out at once on the receipt of this, long before midnight; but I will leave you that amount of margin, not only in the fear of one of those obstacles that can neither be prevented nor foreseen, but because an hour when your servants are in bed is to be preferred for what will then remain to do. At midnight, then, I have to ask you to be alone in your consulting room, to admit with your own hand into the house a man who will present himself in my name, and to place in his hands the drawer that you will have brought with you from my cabinet. Then you will have played your part and earned my gratitude completely. Five minutes afterwards, if you insist upon an explanation, you will have understood that these arrangements are of capital importance; and that by the neglect of one of them, fantastic as they must appear, you might have charged your conscience with my death or the shipwreck of my reason.

'Confident as I am that you will not trifle with this appeal, my heart sinks and my hand trembles at the bare thought of such a possibility. Think

---

[4] There is a certain amount of reserve here that chills Jekyll's fervor a little. Given the urgency of his letter, one would expect more intense hyperbole; a willingness to lay down his life for his friend, for instance, or even the sacrifice of his *right* hand.

[5] Case.

[6] There are, then, six drawers.

[7] A paperbound notebook.

[8] That is, to Lanyon's house.

of me at this hour, in a strange place,[9] laboring under a blackness of distress that no fancy can exaggerate, and yet well aware that, if you will but punctually serve me, my troubles will roll away like a story that is told. Serve me, my dear Lanyon, and save

'Your friend, H.J.

'P.S. I had already sealed this up when a fresh terror struck upon my soul. It is possible that the post office may fail me, and this letter not come into your hands until tomorrow morning. In that case, dear Lanyon, do my errand when it shall be most convenient for you in the course of the day; and once more expect my messenger at midnight. It may then already be too late; and if that night passes without event, you will know that you have seen the last of Henry Jekyll.'

Upon the reading of this letter, I made sure[10] my colleague was insane; but till that was proved beyond the possibility of doubt, I felt bound to do as he requested. The less I understood of this farrago, the less I was in a position to judge of its importance; and an appeal so worded could not be set aside without a grave responsibility. I rose accordingly from table, got into a hansom, and drove straight to Jekyll's house. The butler was awaiting my arrival; he had received by the same post as mine a registered letter of instruction, and had sent at once for a locksmith and a carpenter.[11] The tradesmen came while we were yet speaking; and we moved in a body to old Dr. Denman's surgical theatre, from which (as you are doubtless aware)[12] Jekyll's private cabinet is most conveniently entered. The door was very strong, the lock excellent; the carpenter avowed he would have great trouble and have to do much damage, if force were to be used; and the locksmith was near despair. But this last was a handy fellow, and after two hours' work, the door stood open. The press marked E was unlocked;

---

[9] From a hotel in Portland Street (see page 131).

[10] I was convinced.

[11] Here again, we have an instance of an oversight in the development of Stevenson's plot. The events described here took place on January 9. Surely the drama of a mysterious letter addressed to Poole, the hiring of a carpenter and a locksmith, and the presence of Dr. Lanyon on a mysterious errand should have made the occasion as memorable an event for Poole as it was for Lanyon. And yet, in the previous chapter, "The Last Night," in which Poole involves Utterson in the drama of his master's life, he never mentions this episode. Stranger still, since Poole, in that chapter, is required to break down the red baize door, he does not mention the clever locksmith who, on the earlier occasion, opened the door for them without violence.

[12] Here is more evidence that Utterson, though he gave no indication of it when he was listening to Enfield's story at the beginning of this fiction, was thoroughly familiar with the layout of Jekyll's house.

and I took out the drawer, had it filled up with straw and tied in a sheet, and returned with it to Cavendish Square.

Here I proceeded to examine its contents. The powders were neatly enough made up, but not with the nicety of the dispensing chemist; so that it was plain they were of Jekyll's private manufacture: and when I opened one of the wrappers, I found what seemed to me a simple, crystalline salt of a white colour. The phial, to which I next turned my attention, might have been about half full of a blood-red liquor, which was highly pungent to the sense of smell and seemed to me to contain phosphorus and some volatile either.[13] At the other ingredients, I could make no guess. The book was an ordinary version book[14] and contained little but a series of dates. These covered a period of many years,[15] but I observed that the entries ceased nearly a year ago and quite abruptly. Here and there a brief remark was appended to a date, usually no more than a single word: 'double' occurring perhaps six times in a total of several hundred entries; and once very early in the list and followed by several marks of exclamation, 'total failure!!!' All this, though it whetted my curiosity, told me little that was definite. Here were a phial of some tincture, a paper of some salt, and the record of a series of experiments that had led (like too many of Jekyll's investigations) to no end of practical usefulness.[16] How could the presence of these articles in my house affect either the honour, the sanity or the life of my flighty colleague? If his messenger could go to one place, why could he not go to another? And even granting some impediment, why was this gentleman to be received by me in secret? The more I reflected, the more convinced I grew that I was dealing with a case of cerebral disease;[17] and though I dismissed my servants to bed, I loaded an old revolver that I might be found in some posture of self-defence.

Twelve o'clock had scarce rung out over London, ere the knocker sounded very gently on the door. I went myself at the summons, and found a small man crouching against the pillars of the portico.

'Are you come from Dr. Jekyll?' I asked.

---

[13]   Ether, by its nature, *is* volatile.

[14]   A record book. This is the "paper book" mentioned on page 106.

[15]   Lanyon, on page 45, tells Utterson that ten years have gone by since Jekyll began to go "wrong, wrong in mind . . ." We may then date the beginning of Jekyll's researches to some time ten years before the opening of the narrative. The date on which Jekyll's researches proved successful, we may surmise, is the last entry in the notebook; that is, a year before this January 9. The important implication of all this is that Hyde—as Hyde—is one year old.

[16]   That is, nothing practical came of the experiments.

[17]   The suspicion that Jekyll might be insane has been expressed several times previously.

He told me 'yes' by a constrained gesture; and when I had bidden him enter, he did not obey me without a searching backward glance into the darkness of the square. There was a policeman not far off, advancing with his bull's eye open,[18] and at the sight, I thought my visitor started and made greater haste.

These particulars struck me, I confess, disagreeably; and as I followed him into the bright light of the consulting room, I kept my hand ready on my weapon. Here, at last, I had a chance of clearly seeing him. I had never set eyes on him before, so much was certain. He was small, as I have said; I was struck besides with the shocking expression of his face, with his remarkable combination of great muscular activity and great apparent debility of constitution,[19] and—last but not least—with the odd, subjective disturbance caused by his neighborhood. This bore some resemblance to incipient rigor, and was accompanied by a marked sinking of the pulse.[20] At the time, I set it down to some idiosyncratic, personal distaste, and merely wondered at the acuteness of the symptoms; but I have since had reason to believe the cause to lie much deeper in the nature of man, and to turn on some nobler hinge than the principle of hatred.[21]

This person (who had thus, from the first moment of his entrance, struck in me what I can only describe as a disgustful curiosity) was dressed in a fashion that would have made an ordinary person laughable: his clothes, that is to say, although they were of rich and sober fabric, were enormously too large for him in every measurement—the trousers hanging on his legs and rolled up to keep them from the ground, the waist of the coat below his haunches, and the collar sprawling wide upon his shoulders. Strange to relate, this ludicrous accoutrement was far from moving me to laughter. Rather, as there was something abnormal and misbegotten in the very essence of the creature that now faced me—something seizing, surprising and revolting—this fresh disparity seemed but to fit in with and to rëinforce it; so that to my interest in the man's nature and character, there was added a curiosity as to his origin, his life, his fortune and status in the world.

---

[18] See note 18, page 45.
[19] Though physically weak, his muscles were twitching.
[20] Lanyon turns from describing Hyde's physical symptoms to an account of his own. *Lanyon* is feeling "incipient rigor . . . accompanied by a marked sinking of the pulse."
[21] Throughout this novel, Stevenson has been consistently vague about the source of the strange uneasiness and feelings of repulsion people feel in the presence of Hyde. Lanyon believes that deep in the nature of man there is an instinctive and noble capacity to recognize evil and shrink from it.

These observations, though they have taken so great a space to be set down in, were yet the work of a few seconds. My visitor was, indeed, on fire with sombre excitement.

'Have you got it?' he cried. 'Have you got it?' And so lively was his impatience that he even laid his hand upon my arm and sought to shake me.

I put him back, conscious at his touch of a certain icy pang along my blood. 'Come, sir,' said I. 'You forget that I have not yet the pleasure of your acquaintance. Be seated, if you please.' And I showed him an example, and sat down myself in my customary seat and with as fair an imitation of my ordinary manner to a patient, as the lateness of the hour, the nature of my prëoccupations, and the horror I had of my visitor, would suffer me to muster.

'I beg your pardon, Dr. Lanyon,' he replied civilly enough. 'What you say is very well founded; and my impatience has shown its heels to my politeness.[22] I come here at the instance of your colleague, Dr. Henry Jekyll, on a piece of business of some moment; and I understood . . .' he paused and put his hand to his throat, and I could see, in spite of his collected manner, that he was wrestling against the approaches of the hysteria—'I understood, a drawer . . .'

But here I took pity on my visitor's suspense, and some perhaps on my own growing curiosity.

'There it is, sir,' said I, pointing to the drawer, where it lay on the floor behind a table and still covered with the sheet.

He sprang to it, and then paused, and laid his hand upon his heart; I could hear his teeth grate with the convulsive action of his jaws; and his face was so ghastly to see that I grew alarmed both for his life and reason.

'Compose yourself,' said I.

He turned a dreadful smile to me, and as if with the decision of despair, plucked away the sheet. At sight of the contents, he uttered one loud sob of such immense relief that I sat petrified. And the next moment, in a voice that was already fairly well under control, 'Have you a graduated glass?' he asked.

I rose from my place with something of an effort and gave him what he asked.

---

[22] "My impatience has interfered with my politeness."

    The scene between Lanyon and Hyde in which civility and formality play so large a part has some similarity to that between Utterson and Hyde when they met. What is notable is that Hyde, who has been described as animal-like as recently as four paragraphs earlier, behaves, especially here, with considerable, almost courtly, courtesy. Again, there is the puzzling question: why would Hyde, who relishes evil, be so eager for the potion that will turn him into Jekyll, his drearier self?

He thanked me with a smiling nod, measured out a few minims[23] of the red tincture and added one of the powders. The mixture, which was at first of a reddish hue, began, in proportion as the crystals melted, to brighten in colour, to effervesce audibly, and to throw off small fumes of vapour. Suddenly and at the same moment, the ebullition ceased and the compound changed to a dark purple, which faded again more slowly to a watery green. My visitor, who had watched these metamorphoses with a keen eye, smiled, set down the glass upon the table, and then turned and looked upon me with an air of scrutiny.

'And now,' said he, 'to settle what remains. Will you be wise? will you be guided? will you suffer me to take this glass in my hand and to go forth from your house without further parley? or has the greed of curiosity[24] too much command of you? Think before you answer, for it shall be done as you decide. As you decide, you shall be left as you were before, and neither richer nor wiser, unless the sense of service rendered to a man in mortal distress may be counted as a kind of riches of the soul. Or, if you shall so prefer to choose, a new province of knowledge and new avenues to fame and power shall be laid open to you, here, in this room, upon the instant; and your sight shall be blasted by a prodigy[25] to stagger the unbelief of Satan.'

'Sir,' said I, affecting a coolness that I was far from truly possessing, 'you speak enigmas, and you will perhaps not wonder that I hear you with no very strong impression of belief. But I have gone too far in the way of inexplicable services to pause before I see the end.'

'It is well,' replied my visitor. 'Lanyon, you remember your vows: what follows is under the seal of our profession.[26] And now, you who have so long been bound to the most narrow and material views, you who have denied the virtue of transcendental medicine, you who have derided your superiors—behold!'

He put the glass to his lips and drank at one gulp. A cry followed; he reeled, staggered, clutched at the table and held on, staring with injected

---

[23]   A very small amount.

[24]   On page 109, Lanyon confessed to having a "disgustful curiosity." Here, Hyde names the temptation to which Lanyon will succumb. Note, too, that Utterson's original motivation for pursuing the Hyde matter was "a singularly strong, an almost inordinate curiosity . . ." (page 47).

[25]   Something out of the ordinary.

[26]   If we remember that Lanyon, as long as ten years ago, disapproved of the direction Jekyll's researches were taking, then these paragraphs sound more like Jekyll talking to a medical colleague over whom he means to triumph than anything we might expect from Hyde. Note particularly "Lanyon . . . what follows is under the seal of our profession." Lanyon is a fellow physician of Jekyll's. We never have any indication that Hyde has a profession.

eyes,[27] gasping with open mouth; and as I looked there came, I thought, a change—he seemed to swell—his face became suddenly black, and the features seemed to melt and alter—and the next moment, I had sprung to my feet and leaped back against the wall, my arm raised to shield me from that prodigy, my mind submerged in terror.

'O God!' I screamed, and 'O God!' again and again; for there before my eyes—pale and shaken, and half fainting, and groping before him with his hands, like a man restored from death—there stood Henry Jekyll!

What he told me in the next hour, I cannot bring my mind to set on paper. I saw what I saw, I heard what I heard, and my soul sickened at it; and yet, now when that sight has faded from my eyes, I ask myself if I believe it, and I cannot answer. My life is shaken to its roots; sleep has left me; the deadliest terror sits by me at all hours of the day and night; I feel that my days are numbered, and that I must die; and yet I shall die incredulous. As for the moral turpitude that man unveiled to me, even with tears of penitence, I cannot, even in memory, dwell on it without a start of horror. I will say but one thing, Utterson, and that (if you can bring your mind to credit it) will be more than enough. The creature who crept into my house that night was, on Jekyll's own confession, known by the name of Hyde and hunted for in every corner of the land as the murderer of Carew.

HASTIE LANYON[28]

---

[27] Bulging eyes.

[28] In this allegorical novel, we have often paused to think about what meanings a character's name might imply. Except for Lanyon's ruddy complexion (see page 45), which suggests a choleric nature, nothing we know about him would make us think of him as "hasty." There is, however, a less speculative source for the name Hastie in Stevenson's work. In his historical novel *Kidnapped* (1886), the young woman who helped David Balfour and Alan Breck across the Forth is named Alison Hastie, and she, Stevenson informed his nurse, was one of her ancestors (Balfour, Vol. I, p. 41).

The horror of Jekyll and Hyde *is of a markedly cerebral kind. There are no monstrous creatures, as in* Frankenstein *or* Dracula. *Of course there is Hyde, but he is a projection of Jekyll. This is why the story still interests us:* Jekyll and Hyde *is a pre-Jungian fable, a vivid illustration of the Shadow side of a decent man, that aspect of our natures whose presence we all have to acknowledge. The drug Jekyll takes is not the instrument of Hyde's coming into being, but merely a neutral means of transmission. In Jekyll's words, "The drug had no discriminating action; it was neither diabolical nor divine; but it shook the doors of the prisonhouse of my disposition."*

With these powerful words, Jekyll admits that, had he undertaken his experiment in a nobler spirit, he might have released from within himself "an angel instead of a fiend." How remarkably this reflection of the 1880s recalls comments on the LSD experiments of the 1950s!

The best part of the story resides in the final section, in Jekyll's statement. It's wonderful, a tour de force, although at the same time rather bloodless. Hyde's sins are no more than alluded to. The drug, we are told, cannot be correctly administered, nor its effects controlled; we are reminded of L-dopa in Oliver Sachs's Awakenings, *where any dose proved too little or too much.*

Like Frankenstein *and* Dracula, Jekyll and Hyde *has frequently been filmed. But, where film versions of the former pair are almost parodic versions of the novels, such is not the case with* Jekyll and Hyde. *The horror, as I've said, is too cerebral, too bloodless, for the movies. Injustice must be seen to be done. We have to be shown Fredric March or Spencer Tracy, or whomever, consorting with prostitutes, wielding the stick, being cruel. We have to see the beaker foam with its deadly but seductive brew, to watch the terrible transformation take place. To witness what is at first willed become involuntary.*

I believe Stevenson, the old Teller of Tales, would be pleased that Hollywood reached towards something darker and more disturbing than Treasure Island.

—*Brian W. Aldiss*

Chapter X

❧❧

HENRY JEKYLL'S FULL STATEMENT OF THE CASE

I was born in the year 18— to a large fortune, endowed besides with excellent parts, inclined by nature to industry, fond of the respect of the wise and good among my fellow-men, and thus, as might have been supposed, with every guarantee of an honourable and distinguished future. And indeed the worst of my faults was a certain impatient gaiety of disposi-tion,[1] such as has made the happiness of many, but such as I found it hard to reconcile with my imperious desire to carry my head high, and wear a more than commonly grave countenance before the public. Hence it came about that I concealed my pleasures; and that when I reached years of reflection, and began to look round me and take stock of my progress and position in the world, I stood already committed to a profound duplicity of life. Many a man would have even blazoned such irregularities as I was guilty of; but from the high views that I had set before me, I regarded and hid them with an almost morbid sense of shame. It was thus rather the exacting nature of my aspirations than any particular degradation in my

---

[1] On page 52, we learned from Utterson that Jekyll had been "wild when he was young." And on page 55, we were told that Jekyll was among those who sobered their minds by basking in Utterson's presence "after the expense and strain of gaiety." Here, the word is given heavy and negative resonance; for Jekyll, gaiety interfered with his desire to "to carry [his] head high."

faults, that made me what I was and, with even a deeper trench than in the majority of men, severed in me those provinces of good and ill which divide and compound man's dual nature. In this case, I was driven to reflect deeply and inveterately on that hard law of life,[2] which lies at the root of religion and is one of the most plentiful springs of distress. Though so profound a double-dealer, I was in no sense a hypocrite;[3] both sides of me were in dead earnest; I was no more myself when I laid aside restraint and plunged in shame, than when I laboured, in the eye of day, at the further-ance of knowledge or the relief of sorrow and suffering. And it chanced that the direction of my scientific studies, which led wholly towards the mystic and the transcendental,[4] rëacted and shed a strong light on this consciousness of the perennial war among my members.[5] With every day, and from both sides of my intelligence, the moral and the intellectual, I thus drew steadily nearer to that truth, by whose partial discovery I have been doomed to such a dreadful shipwreck:[6] that man is not truly one, but truly two. I say two, because the state of my own knowledge does not pass beyond that point. Others will follow, others will outstrip me on the same lines; and I hazard the guess that man will be ultimately known for a mere polity of multifarious, incongruous and independent denizens.[7] I for my part, from the nature of my life, advanced infallibly in one direction and in one direction only. It was on the moral side, and in my own person,

---

[2]   That there is a split in the nature of humankind; that good and evil are coexistent in the self.

[3]   A few years after *Jekyll and Hyde* was published, Stevenson, writing to John Paul Bocock in 1887, said that hypocrisy, not his love of women, was Jekyll's chief fault (see the Afterword to this edition).

[4]   The proximity of the words "mystic" and "transcendental," and the somewhat densely developed theory of the relationship between spirit and matter that immediately follows, raises the possibility that Stevenson, the prankster, is remembering the lines in Gilbert and Sullivan's *Patience*:

> You must lie upon the daisies
> and discourse in novel phrases
> of your complicated state of mind.
> The meaning doesn't matter
> if it's only idle chatter
> of a transcendental kind.
> And everyone will say
> As you walk your mystic way,
> "If this young man expresses himself in terms too deep for *me*,
> Why, what a very singularly deep young man this deep young man must be."

[5]   For a fiction in which women are significantly *not* involved, this phrasing is extremely suggestive. Jekyll has been talking about the moral divisions in the self: the war between good and evil. Now he speaks of the war between the members. It sounds suspiciously like Lear's, "But to the girdle do the gods inherit,/The rest is all the fiend's" (*King Lear*, Act IV, Scene 6, lines 128–129).

  Writing to J.A. Symonds in 1886, Stevenson says, "*Jekyll* is a dreadful thing, I own; but the only thing I feel dreadful about is that damned old business of the war in the members. This time it came out; I hope it will stay in, in future" ("The Letters," in Stevenson, R.L., *The Works*, Vol. 2, p. 293).

[6]   Jekyll used the same word in his letter to Lanyon (see page 106).

that I learned to recognise the thorough and primitive duality of man; I saw that, of the two natures that contended in the field of my consciousness, even if I could rightly be said to be either, it was only because I was radically both;[8] and from an early date, even before the course of my scientific discoveries had begun to suggest the most naked possibility of such a miracle, I had learned to dwell with pleasure, as a beloved daydream, on the thought of the separation of these elements. If each, I told myself, could but be housed in separate identities, life would be relieved of all that was unbearable; the unjust might go his way delivered from the aspirations and remorse of his more upright twin; and the just could walk steadfastly and securely on his upward path, doing the good things in which he found his pleasure, and no longer exposed to disgrace and penitence by the hands of this extraneous evil. It was the curse of mankind that these incongruous faggots were thus bound together—that in the agonised womb of consciousness, these polar twins should be continuously struggling.[9] How, then, were they dissociated?

I was so far in my reflections when, as I have said, a side light began to shine upon the subject from the laboratory table. I began to perceive more deeply than it has ever yet been stated, the trembling immateriality, the mist-like transience, of this seemingly so solid body in which we walk attired.[10] Certain agents I found to have the power to shake and to pluck back that fleshly vestment,[11] even as a wind might toss the curtains of a pavilion. For two good reasons, I will not enter deeply into this scientific branch of my confession.[12] First, because I have been made to learn that

---

[7]   Indeed, in the twentieth century, there has been a plethora of multiple personality studies, usually under the rubric of "Multiple Personality Syndrome" (MPS) or Multiple Personality Disorder (MPD). The disorder differs from schizophrenia in that in the schizophrenic there is a lack of cohesion between thought and emotion, not a splitting of different personalities. See the Introduction to this edition.
    Robert Wringhim, the doomed protagonist of Hogg's *Confessions of a Justified Sinner*, says of himself that nothing could dispel "the singular illusion that I was two people at the same time." In Hogg's book, the division is the direct work of a satanic figure, while here Jekyll is the prime mover of his own disaster.

[8]   Jekyll asserts the distinctness of the difference between the two selves, but we will see that his potion does not separate a good Jekyll from a bad Hyde. Hyde is the one of the two who is said to be wholly evil. The Jekyll character always has both aspects and is quite capable of committing evil in his own right.

[9]   This image of the twins struggling in the womb must have readily occurred to a Stevenson, who was deeply read in the Bible and to whom the story of Jacob and Esau was well known. In Genesis 25:22–23, we read of the pregnant Rebekah, Isaac's wife, that "the children struggled together within her . . . And the Lord said unto her, Two nations are in thy womb, and two manner of people shall be separated from thy bowels . . ."

[10]   The entire metaphor seems borrowed from Hamlet's soliloquy: "O, that this too, too solid flesh/ Would melt, thaw, and resolve itself into a dew . . ." (*Hamlet*, Act I, Scene 3, lines 129–130).

[11]   See page 46, where Utterson, musing on Jekyll's situation, imagines the appearance in Jekyll's room of a figure to whom "power is given" and who plucks back the bed curtains.

[12]   There is a third reason Stevenson could not "enter deeply" into any scientific account of Jekyll's researches. Like Mary Shelley, who also spared her readers any pretense of scientific underpinnings to her *Frankenstein*, Stevenson is writing an allegory, not science fiction.
    All the science we are given about Jekyll's potion is contained in Lanyon's account of it on page

the doom and burthen of our life is bound forever on man's shoulders, and when the attempt is made to cast it off, it but returns upon us with more unfamiliar and more awful pressure. Second, because as my narrative will make alas! too evident, my discoveries were incomplete. Enough, then, that I not only recognised my natural body for the mere aura and effulgence of certain of the powers that made up my spirit,[13] but managed to compound a drug by which these powers should be dethroned from their supremacy, and a second form and countenance substituted, none the less natural to me because they were the expression, and bore the stamp, of lower elements in my soul.[14]

I hesitated long before I put this theory to the test of practice. I knew well that I risked death; for any drug that so potently controlled and shook the very fortress of identity, might by the least scruple[15] of an overdose or at the least inopportunity in the moment of exhibition, utterly blot out that immaterial tabernacle[16] which I looked to it to change. But the temptation of a discovery so singular and profound, at last overcame the suggestions of alarm. I had long since prepared my tincture; I purchased at once, from a firm of wholesale chemists, a large quantity of a particular salt which I knew, from my experiments, to be the last ingredient required; and late one accursed night,[17] I compounded the elements, watched them boil and

---

111, where we learn that it contains a red tincture of a "salt" which, after an ebullition, turns purple, then watery green.

[13] The point is that Stevenson conceives an essence which is incorporeal; that essence can project a corporeal "aura" which is, however, a lesser aspect of the self.

[14] Jekyll's metaphysical view seems to be that the soul (or spirit) is made up of powers, the physical body is a mere projection or aura of these powers, and the powers themselves have a hierarchical relationship to each other. The "higher" powers can project a higher physical being or aura. The lower ones can project a lower one. What Jekyll's potion does is to "dethrone" the unifying powers of the spirit so that the higher powers may be separated from the lower ones. Hyde, then, is the aura and effulgence of those lower powers. Hyde, one needs to stress, does not contain Jekyll. Jekyll, on the other hand, *always* contains Hyde.

[15] A measure of (small) weight.

[16] In Stevenson's metaphysics, the body is immaterial, a mere projection or aura of the spirit. The word tabernacle in this context, emphasizes the heretical nature of what Jekyll is about to do. In the Old Testament, the tabernacle was the portable sanctuary in which the Israelites carried their holiest of holies, the Ark of the Covenant. In this context, and in my reading, Stevenson makes the immaterial body the holy container of the soul. Stevenson may also be remembering some New Testament teachings: ". . . Know ye not that ye are the temple [tabernacle] of God and that the spirit of God dwelleth in you? If any man defile the temple of God, him shall God destroy; for the temple of God is holy, which temple ye are" (I Corinthians 3:16–17); as well as, "What? know ye not that your body is the temple of the Holy Ghost which is in you, which ye have of God and ye are not your own?" (I Corinthians 6:19).

[17] The description that follows, which we might call the birth of Hyde, makes illuminating reading set beside a similar creation scene in Mary Shelley's *Frankenstein*, where we read: "It was on a dreary night in November, that I beheld the accomplishment of my toils. . . . It was already one in the morning; the rain pattered dismally against the panes, and my candle was nearly burnt out, when, by the glimmer of the half-extinguished light, I saw the dull yellow eye of the creature open; it breathed hard and a convulsive motion agitated its limbs" (Wolf, *The Essential Frankenstein*, p. 85).

smoke together in the glass, and when the ebullition had subsided, with a strong glow of courage, drank off the potion.

The most racking pangs succeeded: a grinding in the bones, deadly nausea,[18] and a horror of the spirit that cannot be exceeded at the hour of birth or death.[19] Then these agonies began swiftly to subside, and I came to myself as if out of a great sickness. There was something strange in my sensations, something indescribably new and, from its very novelty, incredibly sweet. I felt younger, lighter, happier in body; within I was conscious of a heady recklessness, a current of disordered sensual images running like a mill race in my fancy, a solution of the bonds of obligation, an unknown but not an innocent freedom of the soul. I knew myself, at the first breath of this new life, to be more wicked, tenfold more wicked, sold a slave to my original evil,[20] and the thought, in that moment, braced and delighted me like wine.[21] I stretched out my hands, exulting in the freshness of these sensations; and in the act, I was suddenly aware that I had lost in stature.

There was no mirror, at that date, in my room;[22] that which stands beside me as I write, was brought there later on and for the very purpose of these transformations.[23] The night, however, was far gone into the morning—the morning, black as it was, was nearly ripe for the conception of the day—the inmates of my house were locked in the most rigorous hours of slumber; and I determined, flushed as I was with hope and triumph, to venture in my new shape as far as to my bedroom. I crossed the yard, wherein the constellations looked down upon me, I could have thought, with wonder, the first creature of that sort that their unsleeping vigilance had yet disclosed to them; I stole through the corridors, a stranger in my own house; and coming to my room, I saw for the first time the appearance of Edward Hyde.

---

[18] Utterson, when he was merely thinking about Jekyll's situation (page 52) experienced a "nausea and a distaste of life."

[19] That is, at the entry into and the departure from physical consciousness. Or, to put a spiritual gloss on the phrase, at the points where the soul enters or leaves the tabernacle of the body. Let me emphasize that the birth-death analogy is appropriate whether the transformation is from Jekyll to Hyde or from Hyde to Jekyll.

In a later story, "The Waif Woman" (1893), both Thorgunna, the Waif Woman, and Aud, Finnward's envious wife, experience similar convulsions, but there they are premonitory to the deaths that soon follow.

[20] The idea that Jekyll might be enslaved appears first in Utterson's speculations about him on pages 46 and 47. See also page 122, where Jekyll reiterates the idea.

[21] We have seen that Jekyll, Utterson, and Hyde all have educated palates for wine. Here, for the first time in this story, wine is linked with evil.

[22] Jekyll is speaking of the cabinet. In order to see himself on the occasion of this first transformation, he has to go to his bedroom in his residence (see above).

[23] This answers Utterson's question about the mirror in the cabinet ("What could Jekyll want with it?") on page 101.

Scene from *Dr. Jekyll and Mr. Hyde* (1941)

I must here speak by theory alone, saying not that which I know, but that which I suppose to be most probable. The evil side of my nature, to which I had now transferred the stamping efficacy,[24] was less robust and less developed than the good which I had just deposed. Again, in the course of my life, which had been, after all, nine tenths a life of effort, virtue and control, it had been much less exercised and much less exhausted. And hence, as I think, it came about that Edward Hyde was so much smaller, slighter and younger than Henry Jekyll. Even as good shone upon the countenance of the one, evil was written broadly and plainly on the face of the other. Evil besides (which I must still believe to be the lethal side of man) had left on that body an imprint of deformity and decay.[25] And yet when I looked upon that ugly idol in the glass, I was conscious of no repugnance, rather of a leap of welcome. This, too, was myself.[26] It seemed natural and human. In my eyes it bore a livelier image of the spirit, it seemed more express and single,[27] than the imperfect and divided countenance, I had been hitherto accustomed to call mine. And in so far I was doubtless right. I have observed that when I wore the semblance of Edward Hyde, none could come near to me at first without a visible misgiving of the flesh.[28] This, as I take it, was because all human beings, as we meet them, are commingled out of good and evil: and Edward Hyde, alone in the ranks of mankind, was pure evil.

I lingered but a moment at the mirror: the second and conclusive experiment had yet to be attempted;[29] it yet remained to be seen if I had

---

[24] This is a phrase difficult to understand. One reading, authorized by Stevenson's use of the word "deposed," is that Jekyll is employing a metaphor based on the royal right to coin money. Jekyll is telling us that he has dethroned his good self and turned power over to his evil nature.

[25] See page 41, note 46 on Lombroso's theories. Beyond Lombroso, Oscar Wilde extrapolated on the notion that evil leaves visible marks on the human countenance in his *The Picture of Dorian Gray* (1891). Wilde's book deserves close comparison with *The Strange Case of Dr. Jekyll and Mr. Hyde.*

[26] Here, if anywhere, is the thematic radium center of *Jekyll and Hyde*: Stevenson's recognition that the wholeness of humankind absolutely includes a Hyde. Several years after writing *Jekyll and Hyde*, Stevenson, in "Pulvis et Umbra," would elaborate a grim view of the world and the human condition:

What a monstrous specter is this man, the disease of the agglutinated dust, lifting alternate feet or lying drugged with slumber; killing, feeding, growing, bringing forth small copies of himself; grown upon with hair like grass, fitted with eyes that move and glitter in his face; a thing to set children screaming. . . . (*Memories and Portraits*, in Stevenson, R.L., *The Works*, Vol. 13, p. 162–163).

Dark as that view is, "Pulvis et Umbra" goes on to express admiration for humanity which no matter how low it has fallen, makes some gestures toward honorable behavior.

[27] The point of the phrase is not that Hyde represents the wholeness of a human being but rather that, unlike Jekyll, who is an admixture of good and evil, Hyde is only (singly) evil.

[28] See Lanyon's observation on this matter on page 109.

[29] The first experiment was, of course, the transformation itself. It remained to be seen if he could transform back to Jekyll.

lost my identity beyond redemption and must flee before daylight from a house that was no longer mine; and hurrying back to my cabinet, I once more prepared and drank the cup, once more suffered the pangs of dissolution, and came to myself once more with the character, the stature and the face of Henry Jekyll.

That night I had come to the fatal cross roads. Had I approached my discovery in a more noble spirit, had I risked the experiment while under the empire of generous or pious aspirations, all must have been otherwise, and from these agonies of death and birth, I had come forth an angel instead of a fiend.[30] The drug had no discriminating action; it was neither diabolical nor divine; it but shook the doors of the prisonhouse of my disposition; and like the captives of Philippi;[31] that which stood within ran forth. At that time my virtue slumbered; my evil, kept awake by ambition, was alert and swift to seize the occasion; and the thing that was projected was Edward Hyde.[32] Hence, although I had now two characters as well as two appearances, one was wholly evil, and the other was still the old Henry Jekyll, that incongruous compound of whose reformation and improvement I had already learned to despair. The movement was thus wholly towards the worse.

Even at that time, I had not yet conquered my aversion to the dryness of a life of study. I would still be merrily disposed at times;[33] and as my pleasures were (to say the least) undignified, and I was not only well known and highly considered, but growing towards the elderly man,[34] this incoherency of my life was daily growing more unwelcome. It was on this side that my new power tempted me until I fell in slavery.[35] I had but to drink the cup, to doff at once the body of the noted professor, and to assume, like a thick cloak, that of Edward Hyde. I smiled at the notion; it

---

[30] This is a very shaky premise. Whatever the state of moral purity the experimenter possessed, it could have made no difference on the effect of the potion, which was to separate the parts of the self, one of which was evil. As Jekyll himself points out, "the drug had no discriminating action; it was neither diabolical nor divine." The idea that something good might have come of Jekyll's experiments had he undertaken them with a pure heart seems unconvincing.

[31] When Mark Anthony and Octavius Caesar defeated Brutus and Cassius at Philippi, in Macedonia. In the history of Christianity, Philippi is famous because it was the first place in Europe where St. Paul preached the gospel.

[32] Though one would dearly like to know, Jekyll does not tell us who named Edward Hyde, nor how an identity was established for him.

[33] Utterson has told us that Jekyll was wild when he was young (page 52) and Jekyll (on page 116) describes himself as having "a certain impatient gaiety of disposition."

[34] On page 56, we were told that Jekyll was fifty years old, hardly an elderly man. On the other hand, from Stevenson's thirty-six-year-old vantage point, fifty might have seemed the beginning of old age.

[35] Again the theme of slavery (see page 119).

seemed to me at the time to be humorous; and I made my preparations with the most studious care. I took and furnished that house in Soho, to which Hyde was tracked by the police;[36] and engaged as housekeeper a creature whom I well knew[37] to be silent and unscrupulous. On the other side, I announced to my servants that a Mr. Hyde (whom I described) was to have full liberty and power about my house in the square; and to parry mishaps, I even called and made myself a familiar object, in my second character. I next drew up that will to which you so much objected; so that if anything befell me in the person of Doctor Jekyll, I could enter on that of Edward Hyde without pecuniary loss. And thus fortified, as I supposed, on every side, I began to profit by the strange immunities of my position.

Men have before hired bravos[38] to transact their crimes, while their own person and reputation sat under shelter. I was the first that ever did so for his pleasures. I was the first that could thus plod in the public eye with a load of genial respectability, and in a moment, like a schoolboy, strip off these lendings[39] and spring headlong into the sea of liberty.[40] But for me, in my impenetrable mantle, the safety was complete. Think of it— I did not even exist! Let me but escape into my laboratory door, give me but a second or two to mix and swallow the draught that I had always standing ready; and whatever he had done, Edward Hyde would pass away like the stain of breath upon a mirror;[41] and there in his stead, quietly at home, trimming the midnight lamp[42] in his study, a man who could afford to laugh at suspicion, would be Henry Jekyll.

The pleasures which I made haste to seek in my disguise were, as I have said, undignified;[43] I would scarce use a harder term. But in the hands of Edward Hyde, they soon began to turn towards the monstrous. When I would come back from these excursions, I was often plunged into a kind

---

[36] He was hardly tracked. See page 50, where Hyde, without provocation, gives Utterson his address. Utterson, on the morning after the Carew murder, leads the policeman to Hyde's apartment.

[37] Stevenson gives us fascinating hints about Jekyll's pre-Hyde existence. Obviously this unscrupulous and silent housekeeper had been useful to the pleasure-seeking and hypocritical Jekyll in the past.

[38] Desperadoes, cutthroats.

[39] The phrase echoes King Lear's who, as the storm gathers on the heath, cries "Off, off you lendings! Come, unbutton here into the sea of liberty" (King Lear, Act III, Scene 4, line 114).

[40] The heavy, staid Jekyll plods while the instinctive, youthful Hyde springs.

[41] Having borrowed some diction from King Lear (see note 39, above), Stevenson's mind is still inside the aura of the play. Lear, holding the body of the dead Cordelia in his arms in the famous "Howl, howl, howl!" scene, says, "Lend me a looking glass./If that her breath will mist or stain the stone,/ Why then she lives" (King Lear, Act V, Scene 3, lines 260–262).

[42] Stevenson and his imagined Jekyll lived in an age of oil-burning lamps, whose wicks grew charred and had to be trimmed at intervals with a penknife or scissors.

[43] Here he calls them undignified, but on page 115, half in extenuation of his vices, he also said, "Many a man would have even blazoned such irregularities as I was guilty of," though they filled him "with an almost morbid sense of shame."

of wonder at my vicarious depravity. This familiar[44] that I called out of my own soul, and sent forth alone to do his good pleasure, was a being inherently malign and villainous; his every act and thought centered on self; drinking pleasure with bestial avidity from any degree of torture to another; relentless like a man of stone. Henry Jekyll stood at times aghast before the acts of Edward Hyde; but the situation was apart from ordinary laws, and insidiously relaxed the grasp of conscience. It was Hyde, after all, and Hyde alone, that was guilty. Jekyll was no worse; he woke again to his good qualities seemingly unimpaired; he would even make haste, where it was possible, to undo the evil done by Hyde. And thus his conscience slumbered.

Into the details of the infamy at which I thus connived (for even now I can scarce grant that I committed it) I have no design of entering; I mean but to point out the warnings and the successive steps with which my chastisement approached. I met with one accident which, as it brought on no consequence, I shall no more than mention. An act of cruelty to a child aroused against me the anger of a passer by, whom I recognised the other day in the person of your kinsman;[45] the doctor and the child's family joined him; there were moments when I feared for my life; and at last, in order to pacify their too just resentment, Edward Hyde had to bring them to the door, and pay them in a cheque drawn in the name of Henry Jekyll. But this danger was easily eliminated from the future, by opening an account at another bank in the name of Edward Hyde himself; and when, by sloping my own hand backward, I had supplied my double with a signature, I thought I sat beyond the reach of fate.

Some two months before the murder of Sir Danvers, I had been out for one of my adventures, had returned at a late hour, and woke the next day in bed with somewhat odd sensations. It was in vain I looked about me; in vain I saw the decent furniture and tall proportions of my room in the square; in vain that I recognised the pattern of the bed curtains and the design of the mahogany frame; something still kept insisting that I was not where I was, that I had not wakened where I seemed to be, but in the little room in Soho where I was accustomed to sleep in the body of Edward Hyde. I smiled to myself, and, in my psychological way, began

---

[44] Stevenson again connects Hyde with Satan. In the folklore of witchcraft, a "familiar" was an animal—a dog, cat, raven, or other animal—that lived with a witch and was said to be a demonic guide or attendant. Women accused of witchcraft were often examined for the presence on their bodies of supernumerary nipples which, it was believed, were intended to give suck to their familiar.

[45] Enfield, who is Utterson's cousin. This childish ruse is unworthy of Stevenson and makes a farce of the consultation Utterson has with his chief clerk, Guest, who is described as a handwriting expert.

lazily to inquire into the elements of this illusion, occasionally, even as I did so, dropping back into a comfortable morning doze. I was still so engaged when, in one of my more wakeful moments, my eyes fell upon my hand. Now the hand of Henry Jekyll (as you have often remarked) was professional in shape and size: it was large, firm, white and comely. But the hand which I now saw, clearly enough, in the yellow light of a mid-London morning, lying half shut on the bed clothes, was lean, corded, knuckly, of a dusky pallor and thickly shaded with a swart growth of hair. It was the hand of Edward Hyde.

I must have stared upon it for near half a minute, sunk as I was in the mere stupidity of wonder, before terror woke up in my breast as sudden and startling as the crash of cymbals; and bounding from my bed, I rushed to the mirror. At the sight that met my eyes, my blood was changed into something exquisitely thin and icy. Yes, I had gone to bed Henry Jekyll, I had awakened Edward Hyde. How was this to be explained? I asked myself; and then, with another bound of terror—how was it to be remedied? It was well on in the morning; the servants were up; all my drugs were in the cabinet—a long journey down two pair of stairs,[46] through the back passage, across the open court and through the anatomical theatre, from where I was then standing horror-struck. It might indeed be possible to cover my face;[47] but of what use was that, when I was unable to conceal the alteration in my stature? And then with an overpowering sweetness of relief, it came back upon my mind that the servants were already used to the coming and going of my second self. I had soon dressed, as well as I was able, in clothes of my own size:[48] had soon passed through the house, where Bradshaw stared and drew back at seeing Mr. Hyde at such an hour and in such a strange array; and ten minutes later, Dr. Jekyll had returned to his own shape and was sitting down, with a darkened brow, to make a feint of breakfasting.

Small indeed was my appetite. This inexplicable incident, this reversal of my previous experience, seemed, like the Babylonian finger on the wall; to be spelling out the letters of my judgment;[49] and I began to reflect more seriously than ever before on the issues and possibilities of my double existence. That part of me which I had the power of projecting, had lately been much exercised and nourished; it had seemed to me of late as though

---

[46]   In Jekyll's home.
[47]   On page 94, in the chapter called "The Last Night," the butler, Poole, claims to have seen a figure wearing a mask running upstairs into the cabinet.
[48]   That is, Jekyll's clothes, which is why he appears to Bradshaw in "strange array."

the body of Edward Hyde had grown in stature, as though (when I wore that form) I were conscious of a more generous tide of blood;[50] and I began to spy a danger that, if this were much prolonged, the balance of my nature might be permanently overthrown, the power of voluntary change be forfeited, and the character of Edward Hyde become irrevocably mine. The power of the drug had not been always equally displayed. Once, very early in my career, it had totally failed me; since then I had been obliged on more than one occasion to double,[51] and once, with infinite risk of death, to treble the amount; and these rare uncertainties had cast hitherto the sole shadow on my contentment. Now, however, and in the light of that morning's accident, I was led to remark that whereas, in the beginning, the difficulty had been to throw off the body of Jekyll, it had of late, gradually but decidedly transferred itself to the other side. All things therefore seemed to point to this: that I was slowly losing hold of my original and better self, and becoming slowly incorporated[52] with my second and worse.[53]

Between these two, I now felt I had to choose. My two natures had memory in common, but all other faculties were most unequally shared between them. Jekyll (who was composite) now with the most sensitive apprehensions, now with a greedy gusto, projected and shared in the pleasures and adventures of Hyde; but Hyde was indifferent to Jekyll, or but remembered him as the mountain bandit remembers the cavern in which he conceals himself from pursuit. Jekyll had more than a father's interest, Hyde had more than a son's indifference.[54] To cast in my lot with Jekyll,

---

[49] The story is to be found in Daniel 5:5, 24–31. Belshazzar, the king of Babylon, threw a great feast: "In the same hour came forth fingers of a man's hand, and wrote over against the candlestick upon the plaister of the wall of the king's palace: and the king saw the part of the hand that wrote." The words the mysterious hand wrote were "*Mene, Mene, Tekel, Upharsin*," which Daniel interpreted for Belshazzar as meaning, "*Mene*; God hath numbered the kingdom and finished it. *Tekel*; Thou art weighed in the balance and found wanting. *Peres*; Thy kingdom is divided, and given to the Medes and the Persians."

[50] We have already seen, after the birth pangs of the transformation, the entry into Hyde is an experience much like that of a cocaine rush. Here we are reminded that being Hyde is exciting, sensual, primordial.

[51] See page 108, where Lanyon, inspecting Jekyll's notebooks, sees entries indicating a doubling of a dose. Note that Stevenson uses precisely the same language there as here: "once very early . . ."

[52] The text here begins to verge either on an insoluble problem or to skirt incoherence on Stevenson's part. We are told the original, better self is becoming incorporated with the second, worse self. But that's what Jekyll was before he took the potion: an amiable, solid citizen who hypocritically practiced vices. As if to emphasize that point, we will see later (page 130) that the event precipitating Jekyll's catastrophe is brought on not by the potion that unleashes Hyde but by a sensual itch in the mind of that "ordinary secret sinner," the hypocrite Jekyll.

[53] Jekyll is essentially the voyeur, the tourist into evil. He is titillated by it, gratified by it, but only in the way a tourist is excited by the strangeness of a country he is visiting without ever feeling the need to dwell there. Hyde, on the other hand, is a contented native of the country of evil.

[54] Stevenson's phrasing here is most provocative. Normally, *Jekyll and Hyde* is read as an allegory of the divided human mind (or character). But here we are presented with the idea that father-son tensions

was to die to those appetites which I had long secretly indulged and had of late begun to pamper. To cast it in with Hyde, was to die to a thousand interests and aspirations, and to become, at a blow and forever, despised and friendless. The bargain might appear unequal; but there was still another consideration in the scales; for while Jekyll would suffer smartingly in the fires of abstinence, Hyde would be not even conscious of all that he had lost.[55] Strange as my circumstances were, the terms of this debate are as old and commonplace as man; much the same inducements and alarms cast the die for any tempted and trembling sinner; and it fell out with me, as it falls with so vast a majority of my fellows, that I chose the better part and was found wanting in the strength to keep to it.

Yes, I preferred the elderly and discontented doctor, surrounded by friends and cherishing honest hopes; and bade a resolute farewell to the liberty, the comparative youth, the light step, leaping impulses and secret pleasures, that I had enjoyed in the disguise of Hyde. I made this choice perhaps with some unconscious reservation, for I neither gave up the house in Soho, nor destroyed the clothes of Edward Hyde, which still lay ready in my cabinet.[56] For two months, however, I was true to my determination; for two months, I led a life of such severity as I had never before attained to, and enjoyed the compensations of an approving conscience. But time began at last to obliterate the freshness of my alarm; the praises of conscience began to grow into a thing of course; I began to be tortured with throes and longings, as of Hyde struggling after freedom; and at last, in an hour of moral weakness, I once again compounded and swallowed the transforming draught.[57]

I do not suppose that, when a drunkard reasons with himself upon his vice, he is once out of five hundred times affected by the dangers that he runs through his brutish, physical insensibility; neither had I, long as I had

may also be implicit in the story. See page 129, where the father and son imagery is repeated. See also the Introduction to this edition for commentary on Stevenson's relationship with his father.

[55] The unequal bargain would be that if he chooses Hyde, he will be a social (and moral) outcast. If he chooses Jekyll, he will be scorched by the flames of unfulfilled desire. The element thrown onto the scales, and the one that makes the choice more difficult, is that Hyde would never have Jekyll's moral anguish. To be Hyde would be to be free of the "agenbite of inwit," the remorse of conscience. To put it another way, the gorgeous attraction of being Hyde is that Hyde is guilt free. For Stevenson, raised in the morally suffocating atmosphere of a Calvinist home, what a wonderful freedom that might seem to be. See page 119 for the ecstatic description of Jekyll's feelings as he first experienced being Hyde.

[56] This is a detail we were neither given on page 123, where Jekyll describes setting up the Soho house, nor on page 125, where we see Hyde, dressed in Jekyll's oversized clothing, skulking through the house.

We are not told whether Hyde kept a set of Jekyll's clothes in that house.

[57] This transformation takes place on the night of the Carew murder.

considered my position, made enough allowance for the complete moral insensibility and insensate readiness to evil, which were the leading characters of Edward Hyde. Yet it was by these that I was punished. My devil had been long caged, he came out roaring. I was conscious, even when I took the draught, of a more unbridled, a more furious propensity to ill. It must have been this, I suppose, that stirred in my soul that tempest of impatience with which I listened to the civilities of my unhappy victim; I declare, at least, before God, no man morally sane could have been guilty of that crime upon so pitiful a provocation; and that I struck in no more reasonable spirit than that in which a sick child may break a plaything. But I had voluntarily stripped myself of all those balancing instincts, by which even the worst of us continues to walk with some degree of steadiness among temptations; and in my case, to be tempted, however slightly, was to fall.[58]

Instantly the spirit of hell awoke in me and raged. With a transport of glee, I mauled the unresisting body, tasting delight from every blow; and it was not till weariness had begun to succeed, that I was suddenly, in the top fit of my delirium, struck through the heart by a cold thrill of terror. A mist dispersed; I saw my life to be forfeit; and fled from the scene of these excesses, at once glorying and trembling, my lust of evil gratified and stimulated, my love of life screwed to the topmost peg.[59] I ran to the house in Soho, and (to make assurance doubly sure) destroyed my papers; thence I set out through the lamplit streets, in the same divided ecstasy of mind, gloating on my crime, light-headedly devising others in the future, and yet still hastening and still hearkening in my wake for the steps of the avenger. Hyde had a song upon his lips as he compounded the draught, and as he drank it, pledged the dead man. The pangs of transformation had not done tearing him, before Henry Jekyll, with streaming tears of gratitude and remorse, had fallen upon his knees and lifted his clasped hands to God.

---

[58] Stevenson frequently used wine, laudanum, and hashish to get him through illness-induced sleepless nights. This paragraph, built on such feelings, like an alcoholic resisting and finally succumbing to temptation, therefore has a particularly convincing ring to it.

[59] From a psychological point of view, this ecstatic moment is the key to the meaning of Hyde. Two emotions are recorded: exhilaration and fear. As we have seen, there is no question of remorse. Instead, he tasted "delight from every blow." In the very moment that Hyde kills, he feels his "love of life screwed to the topmost peg." And flushed with that feeling, still "gloating on [his] crime," he focuses on flight and safety.

Note that Gil Martin, T.J. Hogg's satanic figure in *Confessions of a Justified Sinner*, has a similar excess of vibrant excitement after the murder of the kindly preacher, Blanchard.

At this point, we are given a reason why Hyde would choose to become Jekyll again. Jekyll's persona, as we were told on page 126, served Hyde as a fortress within which he was safe from pursuit. See also page 129, where Jekyll is described as "[Hyde's] city of refuge."

The veil of self-indulgence was rent from head to foot, I saw my life as a whole: I followed it up from the days of childhood, when I had walked with my father's hand, and through the self-denying toils of my professional life, to arrive again and again, with the same sense of unreality, at the damned horrors of the evening. I could have screamed aloud; I sought with tears and prayers to smother down the crowd of hideous images and sounds with which my memory swarmed against me; and still, between the petitions, the ugly face of my iniquity stared into my soul. As the acuteness of this remorse began to die away, it was succeeded by a sense of joy. The problem of my conduct was solved. Hyde was thenceforth impossible; whether I would or not, I was now confined to the better part of my existence; and O, how I rejoiced to think it! with what willing humility, I embraced anew the restrictions of natural life! with what sincere renunciation, I locked the door by which I had so often gone and come, and ground the key under my heel![60]

The next day, came the news that the murder had been overlooked,[61] that the guilt of Hyde was patent to the world, and that the victim was a man high in public estimation. It was not only a crime, it had been a tragic folly. I think I was glad to know it; I think I was glad to have my better impulses thus buttressed and guarded by the terrors of the scaffold. Jekyll was now my city of refuge; let but Hyde peep out an instant, and the hands of all men would be raised to take and slay him.

I resolved in my future conduct to redeem the past; and I can say with honesty that my resolve was fruitful of some good. You know yourself how earnestly in the last months of last year,[62] I laboured to relieve suffering; you know that much was done for others, and that the days passed quietly, almost happily for myself. Nor can I truly say that I wearied of this beneficent and innocent life; I think instead that I daily enjoyed it more completely; but I was still cursed with my duality of purpose; and as the first edge of my penitence wore off, the lower side of me, so long indulged, so recently chained down, began to growl for license.[63] Not that I dreamed of resuscitating Hyde; the bare idea of that would startle me to frenzy: no, it was in my own person,[64] that I was once more tempted to trifle with

---

[60] See pages 100–101.
[61] Observed.
[62] November and December.
[63] See page 128, where Hyde is described as the "devil [who] had been long caged . . . came out roaring." When Hyde is not bestial he is satanic. The distinction is important: beasts, while they can do harm, cannot—since they have no souls—do evil. Satan—and his minions—are always God's willing antagonists.
[64] Stevenson is emphatic here. Jekyll's final and irremediable fall has *nothing* to do with the potion

129

my conscience; and it was as an ordinary secret sinner, that I at last fell before the assaults of temptation.

There comes an end to all things; the most capacious measure is filled at last; and this brief condescension to my evil finally destroyed the balance of my soul. And yet I was not alarmed; the fall seemed natural, like a return to the old days before I had made my discovery. It was a fine, clear, January day, wet under foot where the frost had melted, but cloudless overhead; and the Regent's Park was full of winter chirruppings and sweet with spring odours.[65] I sat in the sun on a bench; the animal within me licking the chops of memory;[66] the spiritual side a little drowsed, promising subsequent penitence, but not yet moved to begin. After all, I reflected I was like my neighbours; and then I smiled, comparing myself with other men, comparing my active goodwill with the lazy cruelty of their neglect. And at the very moment of that vainglorious thought, a qualm came over me, a horrid nausea and the most deadly shuddering. These passed away, and left me faint; and then as in its turn the faintness subsided, I began to

---

(see the Introduction to this edition). Nowhere in the text of *Jekyll and Hyde* are we ever told specifically which vices Jekyll or Hyde practiced. In a latter to his friend John Paul Bocock, November 1887, Stevenson asserts specifically that hypocrisy, not sexual temptation, was Jekyll's problem:

> There is no harm in a voluptuary; and none, with my hand on my heart and in the sight of God, none—no harm whatever—in what prurient fools call "immorality." The harm was in Jekyll, because he was a hypocrite—not because he was fond of women; he says so himself; but people are so filled full of folly and inverted lust, that they can think of nothing but sexuality. The hypocrite let out the beast Hyde—who is no more sensual than another, but who is the essence of cruelty and malice, and selfishness and cowardice; and these are the diabolic in man—not this poor wish to have a woman, that they make such a cry about. I know, and I dare to say, you know as well as I, that good and bad, even to our human eyes, has no more connection with what is called dissipation than it has to do with flying kites. But the sexual field and the business field are perhaps the two best fitted for the display of cruelty and cowardice and selfishness. That is what people see; and then they confound. (Maixner, p. 231).

Evidently, apart from his fiction and writing to a friend, Stevenson was willing to suppose that people read Jekyll as a womanizer, but in the text of *Jekyll and Hyde* there is nothing to show what sexual wickedness or with which gender Jekyll or Hyde may have committed their iniquities.

[65] Regent's Park was designed by John Nash in 1814 and named for the Prince Regent. The park is the site of London's zoo, where Dracula, in a famous scene in Bram Stoker's novel, found refuge by inhabiting the body of a wolf named Berserker.

[66] This image of Jekyll sitting in Regent's Park and sleepily savoring the memory of some delicious sin bears comparison with the occasional glimpses we are given of the decayed noblewoman who is the vampire in Stevenson's short story "Olalla," written a year earlier than *Jekyll and Hyde*. There, she is described as lying "luxuriously folded on herself and sunk in sloth and pleasure" (Bell, *Robert Louis Stevenson: The Complete Short Stories*, p. 235). Or else,

> . . . I marked her make infinitesimal changes in her posture, savoring and lingering on the bodily pleasure of the movement. . . . She lived in her body; and her consciousness was all sunk into and disseminated through her members, where it luxuriously dwelt (Ibid.).

Like Hyde's, her voice has a "broken hoarseness."

be aware of a change in the temper of my thoughts, a greater boldness, a contempt of danger, a solution[67] of the bonds of obligation. I looked down; my clothes hung formlessly on my shrunken limbs; the hand that lay on. my knee was corded and hairy. I was once more Edward Hyde. A moment before I had been safe of all men's respect, wealthy, beloved—the cloth laying for me in the dining room at home; and now I was the common quarry of mankind, hunted, houseless, a known murderer, thrall to the gallows.

My reason wavered, but it did not fail me utterly. I have more than once observed that, in my second character, my faculties seemed sharpened to a point and my spirits more tensely elastic; thus it came about that, where Jekyll perhaps might have succumbed, Hyde rose to the importance of the moment. My drugs were in one of the presses of my cabinet; how was I to reach them? That was the problem that (crushing my temples in my hands) I set myself to solve. The laboratory door I had closed. If I sought to enter by the house, my own servants would consign me to the gallows. I saw I must employ another hand, and thought of Lanyon. How was he to be reached? how persuaded? Supposing that I escaped capture in the streets, how was I to make my way into his presence? and how should I, an unknown and displeasing visitor, prevail on the famous physician to rifle the study of his colleague, Dr. Jekyll? Then I remembered that of my original character, one part remained to me: I could write my own hand; and once I had conceived that kindling spark, the way that I must follow became lighted up from end to end.

Thereupon, I arranged my clothes as best I could, and summoning a passing hansom, drove to an hotel in Portland street,[68] the name of which I chanced to remember. At my appearance (which was indeed comical enough, however tragic a fate these garments covered) the driver could not conceal his mirth. I gnashed my teeth upon him with a gust of devilish fury; and the smile withered from his face—happily for him—yet more happily for myself, for in another instant I had certainly dragged him from his perch. At the inn, as I entered, I looked about me with so black a countenance as made the attendants tremble; not a look did they exchange in my presence; but obsequiously took my orders, led me to a private room, and brought me wherewithal to write.[69] Hyde in danger of his life

---

[67] Dissolution.

[68] Portland Street runs parallel to Regent's Park. It intersects Oxford Street near Soho, where Hyde had his rooms.

[69] The end of this sentence marks the beginning of an interval in the course of which Jekyll abandons his first-person narrative and speaks of Hyde as a separate entity. It will be resumed again on page 132 with the paragraph that begins, "When I came to myself . . ."

was a creature new to me: shaken with inordinate anger, strung to the pitch of murder, lusting to inflict pain. Yet the creature was astute;[70] mastered his fury with a great effort of the will; composed, his two important letters, one to Lanyon and one to Poole; and that he might receive actual evidence of their being posted, sent them out with directions that they should be registered.

Thenceforward, he sat all day over the fire in the private room, gnawing his nails; there he dined, sitting alone with his fears, the waiter visibly quailing before his eye; and thence, when the night was fully come, he set forth in the corner of a closed cab, and was driven to and fro about the streets of the city. He, I say—I cannot say, I. That child of Hell had nothing human; nothing lived in him but fear and hatred. And when at last, thinking the driver had begun to grow suspicious, he discharged the cab and ventured on foot, attired in his misfitting clothes, an object marked out for observation, into the midst of the nocturnal passengers, these two base passions[71] raged within him like a tempest. He walked fast, hunted by his fears, chattering to himself, skulking through the less frequented thoroughfares, counting the minutes that still divided him from midnight. Once a woman spoke to him,[72] offering, I think, a box of lights. He smote her in the face, and she fled.[73]

When I came to myself at Lanyon's, the horror of my old friend perhaps affected me somewhat: I do not know; it was at least but a drop in the sea to the abhorrence with which I looked back upon these hours. A change had come over me. It was no longer the fear of the gallows, it was the horror of being Hyde that racked me. I received Lanyon's condemnation partly in a dream; it was partly in a dream that I came home to

---

[70] For a Hyde who is frequently presented as beastlike, he is shown here, in the midst of the profoundest crisis of his short life, as astute and controlled.

[71] Fear and hatred: see several lines above. See also page 128, where Hyde is described as experiencing a "divided ecstasy" made up of fear and gloating.

[72] Some critics have supposed that this woman is a prostitute because she accosts Hyde late at night. The imprecision of the language describing what she offers Hyde, "I think, a box of lights," encourages such speculation.

What seems to me more meaningful, however, is that Stevenson, bringing his story to its end, gives us a symmetry that is symbolic: our story began with Hyde abusing a female child; now, as it ends, Hyde is shown taking a swipe at a grown woman.

Though I have stressed that women have little or no effective part in this story, it is worth noting that thin though it is, there *is* a thread of femininity woven into this fiction. As the story comes to its end, we can count a minimum of six females in it: the little girl whom Hyde trampled; Jekyll's cook; his housemaid; the maid servant, who witnessed Sir Danvers Carew's murder; Hyde's evil housekeeper; and this woman whose face Hyde slaps. There may actually be more. In Chapter I, Stevenson referred to the women relatives of the little girl Hyde stomped on, but, except for telling us that they had to be restrained from harming Hyde, we are not told how many of them there were.

[73] After these words, the story again becomes a first-person narrative.

my own house and got into bed. I slept after the prostration of the day, with a stringent and profound slumber which not even the nightmares that wrung me could avail to break. I awoke in the morning shaken, weakened, but refreshed. I still hated and feared the thought of the brute that slept within me, and I had not of course forgotten the appalling dangers of the day before; but I was once more at home, in my own house and close to my drugs; and gratitude for my escape shone so strong in my soul that it almost rivalled the brightness of hope.

I was stepping leisurely across the court after breakfast, drinking the chill of the air with pleasure, when I was seized again with those indescribable sensations that heralded the change; and I had but the time to gain the shelter of my cabinet, before I was once again raging and freezing with the passions of Hyde. It took on this occasion a double dose to recall me to myself; and alas, six hours after, as I sat looking sadly in the fire, the pangs returned, and the drug had to be re-administered. In short, from that day forth[74] it seemed only by a great effort as of gymnastics, and only under the immediate stimulation of the drug, that I was able to wear the countenance of Jekyll. At all hours of the day and night, I would be taken with the premonitory shudder;[75] above all, if I slept, or even dozed for a moment in my chair, it was always as Hyde that I awakened. Under the strain of this continually impending doom and by the sleeplessness to which I now condemned myself, ay, even beyond what I had thought possible to man, I became, in my own person a creature eaten up and emptied by fever, languidly weak both in body and mind, and solely occupied by one thought: the horror of my other self. But when I slept, or when the virtue of the medicine wore off, I would leap almost without transition (for the pangs of transformation grew daily less marked) into the possession of a fancy brimming with images of terror,[76] a soul boiling with causeless hatreds and a body that seemed not strong enough to contain the raging energies of life.[77] The powers of Hyde[78] seemed to have grown with the sickliness of Jekyll. And certainly the hate that now divided them was equal on each side. With Jekyll, it was a thing of vital instinct. He had now seen the full deformity of that creature that shared with him some of the phenomena of consciousness, and was co-heir with him to death: and beyond these links of community, which in themselves made the most poignant part of his

---

[74] That is, from January 10 on.

[75] These shudders strongly resemble the aura some epilepsy sufferers experience just before the onset of a seizure. Indeed, the violence with which the personality changes are accompanied has much in common with *grand mal* epilepsy seizures. Note that Jekyll-Hyde is left "languidly weak both in body and mind. . . ."

distress, he thought of Hyde, for all his energy of life, as of something not only hellish but inorganic. This was the shocking thing; that the slime of the pit seemed to utter cries and voices; that the amorphous dust gesticulated and sinned;[79] that what was dead, and had no shape, should usurp the offices of life.[80] And this again, that that insurgent horror was knit to him

---

[76] Stevenson, from a very early age, was familiar with nightmare images. In his "Chapter on Dreams," writing in the third person, he tells us:

> He was from a child an ardent and uncomfortable dreamer. When he had a touch of fever at night, and the room swelled and shrank, and his clothes, hanging on a nail, now loomed up instant to the bigness of a church, and now drew away into a horror of infinite distance and infinite littleness, the poor soul was very well aware of what must follow . . . sooner or later the night-hag would have him by the throat, and pluck him, strangling and screaming, from his sleep. His dreams were at times commonplace enough, at times very strange: at times they were almost formless, he would be haunted, for instance, by nothing more definite than a certain hue of brown, which he did not mind in the least while he was awake, but he feared and loathed while he was dreaming; at times, again, they took on every detail of circumstance, as when once he supposed he must swallow the populous world, and awoke screaming with the horror of the thought. (*Memories and Portraits*, in Stevenson, R.L., *The Works*, Vol. 13, p. 162–163).

[77] Throughout the story, Hyde has been perceived as supremely vital. But, like Milton's Satan, or Bram Stoker's Dracula, his is energy without grace, power without responsibility. And yet, as with those heroes of iniquity, energy arouses envy.
Stevenson, in a somewhat forced poem, expressed that admiration for vigor:

> Away with funeral music—
> Set the pipe to powerful lips—
> The cup of life's for him that drinks
> And not for him that sips.
> ("Poems," in Stevenson, R.L., *The Works*, Vol. 2, p. 116.)

In another poem expressing similar bravado he writes,

> Oh, fine, religious, decent folk,
> In VIRTUES flaunting golden scarlet
> I sneer between two puffs of smoke,—
> Give me the publican and harlot.
> (Ibid., Vol. 3, p. 248.)

Years after *Jekyll and Hyde*, Stevenson was still very aware of the "raging" aspect of such primordial power. In a letter to Colvin describing work he was doing in the garden at Vailima, Stevenson wrote: "I wonder if anyone had ever the same attitude to Nature as I hold, and have held for so long? This business fascinates me like a tune or a passion; yet all the while I thrill with a strong distaste. The horror of the thing, objected and subjected, is always present to my mind; the horror of creeping things, the superstitious horror of the void and the powers about me, the horror of my own devastation and continual murder" ("The Letters," in Stevenson, R.L., *The Works*, Vol. 3, p. 249).
[78] Stevenson has switched back to a third-person narrative which continues until page 135 with the words: ". . . that he would play me."
The alternating shifts in point of view from first-person narrative to third-person and then back again do two things. First, they mimic in feeling the dizzying pace of the oscillations that are now going on between Jekyll and Hyde, and second, they reflect the revulsion Jekyll feels for his counterpart. Jekyll is using language to put as much distance between himself and his "other" as he can.
Compare these shifts between first-person and third-person narration to the straightforward first-person account Jekyll gives us about how he felt being Hyde on page 119, where the language describing the first transformation is exhilarated, ebullient, triumphant, and sensual.

closer than a wife, closer than an eye; lay caged in his flesh,[81] where he heard it mutter and felt it struggle to be born; and at every hour of weakness, and in the confidence of slumber, prevailed against him, and deposed him out of life. The hatred of Hyde for Jekyll, was of a different order. His terror of the gallows drove him continually to commit temporary suicide, and return to his subordinate station of a part instead of a person; but he loathed the necessity, he loathed the despondency into which Jekyll was now fallen, and he resented the dislike with which he was himself regarded. Hence the apelike tricks that he would play me, scrawling in my own hand blasphemies on the pages of my books,[82] burning the letters and destroying the portrait of my father; and indeed, had it not been for his fear of death, he would long ago have ruined himself in order to involve me in the ruin. But his love of life is wonderful; I go further: I, who sicken and freeze at the mere thought of him, when I recall the abjection and passion of this attachment,[83] and when I know how he fears my power to cut him off by suicide, I find it in my heart to pity him.

It is useless, and the time awfully fails me, to prolong this description; no one has ever suffered such torments, let that suffice; and yet even to these, habit brought—no, not alleviation—but a certain callousness of soul, a certain acquiescence of despair; and my punishment might have gone on for years, but for the last calamity which has now fallen, and which has finally severed me from my own face and nature.[84] My provision of the

---

[79] Stevenson's prose, from page 133 to the end of this very long paragraph, is at once rich and terrifying. It is as if here, in the penultimate moments of his fiction, Stevenson has found not only the voice but the music needed to give expression to the spiritual ghastliness of Jekyll's situation.

    If we keep in mind that Jekyll is describing Hyde, the paragraph—like a fine poem—vibrates with allusion. "That the slime of the pit seemed to utter cries and voices," recalls Poole's description of Jekyll-Hyde, "weeping like a . . . lost soul" (page 98). The "slime of the pit" refers to the biblical tar pits known as the Vale of Siddim (Genesis 14:3, 8, 10). Finally, we note that the "amorphous dust [that] gesticulated and sinned" describes Adam, who was made from dust (see Genesis 4:7) and therefore, by extension, describes what all the rest of humanity is made of.

[80] In 1881, Stevenson developed this theme in the short story "Thrawn Janet." See Appendix A, page 149 in this edition.

[81] This imagery announces the imminent closure of a circle. Our story began with Jekyll's desire to separate the moral aspects of his self so that he might have vibrant, voluptuous, and wicked experiences without remorse. The cost of that pilgrimage, however, has been a deadly reversal of dominance—as we will soon see.

[82] See page 101, note 47.

[83] To life.

[84] Whose face, and whose nature? In this paragraph, more clearly than elsewhere, we see the contradiction implicit in Stevenson's controlling metaphor. Jekyll tells us that he is the author of the lines we are reading. He tells us, too, that though he made a potion with a fresh supply of the salt, it was without efficacy. But that leaves us at the center of the conceptual problem: If the writer was Jekyll, why would he drink the potion to turn him into Hyde, whom he detests? And if it was Hyde who, according to Jekyll, is a pure precipitate of all that is humanly evil, why would he ransack London to find the chemicals needed to turn him into Jekyll, whom *he* detests?

salt, which had never been renewed since the date of the first experiment, began to run low. I sent out for a fresh supply, and mixed the draught; the ebullition followed, and the first change of colour, not the second; I drank it and it was without efficiency. You will learn from Poole how I have had London ransacked; it was in vain; and I am now persuaded that my first supply was impure, and that it was that unknown impurity which lent efficacy to the draught.

About a week has passed, and I am now finishing this statement under the influence of the last of the old powders. This, then, is the last time, short of a miracle, that Henry Jekyll can think his own thoughts or see his own face (now how sadly altered!) in the glass. Nor must I delay too long to bring my writing to an end; for if my narrative has hitherto escaped destruction, it has been by a combination of great prudence and great good luck. Should the throes of change take me in the act of writing it, Hyde will tear it in pieces; but if some time shall have elapsed after I have laid it by,[85] his wonderful selfishness and circumscription to the moment will probably save it once again from the action of his apelike spite.[86] And indeed the doom that is closing on us both, has already changed and crushed him. Half an hour from now, when I shall again and forever reindue[87] that hated personality, I know how I shall sit shuddering and weeping in my chair, or continue, with the most strained and fearstruck ecstasy of listening, to pace up and down this room (my last earthly refuge) and give ear to every sound of menace. Will Hyde die upon the scaffold? or will he find courage to release himself at the last moment? God knows; I am careless;[88] this is my true hour of death, and what is to follow concerns another than myself. Here then, as I lay down the pen and proceed to seal up my confession, I bring the life of that unhappy Henry Jekyll to an end.

---

[85] Hidden it. Hyde, being caught up in the moment, may not look for it.

[86] Here, in a penultimate moment of his fiction, Stevenson alludes once again to Hyde as an unevolved creature.

[87] Put back on. This is a very important moment. Jekyll, either by means of what is left of the old potion, or by the unstable action of the potion he has already imbibed, knows that he will soon turn into Hyde. What is wonderful to see is how Stevenson, by the simple change of pronoun in the course of two sentences, lets us know that Jekyll and Hyde will have accomplished their pilgrimage, which took them first away from and then toward each other to become one.

[88] Indifferent. That is, he does not care.

Afterword

"... as I lay down the pen and proceed to seal up my confession, I bring the life of that unhappy Henry Jekyll to an end."

So writes Henry Jekyll as himself and under the "influence of the last of the old powders." His tone is weary and resigned. For the duration of the final chapter, he has been explaining, clarifying, revealing. But as we turn the last page of Stevenson's ingeniously crafted fiction, we know that the story is not altogether over.

Because the story's end came long ago, in Chapter VIII, where we learned, without then knowing it, what happened *after* Henry Jekyll laid down his pen. There, in that chapter, we get a quite different Hyde from the dwarflike evil troglodyte. The Hyde behind the locked door of Henry Jekyll's cabinet has spent eight days in abject despair. Writing to an unknown chemist, his raw emotion breaks out and his pen splutters as he cries, "For God's sake, find me some of the old." He is a man pacing, weeping "like a woman or a lost soul."

As a piece of fictional plotting, what Stevenson has pulled off is a tour de force, creating a rich ambiguity in the midst of his story and then to putting it on hold until our own memory, not Stevenson's text, recalls it at the end. The poignancy and the pathos with which Stevenson has imbued Jekyll's confession then creates a dark stain that tinges our feelings about both Jekyll and Hyde.

Stevenson has managed to make both men's predicaments, though not both men, real. Having created a couple of two-dimensional figures, he has confronted them with a three-dimensional dilemma. And there's the trick that turned the easy "shilling shocker" of the first draft he threw into the fire into the complex and tragic tale we have just read.

The work, like Stevenson himself, is full of contradictions. Over and over again, I have complained in my notes that Stevenson gives us insufficient detail. Readers who know Stevenson as a superb writer about the natural world—trees, mountains, valleys, rivers, clouds, or the sea—must feel baffled by the curious placelessness of *Jekyll and Hyde*. Though we are told that the action takes place in London, we get very little information about the city. G.K. Chesterton sensed that Stevenson was actually writing about Edinburgh, but even that city does not come properly into focus. There's a hermetic quality to Stevenson's urban landscape, as if the story was taking place inside one of those glass spheres in which one sees a tiny cottage under water, and when one shakes the sphere, snow swirls down. We keep being told that one can hear the hum of the city, but there is hardly any description of traffic or street noises.

The book's characters, too, lack detail. We hardly receive any details about clothing. Jekyll is well dressed; Hyde's clothes, when they are Jekyll's, are too big for him. Jekyll's hall is one of the finest in London, but we have no idea how it is furnished. There are very few colors mentioned beyond Poole's red handkerchief, the red baize door, and the changing colors of the potion. We have no idea of the color of anybody's eyes or hair. Even the wine that is frequently mentioned is left unidentified.

Nor are Stevenson's characters fully rounded: the five major characters, Jekyll-Hyde, Utterson, Dr. Lanyon, Sir Danvers Carew, and Enfield, are all prosperous middle-aged or older bachelors. Jekyll refers once to his father; Utterson is Enfield's cousin; Jekyll and Lanyon were once schoolfellows; Sir Danvers Carew mails a letter at night—that constitutes all the history we have about any of the book's characters. And yet, if the book is sparsely detailed, such detail as we get is always significant. The fact, to repeat, that all the major characters are middle-aged bachelors, or the description of the architecture of Jekyll-Hyde's house, for instance. The presence of wine and a good rug on the floor in Hyde's rooms in Soho. Enfield's characterization as a man about town. The pretty manners of Sir Danvers Carew. What is remarkable is that the lack of complex description does not keep us from being swept along by the need to know what happens next. Vladimir Nabokov says in his 1980 essay on the novel that

Robert Louis Stevenson in France (above), and a similarly-posed mask of
Stevenson sculpted by Gertrude Amidar in 1970

it is because Stevenson is a great stylist; he makes light of the importance of allegory in the fiction. I share Nabokov's view that Stevenson in this work is a great stylist, but I think the allegory matters a great deal.

We tend to know more about Utterson than about anyone else but Jekyll-Hyde. He is a man in middle life, a tight-lipped but feelingful attorney, who, though he loves wine, perversely drinks gin; who loves the theater but will not go to it. Quiet and sedentary though he is, he is something of a British bulldog when, with Poole beside him, he wields an ax against the red baize door of Jekyll's study. We are told that he is valued by a circle of friends who are mostly blood relatives or people whom he has known for a long time. And yet, this decent, respectable, and loyal friend treats his kinsman Enfield with shabby, even unpardonable, levity. Why, as Chapter I ends, does he not simply tell Enfield that Jekyll owns the house into which Hyde disappeared?

Stevenson asks us to believe that Enfield is a man about town, a phrase that lets us imagine as much or as little as we like about his proclivities. Presumably, a man who tells us that he was returning from "some place at the end of the world" at three o'clock in the morning may be supposed to have an interesting present life and, very likely, something of a past. Here again, we are left without detail. We might, for instance, think that if Enfield was a man about town, he would be a young man. On the other hand, why should this be so? There are wicked old roués aplenty in the world, and there's no reason why Enfield may not be one of them.

What is most troubling about Enfield's fate is the way that Stevenson seems to set him up as an important character, the first witness to Hyde's depravity, and then, after Chapter I, allows him to disappear from the novel except for a brief return in Chapter VIII, in which he gets to speak a total of five short sentences and then disappears entirely from the story.

More interesting than Enfield's short shrift is the fact that Stevenson gives him some of the finest descriptive speeches in the story. In one of the longest paragraphs in the book (nearly four and a half pages in the original printing), Enfield gives Utterson a vivid account of Hyde's brutal encounter with the little girl.

We meet next a handful of minor characters. There is, first, the unnamed doctor who arrives on the scene and looks after the little girl whom Hyde has injured. Though Stevenson tells us that he "is a man of no particular age or color," he is a fairly important figure if for no other reason than that in a novel whose protagonist is a doctor, every doctor we meet bears scrutiny. What we learn about him before he passes from the scene is that he represses murderous instincts, and that he is quite willing to do the wrong thing for the right reason: blackmail Hyde so that the little girl's family can be recompensed for her fear and pain. The fact that he goes off with Enfield and Hyde, leaving untended whoever the patient was that caused him to be sent for in the first place, seems to me less a flaw in his character than a plotting error on Stevenson's part.

We come next to the two butlers. Dr. Lanyon's unnamed butler, merely solemn, comes in briefly in Chapter III. On the other hand, Poole, who is Dr. Jekyll's butler, is of the race of stalwart, honest serving-men beloved by class-conscious British writers. But he is not simply a biddable servant. He is astute enough to recognize that his master is in deep trouble, and he has both the imagination and the courage to do something about it.

Dr. Lanyon, the second of the three doctors we meet, is sketched in with great economy: ". . . a hearty, healthy, dapper, red-faced gentleman, with a shock of hair prematurely white, and a boisterous and decided manner." That rubicund face and boisterous manner, as well as the image of him sitting alone over his wine, gives us a quick peek into his life. As well as being a great physician, he is something of a bon vivant. His health is a very important detail, because it is precisely this paragon of fleshly, sensuous vigor who, when the Jekyll-Hyde secret is revealed, is sickened unto death by the knowledge. One ought to wonder why knowing about another man's sins or crimes should inflict a death wound. And the answer can only be, as Stevenson in his deep wisdom knew, that the view into the abyss Jekyll revealed to Lanyon included in it a glimpse of his own soul. Lanyon doesn't sicken and die because of Jekyll's depravity, but because of what he has learned about himself and the human condition. Stevenson says,

> The rosy man had grown pale; his flesh had fallen away; he was visibly balder and older; and yet it was not so much these tokens of a swift physical decay that arrested the lawyer's [Utterson's] notice, as a look in the eye and quality of manner that seemed to testify to some deep-seated terror of the mind (p. 80).

Sir Danvers Carew is another of those figures in *Jekyll and Hyde* who pass before us so briefly that we are tempted to think of them as stick figures invented simply to move the plot along. For one thing, he is not described directly. All we know about him is what we get from the testimony of the maid servant who witnessed his murder. What she tells us is that he was an aged and beautiful gentleman with white hair, who said something to Hyde "with a very pretty manner of politeness"; that when the moon shone on his face "it seemed to breathe such an innocent and old-world kindness of disposition, yet with something high too, as of a well-founded self-content." Beyond a sentence more about the old gentleman's surprise at Hyde's outburst of anger, that is all we have from Stevenson's pen about Sir Danvers Carew.

Not quite all. After his death, a stamped and sealed letter addressed to Utterson which "he had been probably carrying to the post" is found on his body. Again, the sparseness of detail stimulates speculations. Since in this novel, every major character (except Hyde) at some point confides in the close-mouthed attorney, we cannot help wondering about the contents of that letter. Did Sir Danvers Carew also have something desperate or guilty—some secret involving Hyde—to tell him? Surely that would go far to explaining the scene in which the aged and beautiful Sir Danvers accosts a small, hurrying *young* stranger "with a very pretty manner of politeness . . ." and is answered by a storm of rage so violent that it ends in murder? For Stevenson and his Victorian readers, the murder is what it appears to be: a defining instance of Hyde's wickedness. For us, more than a hundred years after the book was written, the ambiguous diction describing the scene stirs our suspicion that we are witnessing a scene that begins as gay-bashing and ends in death.

To make that point more effectively, I need to shift the direction of the discussion for a moment.

The novel's focus on the lives of half a dozen middle-aged bachelors, and its effective absence of women, have naturally enough raised the question of the degree to which homosexuality is an issue in *Jekyll and Hyde*. We have, for instance, Jekyll and Lanyon's friendship compared with that of Damon and Pythias; we have Utterson's dark speculations about blackmail, Jekyll's "enslavement" to Hyde, the unspecified sins of Jekyll's youth, and the lack of specificity about his present wickednesses. All of this, combined with the suggestive language of the Carew-Hyde episode, can stir questions.

To which the simplest answer may be the best: Stevenson, as we have seen, was aware that he did not write well about women, and so chose to write about what he knew best: men. It's the same choice he made when he wrote *Treasure Island*, another of his fictions in which there are no women to speak of. In *The Strange Case of Dr. Jekyll and Mr. Hyde*, he focused on a milieu he knew well: the clubby, middle-class world of powerful men in Edinburgh and London. And what he knew best about that milieu was that it was a world in which facade counted—the cut of one's suit, the social status of one's friends. Appearance, not substance. If Stevenson has any single target, it is hypocrisy—not heterosexual or homosexual sin.

Still, it would be naive not to take into account in our reading Stevenson's life experience. Two of his friends, Edmund Gosse and John Aldington Symonds, were homosexuals. Aldington was particularly upset when he read *Jekyll and Hyde*. In a letter to Stevenson, he complained,

> I doubt whether anyone has a right so to scrutinize the abysmal depths of personality. . . . At least I think he ought to bring more of the distinct belief in the resources of human nature, more faith, more sympathy with our frailty, into the matter than you have done. . . . I seem to have lost you so utterly that I can afford to fling truth of the crudest in your face. And yet I love you and think of you daily.

Stevenson's reply is gentle enough:

> Jekyll is a dreadful thing, I own; but the only thing I feel dreadful about is that damned old business of the war in the members. This time it came out; and I hope it will stay in, in future.

There are a couple of other minor characters. We have Mr. Guest, Utterson's head clerk, who is pleased to share "a bottle of a particular old wine" with him, and who is said to have some skill as a handwriting analyst, though the single document he is asked to look at is hardly a test of his acumen. There is very little that can be said about Guest, as Stevenson seems not to have thought much about him. He is a weak invention at best in what is certainly the weakest chapter in the novel.

More memorable than Guest is Hyde's silvery-haired, ivory-faced housekeeper who, in Stevenson's brilliant shorthand, stands vividly before us, though Stevenson devotes less than two short paragraphs to her. Wonderfully, she manages to resemble both Hyde and Jekyll. Like Hyde, she has an evil face; like Jekyll, her face is smoothed by hypocrisy, and like him, she has excellent manners. Her odious joy at the suggestion that Hyde might be in trouble tells us all we need to know about her relationship to her employer.

Inspector Newcomen of Scotland Yard is merely a presence in the fiction. Apparently, though not certainly, it is he who brings the mysterious letter found on Sir Danvers Carew's body to Utterson. One guesses that he stands or sits patiently waiting for Utterson to finish his breakfast and then rides with him to the police station where Utterson identifies the body. One guesses, too, that Stevenson, who allows him to be anonymous from page 64 until page 66, named him as an afterthought. He is given two brief speeches, the first of which is fatuous (page 64) and the second optimistic but entirely mistaken (page 67).

Let us finally turn to Dr. Jekyll and Mr. Hyde. Since, as G.K. Chesterton pointed out as early as 1927, "The real stab of the story is not in the discovery that one man is two men; but in the discovery that the two men are one man," let me continue to treat them as separate characters. That makes the story, on the face of it, fairly simple. The wealthy, distinguished, reputable do-gooder scientist Dr. Henry Jekyll has, for some ten years, been pursuing researches that, according to his old friend and colleague, Dr. Lanyon, were too fanciful and that proved that he had begun "to go wrong, wrong in mind." Jekyll tells us that the worst of his own faults was "a certain impatient gaiety of disposition" that fills him with such morbid shame that he sedulously conceals his pleasures from the world. And from Utterson we learn that Jekyll was "wild when he was young."

The violence of the transformation from Jekyll to Hyde and the remarkable physical differences between the upright, middle-aged Jekyll and the somehow dwarfish, much younger Hyde can easily mislead readers into accepting that they are, morally speaking, polar opposites. The error is compounded by Jekyll's later insistence that Hyde is absolutely and only evil.

The point, stressed in the notes, has been that the potion does not create Hyde, it releases him. Jekyll says:

> The drug had no discriminating action; it was neither diabolical nor divine; it but shook the doors of the prisonhouse of my disposition . . . Hence, although I had now two characters as well as two appearances, one was wholly evil, and the other was still the old Henry Jekyll, *that incongruous compound of whose reformation and improvement I had already learned to despair.* (p. 122, italics added).

If we remember, as we are meant to, that Hyde *is* Jekyll, we will not fall into Jekyll's easy assumption that the separation has been accomplished. Jekyll for a while flatters himself that it has: "It was Hyde after all, and Hyde alone, that was guilty. Jekyll was no worse; he woke again to his good qualities *seemingly* unimpaired" (the italics for "seemingly" are, again, mine).

Stevenson goes to great pains to make clear that the final transformation leading to Jekyll's downfall comes about not because of the ineffectiveness or failure of the potion but because Jekyll on his own and in his proper shape yields to a Jekyllian temptation: "Not that I dreamed of resuscitating Hyde; the bare idea of that would startle me to frenzy; no, it was in my own person, that I was once more tempted to trifle with my conscience; and it was as an ordinary secret sinner, that I at last fell before the assaults of temptation" (p. 129–130). As he is sitting in Regent's Park, savoring the memory of whatever the delicious sin it was that he has committed and lazily repeating to himself the solid citizen's usual excuse for vice, "After all . . . I was like my neighbours . . ." the transformation comes that drives him to seek refuge in the hotel on Portland Street, after which there is the meeting with Lanyon and the sequence of uncontrollable transformations that mark the beginning of the tragic end.

Hyde, recounting the murder of Sir Danvers Carew, speaks so exultantly of the delight he took in breaking the old man's bones that we are inclined to accept Jekyll's judgment that Hyde is pure evil. But there is an intractable puzzle here. If Hyde is so happy being a purely evil monster, why would he ever choose to take the draught that would turn him back again into the middle-aging, dreary, sedate bourgeois named Jekyll? Except for just after the murder of Sir Danvers Carew, when Jekyll's identity serves him as a sort of hiding place from the police, he has no motivation to return to his Jekyll self. Hyde, after all, is the one who has more fun.

The problem is only solved if we suggest either that Stevenson made a major plotting error, which gets obscured because of his superb narrative and stylistic skills, or that Hyde is not as purely evil as Jekyll insists. Vladimir Nabokov is attracted to both explanations, and I can see why. From the point of view of a novelist organizing an allegoric fiction, an absolutely evil Hyde is an attractive choice. In children's tales, the Wicked Stepmother, the Cruel Witch, the Ferocious Ogre, and the Horrid Dragon are immediately present and memorable. From a reader's point of view, too, how pleasant it is to have so simple a moral dichotomy as a good Jekyll and a bad Hyde. But if we look hard at the way the story ends, we see that Jekyll disappears from our view essentially unchanged.

Jekyll, without the potion, was always the Hypocrite-Jekyll-Containing-Hyde. But what about the Hyde who weeps as pitifully as a woman or a lost soul behind the locked door of Jekyll's cabinet in the week that Poole

Fanny Stevenson

is sent haring over London from one chemist's shop to another? Or the Hyde who downs the redeeming cyanide at the end?

What, finally, can we conclude about this strange tale that refuses to behave either like the simple allegory of good and evil or the equally simple mad-scientist novel it is most often taken to be? It is, after all, such a minimal book; a short novel in which there are no richly developed characters, no fine writing about places, no astute analyses of manners. The answer is that in this, of all of Stevenson's novels, less is more. What we succumb to is the skill of a first-rate storyteller who has managed to infuse an allegory with the sort of fascinating life other writers give to the people they invent. Instead, what we have is a tale within which a reader will discern not only how complex the struggle between good and evil is, but also the shadowy outlines of the other struggles constantly going on within ourselves. Yes, there is good versus evil, but there is also repression against gratification, friendship versus betrayal, fathers against sons, youth versus youth, love against hate, civility wrestling with instinct.

And all of that is framed by compassion, as if in writing *The Strange Case of Dr. Jekyll and Mr. Hyde* Stevenson had found the fictional way to distill the wisdom he passed on to his friend Sidney Colvin the following year:

You believe in unbelief; don't, it's not worth while. The world has been going on long enough for us to *know* we are wrong; yet something is meant by everything, . . . I am sir, your obedient servant

Andrew Crossmyloof

Gallio [sic]

Julius Caesar

Archbishop Sharpe

My Uncle Toby

and

The Man in the Moon.

Everything is true; only the opposite is true too; you must believe both equally or be damned.

Whimsically put though it is, it is a health-asserting credo in keeping with the willed optimism of a man who has spent his life drifting in and out of painful and life-threatening illness. "To me," he wrote to William Archer, "the medicine bottles on my chimney and the blood on my handkerchief are accidents; they do not colour my view of life . . . they do not exist in my prospect; I would as soon drag them under the eyes of my readers as I would mention a pimple I might chance to have (saving your presence) on my posteriors. What does it prove? What does it change? it has not hurt, it has not changed me in any essential part . . ." Stevenson's willed optimism has nothing in common with Panglossian cheerfulness. It is the optimism of gritted teeth based on the consoling knowledge that the only progress the pilgrim who walks on a treadmill can make is toward himself. To paraphrase Melville, "Ah Jekyll, ah, humanity."

147

Appendix A
Stevenson's Short Stories

Thrawn Janet

The Reverend Murdoch Soulis was long minister of the moorland parish of Balweary, in the vale of Dule. A severe, bleak-faced old man, dreadful to his hearers, he dwelt in the last years of his life, without relative or servant or any human company, in the small and lonely manse under the Hanging Shaw.[1] In spite of the iron composure of his features, his eye was wild, scared, and uncertain; and when he dwelt, in private admonition, on the future of the impenitent, it seemed as if his eye pierced through the storms of time to the terrors of eternity. Many young persons, coming to prepare themselves against the season of the Holy Communion, were dreadfully affected by his talk. He had a sermon on 1st Peter, v. and 8th,[2] 'The devil as a roaring lion', on the Sunday after every seventeenth of August, and he was accustomed to surpass himself upon that text both by the appalling nature of the matter and the terror of his bearing in the pulpit. The children were frightened into fits, and the old looked more

---

[1]   A thicket or small wood.
[2]   The verse reads, "Be sober, be vigilant; because your adversary the devil, as a roaring lion, walketh about, seeking whom he may devour . . ."

than usually oracular, and were, all that day, full of those hints that Hamlet deprecated. The manse itself, where it stood by the water of Dule among some thick trees, with the Shaw overhanging it on the one side, and on the other many cold, moorish[3] hilltops rising toward the sky, had begun, at a very early period of Mr Soulis's ministry, to be avoided in the dusk hours by all who valued themselves upon their prudence; and guidmen[4] sitting at the clachan[5] alehouse shook their heads together at the thought of passing late by that uncanny neighbourhood. There was one spot, to be more particular, which was regarded with especial awe. The manse stood between the high road and the water of Dule, with a gable to each; its back was towards the kirktown[6] of Balweary, nearly half a mile away; in front of it, a bare garden, hedged with thorn, occupied the land between the river and the road. The house was two storeys high, with two large rooms on each. It opened not directly on the garden, but on a causewayed path, or passage, giving on the road on the one hand, and closed on the other by the tall willows and elders that bordered on the stream. And it was this strip of causeway that enjoyed among the young parishioners of Balweary so infamous a reputation. The minister walked there often after dark, sometimes groaning aloud in the instancy of his unspoken prayers; and when he was from home, and the manse door was locked, the more daring schoolboys ventured, with beating hearts, to 'follow my leader' across that legendary spot.

This atmosphere of terror, surrounding, as it did, a man of God of spotless character and orthodoxy, was a common cause of wonder and subject of inquiry among the few strangers who were led by chance or business into that unknown, outlying country. But many even of the people of the parish were ignorant of the strange events which had marked the first year of Mr Soulis's ministrations; and among those who were better informed, some were naturally reticent, and others shy of that particular topic. Now and again, only, one of the older folk would warm into courage over his third tumbler, and recount the cause of the minister's strange looks and solitary life.

Fifty years syne, when Mr Soulis cam' first into Ba'weary, he was still a young man—a callant,[7] the folk said—fu' o' book-learnin' an' grand at

---

3   As on a moor.
4   Goodmen.
5   A small village.
6   The village in which the parish church is located.
7   Fellow, lad, a youth.

the exposition, but, as was natural in sae young a man, wi' nae leevin'[8] experience in religion. The younger sort were greatly taken wi' his gifts and his gab; but auld, concerned, serious men and women were moved even to prayer for the young man, whom they took to be a self-deceiver, and the parish that was like to be sae ill-supplied. It was before the days o' the moderates—weary fa' them[9]; but ill things are like guid—they baith come bit by bit, a pickle[10] at a time; and there were folk even then that said the Lord had left the college professors to their ain devices, an' the lads that went to study wi' them wad hae done mair an' better sittin' in a peatbog, like their forbears of the persecution, wi' a Bible under their oxter[11] an' a speerit o' prayer in their heart. There was nae doubt, onyway, but that Mr Soulis had been ower hand at the college. He was careful and troubled for mony things besides the ae thing needful. He had a feck[12] o' books wi' him—mair than had ever been seen before in a' that presbytery; and a sair[13] wark the carrier had wi' them, for they were a like to have smoored[14] in the Deil's Hag[15] between this and Kilmackerlie. They were books o' divinity, to be sure, or so they c'ad them; but the serious were o' opinion there was little service for sae mony, when the hail o' God's Word would gang in the neuk o' a plaid.[16] Then he wad sin half the day and half the nicht forbye, which was scant decent—writin' nae less; an' first they were feared he wad read his sermons; an' syne it proved he was writin' a book himsel', which was surely no' fittin' for ane o' his years an' sma' experience.

Onyway it behoved him to get an auld, decent wife to keep the manse for him an' see to his bit denners; an' he was recommended to an auld limmer[17]—Janet M'Clour, they ca'd her—an' sae far left to himsel' as to be ower persuaded. There was mony advised him to the contrary for Janet was mair than suspeckit by the best folk in Ba'weary. Lang o' that,[18] she had had a wean to a dragoon;[19] she hadna come forrit[20] for maybe thretty

8 Living.
9 A curse on them.
10 A little.
11 The underarm, or armpit.
12 A quantity.
13 Hard.
14 Smothered.
15 A hill of firmer ground in a bog.
16 The whole of God's Word would go [fit] into the corner of a plaid.
17 As applied to a woman, the word means strumpet, hussy, jade.
18 Beyond all that. . .
19 Had a dragoon's baby.
20 Ian Bell says the phrase in this context means, "to offer oneself as a communicant."

year; and bairns had seen her mumblin' to hersel' up on Key' Loan[21] in the gloamin', whilk was an unco time[22] an' place for a God fearin' woman. Howsoever, it was the laird himsel' that had first tauld the minister o' Janet; an' in thae days he wad hae gane a far gate[23] to pleesure the laird. When folk tauld him that Janet was sib to the de'il,[24] it was a' superstition by his way o' it; an' when they cast up the Bible to him an' the witch of Endor, he wad threep it doun their thrapples[25] that thir days[26] were a' gane by, an' the de'il was mercifully restrained.

Weel, when it got about the clachan that Janet M'Clour was to be servant at the manse, the folk were fair mad wi' her an' him thegither an' some o' the guidwives had nae better to dae than get round her doorcheeks[27] and chairge her wi' a' that was ken't again' her, frae the sodger's bairn to John Tamson's taw kye.[28] She was nae great speaker folk usually let her gang her ain gate,[29] an' she let them gang theirs, with neither Fairguid-een nor Fair-guid-day; but when she buckled to,[30] she had a tongue to deave the miller.[31] Up she got, an' there wasna an auld story in Ba'weary but she gart somebody lowp for it[32] that day; they couldna say ae thing but she could say twa to it; till, at the hinder end, the guidwives up an' claucht haud[33] of her, an' clawed the coats aff her back, and pu'd her doun the clachan to the water o' Dule, to see if she were a witch or no, soom or droun.[34] The carline skirled[35] till ye could hear her at the Hangin' Shaw, an' she focht like ten; there was mony a guidwife bure the mark o' her neist day an' mony a lang day after; an' just in the hettest o' the collieshangie,[36] wha suld come up (for his sins) but the new minister!

'Women,' said he (an' he had a grand voice), 'I charge you in the Lord's name to let her go.'

Janet ran to him—she was fair wud wi' terror—an' clang to him, an'

---

21 A lane or by-road to a farm.
22 Which was a strange time. . . .
23 Gone a far way or distance.
24 The devil's kin.
25 Force one's opinion down their throats.
26 Their days.
27 Door-posts.
28 The soldier's child to John Amson's two cows.
29 Went her own way.
30 To set to work.
31 To deafen the miller.
32 Made somebody leap for it.
33 Clutched or grasped hold of her.
34 Swim or drown. This is the time-honored way to test whether anyone was a witch. If the suspected person floated or swam, he or she was considered guilty. Drowning was the only exculpation.
35 The old woman shrieked.
36 Noisy quarrel.

prayed him, for Christ's sake, save her frae the cummers;[37] an' they, for their pairt, tauld him a' that was ken't, an' maybe mair.

'Woman,' says he to Janet, 'is this true?'

'As the Lord sees me,' says she, 'as the Lord made me, no' a word o't. Forbye the bairn,'[38] says she, 'I've been a decent woman a' my days.'

'Will you,' says Mr Soulis, 'in the name of God, and before me, His unworthy minister, renounce the devil and his works?'

Weel, it wad appear that when he askit that, she gave a girn that fairly frichit them[39] that saw her, an' they could hear her teeth play dirl thegither in her chafts;[40] but there was naething for it but the ae way or the ither; an' Janet lifted up her hand an' renounced the de'il before them a'.

'And now,' says Mr Soulis to the guidwives, 'home with ye, one and all, and pray to God for His forgiveness.'

An' he gied Janet his arm, though she had little on her but a sark,[41] and took her up the clachan to her ain door like a leddy o' the land; an' her screighin' an' laughin' as was a scandal to be heard.

There were mony grave folk lang ower their prayers that nicht; but when the morn cam' there was sic a fear full upon a' Ba'weary that the bairns hid theirsels, an' even the menfolk stood an' keekit[42] frae their doors. For there was Janet comin' doun the clachan—her or her likeness, nane could tell—wi' her neck thrawn,[43] an' her heid on ae side, like a body that has been hangit, an' a girn on her face like an unstreakit corp. By an' by they got used wi' it, an' even speered[44] at her to ken what was wrang; but frae that day forth she couldna speak like a Christian woman, but slavered an' played click wi' her teeth like a pair o' shears; an' frae that day forth the name o' God cam' never on her lips. Whiles she wad try to say it, but it michtna be.[45] Them that kenned best said least; but they never gied that Thing the name o' Janet M'Clour; for the auld Janet, by their way o't, was in muckle hell[46] that day. But the minister was neither to haud nor to bind;[47] he preached about naething but the folk cruelty that had gi'en her a stroke of the palsy; he skelpit[48] the bairns that meddled

---

[37] The midwives, or women, or gossips.
[38] Except for the child.
[39] A grimace that fairly frightened them.
[40] Vibrate or grind together in her cheeks.
[41] Shirt or chemise.
[42] Peeped.
[43] Twisted, crooked, warped.
[44] Questioned.
[45] It might not be.
[46] According to them, was in the deepest hell. . . .
[47] Was neither to be held nor bound.

her; an' he had her up to the manse that same nicht, an' dwalled there a' his lane wi' her under the Hangin' Shaw.

Weel, time gaed by: and the idler sort commenced to think mair lichtly o' that black business. The minister was weel thocht o'; he was aye late at the writing, folk wad see his can'le doon by the Dule water after twal' at e'en; and he seemed pleased wi' himself an' upsitten[49] as at first, though a'-body could see that he was dwining.[50] As for Janet, she cam' an' she gaed; if she didna speak muckle afore it, it was reason she should speak less then; she meddled naebody; but she was an eldritch[51] thing to see, an' nane wad hae mistrysted[52] wi' her for Ba'weary glebe.[53]

About the end o' July there cam' a spell o' weather, the like o't never was in that country-side; it was lown[54] an' het an' heartless; the herds couldna win up the Black Hill, the bairns were ower weariet to play; an' yet it was gousty[55] too, wi' claps o' het wun that rumm'led[56] in the glens, and bits o'shouers that slockened[57] naething. We aye thoucht it but to thun'er to the morn; but the morn cam' an' the morn's morning, an' it was aye the same uncanny weather, sair on folks and bestial.[58] O' a' that were the waur, nane suffered like Mr Soulis; he could neither sleep nor eat, he tauld his elders; an' when he wasna writin' at his weary book, he wad be stravaguin' ower[59] a' the country-side like a man possessed, when a'-body else was blithe to keep caller[60] ben the house.

Abune Hangin' Shaw, in the bield[61] o' the Black Hill, there's a bit enclosed grund wi' an iron yett; an' it seems, in the auld days, that was the kirkyaird o' Ba'weary, an' consecrated by the Papists before the blessed licht shone upon the kingdom. It was a great howff,[62] o' Mr Soulis's ony-way; there he wad sit and consider his sermons; an' indeed it's a bieldy bit. Weel, as he cam' ower the waist end o' the Black Hill, ae day, he

---

[48] Slapped.
[49] Sitting up at night.
[50] Pining away or wasting away as during an illness.
[51] Unnatural, frightful, hideous.
[52] To fail to keep an appointment.
[53] A plot or piece of land.
[54] Still, calm, quiet.
[55] Gusty.
[56] With bursts of hot wind that rumbled. . . .
[57] Slaked, quenched.
[58] Hard on people and beasts.
[59] Wandering aimlessly.
[60] Keep cool.
[61] Shelter.
[62] A place of resort. A favorite place at which one goes.

saw first twa, an' syne fower, an' syne seeven corbie craws fleein' round an' round abune the auld kirkyaird. They flew laigh an' heavy, an' squawked to ither as they gaed;[63] an' it was clear to Mr Soulis that something had put them frae their ordinar. He wasna easy fleyed,[64] an' gaed straucht up to the wa's; an' what suld he find there but a man, or the appearance o' a man, sittin' in the inside upon a grave. He was of a great stature, an' black as hell, and his e'en were singular to see.[65] Mr Soulis had heard tell o' black men, mony's the time; but there was something unco about this black man that daunted him. Het as he was, he took a kind o' cauld grue[66] in the marrow o' his banes; but up he spak for a' that; an' says he: 'My friend, are you a stranger in this place?' The black man answered never a word; he got upon his feet, an' begoud on to hirsle to the wa'[67] on the far side; but he aye lookit at the minister; an' the minister stood an' lookit back; till a' in a meenit the black man was ower the wa' an' rinnin' for the bield o' the trees. Mr Soulis, he hardly kenned why, ran after him; but he was fair forjeskit[68] wi' his walk an' the het, unhalesome weather; an' rin as he likit, he got nae mair than a glisk[69] o' the black man amang the birks,[70] till he won doun to the foot o' the hillside, an' there he saw him ance mair, gaun, hap-step-an'-lawp,[71] ower Dule water to the manse.

Mr Soulis wasna weel pleased that this fearsome gangrel[72] suld mak' sae free wi' Ba'weary manse; an' he ran the harder, an', wet shoon, ower the burn, an' up the walk; but the de'il a black man was there to see. He stepped out upon the road, but there was naebody there; he gaed a' ower the gairden, but na, nae black man. At the hinder end, an'a bit feared as was but natural, he lifted the hasp an' into the manse; and there was Janet M'Clour before his e'en, wi' her thrawn craig,[73] an' nane sae pleased to see him. An' he aye minded sinsyne,[74] when first he set his e'en upon her, he had the same cauld and deidly grue.

---

[63] He saw first two, and then four, and then seven ravens flying round and round above the old churchyard. They flew low and heavy and squawked to each other as they went.
[64] Frightened.
[65] Ian Bell makes the point that this black man derives from Scottish religious folklore in which the devil is frequently described as black.
[66] A shudder, shivering, of horror or disgust.
[67] Began to clamber clumsily over the wall.
[68] Weary, exhausted.
[69] Glimpse, or glance.
[70] Birches.
[71] Hop, step, and leap.
[72] Tramp, vagabond.
[73] Twisted neck.
[74] Since that time.

'Janet,' says he, 'have you seen a black man?'

'A black man!' quo' she 'Save us a'! Ye're no wise, minister. There's nae black man in a' Ba'weary.'

But she didna speak plain, ye maun understand; but yam-yam-mered, like a powney wi' the bit in its moo.[75]

'Weel,' says he, 'Janet, if there was nae black man, I have spoken with the Accuser of the Brethren.'

An' he sat doun like ane wi' a fever, an' his teeth chittered in his heid.

'Hoots,'[76] says she, 'think shame to yoursel', minister'; an' gied him a drap brandy that she keept aye by her.

Syne Mr Soulis gaed into his study amang a' his books. It's a lang, laigh, mirk chalmer,[77] perishin' cauld in winter, an' no' very dry even in the top o' the simmer, for the manse stands near the burn. Sae doun he sat, and thocht of a' that had come an' gane since he was in Ba'weary, an' his name, an' the days when he was a bairn an' ran daffin' on the braes;[78] an' that black man aye ran in his heid like the owercome[79] of a sang. Aye the mair he thocht, the mair he thocht o' the black man. He tried the prayer, an' the words wouldna come to him; an' he tried, they say, to write at his book, but he couldna mak' nae mair o' that. There was whiles he thocht the black man was at his oxter, an' the swat stood upon him cauld as well-water; and there was ither whiles, when he cam' to himsel' like a christened bairn an' minded naething.

The upshot was that he gaed to the window an' stood glowerin' at Dule water. The trees are unco thick, an' the water lies deep an' black under the manse; an' there was Janet washin' the cla'es wi' her coats kilted.[80] She had her back to the minister, an' he, for his pairt, hardly kenned what he was lookin' at. Syne she turned round, an' shawed her face; Mr Soulis had the same cauld grue as twice that day afore, an' it was borne in upon him what folks said, that Janet was deid lang syne, an' this was a bogle[81] in her clay-cauld flesh. He drew back a pickle and he scanned her narrowly. She was tramp-trampin' in the cla'es croonin' to hersel'; and eh! Gude guide us, but it was a fearsome face. While she sang louder, but there was nae man born o' woman that could tell the words o' her sang;

---

[75]   Like a pony with the bit in its mouth.
[76]   An interjection expressing impatience.
[77]   Long, low, dark chamber.
[78]   Being merry on the hilltops.
[79]   Repeated phrasing.
[80]   Petticoats gathered up.
[81]   An apparition. A goblin.

an' whiles[82] she lookit side-lang doun, but there was naething there for her to look at. There gaed a scunner[83] through the flesh upon his banes; an' that was Heeven's advertisement.[84] But Mr Soulis just blamed himsel', he said, to think sae ill o' a puir, auld afflicted wife that hadna a freend forbye himsel'; an' he put up a bit prayer for him an' her, an' drank a little caller[85] water—for his heart rose again' the meat—an' gaed up to his naked bed in the gloamin'.

That was a nicht that has never been forgotten in Ba'weary, the nicht o' the seventeenth o' August, seventeen hun'er an' twal'. It has been het afore, as I hae said, but that nicht it was hetter than ever. The sun gaed doun amang unco-lookin' clouds; it fell as mirk as the pit; no' a star, no' a breath o' wund; ye couldna see your han' afore your face, an' even the auld folk cuist the covers frae their beds an' lay pechin'[86] for their breath. Wi' a' that he had upon his mind, it was gey[87] an' unlikely Mr Soulis wad get muckle sleep. He lay an' he tummled; the gude, caller bed that he got into brunt his very banes; whiles he slept, an' whiles he waukened; whiles he heard the time o' nicht, an' whiles a tyke[88] yowlin' up the muir,[89] as if somebody was deid; whiles he thocht he heard bogles claverin'[90] in his lug,[91] an' whiles he saw spunkies[92] in the room. He behoved, he judged, to be sick; an' sick he was—little he jaloosed[93] the sickness.

At the hinder end, he got a clearness in his mind, sat up in his sark on the bed-side, an' fell thinkin' ance mair o' the black man an' Janet. He couldna weel tell how—maybe it was the cauld to his feet—but it cam' in upon him wi' a spate that there was some connection between thir twa, an' that either or baith o' them were bogles. An' just at that moment, in Janet's room, which was neist to his, there cam' a stramp[94] o' feet as if men were wars'lin',[95] an' then a loud bang; an' then a wund gaed reishling[96] round the fower quarters o' the house; an' then a' was ance mair as seelent as the grave.

---

82 From time to time.
83 Disgusted irritation.
84 Heaven's warning.
85 Fresh.
86 Panting.
87 Rather, very, considerably.
88 A mongrel dog.
89 Moor.
90 Chattering, gossiping.
91 Ear.
92 Deceptive lights, *ignis fatuus*, will-o'-the-wisp.
93 Suspected, surmised.
94 Stamp.
95 Wrestling.
96 Rushing.

Mr Soulis was feared for neither man nor de'il. He got his tinderbox, an' lit a can'le, an' made three steps o' tower to Janet's door. It was on the hasp, an' he pushed it open an' keeked bauldly in. It was a big room, as big as the minister's ain, an' plenished wi' grand, auld solid gear, for he had naething else. There was a fower-posted bed wi' auld tapestry; an' a braw[97] cabinet o' aik,[98] that was fu' o' the minister's divinity books, an' put there to be out o' the gate;[99] an' a wheen[100] duds o' Janet's lying here an' there about the floor. But nae Janet could Mr Soulis see; nor any sign o' a contention. In he gaed (an' there's few that wad hae followed him) an' lookit a' round, an' listened. But there was naething to be heard, neither inside the manse nor in a' Ba'weary parish, an' naething to be seen but the muckle shadows turnin' round the can'le. An' then, a' at aince, the minister's heart played dunt[101] an' stood stockstill; an' a cauld wund blew amang the hairs o' his heid. Whaten a weary sicht[102] was that for the puir man's e'en! For there was Janet hangin' frae a nail beside the auld aik cabinet: her heid aye lay on her shouther, her e'en were steekit,[103] the tongue projected frae her mouth, an' her heels were twa feet clear abune the floor.

'God forgive us all!' thocht Mr Soulis, 'poor Janet's dead.'

He cam' a step nearer to the corp; an' then his heart fair whammled[104] in his inside. For by what cantrip[105] it wad ill beseem a man to judge, she was hangin' frae a single nail an' by a single wursted thread for darnin' hose.

It's a awfu' thing to be your lane at nicht wi' siccan[106] prodigies of darkness; but Mr Soulis was strong in the Lord. He turned and gaed his ways oot o' that room, an' lockit the door ahint him; and step by step, dount the stairs, as heavy as leed; and set dount the can'le on the table at the stair-foot. He couldna pray, he couldna think, he was dreepin' wi' caul' swat, an' naething could he hear but the dunt-dunt-duntin' o' his ain heart. He micht maybe hae stood there an hour, or maybe twa, he minded sae little; when a' o' a sudden he heard a laigh, uncanny steer[107] upstairs; a foot gaed to an' fro in the chalmer whaur the corp was hangin'; syne the

---

[97] Fine.
[98] Oak.
[99] Of the way.
[100] Some.
[101] Throb, beat rapidly.
[102] What a miserable sight.
[103] Protruding.
[104] Overturned, turned inside out, stumbled.
[105] Spell or charm.
[106] Such.
[107] Stir, disturbance.

door was opened, though he minded weel that he had lockit in an' syne there was a step upon the landin', an' it seemed to him as if the corp was lookin' ower the rail and doun upon him whaur he stood.

He took up the can'le again (for he couldna want the licht) an as saftly as ever he could, gaed straucht out o' the manse an' to the far end o' the causeway. It was aye pit-mirk; the flame o' the can'le, when he set it on the grund, brunt steedy and clear as in a room; naething moved, but the Dule water seepin' and sabbing doun the glen, an' yon unhaly footstep that cam' ploddin' doun the stairs inside the manse. He kenned the foot ower weel, for it was Janet's; an' at ilka step that cam' a wee thing nearer, the cauld got deeper in his vitals. He commended his soul to Him that made an' keepit him; 'and, O Lord,' said he, 'give me strength this night to war against the powers of evil.'

By this time the foot was comin', though the passage for the door; he could hear a hand skirt alang the wa', as if the fearsome thing was feelin' for its way. The saughs[108] tossed an' maned thegither, a long sigh cam' ower the hills, the flame o' the can'le was blawn aboot; an' there stood the corp of Thrawn Janet, wi' her grogram goun[109] an' her black mutch,[110] wi' the heid aye upon the shouther an' the girn still upon the face o't— leevin', ye wad hae said—deid, as Mr Soulis weel kenned[111]—upon the threshold o' the manse.

It's a strange thing that the soul of man should be that thirled into his perishable body; but the minister saw that, an' his heart didna break.

She didna stand there lang; she began to move again an' cam' slowly towards Mr Soulis whaur he stood under the saughs. A' the life o' his body, a' the strength o' his speerit, were glowerin' frae his e'en. It seemed she was gaun to speak, but wanted words, an' made a sign wi' the left hand. There cam' a clap o' wund, like a cat's fuff;[112] oot gaed the can'le, the saughs skreighed[113] like folk; an' Mr Soulis kenned, that, live or die, this was the end o't.

'Witch, beldame, devil!' he cried, 'I charge you, by the power of God, begone—if you be dead, to the grave—if you be damned, to hell.'

An' at that moment the Lord's ain hand out o' the heevens struck the Horror whaur it stood; the auld, deid desecrated corp o' the witch-wife,

---

108 Willows.
109 Gown made of coarse, loosely woven cloth—gros grain.
110 A close-fitting cap.
111 Living, you would have said—dead, as Mr. Soulis well knew.
112 Hiss.
113 Screeched or screamed.

sae lang keepit frae the grave and hirsled[114] round by de'ils, lowed up[115] like a brunstane spunk[116] an' fell in ashes to the grund; the thunder followed, peal on dirlin'[117] peal, the rairin' rain upon the back o' that; and Mr Soulis lowped through the garden hedge, an' ran, wi' skelloch[118] upon skelloch, for the clachan.

That same mornin', John Christie saw the Black Man pass the Muckle Cairn as it was chappin' six; before eicht, he gaed by the change-house at Knockdow; an' no' lang after, Sandy M'Lellan saw him gaun linkin'[119] doun the braes frae Kilmackerlie. There's little doubt but it was him that dwalled sae lang in Janet's body; but he was awa' at last; an' sinsyne the de'il has never fashed[120] us in Ba'weary.

But it was a sair dispensation for the minister; lang, lang he lay ravin' in his bed; an' frae that hour to this, he was the man ye ken the day.

---

[114] To move or slide with grazing or friction.
[115] Flared up.
[116] Brimstone spark.
[117] A vibrating or a ringing sound.
[118] Scream.
[119] To trip along; move smartly.
[120] Bothered.

The Body Snatcher

Every night in the year, four of us sat in the small parlour of the George at Debenham—the undertaker, and the landlord, and Fettes, and myself. Sometimes there would be more; but blow high, blow low, come rain or snow or frost, we four would be each planted in his own particular armchair. Fettes was an old drunken Scotchman, a man of education obviously, and a man of some property, since he lived in idleness. He had come to Debenham years ago, while still young, and by a mere continuance of living had grown to be an adopted townsman. His blue camlet[1] cloak was a local antiquity, like the church spire. His place in the parlour at the George, his absence from church, his old, crapulous, disreputable vices, were all things of course in Debenham. He had some vague Radical opinions and some fleeting infidelities, which he would now and again set forth and emphasise with tottering slaps upon the table. He drank rum—five glasses regularly every evening; and for the greater portion of his nightly visit to the George sat, with his glass in his right hand, in a state of melancholy alcoholic saturation. We called him the doctor, for he was supposed to have some special knowledge of medicine, and had been known, upon a pinch, to set a fracture or reduce a dislocation; but, beyond these slight particulars, we had no knowledge of his character and antecedents.

---

[1] Cloth marked in wavy lines, like watered silk.

One dark winter night—it had struck nine some time before the landlord joined us—there was a sick man in the George, a great neighbouring proprietor suddenly struck down with apoplexy on his way to Parliament; and the great man's still greater London doctor had been telegraphed to his bedside. It was the first time that such a thing had happened in Debenham, for the railway was but newly open, and we were all proportionately moved by the occurrence.

'He's come,' said the landlord, after he had filled and lighted his pipe.

'He?' said I. 'Who?—not the doctor?'

'Himself,' replied our host.

'What is his name?'

'Dr Macfarlane,' said the landlord.

Fettes was far through his third tumbler, stupidly fuddled, now nodding over, now staring mazily around him; but at the last word he seemed to awaken, and repeated the name 'Macfarlane' twice, quietly enough the first time, but with sudden emotion at the second.

'Yes,' said the landlord, 'that's his name, Dr Wolfe Macfarlane.'

Fettes became instantly sober; his eyes awoke, his voice became clear, loud, and steady, his language forcible and earnest. We were all startled by the transformation, as if a man had risen from the dead.

'I beg your pardon,' he said; 'I am afraid I have not been paying much attention to your talk. Who is this Wolfe Macfarlane?' And then, when he had heard the landlord out, 'It cannot be, it cannot be,' he added; 'and yet I would like well to see him face to face.'

'Do you know him, doctor?' asked the undertaker, with a gasp.

'God forbid!' was the reply. 'And yet the name is a strange one; it were too much to fancy two. Tell me, landlord, is he old?'

'Well,' said the host, 'he's not a young man, to be sure, and his hair is white; but he looks younger than you.'

'He is older, though; years older. But,' with a slap upon the table, 'it's the rum you see in my face—rum and sin. This man, perhaps, may have an easy conscience and a good digestion. Conscience! Hear me speak. You would think I was some good, old, decent Christian, would you not? But no, not I; I never canted.[2] Voltaire might have canted if he'd stood in my shoes; but the brains'—with a rattling fillip on his bald head—'the brains were clear and active, and I saw and made no deductions.'

---

[2] Talked with an affectation of piety.

'If you know this doctor,' I ventured to remark, after a somewhat awful pause, 'I should gather that you do not share the landlord's good opinion.'

Fettes paid no regard to me.

'Yes,' he said, with sudden decision, 'I must see him face to face.'

There was another pause, and then a door was closed rather sharply on the first floor, and a step was heard upon the stair.

'That's the doctor,' cried the landlord. 'Look sharp, and you can catch him.'

It was but two steps from the small parlour to the door of the old George Inn; the wide oak staircase landed almost in the street; there was a room for a Turkey rug[3] and nothing more between the threshold and the last round of the descent; but this little space was every evening brilliantly lit up, not only by the light upon the stair and the great signal-lamp below the sign, but by the warm radiance of the bar-room window. The George thus brightly advertised itself to passers-by in the cold street. Fettes walked steadily to the spot, and we, who were hanging behind, beheld the two men meet, as one of them had phrased it, face to face. Dr Macfarlane was alert and vigorous. His white hair set off his pale and placid, although energetic, countenance. He was richly dressed in the finest of broadcloth and the whitest of linen, with a great gold watch-chain, and studs and spectacles of the same precious material. He wore a broad-folded tie, white and speckled with lilac, and he carried on his arm a comfortable driving coat of fur. There was no doubt but he became his years, breathing, as he did, of wealth and consideration; and it was a surprising contrast to see our parlour sot—bald, dirty, pimpled, and robed in his old camlet cloak—confront him at the bottom of the stairs.

'Macfarlane!' he said somewhat loudly, more like a herald than a friend.

The great doctor pulled up short on the fourth step, as though the familiarity of the address surprised and somewhat shocked his dignity.

'Toddy Macfarlane!'[4] repeated Fettes.

The London man almost staggered. He stared for the swiftest of seconds at the man before him, glanced behind him with a sort of scare, and then in a startled whisper, 'Fettes!' he said, 'you!'

'Ay,' said the other, 'me! Did you think I was dead, too? We are not so easy shut of our acquaintance.'

---

[3] Turkish rug.

[4] Toddy is an alcoholic drink usually spiced with cloves, cinnamon or nutmeg. Presumably it is Macfarlane's nickname because it was his beverage. Note, too, that he hates the nickname (see page 170).

'Hush, hush!' exclaimed the doctor. 'Hush, hush! this meeting is so unexpected—I can see you are unmanned. I hardly knew you, I confess, at first; but I am overjoyed—overjoyed to have this opportunity. For the present it must be how-d'ye-do and goodbye in one, for my fly[5] is waiting, and I must not fail the train; but you shall—let me see—yes—you shall give me your address, and you can count on early news of me. We must do something for you, Fettes. I fear you are out at elbows; but we must see to that for auld lang syne, as once we sang at suppers.'

'Money!' cried Fettes; 'money from you! The money that I had from you is lying where I cast it in the rain.'

Dr Macfarlane had talked himself into some measure of superiority and confidence, but the uncommon energy of this refusal cast him back into his first confusion.

A horrible, ugly look came and went across his almost venerable countenance. 'My dear fellow,' he said, 'be it as you please; my last thought is to offend you. I would intrude on none. I will leave you my address, however—'

'I do not wish it—I do not wish to know the roof that shelters you,' interrupted the other. 'I heard your name; I feared it might be you; I wished to know if, after all, there were a God; I know now that there is none. Begone!'

He still stood in the middle of the rug, between the stair and doorway; and the great London physician, in order to escape, would be forced to step to one side. It was plain that he hesitated before the thought of this humiliation. White as he was, there was a dangerous glitter in his spectacles; but, while he still paused uncertain, he became aware that the driver of his fly was peering in from the street at this unusual scene, and caught a glimpse at the same time of our little body from the parlour, huddled by the corner of the bar. The presence of so many witnesses decided him at once to flee. He crouched together, brushing on the wainscot, and made a dart like a serpent, striking for the door. But his tribulation was not yet entirely at an end, for even as he was passing Fettes clutched him by the arm and these words came in a whisper, and yet painfully distinct, 'Have you seen it again?'

The great rich London doctor cried out aloud with a sharp, throttling cry; he dashed his questioner across the open space, and, with his hands over his head, fled out of the door like a detected thief. Before it had

---

[5] A horse-drawn public coach.

occurred to one of us to make a movement the fly was already rattling toward the station. The scene was over like a dream, but the dream had left proofs and traces of its passage. Next day the servant found the fine gold spectacles broken on the threshold, and that very night we were all standing breathless by the bar-room window, and Fettes at our side, sober, pale, and resolute in look.

'God protect us, Mr Fettes!' said the landlord, coming first into possession of his customary senses. 'What in the universe is all this? These are strange things you have been saying.'

Fettes turned toward us; he looked us each in succession in the face. 'See if you can hold your tongues,' said he. 'That man Macfarlane is not safe to cross; those that have done so already have repented it too late.'

And then, without so much as finishing his third glass, far less waiting for the other two, he bade us goodbye and went forth, under the lamp of the hotel, into the black night.

We three turned to our places in the parlour, with the big red fire and four clear candles; and, as we recapitulated what had passed, the first chill of our surprise soon changed into a glow of curiosity. We sat late; it was the latest session I have known in the old George. Each man, before we parted, had his theory that he was bound to prove; and none of us had any nearer business in this world than to track out the past of our condemned companion, and surprise the secret that he shared with the great London doctor. It is no great boast, but I believe I was a better hand at worming out a story than either of my fellows at the George; and perhaps there is now no other man alive who could narrate to you the following foul and unnatural events.

In his young days Fettes studied medicine in the schools of Edinburgh. He had talent of a kind, the talent that picks up swiftly what it hears and readily retails it for its own. He worked little at home; but he was civil, attentive, and intelligent in the presence of his masters. They soon picked him out as a lad who listened closely and remembered well; nay, strange as it seemed to me when I first heard it, he was in those days well favoured, and pleased by his exterior. There was, at that period, a certain extramural[6] teacher of anatomy, whom I shall here designate by the letter K. His name was subsequently too well known. The man who bore it skulked through the streets of Edinburgh in disguise, while the mob that applauded at the execution of Burke[7] called loudly for the blood of his employer. But Mr

---

[6] Teaching extension courses.

[7] William Burke, an Irishman executed in 1829 in Edinburgh for his part in a criminal enterprise that

K—was then at the top of his vogue; he enjoyed a popularity due partly to his own talent and address, partly to the incapacity of his rival, the university professor. The students, at least, swore by his name, and Fettes believed himself, and was believed by others, to have laid the foundations of success when he had acquired the favour of this meteorically famous man. Mr K—was a *bon vivant* as well as an accomplished teacher; he liked a sly illusion no less than a careful preparation. In both capacities Fettes enjoyed and deserved his notice, and by the second year of his attendance he held the half-regular position of second demonstrator or sub-assistant in his class.

In this capacity the charge of the theatre and lecture-room devolved in particular upon his shoulders. He had to answer for the cleanliness of the premises and the conduct of the other students, and it was a part of his duty to supply, receive, and divide the various subjects. It was with a view to this last—at that time very delicate—affair that he was lodged by Mr K—in the same wynd,[8] and at last in the same building, with the dissecting-rooms. Here, after a night of turbulent pleasures, his hand still tottering, his sight still misty and confused, he would be called out of bed in the black hours before the winter dawn by the unclean and desperate interlopers who supplied the table. He would open the door to these men, since infamous throughout the land.[9] He would help them with their tragic burden, pay them their sordid price, and remain alone, when they were gone, with the unfriendly relics of humanity. From such a scene he would return to snatch another hour or two of slumber, to repair the abuses of the night, and refresh himself for the labours of the day.

Few lads could have been more insensible to the impressions of a life thus passed among the ensigns of mortality. His mind was closed against all general considerations. He was incapable of interest in the fate and fortunes of another, the slave of his own desires and low ambitions. Cold, light, and selfish in the last resort, he had that modicum of prudence, miscalled morality which keeps a man from inconvenient drunkenness or punishable theft.[10] He coveted, besides, a measure of consideration from his masters and his fellow-pupils, and he had no desire to fail conspicuously

provided medical schools with corpses for dissection. He and his accomplice, William Hare, smothered their victims. Hare escaped the gallows.

The name "Burke" has become a verb meaning to murder by strangling.

[8] A narrow lane or alley.

[9] Burke and Hare (see above, note 7).

[10] This brilliant description of hypocrisy seems remarkably to anticipate Stevenson's judgment of Jekyll in *Jekyll and Hyde*.

in the external parts of life. Thus he made it his pleasure to gain some distinction in his studies, and day after day rendered the unimpeachable eye-service to his employer, Mr K——. For his day of work he indemnified himself by nights of roaring, blackguardly enjoyment; and when that balance had been struck, the organ that he called his conscience declared itself content.

The supply of subjects was a continual trouble to him as well as to his master. In that large and busy class, the raw material of the anatomists kept perpetually running out; and the business thus rendered necessary was not only unpleasant in itself, but threatened dangerous consequences to all who were concerned. It was the policy of Mr K—— to ask no questions in his dealings with the trade. 'They bring the body, and we pay the price,' he used to say, dwelling on the alliteration—'quid pro quo'. And, again, and somewhat profanely, 'Ask no questions,' he would tell his assistants, 'for conscience' sake.' There was no understanding that the subjects were provided by the crime of murder. Had that idea been broached to him in words, he would have recoiled in horror; but the lightness of his speech upon so grave a matter was, in itself, an offence against good manners, and a temptation to the men with whom he dealt. Fettes, for instance, had often remarked to himself upon the singular freshness of the bodies. He had been struck again and again by the hang-dog, abominable looks of the ruffians who came to him before the dawn; and, putting things together clearly in his private thoughts, he perhaps attributed a meaning too immoral and too categorical to the unguarded counsels of his master. He understood his duty, in short, to have three branches: to take what was brought, to pay the price, and to avert the eye from any evidence of crime.

One November morning this policy of silence was put sharply to the test. He had been awake all night with a racking toothache—pacing his room like a caged beast or throwing himself in fury on his bed—and had fallen at last into that profound, uneasy slumber that so often follows on a night of pain, when he was awakened by the third or fourth angry repetition of the concerted signal. There was a thin, bright moonshine; it was bitter cold, windy, and frosty; the town had not yet awakened, but an indefinable stir already preluded the noise and business of the day. The ghouls had come later than usual, and they seemed more than usually eager to be gone. Fettes, sick with sleep, lighted them upstairs. He heard their grumbling Irish voices through a dream; and as they stripped the sack from their sad merchandise he leaned dozing, with his shoulder propped against the wall; he had to shake himself to find the men their money. As he did so his eyes lighted on the dead face. He started; he took two steps nearer, with the candle raised.

'God Almighty!' he cried. 'That is Jane Galbraith!'

The men answered nothing, but they shuffled nearer the door.

'I know her, I tell you,' he continued. 'She was alive and hearty yesterday. It's impossible she can be dead; it's impossible you should have got this body fairly.'

'Sure, sir, you're mistaken entirely,' said one of the men.

But the other looked Fettes darkly in the eyes, and demanded the money on the spot.

It was impossible to misconceive the threat or to exaggerate the danger. The lad's heart failed him. He stammered some excuses, counted out the sum, and saw his hateful visitors depart. No sooner were they gone than he hastened to confirm his doubts. By a dozen unquestionable marks he identified the girl he had jested with the day before. He saw, with horror, marks upon her body that might well betoken violence. A panic seized him, and he took refuge in his room. There he reflected at length over the discovery that he had made; considered soberly the bearing of Mr K—'s instructions and the danger to himself of interference in so serious a business, and at last, in sore perplexity, determined to wait for the advice of his immediate superior, the class assistant.

This was a young doctor, Wolfe Macfarlane, a high favourite among all the reckless students, clever, dissipated, and unscrupulous to the last degree. He had travelled and studied abroad. His manners were agreeable and a little forward. He was an authority on the stage, skilful on the ice or the links with skate or golf-club; he dressed with nice audacity, and, to put the finishing touch upon his glory, he kept a gig[11] and a strong trotting-horse. With Fettes he was on terms of intimacy; indeed, their relative positions called for some community of life; and when subjects were scarce the pair would drive far into the country in Macfarlane's gig, visit and desecrate some lonely graveyard, and return before dawn with their booty to the door of the dissecting-room.

On that particular morning Macfarlane arrived somewhat earlier than his wont. Fettes heard him, and met him on the stairs, told him his story, and showed him the cause of his alarm. Macfarlane examined the marks on her body.

'Yes,' he said with a nod, 'it looks fishy.'

---

[11]   A light, two-wheeled horse-drawn carriage.

'Well, what should I do?' asked Fettes.

'Do?' repeated the other. 'Do you want to do anything? Least said soonest mended, I should say.'

'Someone else might recognise her,' objected Fettes. 'She was as well known as the Castle Rock.'

'We'll hope not,' said Macfarlane, 'and if anybody does—well, you didn't, don't you see, and there's an end. The fact is, this has been going on too long. Stir up the mud, and you'll get K— into the most unholy trouble; you'll be in a shocking box yourself. So will I, if you come to that. I should like to know how any one of us would look, or what the devil we should have to say for ourselves, in any Christian witness-box. For me, you know, there's one thing certain—that, practically speaking, all our subjects have been murdered.'

'Macfarlane!' cried Fettes.

'Come now!' sneered the other. 'As if you hadn't suspected yourself!'

'Suspecting is one thing—'

'And proof another. Yes, I know; and I'm as sorry as you are tha' should have come here,' tapping the body with his cane. 'The next best thing for me is not to recognise it; and,' he added coolly, 'I don't. You may, if you please. I don't dictate, but I think a man of the world would do as I do; and, I may add, I fancy that is what K— would look for at our hands. The question is, Why did he choose us two for his assistants? And I answer, Because he didn't want old wives.'

This was the tone of all others to affect the mind of a lad like Fettes. He agreed to imitate Macfarlane. The body of the unfortunate girl was duly dissected, and no one remarked or appeared to recognise her.

One afternoon, when his day's work was over, Fettes dropped into a popular tavern and found Macfarlane sitting with a stranger. This was a small man, very pale and dark, with coal-black eyes. The cut of his features gave a promise of intellect and refinement which was but feebly realised in his manners, for he proved, upon a nearer acquaintance, coarse, vulgar, and stupid. He exercised, however, a very remarkable control over Macfarlane; issued orders like the Great Bashaw; became inflamed at the least discussion or delay, and commented rudely on the servility with which he was obeyed. This most offensive person took a fancy to Fettes on the spot, plied him with drinks, and honoured him with unusual confidences on his past career. If a tenth part of what he confessed were true, he was a very loathsome rogue; and the lad's vanity was tickled by the attention of so experienced a man.

'I'm a pretty bad fellow myself,' the stranger remarked, 'but Macfarlane is the boy—Toddy Macfarlane I call him. Toddy, order your friend another glass.' Or it might be, 'Toddy, you jump up and shut the door.' 'Toddy hates me,' he said again. 'Oh, yes, Toddy, you do!'

'Don't you call me that confounded name,' growled Macfarlane.

'Hear him! Did you ever see the lads play knife?[12] He would like to do that all over my body,' remarked the stranger.

'We medicals have a better way than that,' said Fettes. 'When we dislike a dead friend of ours, we dissect him.'

Macfarlane looked up sharply, as though this jest were scarcely to his mind.

The afternoon passed. Gray, for that was the stranger's name, invited Fettes to join them at dinner, ordered a feast so sumptuous that the tavern was thrown into commotion, and when all was done commanded Macfarlane to settle the bill. It was late before they separated; the man Gray was incapably drunk. Macfarlane, sobered by his fury, chewed the cud of the money he had been forced to squander and the slights he had been obliged to swallow. Fettes, with various liquors singing in his head, returned home with devious footsteps and a mind entirely in abeyance. Next day Macfarlane was absent from the class, and Fettes smiled to himself as he imagined him still squiring the intolerable Gray from tavern to tavern. As soon as the hour of liberty had struck, he posted from place to place in quest of his last night's companions. He could find them, however, nowhere; so returned early to his rooms, went early to bed, and slept the sleep of the just.

At four in the morning he was awakened by the well-known signal. Descending to the door, he was filled with astonishment to find Macfarlane with his gig, and in the gig one of those long and ghastly packages with which he was so well acquainted.

'What?' he cried. 'Have you been out alone? How did you manage?'

But Macfarlane silenced him roughly, bidding him turn to business. When they had got the body upstairs and laid it on the table, Macfarlane made at first as if he were going away. Then he paused and seemed to hesitate; and then, 'You had better look at the face,' said he, in tones of some constraint. 'You had better,' he repeated, as Fettes only stared at him in wonder.

'But where, and how, and when did you come by it?' cried the other.

'Look at the face,' was the only answer.

Fettes was staggered; strange doubts assailed him. He looked from the

---

[12] Another name for mumbledy-peg, a game in which the players throw knives into the ground from various positions.

young doctor to the body, and then back again. At last, with a start, he did as he was bidden. He had almost expected the sight that met his eyes, and yet the shock was cruel. To see, fixed in the rigidity of death and naked on that coarse layer of sackcloth, the man whom he had left well clad and full of meat and sin upon the threshold of a tavern, awoke, even in the thoughtless Fettes, some of the terrors of the conscience. It was a *cras tibi* which re-echoed in his soul, that two whom he had known should have come to lie upon these icy tables. Yet these were only secondary thoughts. His first concern regarded Wolfe. Unprepared for a challenge so momentous, he knew not how to look his comrade in the face. He durst not meet his eye, and he had neither words nor voice at his command.

It was Macfarlane himself who made the first advance. He came up quietly behind and laid his hand gently but firmly on the other's shoulder.

'Richardson,' said he, 'may have the head.'

Now, Richardson was a student who had long been anxious for that portion of the human subject to dissect. There was no answer, and the murderer resumed: 'Talking of business, you must pay me; your accounts, you see, must tally.'

Fettes found a voice, the ghost of his own: 'Pay you!' he cried. 'Pay you for that?'

'Why, yes, of course you must. By all means and on every possible account, you must,' returned the other. 'I dare not give it for nothing, you dare not take it for nothing; it would compromise us both. This is another case like Jane Galbraith's. The more things are wrong, the more we must act as if all were right. Where does old K— keep his money?'

'There,' answered Fettes hoarsely, pointing to a cupboard in the corner.

'Give me the key, then,' said the other calmly, holding out his hand.

There was an instant's hesitation, and the die was cast. Macfarlane could not suppress a nervous twitch, the infinitesimal mark of an immense relief, as he felt the key between his fingers. He opened the cupboard, brought out pen and ink and a paper-book that stood in one compartment, and separated from the funds in a drawer a sum suitable to the occasion.

'Now, look here,' he said, 'there is the payment made—first proof of your good faith: first step to your security. You have now to clinch it by a second. Enter the payment in your book, and then you for your part may defy the devil.'

The next few seconds were for Fettes an agony of thought; but in balancing his terrors it was the most immediate that triumphed. Any future difficulty seemed almost welcome if he could avoid a present quarrel with

Macfarlane. He set down the candle which he had been carrying all this time, and with a steady hand entered the date, the nature, and the amount of the transaction.

'And now,' said Macfarlane, 'it's only fair that you should pocket the lucre. I've had my share already. By the by, when a man of the world falls into a bit of luck, has a few shillings extra in his pocket—I'm ashamed to speak of it, but there's a rule of conduct in the case. No treating, no purchase of expensive class-books, no squaring of old debts; borrow, don't lend.'

'Macfarlane,' began Fettes, still somewhat hoarsely, 'I have put my neck in a halter to oblige you.'

'To oblige me?' cried Wolfe. 'Oh, come! You did, as near as I can see the matter, what you downright had to do in self-defence. Suppose I got into trouble, where would you be? This second little matter flows clearly from the first. Mr Gray is the continuation of Miss Galbraith. You can't begin and then stop. If you begin, you must keep on beginning; that's the truth. No rest for the wicked.'

A horrible sense of blackness and the treachery of fate seized hold upon the soul of the unhappy student.

'My God!' he cried, 'but what have I done? and when did I begin? To be made a class assistant—in the name of reason, where's the harm in that? Service wanted the position; Service might have got it. Would *he* have been where *I* am now?'

'My dear fellow,' said Macfarlane, 'what a boy you are! What harm *has* come to you? What harm *can* come to you if you hold your tongue? Why, man, do you know what this life is? There are two squads of us— the lions and the lambs. If you're a lamb, you'll come to lie upon these tables like Gray or Jane Galbraith; if you're a lion, you'll live and drive a horse like me, like K—, like all the world with any wit or courage. You're staggered at the first. But look at K—! My dear fellow, you're clever, you have pluck. I like you, and K— likes you. You were born to lead the hunt; and I tell you, on my honour and my experience of life, three days from now you'll laugh at all these scarecrows like a High School boy at a farce.'

And with that Macfarlane took his departure and drove off up the wynd in his gig to get under cover before daylight. Fettes was thus left alone with his regrets. He saw the miserable peril in which he stood involved. He saw, with inexpressible dismay, that there was no limit to his weakness, and that, from concession to concession, he had fallen from the arbiter of

Macfarlane's destiny to his paid and helpless accomplice. He would have given the world to have been a little braver at the time, but it did not occur to him that he might still be brave. The secret of Jane Galbraith and the cursed entry in the day-book closed his mouth.

Hours passed; the class began to arrive; the members of the unhappy Gray were dealt out to one and to another, and received without remark. Richardson was made happy with the head; and, before the hour of freedom rang, Fettes trembled with exultation to perceive how far they had already gone toward safety.

For two days he continued to watch, with an increasingly joy, the dreadful process of disguise.

On the third day Macfarlane made his appearance. He had been ill, he said; but he made up for lost time by the energy with which he directed the students. To Richardson in particular he extended the most valuable assistance and advice, and that student, encouraged by the praise of the demonstrator, burned high with ambitious hopes, and saw the medal already in his grasp.

Before the week was out Macfarlane's prophecy had been fulfilled. Fettes had outlived his terrors and had forgotten his baseness. He began to plume himself upon his courage, and had so arranged the story in his mind that he could look back on these events with an unhealthy pride. Of his accomplice he saw but little. They met, of course, in the business of the class; they received their orders together from Mr K——. At times they had a word or two in private, and Macfarlane was from first to last particularly kind and jovial. But it was plain that he avoided any reference to their common secret; and even when Fettes whispered to him that he had cast in his lot with the lions and forsworn the lambs, he only signed to him smilingly to hold his peace.

At length an occasion arose which threw the pair once more into a closer union. Mr K—— was again short of subjects; pupils were eager, and it was a part of his teacher's pretensions to be always well supplied. At the same time there came the news of a burial in the rustic graveyard of Glencorse. Time has little changed the place in question. It stood then, as now, upon a cross-road, out of call of human habitations, and buried fathoms deep in the foliage of six cedar-trees. The cries of the sheep upon the neighbouring hills, the streamlets upon either hand, one loudly singing among pebbles, the other dripping furtively from pond to pond, the stir of the wind in mountainous old flowering chestnuts, and once in seven days the voice of the bell and the old tunes of the precentor, were the only sounds that disturbed the silence around the rural church. The Resurrection Man[13]—to use a byname of the period—was not to be deterred by any of the sanctities of customary piety. It was part of his trade to despise and desecrate the scrolls and trumpets of old tombs, the paths worn by the feet of worshippers and mourners, and the offerings and the inscriptions of bereaved affection. To rustic neighbourhoods where love is more than commonly tenacious, and where some bonds of blood or fellowship unite the entire society of a parish, the body snatcher, far from being repelled by natural respect, was attracted by the ease and safety of the task. To bodies that had been laid in earth, in joyful expectation of a far different awakening, there came that hasty, lamp-lit, terror-haunted resurrection of the spade and mattock. The coffin was forced, the cerements torn, and the melancholy relics, clad in sack-cloth, after being rattled for hours on moonless by-ways, were at length exposed to uttermost indignities before a class of gaping boys.

Somewhat as two vultures may swoop upon a dying lamb, Fettes and Macfarlane were to be let loose upon a grave in that green and quiet resting-place. The wife of a farmer, a woman who had lived for sixty years, and been known for nothing but good butter and a godly conversation, was to be rooted from her grave at midnight and carried, dead and naked, to that far-away city that she had always honoured with her Sunday's best; the place beside her family was to be empty till the crack of doom; her innocent and almost venerable members to be exposed to that last curiosity of the anatomist.

Late one afternoon the pair set forth, well wrapped in cloaks and furnished with a formidable bottle. It rained without remission—a cold, dense, lashing rain. Now and again there blew a puff of wind, but these sheets of falling water kept it down. Bottle and all, it was a sad and silent drive as far as Penicuik, where they were to spend the evening. They stopped once, to hide their implements in a thick bush not far from the churchyard, and once again at the Fisher's Tryst, to have a toast before the kitchen fire and vary their nips of whisky with a glass of ale. When they reached their journey's end the gig was housed, the horse was fed and comforted, and the two young doctors in a private room sat down to the best dinner and the best wine the house afforded. The lights, the fire, the beating rain upon the window, the cold, incongruous work that lay before them, added zest to their enjoyment of the meal. With every glass their

---

[13] The name given to grave robbers. The name was first applied to Burke and Hare.

cordiality increased. Soon Macfarlane handed a little pile of gold to his companion.

'A compliment,' he said. 'Between friends these little d—d accommodations ought to fly like pipe-lights.'[14]

Fettes pocketed the money, and applauded the sentiment to the echo. 'You are a philosopher,' he cried. 'I was an ass till I knew you. You and K— between you, by the Lord Harry! but you'll make a man of me.'

'Of course we shall,' applauded Macfarlane. 'A man? I tell you, it required a man to back me up the other morning. There are some big, brawling, forty-year-old cowards who would have turned sick at the look of the d—d thing; but not you—you kept your head. I watched you.'

'Well, and why not?' Fettes thus vaunted himself. 'It was no affair of mine. There was nothing to gain on the one side but disturbance, and on the other I could count on your gratitude, don't you see?' And he slapped his pocket till the gold pieces rang.

Macfarlane somehow felt a certain touch of alarm at these unpleasant words. He may have regretted that he had taught his young companion so successfully, but he had no time to interfere, for the other noisily continued in this boastful strain:

'The great thing is not to be afraid. Now, between you and me, I don't want to hang—that's practical; but for all cant,[15] Macfarlane, I was born with a contempt. Hell, God, devil, right, wrong, sin, crime, and all the old gallery of curiosities—they may frighten boys, but men of the world, like you and me, despise them. Here's to the memory of Gray!'[16]

It was by this time growing somewhat late. The gig, according to order, was brought round to the door with both lamps brightly shining, and the young men had to pay their bill and take the road. They announced that they were bound for Peebles, and drove in that direction till they were clear of the last houses of the town; then, extinguishing the lamps, returned upon their course, and followed a byroad toward Glencorse. There was no sound but that of their own passage, and the incessant, strident pouring of the rain. It was pitch dark; here and there a white gate or a white stone in the wall guided them for a short space across the night; but for the most part it was at a foot pace, and almost groping, that they picked their way through that resonant blackness to their solemn and isolated destination. In the sunken woods that traverse the neighbourhood of the burying-ground

---

[14] Folded or twisted paper used to light a pipe.
[15] See page 162, note 2.
[16] The reader will recall Hyde's toast to the murdered Sir Danvers Carew (page 128).

the last glimmer failed them, and it became necessary to kindle a match and re-illuminate one of the lanterns of the gig. Thus, under the dripping trees, and environed by huge and moving shadows, they reached the scene of their unhallowed labours.

They were both experienced in such affairs, and powerful with the spade; and they had scarce been twenty minutes at their task before they were rewarded by a dull rattle on the coffin-lid. At the same moment, Macfarlane, having hurt his hand upon a stone, flung it carelessly above his head. The grave, in which they now stood almost to the shoulders, was close to the edge of the plateau of the graveyard; and the gig lamp had been propped, the better to illuminate their labours, against a tree, and on the immediate verge of the steep bank descending to the stream. Chance had taken a sure aim with the stone. Then came a clang of broken glass; night fell upon them; sounds alternately dull and ringing announced the bounding of the lantern down the bank, and its occasional collision with the trees. A stone or two, which it had dislodged in its descent, rattled behind it into the profundities of the glen; and then silence, like night, resumed its sway; and they might bend their hearing to its utmost pitch, but naught was to be heard except the rain, now marching to the wind, now steadily falling over miles of open country.

They were so nearly at an end of their abhorred task that they judged it wisest to complete it in the dark. The coffin was exhumed and broken open; the body inserted in the dripping sack and carried between them to the gig; one mounted to keep it in its place, and the other, taking the horse by the mouth, groped along by wall and bush until they reached the wider road by the Fisher's Tryst. Here was a faint, diffused radiancy, which they hailed like daylight; by that they pushed the horse to a good pace and began to rattle along merrily in the direction of the town.

They had both been wetted to the skin during their operations, and now, as the gig jumped among the deep ruts, the thing that stood propped between them fell now upon one and now upon the other. At every repetition of the horrid contact each instinctively repelled it with the greater haste; and the process, natural although it was, began to tell upon the nerves of the companions. Macfarlane made some ill-favoured jest about the farmer's wife, but it came hollowly from his lips, and was allowed to drop in silence. Still their unnatural burden bumped from side to side; and now the head would be laid, as if in confidence, upon their shoulders, and now the drenching sack-cloth would flap icily about their faces. A creeping chill began to possess the soul of Fettes. He peered at the bundle, and it seemed somehow larger than at first. All over the country-side, and from every degree of distance, the farm dogs accompanied their passage with tragic ululations; and it grew and grew upon his mind that some unnatural miracle had been accomplished, that some nameless change had befallen the dead body, and that it was in fear of their unholy burden that the dogs were howling.

'For God's sake,' said he, making a great effort to arrive at speech, 'for God's sake, let's have a light!'

Seemingly Macfarlane was affected in the same direction; for, though he made no reply, he stopped the horse, passed the reins to his companion, got down, and proceeded to kindle the remaining lamp. They had by that time got no farther than the cross-road down to Auchenclinny. The rain still poured as though the deluge were returning, and it was no easy matter to make a light in such a world of wet and darkness. When at last the flickering blue flame had been transferred to the wick and began to expand and clarify, and shed a wide circle of misty brightness round the gig, it became possible for the two young men to see each other and the thing they had along with them. The rain had moulded the rough sacking to the outlines of the body underneath; the head was distinct from the trunk, the shoulders plainly modelled; something at once spectral and human riveted their eyes upon the ghastly comrade of their drive.

For some time Macfarlane stood motionless, holding up the lamp. A nameless dread was swathed, like a wet sheet, about the body, and tightened the white skin upon the face of Fettes; a fear that was meaningless, a horror of what could not be, kept mounting to his brain. Another beat of the watch, and he had spoken.[17] But his comrade forestalled him.

'That is not a woman,' said Macfarlane, in a hushed voice.

'It was a woman when we put her in,' whispered Fettes.

'Hold that lamp,' said the other. 'I must see her face.'

And as Fettes took the lamp from his companion untied the fastenings of the sack and drew down the cover from the head. The light fell very clear upon the dark, well-moulded features and smooth-shaven cheeks of a too familiar countenance, often beheld in dreams of both of these young men. A wild yell rang up into the night; each leaped from his own side into the roadway: the lamp fell, broke, and was extinguished; and the horse, terrified by this unusual commotion, bounded and went off toward Edinburgh at a gallop, bearing along with it, sole occupant of the gig, the body of the dead and long-dissected Gray.

[17] He would have spoken.

177

Markheim

'Yes,' said the dealer, 'our windfalls are of various kinds. Some customers are ignorant, and then I touch a dividend on my superior knowledge. Some are dishonest,' and here he held up the candle, so that the light fell strongly on his visitor, 'and in that case,' he continued, 'I profit by my virtue.'

Markheim had but just entered from the daylight streets, and his eyes had not yet grown familiar with the mingled shine and darkness in the shop. At these pointed words, and before the near presence of the flame, he blinked painfully and looked aside.

The dealer chuckled. 'You come to me on Christmas Day,' he resumed, 'when you know that I am alone in my house, put up my shutters, and make a point of refusing business. Well, you will have to pay for that; you will have to pay for my loss of time, when I should be balancing my books; you will have to pay, besides, for a kind of manner that I remark in you today very strongly. I am the essence of discretion, and ask no awkward questions; but when a customer cannot look me in the eye, he has to pay for it.' The dealer once more chuckled; and then, changing to his usual business voice, though still with a note of irony, 'You can give, as usual, a clear account of how you came into the possession of the object?' he continued. 'Still your uncle's cabinet? A remarkable collector, sir!'

And the little pale, round-shouldered dealer stood almost on tiptoe, looking over the top of his gold spectacles, and nodding his head with every mark of disbelief. Markheim returned his gaze with one of infinite pity, and a touch of horror.

'This time,' said he, 'you are in error. I have not come to sell, but to buy. I have no curios to dispose of; my uncle's cabinet is bare to the wainscot; even were it still intact, I have done well on the Stock Exchange, and should more likely add to it than otherwise, and my errand today is simplicity itself. I seek a Christmas present for a lady,' he continued, waxing more fluent as he struck into the speech he had prepared; 'and certainly I owe you every excuse for thus disturbing you upon so small a matter. But the thing was neglected yesterday; I must produce my little compliment at dinner; and, as you very well know, a rich marriage is not a thing to be neglected.'

There followed a pause, during which the dealer seemed to weigh this statement incredulously. The ticking of many clocks among the curious lumber[1] of the shop, and the faint rushing of the cabs in a near thoroughfare, filled up the interval of silence. 'Well, sir,' said the dealer, 'be it so. You are an old customer after all; and if, as you say, you have the chance of a good marriage, far be it from me to be an obstacle. Here is a nice thing for a lady now,' he went on, 'this hand-glass—fifteenth century, warranted; comes from a good collection, too; but I reserve the name, in the interests of my customer, who was just like yourself, my dear sir, the nephew and sole heir of a remarkable collector.'

The dealer, while he thus ran on in his dry and biting voice, had stooped to take the object from its place; and, as he had done so, a shock had passed through Markheim, a start both of hand and foot, a sudden leap of many tumultuous passions to the face. It passed as swiftly as it came, and left no trace beyond a certain trembling of the hand that now received the glass.

'A glass,' he said hoarsely, and then paused, and repeated it more clearly. 'A glass? For Christmas? Surely not?'

'And why not?' cried the dealer. 'Why not a glass?'

Markheim was looking upon him with an indefinable expression. 'You ask me why not?' he said. 'Why, look here—look in it—look at yourself! Do you like to see it? No! nor I—nor any man.'

The little man had jumped back when Markheim had so suddenly con-

---

[1] Stored, disused articles.

fronted him with the mirror; but now, perceiving there was nothing worse on hand, he chuckled. 'Your future lady, sir, must be pretty hard-favoured,' said he.

'I ask you,' said Markheim, 'for a Christmas present, and you give me this—this damned reminder of years, and sins and follies—this hand-conscience! Did you mean it? Had you a thought in your mind? Tell me. It will be better for you if you do. Come, tell me about yourself. I hazard a guess now, that you are in secret a very charitable man?'

The dealer looked closely at his companion. It was very odd, Markheim did not appear to be laughing; there was something in his face like an eager sparkle of hope, but nothing of mirth.

'What are you driving at?' the dealer asked.

'Not charitable?' returned the other gloomily. 'Not charitable; not pious; not scrupulous; unloving, unbeloved; a hand to get money, a safe to keep it. Is that all? Dear God, man, is that all?'

'I will tell you what it is,' began the dealer, with some sharpness, and then broke off again into a chuckle. 'But I see this is a love match of yours, and you have been drinking the lady's health.'

'Ah!' cried Markheim, with a strange curiosity. 'Ah, have you been in love? Tell me about that.'

'I,' cried the dealer. 'I in love! I never had the time, nor have I the time today for all this nonsense. Will you take the glass?'

'Where is the hurry?' returned Markheim. 'It is very pleasant to stand here talking; and life is so short and insecure that I would not hurry away from any pleasure—no, not even from so mild a one as this. We should rather cling, cling to what little we can get, like a man at a cliff's edge. Every second is a cliff, if you think upon it—a cliff a mile high—high enough, if we fall, to dash us out of every feature of humanity. Hence it is best to talk pleasantly. Let us talk of each other: why should we wear this mask? Let us be confidential. Who knows, we might become friends?'

'I have just one word to say to you,' said the dealer. 'Either make your purchase, or walk out of my shop!'

'True, true,' said Markheim. 'Enough fooling. To business. Show me something else.'

The dealer stooped once more, this time to replace the glass upon the shelf, his thin blond hair falling over his eyes as he did so. Markheim moved a little nearer, with one hand in the pocket of his greatcoat; he drew himself up and filled his lungs; at the same time many different emotions were depicted together on his face—terror, horror, and resolve, fascination and a physical repulsion; and through a haggard lift of his upper lip, his teeth looked out.

'This, perhaps, may suit,' observed the dealer: and then, as he began to re-arise, Markheim bounded from behind upon his victim. The long, skewer-like dagger flashed and fell. The dealer struggled like a hen, striking his temple on the shelf, and then tumbled on the floor in a heap.

Time had some score of small voices in that shop, some stately and slow, as was becoming to their great age; others garrulous and hurried. All these told out the seconds in an intricate chorus of tickings. Then the passage of a lad's feet, heavily running on the pavement, broke in upon these smaller voices and startled Markheim into the consciousness of his surroundings. He looked about him awfully. The candle stood on the counter, its flame solemnly wagging in a draught; and by that inconsiderable movement, the whole room was filled with noiseless bustle and kept heaving like a sea: the tall shadows nodding, the gross blots of darkness swelling and dwindling as with respiration, the faces of the portraits and the china gods changing and wavering like images in water. The inner door stood ajar, and peered into that leaguer of shadows with a long slit of daylight like a pointing finger.

From these fear-stricken rovings, Markheim's eyes returned to the body of his victim, where it lay both humped and sprawling, incredibly small and strangely meaner than in life. In these poor, miserly clothes, in that ungainly attitude, the dealer lay like so much sawdust. Markheim had feared to see it, and, lo! it was nothing. And yet, as he gazed, this bundle of old clothes and pool of blood began to find eloquent voices. There it must lie; there was none to work the cunning hinges or direct the miracle of locomotion—there it must lie till it was found. Found! ay, and then? Then would this dead flesh lift up a cry that would ring over England, and fill the world with the echoes of pursuit. Ay, dead or not, this was still the enemy. 'Time was that when the brains were out,'[2] he thought; and the first word struck into his mind. Time, now that the deed was accomplished—time, which had closed for the victim, had become instant and momentous for the slayer.

The thought was yet in his mind, when, first one and then another, with every variety of pace and voice—one deep as the bell from a cathedral

---

[2] This sounds suspiciously like Shakespeare's *Merry Wives of Windsor*, Act III, Scene 5, line 7: "If I be served another such trick, I'll have my brains ta'en out, and buttered and give them to a dog for a new year's gift."

turret, another ringing on its treble notes the prelude of a waltz—the clocks began to strike the hour of three in the afternoon.[3]

The sudden outbreak of so many tongues in that dumb chamber staggered him. He began to bestir himself, going to and fro with the candle, beleaguered by moving shadows and startled to the soul by chance reflections. In many rich mirrors,[4] some of home design, some from Venice or Amsterdam, he saw his face repeated and repeated, as it were an army of spies; his own eyes met and detected him; and the sound of his own steps, lightly as they fell, vexed the surrounding quiet. And still, as he continued to fill his pockets, his mind accused him, with a sickening iteration, of the thousand faults of his design. He should have chosen a more quiet hour; he should have prepared an alibi; he should not have used a knife; he should have been more cautious, and only bound and gagged the dealer, and not killed him; he should have been more bold, and killed the servant also; he should have done all things otherwise: poignant regrets, weary, incessant toiling of the mind to change what was unchangeable, to plan what was now useless, to be the architect of the irrevocable past. Meanwhile, and behind all this activity, brute terrors, like the scurrying of rats in a deserted attic, filled the more remote chambers of his brain with riot; the hand of the constable would fall heavy on his shoulder, and his nerves would jerk like a hooked fish; or he beheld, in galloping defile, the dock, the prison, the gallows, and the black coffin.

Terror of the people in the street sat down before his mind like a besieging army. It was impossible, he thought, but that some rumour of the struggle must have reached their ears and set on edge their curiosity, and now, in all the neighbouring houses, he divined them sitting motionless and with uplifted ear—solitary people, condemned to spend Christmas dwelling alone on memories of the past, and now startingly recalled from that tender exercise; happy family parties, struck into silence round the table, the mother still with raised finger: every degree and age and humour, but all, by their own hearths, prying and hearkening and weaving the rope that was to hang him. Sometimes it seemed to him he could not move too softly; the clink of the tall Bohemian goblets rang out loudly like a bell; and alarmed by the bigness of the ticking, he was tempted to stop the clocks. And then, again, with a swift transition of his terrors, the very silence of the place appeared a source of peril, and a thing to strike and freeze the passer-by; and he would step more boldly, and bustle aloud

---

[3] See *Jekyll and Hyde*, page 46, regarding bells.
[4] The theme of the multiplicity of the selves is, of course, developed more fully in *Jekyll and Hyde*.

among the contents of the shop, and imitate, with elaborate bravado, the movements of a busy man at ease in his own house.

But he was now so pulled about by different alarms that, while one portion of his mind was still alert and cunning, another trembled on the brink of lunacy. One hallucination in particular took a strong hold on his credulity. The neighbour hearkening with white face beside his window, the passer-by arrested by a horrible surmise on the pavement—these could at worst suspect, they could not know; through the brick walls and shuttered windows only sounds could penetrate. But here, within the house, was he alone? He knew he was; he had watched the servant set forth sweethearting, in her poor best, 'out for the day' written in every ribbon and smile. Yes, he was alone, of course; and yet, in the bulk of empty house above him, he could surely hear a stir of delicate footing—he was surely conscious, inexplicably conscious of some presence. Ay, surely; to every room and corner of the house his imagination followed it; and now it was a faceless thing, and yet had eyes to see with; and again it was a shadow of himself; and yet again behold the image of the dead dealer, reinspired with cunning and hatred.

At times, with a strong effort, he would glance at the open door which still seemed to repel his eyes. The house was tall, the skylight small and dirty, the day blind with fog; and the light that filtered down to the ground storey was exceedingly faint, and showed dimly on the threshold of the shop. And yet, in that strip of doubtful brightness, did there not hang wavering a shadow?

Suddenly, from the street outside, a very jovial gentleman began to beat with a staff on the shop door, accompanying his blows with shouts and railleries in which the dealer was continually called upon by name. Markheim, smitten into ice, glanced at the dead man. But no! he lay quite still; he was fled away far beyond earshot of these blows and shoutings; he was sunk beneath seas of silence; and his name, which would once have caught his notice above the howling of a storm, had become an empty sound. And presently the jovial gentleman desisted from his knocking and departed.

Here was a broad hint to hurry what remained to be done, to get forth from this accusing neighbourhood, to plunge into a bath of London multitudes, and to reach, on the other side of day, that haven of safety and apparent innocence—his bed. One visitor had come; at any moment another might follow and be more obstinate. To have done the deed, and yet not to reap the profit, would be too abhorrent a failure. The money, that was now Markheim's concern; and as a means to that, the keys.

He glanced over his shoulder at the open door, where the shadow was still lingering and shivering; and with no conscious repugnance of the mind, yet with a tremor of the belly, he drew near the body of his victim. The human character had quite departed. Like a suit half-stuffed with bran, the limbs lay scattered, the trunk doubled, on the floor; and yet the thing repelled him. Although so dingy and inconsiderable to the eye, he feared it might have more significance to the touch. He took the body by the shoulders, and turned it on its back. It was strangely light and supple, and the limbs, as if they had been broken, fell into the oddest postures. The face was robbed of all expression; but it was as pale as wax, and shockingly smeared with blood about one temple. That was, for Markheim, the one displeasing circumstance. It carried him back, upon the instant, to a certain fair-day in a fishers' village: a grey day, a piping wind, a crowd upon the street, the blare of brasses, the booming of drums, the nasal voice of a ballad-singer; and a boy going to and fro, buried overhead in the crowd and divided between interest and fear, until, coming out upon the chief place of concourse, he beheld a booth and a great screen with pictures, dismally designed, garishly coloured: Brownrigg[5] with her apprentice; the Mannings[6] with their murdered guest; Weare in the death-grip of Thurtell; and a score besides of famous crimes. The thing was as clear as an illusion; he was once again that little boy; he was looking once again, and with the same sense of physical revolt, at these vile pictures; he was still stunned by the thumping of the drums. A bar of that day's music returned upon his memory; and at that, for the first time, a qualm came over him, a breath of nausea, a sudden weakness of the joints, which he must instantly resist and conquer.

He judged it more prudent to confront than to flee from these consider-

---

[5] Elizabeth Brownrigg, 1720–1767, an English sadist and murderer who was given three girls to look after by a foundling hospital. Over an extended period of time, she starved and abused them. One of the girls, Mary Clifford, was tied naked to a ceiling hook and whipped till she bled, while Elizabeth Brownrigg's husband and son, James and John, looked on and applauded.

Elizabeth Brownrigg was hanged at Tyburn on September 14, 1767. Her execution was watched by the largest crowd ever to witness a hanging to that time. James and John were each fined one shilling and sentenced to serve six months in jail.

[6] A husband and wife murder team. The husband was Frederick Manning and the wife Maria de Roux Manning. Their victim, a wealthy fifty-year-old dock laborer named O'Connor, was enticed by Maria to the Mannings' house, where he was drugged and beaten to death with a crowbar. Maria was apprehended in Edinburgh. Though the husband testified that it was Maria who wielded the crowbar, both of them were executed.

ations; looking the more hardily in the dead face, bending his mind to realise the nature and greatness of his crime. So little a while ago that face had moved with every change of sentiment, that pale mouth had spoken, that body had been all on fire with governable energies; and now, and by his act, that piece of life had been arrested, as the horologist, with interjected finger, arrests the beating of the clock. So he reasoned in vain; he could rise to no more remorseful consciousness; the same heart which had shuddered before the painted effigies of crime, looked on its reality unmoved. At best, he felt a gleam of pity for one who had been endowed in vain with all those faculties that can make the world a garden of enchantment, one who had never lived and who was now dead. But of penitence, no, not a tremor.

With that, shaking himself clear of these considerations, he found the keys and advanced towards the open door of the shop. Outside, it had begun to rain smartly; and the sound of the shower upon the roof had banished silence. Like some dripping cavern, the chambers of the house were haunted by an incessant echoing, which filled the ear and mingled with the ticking of the clocks. And, as Markheim approached the door, he seemed to hear, in answer to his own cautious tread, the steps of another foot withdrawing up the stair. The shadow still palpitated loosely on the threshold. He threw a ton's weight of resolve upon his muscles, and drew back the door.

The faint, foggy daylight glimmered dimly on the bare floor and stairs;[7] on the bright suit of armour posted, halbert in hand, upon the landing; and on the dark wood-carvings, and framed pictures that hung against the yellow panels of the wainscot. So loud was the beating of the rain through all the house that, in Markheim's ears, it began to be distinguished into many different sounds. Footsteps and sighs, the tread of regiments marching in the distance, the chink of money in the counting, and the creaking of doors held stealthily ajar, appeared to mingle with the patter of the drops upon the cupola and the gushing of the water in the pipes. The sense that he was not alone grew upon him to the verge of madness. On every side he was haunted and begirt by presences. He heard them moving in the

[7] The three paragraphs following are a surprising display of fine writing as plot gives way to texture and tone. The changing, mingling images work the way a contemporary film can work, with shifts in time and focus, producing a web of feeling by a means that today we would call surreal.

Most amazing is the way we find in this interior monologue of Markheim's a precursor to the last phrase Stevenson was to dictate on the day of his death: "He feared tenfold more, with a slavish, superstitious terror, some scission in the continuity of man's experience, some willful illegality of nature." The last words of *The Weir of Hermiston*, it will be recalled, are "a willful convulsion of brute nature."

upper chambers; from the shop, he heard the dead man getting to his legs; and as he began with a great effort to mount the stairs, feet fled quietly before him and followed stealthily behind. If he were but deaf, he thought, how tranquilly he would possess his soul! And then again, and hearkening with ever fresh attention, he blessed himself for that unresting sense which held the outposts and stood a trusty sentinel upon his life. His head turned continually on his neck; his eyes, which seemed starting from their orbits, scouted on every side, and on every side were half-rewarded as with the tail of something nameless vanishing. The four-and-twenty steps to the first floor were four-and-twenty agonies.

On that first storey, the doors stood ajar, three of them like three ambushes, shaking his nerves like the throats of cannon. He could never again, he felt, be sufficiently immured and fortified from men's observing eyes; he longed to be home, girt in by walls, buried among bedclothes, and invisible to all but God. And at that thought he wondered a little, recollecting tales of other murderers and the fear they were said to entertain of heavenly avengers. It was not so, at least, with him. He feared the laws of nature, lest, in their callous and immutable procedure, they should preserve some damning evidence of his crime. He feared tenfold more, with a slavish, superstitious terror, some scission in the continuity of man's experience, some wilful illegality of nature. He played a game of skill, depending on the rules, calculating consequence from cause; and what if nature, as the defeated tyrant overthrew the chess-board, should break the mould of their succession? The like had befallen Napoleon (so writers said) when the winter changed the time of its appearance. The like might befall Markheim: the solid walls might become transparent and reveal his doings like those of bees in a glass hive; the stout planks might yield under his foot like quicksands and detain him in their clutch; ay, and there were soberer accidents that might destroy him; if, for instance, the house should fall and imprison him beside the body of his victim; or the house next door should fly on fire, and the firemen invade him from all sides. These things he feared; and, in a sense, these things might be called the hands of God reached forth against sin. But about God Himself he was at ease; his act was doubtless exceptional, but so were his excuses, which God knew; it was there, and not among men, that he felt sure of justice.

When he had got safe into the drawing-room, and shut the door behind him, he was aware of a respite from alarms. The room was quite dismantled, uncarpeted besides, and strewn with packing-cases and incongruous furniture;[8] several great pier-glasses, in which he beheld himself at various angles, like an actor on a stage; many pictures, framed and unframed, standing, with their faces to the wall; a fine Sheraton sideboard, a cabinet of marquetry, and a great old bed, with tapestry hangings. The windows opened to the floor; but by great good fortune the lower part of the shutters had been closed, and this concealed him from the neighbours. Here, then, Markheim drew in a packing-case before the cabinet, and began to search among the keys. It was a long business, for there were many; and it was irksome, besides; for, after all, there might be nothing in the cabinet, and time was on the wing. But the closeness of the occupation sobered him. With the tail of his eye he saw the door—even glanced at it from time to time directly, like a besieged commander pleased to verify the good estate of his defences. But in truth he was at peace. The rain falling in the street sounded natural and pleasant. Presently, on the other side, the notes of a piano were wakened to the music of a hymn, and the voices of many children took up the air and words. How stately, how comfortable was the melody! How fresh the youthful voices! Markheim gave ear to it smilingly, as he sorted out the keys; and his mind was thronged with answerable ideas and images; church-going children and the pealing of the high organ; children afield, bathers by the brookside, ramblers on the brambly common, kite-flyers in the windy and cloud-navigated sky; and then, at another cadence of the hymn, back again to church, and the somnolence of summer Sundays, and the high genteel voice of the parson (which he smiled a little to recall) and the painted Jacobean tombs, and the dim lettering of the Ten Commandments in the chancel.

And as he sat thus, at once busy and absent, he was startled to his feet. A flash of ice, a flash of fire, a bursting gush of blood, went over him, and then he stood transfixed and thrilling. A step mounted the stair slowly and steadily, and presently a hand was laid upon the knob, and the lock clicked, and the door opened.

Fear held Markheim in a vice. What to expect he knew not, whether the dead man walking, or the official ministers of human justice, or lived to serve me, to spread black looks under colour of religion, or to sow tares in the wheat-field, as you do, in a course of weak compliance with desire. Now that he draws so near to his deliverance, he can add but one act of service—to repent, to die smiling, and thus to build up in confidence and hope the more timorous of my surviving followers. 'I am not so hard a master. Try me. Accept my help. Please yourself in life as you have done

---

[8] See page 92, of *Jekyll and Hyde*, where similar clutter is described in the surgical theater.

hitherto; please yourself more amply, spread your elbows at the board; and when the night begins to fall and the curtains to be drawn, I tell you, for your greater comfort, that you will find it even easy to compound your quarrel with your conscience, and to make a truckling peace with God. I came but now from such a death-bed, and the room was full of sincere mourners, listening to the man's last words: and when I looked into that face, which had been set as a flint against mercy, I found it smiling with hope.'

'And do you, then, suppose me such a creature?' asked Markheim. 'Do you think I have no more generous aspirations than to sin, and sin, and sin, and, at the last, sneak into heaven? My heart rises at the thought. Is this, then, your experience of mankind? or is it because you find me with red hands that you presume such baseness? and is this crime of murder indeed so impious as to dry up the very springs of good?'

'Murder is to me no special category,' replied the other. 'All sins are murder, even as all life is war. I behold your race, like starving mariners on a raft, plucking crusts out of the hands of famine and feeding on each other's lives. I follow sins beyond the moment of their acting; I find in all that the last consequence is death; and to my eyes, the pretty maid who thwarts her mother with such taking graces on a question of a ball, drips no less visibly with human gore than such a murderer as yourself. Do I say that I follow sins? I follow virtues also; they differ not by the thickness of a nail, they are both scythes for the reaping angel of Death. Evil, for which I live, consists not in action but in character. The bad man is dear to me; not the bad act, whose fruits, if we could follow them far enough down the hurtling cataract of the ages, might yet be found more blessed than those of the rarest virtues. And it is not because you have killed a dealer, but because you are Markheim, that I offer to forward your escape.'

'I will lay my heart open to you,' answered Markheim. 'This crime on which you find me is my last. On my way to it I have learned many lessons; itself is a lesson, a momentous lesson. Hitherto I have been driven with revolt to what I would not; I was a bond-slave to poverty, driven and scourged. There are robust virtues that can stand in these temptations; mine was not so: I had a thirst of pleasure. But today, and out of this deed, I pluck both warning and riches—both the power and a fresh resolve to be myself. I become in all things a free actor in the world; I begin to see myself all changed, these hands the agents of good, this heart at peace. Something comes over me out of the past; something of what I have dreamed on Sabbath evenings to the sound of the church organ, of what I

189

forecast when I shed tears over noble books, or talked, an innocent child, with my mother. There lies my life; I have wandered a few years, but now I see once more my city of destination.'

'You are to use this money on the Stock Exchange, I think?' remarked the visitor; 'and there, if I mistake not, you have already lost some thousands?'

'Ah,' said Markheim, 'but this time I have a sure thing.'

'This time, again, you will lose,' replied the visitor quietly.

'Ah, but I keep back the half!' cried Markheim.

'That also you will lose,' said the other.

The sweat started upon Markheim's brow. 'Well, then, what matter?' he exclaimed. 'Say it be lost, say I am plunged again in poverty, shall one part of me, and that the worse, continue until the end to override the better? Evil and good run strong in me, haling me both ways. I do not love the one thing, I love all. I can conceive great deeds, renunciations, martyrdoms; and though I be fallen to such a crime as murder, pity is no stranger to my thoughts. I pity the poor; who knows their trials better than myself? I pity and help them; I prize love, I love honest laughter; there is no good thing nor true thing on earth but I love it from my heart. And are my vices only to direct my life, and my virtues to lie without effect, like some passive lumber of the mind? Not so; good, also, is a spring of acts.'

But the visitant raised his finger. 'For six-and-thirty years that you have been in this world,' said he, 'through many changes of fortune and varieties of humour, I have watched you steadily fall. Fifteen years ago you would have started at a theft. Three years back you would have some chance witness blindly stumbling in to consign him to the gallows.' But when a face was thrust into the aperture, glanced round the room, looked at him, nodded and smiled as if in friendly recognition, and then withdrew again, and the door closed behind it, his fear broke loose from his control in a hoarse cry. At the sound of this the visitant returned.

'Did you call me?' he asked pleasantly, and with that he entered the room and closed the door behind him.

Markheim stood and gazed at him with all his eyes. Perhaps there was a film upon his sight, but the outlines of the newcomer seemed to change and waver like those of the idols in the wavering candle-light of the shop; and at times he thought he knew him; and at times he thought he bore a likeness to himself;[9] and always, like a lump of living terror, there lay in his bosom the conviction that this thing was not of the earth and not of God.

And yet the creature had a strange air of the commonplace, as he stood looking on Markheim with a smile; and when he added: 'You are looking for the money, I believe?' it was in the tones of everyday politeness.

Markheim made no answer.

'I should warn you,' resumed the other, 'that the maid has left her sweetheart earlier than usual and will soon be here. If Mr Markheim be found in this house, I need not describe to him the consequences.'

'You know me?' cried the murderer.

The visitor smiled. 'You have long been a favourite of mine,' he said; 'and I have long observed and often sought to help you.'

'What are you?' cried Markheim: 'the devil?'

'What I may be,' returned the other, 'cannot affect the service I propose to render you.'

'It can,' cried Markheim; 'it does! Be helped by you? No, never; not by you! You do not know me yet; thank God, you do not know me!'

'I know you,' replied the visitant, with a sort of kind severity or rather firmness. 'I know you to the soul.'

'Know me!' cried Markheim. 'Who can do so? My life is but a travesty and slander on myself. I have lived to belie my nature. All men do; all men are better than this disguise that grows about and stifles them. You see each dragged away by life, like one whom bravos[10] have seized and muffled in a cloak. If they had their own control—if you could see their faces, they would be altogether different, they would shine out for heroes and saints! I am worse than most; myself is more overlaid; my excuse is known to me and God. But, had I the time, I could disclose myself.'

'To me?' inquired the visitant.

'To you before all,' returned the murderer. 'I supposed you were intelligent. I thought—since you exist—you would prove a reader of the heart. And yet you would propose to judge me by my acts! Think of it; my acts! I was born and I have lived in a land of giants; giants have dragged me by the wrists since I was born out of my mother—the giants of circumstance. And you would judge me by my acts! But can you not look within? Can you not understand that evil is hateful to me? Can you not see within me the clear writing of conscience, never blurred by any wilful sophistry, although too often disregarded? Can you not read me for a thing that surely must be common as humanity—the unwilling sinner?'

'All this is very feelingly expressed,' was the reply, 'but it regards me

---

[9] This brief, almost glancing reference to the way the visitor looked—that is, that Markheim "thought he bore a likeness to himself"—hints at a theme *Jekyll and Hyde* elaborates: one of the places to seek for the satanic is within the self.

[10] Villains, desperadoes. Hired assassins.

not. These points of consistency are beyond my province, and I care not in the least by what compulsion you may have been dragged away, so as you are but carried in the right direction. But time flies; the servant delays, looking in the faces of the crowd and at the pictures on the hoardings,[11] but still she keeps moving nearer; and remember, it is as if the gallows itself was striding towards you through the Christmas streets! Shall I help you; I, who know all? Shall I tell you where to find the money?'

'For what price?' asked Markheim.

'I offer you the service for a Christmas gift,' returned the other.

Markheim could not refrain from smiling with a kind of bitter triumph. 'No,' said he, 'I will take nothing at your hands; if I were dying of thirst, and it was your hand that put the pitcher to my lips, I should find the courage to refuse. It may be credulous, but I will do nothing to commit myself to evil.'

'I have no objection to a death-bed repentance,' observed the visitant.

'Because you disbelieve their efficacy!' Markheim cried.

'I do not say so,' returned the other; 'but I look on these things from a different side, and when the life is done my interest falls. The man has blenched at the name of murder. Is there any crime, is there any cruelty or meanness, from which you still recoil?—five years from now I shall detect you in the fact! Downward, downward, lies your way; nor can anything but death avail to stop you.'

'It is true,' Markheim said huskily, 'I have in some degree complied with evil. But it is so with all: the very saints, in the mere exercise of living, grow less dainty, and take on the tone of their surroundings.'

'I will propound to you one simple question,' said the other; 'and as you answer, I shall read to you your moral horoscope. You have grown in many things more lax; possibly you do right to be so; and at any account, it is the same with all men. But granting that, are you in any one particular, however trifling, more difficult to please with your own conduct, or do you go in all things with a looser rein?'

'In any one?' repeated Markheim, with an anguish of consideration. 'No,' he added, with despair, 'in none! I have done down in all.'

'Then,' said the visitor, 'content yourself with what you are, for you will never change; and the words of your part on this stage are irrevocably written down.'

Markheim stood for a long while silent, and indeed it was the visitor

---

[11] A temporary board fence around a construction site.

who first broke the silence. 'That being so,' he said, 'shall I show you the money?'

'And grace?' cried Markheim.

'Have you not tried it?' returned the other. 'Two or three years ago, did I not see you on the platform of revival meetings, and was not your voice the loudest in the hymn?'

'It is true,' said Markheim; 'and I see clearly what remains for me by way of duty. I thank you for these lessons from my soul; my eyes are opened, and I behold myself at last for what I am.'

At this moment, the sharp note of the door-bell rang through the house; and the visitant, as though this were some concerted signal for which he had been waiting, changed at once in his demeanour.

'The maid!' he cried. 'She has returned, as I forewarned you, and there is now before you one more difficult passage. Her master, you must say, is ill; you must let her in, with an assured but rather serious countenance— no smiles, no overacting, and I promise you success! Once the girl within, and the door closed, the same dexterity that has already rid you of the dealer will relieve you of this last danger in your path. Thenceforward you have the whole evening—the whole night, if needful—to ransack the trea- sures of the house and to make good your safety. This is help that comes to you with the mask of danger. Up!' he cried; 'up, friend; your life hangs trembling in the scales: up, and act!'

Markheim steadily regarded his counsellor. 'If I be condemned to evil acts,' he said, 'there is still one door of freedom open—I can cease from action. If my life be an ill thing, I can lay it down. Though I be, as you say truly, at the beck of every small temptation, I can yet, by one decisive gesture, place myself beyond the reach of all. My love of good is damned to barrenness; it may, and let it be! But I have still my hatred of evil, and from that, to your galling disappointment, you shall see that I can draw both energy and courage.'

The features of the visitor[12] began to undergo a wonderful and lovely change:[13] they brightened and softened with a tender triumph, and, even as they brightened, faded and dislimned.[14] But Markheim did not pause to

---

[12]   If we have assumed, as Markheim has, that the visitor is a demonic messenger, what happens here is meant, I think, to reverse that perception. The language describing his features is entirely gentle. The change in him is "wonderful and lovely," his features "brightened and softened with a tender triumph. . . ." Because the earlier glancing suggestion as to who the visitor might be (see page 191, note 9) is now confirmed. He is an aspect of Markheim, that aspect that has found his way out of the human conundrum by heading toward "the farther side," where "he perceived a quiet haven for his bark."

watch or understand the transformation. He opened the door and went downstairs very slowly, thinking to himself. His past went soberly before him; he beheld it as it was, ugly and strenuous like a dream, random as chance-medley—a scene of defeat. Life, as he thus reviewed it, tempted him on longer; but on the farther side he perceived a quiet haven for his bark. He paused in the passage, and looked into the shop, where the candle still burned by the dead body. It was strangely silent. Thoughts of the dealer swarmed into his mind, as he stood gazing. And then the bell once more broke out into impatient clamour.

He confronted the maid upon the threshold with something like a smile.

'You had better go for the police,' said he: 'I have killed your master.'

---

[13] As "Markheim" comes to its close, was see more clearly how it structurally resembles *Jekyll and Hyde*. There, too, if we remind ourselves that Jekyll and Hyde are always one, that totality acts out the import of these words, as if Hyde were to say "If my life be an ill thing . . . " and Jekyll chimed in with, "I can lay it down." And again, Hyde might be the one to say, "My love of good is damned to barrenness . . . " with Jekyll adding, "But I have still my hatred of evil."

[14] Dimmed.

The Merry Men

Chapter I
EILEAN AROS[1]

It was a beautiful morning in the late July when I set forth on foot for the last time for Aros. A boat had put me ashore the night before at Grisapol;[2] I had such breakfast as the little inn afforded, and, leaving all my baggage till I had an occasion to come round for it by sea, struck right across the promontory with a cheerful heart.

I was far from being a native of these parts, springing, as I did, from an unmixed lowland stock. But an uncle of mine, Gordon Darnaway, after a poor, rough youth, and some years at sea, had married a young wife in the islands; Mary Maclean she was called, the last of her family; and when she died in giving birth to a daughter, Aros, the sea-girt farm, had remained in his possession. It brought him in nothing but the means of life, as I was well aware; but he was a man whom ill-fortune had pursued; he feared, cumbered as he was with the young child, to make a fresh adventure upon life; and remained in Aros, biting his nails at destiny. Years passed over his head in that isolation, and brought neither help nor contentment. Meantime our family was dying out in the lowlands; there is little luck for any

---

[1] The island Aros, Stevenson told Henley, "is Earraid, where I lived lang syne. . . ."
[2] Mull.

of that race; and perhaps my father was the luckiest of all, for not only was he one of the last to die, but he left a son to his name and a little money to support it. I was a student of Edinburgh University,[3] living well enough at my own charges, but without kith or kin; when some news of me found its way to Uncle Gordon on the Ross of Grisapol;[4] and he, as he was a man who held blood thicker than water, wrote to me the day he heard of my existence, and taught me to count Aros as my home. Thus it was that I came to spend my vacations in that part of the country, so far from all society and comfort, between the codfish and the moorcocks; and thus it was that now, when I had done with my classes, I was returning thither with so light a heart that July day.

The Ross, as we call it, is a promontory neither wide nor high, but as rough as God made it to this day; the deep sea on either hand of it, full of rugged isles and reefs most perilous to seamen—all overlooked from the eastward by some very high cliffs and the great peak of Ben Kyaw. *The Mountain of the Mist*, they say the words signify in the Gaelic tongue; and it is well named. For that hilltop, which is more than three thousand feet in height, catches all the clouds that come blowing from the seaward; and, indeed, I used often to think that it must make them for itself; since when all heaven was clear to the sea level, there would ever be a streamer on Ben Kyaw. It brought water, too, and was mossy[5] to the top in consequence. I have seen us sitting in broad sunshine on the Ross, and the rain falling black like crape upon the mountain. But the wetness of it made it often appear more beautiful to my eyes; for when the sun struck upon the hillsides, there were many wet rocks and watercourses that shone like jewels even as far as Aros, fifteen miles away.

The road that I followed was a cattle-track. It twisted so as nearly to double the length of my journey; it went over rough boulders so that a man had to leap from one to another, and through soft bottoms where the moss came nearly to the knee. There was no cultivation anywhere, and not one house in the ten miles from Grisapol to Aros. Houses of course there were—three at least; but they lay so far on the one side or the other that no stranger could have found them from the track. A large part of the Ross is covered with big granite rocks, some of them larger than a two-

---

[3] Stevenson was a graduate of Edinburgh University. Strangely enough, at the time that he was writing "The Merry Men," a work remarkable for its descriptions of natural—especially seaside—scenery, Stevenson was trying to get himself appointed to a chair in the law school at Edinburgh University. Despite drummed-up letters of support from influential people, the appointment did not come through.
[4] Stevenson identified the "Ross of Grisapol" as the Ross of Mull. Ross means "county."
[5] Boggy.

roomed house, one beside another, with fern and deep heather in between them where the vipers breed. Any way the wind was, it was always sea-air, as salt as on a ship; the gulls were as free as moorfowl over all the Ross; and whenever the way rose a little, your eye would kindle with the brightness of the sea. From the very midst of the land, on a day of wind and a high spring, I have heard the Roost[6] roaring like a battle where it runs by Aros, and the great and fearful voices of the breakers that we call the Merry Men.

Aros itself—Aros Jay, I have heard the natives call it, and they say it means *the House of God*—Aros itself was not properly a piece of the Ross, nor was it quite an islet. It formed the south-west corner of the land, fitted close to it, and was in one place only separated from the coast by a little gut of the sea, not forty feet across the narrowest. When the tide was full, this was clear and still, like a pool on a land river; only there was a difference in the weeds and fishes, and the water itself was green instead of brown; but when the tide went out, in the bottom of the ebb, there was a day or two in every month when you could pass dryshod from Aros to the mainland. There was some good pasture, where my uncle fed the sheep he lived on; perhaps the feed was better because the ground rose higher on the islet than the main level of the Ross, but this I am not skilled enough to settle. The house was a good one for that country, two storeys high. It looked westward over a bay, with a pier hard by for a boat, and from the door you could watch the vapours blowing on Ben Kyaw.

On all this part of the coast, and especially near Aros, these great granite rocks that I have spoken of go down together in troops into the sea, like cattle on a summer's day. There they stand, for all the world like their neighbours ashore; only the salt water sobbing between them instead of the quiet earth, and clots of sea-pink blooming on their sides instead of heather; and the great sea-conger to wreathe about the base of them instead of the poisonous viper of the land. On calm days you can go wandering between them in a boat for hours, echoes following you about the labyrinth; but when the sea is up, Heaven help the man that hears that cauldron boiling.

Off the south-west end of Aros these blocks are very many, and much greater in size. Indeed, they must grow monstrously bigger out to sea, for there must be ten sea miles of open water sown with them as thick as a

---

[6] The *Oxford English Dictionary*'s definition is almost as vibrant as Stevenson's prose. It says that a "roost" is "a tumultuous tidal race formed by the meeting of conflicting currents off various parts of the Orkney and Shetland Islands."

country place with houses, some standing thirty feet above the tides, some covered, but all perilous to ships; so that on a clear, westerly blowing day, I have counted, from the top of Aros, the great rollers breaking white and heavy over as many as six-and-forty buried reefs. But it is nearer in shore that the danger is worst; for the tide, here running like a mill-race, makes a long belt of broken water—a *Roost* we call it—at the tail of the land. I have often been out there in a dead calm at the slack of the tide; and a strange place it is, with the sea swirling and combing up and boiling like the cauldrons of a linn,[7] and now and again a little dancing mutter of sound as though the *Roost* were talking to itself. But when the tide begins to run again, and above all in heavy weather, there is no man could take a boat within half a mile of it, nor a ship afloat that could either steer or live in such a place. You can hear the roaring of it six miles away. At the seaward end there comes the strongest of the bubble; and it's here that these big breakers dance together—the dance of death, it may be called—that have got the name, in these parts, of the Merry Men. I have heard it said that they run fifty feet high; but that must be the green water only, for the spray runs twice as high as that. Whether they got the name from their movements, which are swift and antic, or from the shouting they make about the turn of the tide, so that all Aros shakes with it, is more than I can tell.

The truth is, that in a south-westerly wind that part of our archipelago is no better than a trap. If a ship got through the reefs, and weathered the Merry Men, it would be to come ashore on the south coast of Aros, in Sandag Bay, where so many dismal things befell our family, as I propose to tell. The thought of all these dangers, in the place I knew so long, makes me particularly welcome the works now going forward to set lights upon the headlands and buoys along the channels of our iron-bound, inhospitable islands.

The country people had many a story about Aros, as I used to hear from my uncle's man, Rorie, an old servant of the Macleans, who had transferred his services without afterthought on the occasion of the marriage. There was some tale of an unlucky creature, a sea-kelpie,[8] that dwelt and did business in some fearful manner of his own among the boiling breakers of the Roost. A mermaid had once met a piper on Sandag beach, and there sang to him a long, bright midsummer's night, so that in the morning he was found stricken crazy, and from thenceforward, till the day he died,

---

[7] A pool or collection of water.
[8] In Scottish folklore, a spirit of the waters in the form of a horse.

said only one form of words; what they were in the original Gaelic I cannot tell, but they were thus translated; 'Ah, the sweet singing out of the sea.' Seals that haunted on that coast have been known to speak to man in his own tongue, presaging great disasters. It was here that a certain saint first landed on his voyage out of Ireland to convert the Hebrideans. And, indeed, I think he had some claim to be called saint; for, with the boats of that past age, to make so rough a passage, and land on such a ticklish coast, was surely not far short of the miraculous. It was to him, or to some of his monkish underlings who had a cell there, that the islet owes its holy and beautiful name, the House of God.

Among these old wives' stories there was one which I was inclined to hear with more credulity. As I was told, in that tempest which scattered the ships of the Invincible Armada[9] over all the north and west of Scotland, one great vessel came ashore on Aros, and before the eyes of some solitary people on a hilltop, went down in a moment with all hands, her colours flying even as she sank. There was some likelihood in this tale; for another of that fleet lay sunk on the north side, twenty miles from Grisapol. It was told, I thought, with more detail and gravity than its companion stories, and there was one particularity which went far to convince me of its truth: the name, that is, of the ship was still remembered, and sounded, in my ears, Spanishly. The *Espirito Santo* they called it, a great ship of many decks of guns, laden with treasure and grandees of Spain, and fierce soldadoes, that now lay fathom deep to all eternity, done with her wars and voyages, in Sandag Bay, upon the west of Aros. No more salvos of ordnance for that tall ship, the 'Holy Spirit', no more fair winds or happy ventures; only to rot there deep in the sea-tangle and hear the shoutings of the Merry Men as the tide ran high about the island. It was a strange thought to me first and last, and only grew stranger as I learned the more of Spain, from which she had set sail with so proud a company, and King Philip, the wealthy king, that sent her on that voyage.

And now I must tell you, as I walked from Grisapol that day, the *Espirito Santo* was very much in my reflections. I had been favourably remarked by our then Principal in Edinburgh College, that famous writer, Dr Robertson, and by him had been set to work on some papers of an ancient date to rearrange and sift of what was worthless; and in one of these, to my great wonder, I found a note of this very ship, the *Espirito Santo*, with her captain's name, and how she carried a great part of the Spaniards' treasure,

[9] In Spain's war with England, 1588, King Phillip II of Spain outfitted a fleet of 130 ships intended for the conquest of England. The fleet was defeated in battle by the English fleet and dispersed.

and had been lost upon the Ross of Grisapol; but in what particular spot, the wild tribes of that place and period would give no information to the king's inquiries. Putting one thing with another, and taking our island tradition together with this note of old King Jamie's[10] perquisitions after wealth, it had come strongly on my mind that the spot for which he sought in vain could be no other than the small bay of Sandag on my uncle's land; and being a fellow of a mechanical turn, I had ever since been plotting how to weigh that good ship up again with all her ingots, ounces, and doubloons, and bring back our house of Darnaway to its long-forgotten dignity and wealth.

This was a design of which I soon had reason to repent. My mind was sharply turned on different reflections; and since I became the witness of a strange judgment of God's, the thought of dead men's treasures has been intolerable to my conscience. But even at that time I must acquit myself of sordid greed; for if I desired riches, it was not for their own sake, but for the sake of a person who was dear to my heart—my uncle's daughter, Mary Ellen. She had been educated well, and had been a time to school upon the mainland; which, poor girl, she would have been happier without. For Aros was no place for her, with old Rorie the servant, and her father, who was one of the unhappiest men in Scotland, plainly bred up in a country place among Cameronians,[11] long a skipper sailing out of the Clyde about the islands, and now, with infinite discontent, managing his sheep and a little 'long shore fishing for the necessary bread. If it was sometimes weariful to me, who was there but a month or two, you may fancy what it was to her who dwelt in that same desert all the year round, with the sheep and flying sea-gulls, and the Merry Men singing and dancing in the Roost!

Chapter II
WHAT THE WRECK HAD BROUGHT TO AROS

It was half-flood when I got the length of Aros; and there was nothing for it but to stand on the far shore and whistle for Rorie with the boat. I

---

[10] King James II of England, who was driven from power in 1688 and was succeeded by William and Mary, 1689.

[11] Followers of Richard Cameron of Scotland, who were ardent Covenanters and refused to give their allegiance to Charles II. They later formed the Reformed Presbyterian Church of Scotland.

had no need to repeat the signal. At the first sound, Mary was at the door flying a handkerchief by way of answer, and the old long-legged serving-man was shambling down the gravel to the pier. For all his hurry, it took him a long while to pull across the bay; and I observed him several times to pause, go into the stern, and look over curiously into the wake. As he came nearer, he seemed to me aged and haggard, and I thought he avoided my eye. The coble[12] had been repaired, with two new thwarts and several patches of some rare and beautiful foreign wood, the name of it unknown to me.

'Why, Rorie,' said I, as we began the return voyage, 'this is fine wood. How came you by that?'

'It will be hard to cheesel,' Rorie opined reluctantly; and just then, dropping the oars, he made another of those dives into the stern which I had remarked as he came across to fetch me, and, leaning his hand on my shoulder, stared with an awful look into the waters of the bay.

'What is wrong?' I asked, a good deal startled.

'It will be a great fresh,' said the old man, returning to his oars; and nothing more could I get out of him, but strange glanced and an ominous nodding of the head. In spite of myself, I was infected with a measure of uneasiness; I turned also, and studied the wake. The water was still and transparent, but, out here in the middle of the bay, exceedingly deep. For some time I could see naught; but at last it did seem to me as if something dark—a great fish, or perhaps only a shadow—followed studiously in the track of the moving coble. And then I remembered one of Rorie's superstitions: how in a ferry in Morven, in some great, exterminating feud among the clans, a fish, the like of it unknown in all our waters, followed for some years the passage of the ferry-boat, until no man dared to make the crossing.

'He will be waiting for the right man,' said Rorie.

Mary met me on the beach, and led me up the brae[13] and into the house of Aros. Outside and inside there were many changes. The garden was fenced with the same wood that I had noted in the boat; there were chairs in the kitchen covered with strange brocade; curtains of brocade hung from the window; a clock stood silent on the dresser; a lamp of brass was swinging from the roof; the table was set for dinner with the finest of linen and silver; and all these new riches were displayed in the plain of old kitchen that I knew so well, with the high-backed settle, and the stools,

---

[12]   A short, flat-bottomed boat.
[13]   Hillside.

and the closet bed for Rorie; with the wide chimney the sun shone into, and the clear-smouldering peats; with the pipes on the mantelshelf and the three-cornered spittoons, filled with sea-shells instead of sand, on the floor; with the bare stone walls and the bare wooden floor, and the three patch-work rugs that were of yore its sole adornment—poor man's patchwork, the like of it unknown in cities, woven with homespun, and Sunday black, and sea-cloth polished on the bench of rowing. The room, like the house, had been a sort of wonder in that country-side, it was so neat and habitable; and to see it now, shamed by these incongruous additions, filled me with indignation and a kind of anger. In view of the errand I had come upon to Aros, the feeling was baseless and unjust; but it burned high, at the first moment, in my heart.

'Mary, girl,' said I, 'this is the place I had learned to call my home, and I do not know it.'

'It is my home by nature, not by the learning,' she replied; 'the place I was born and the place I'm like to die in; and I neither like these changes, nor the way they came, nor that which came with them. I would have liked better, under God's pleasure, they had gone down into the sea, and the Merry Men were dancing on them now.'

Mary was always serious; it was perhaps the only trait that she shared with her father; but the tone with which she uttered these words was even graver than of custom.

'Ay,' said I, 'I feared it came by wreck, and that's by death; yet when my father died, I took his goods without remorse.'

'Your father died a clean-strae[14] death, as the folk say,' said Mary.

'True,' I returned; 'and a wreck is like a judgment. What was she called?'

'They ca'd her the *Christ-Anna*,' said a voice behind me; and, turning round, I saw my uncle standing in the doorway.

He was a sour, small, bilious man, with a long face and very dark eyes; fifty-six years old, sound and active in the body, and with an air somewhat between that of a shepherd and that of a man following the sea. He never laughed, that I heard; read long at the Bible; prayed much, like the Cam-eronians he had been brought up among; and indeed, in many ways, used to remind me of one of the hill-preachers in the killing times before the Revolution. But he never got much comfort, nor even, as I used to think, much guidance, by his piety. He had his black fits when he was afraid of

---

[14] A clean straw death; that is, a peaceful death, on his own mattress, in his own bed.

hell; but he had led a rough life, to which he would look back with envy, and was still a rough, cold, gloomy man.

As he came in at the door out of the sunlight, with his bonnet on his head and a pipe hanging in his button-hole, he seemed, like Rorie, to have grown older and paler, the lines were deeplier ploughed upon his face, and the whites of his eyes were yellow, like old stained ivory, or the bones of the dead.

'Ay,' he repeated, dwelling upon the first part of the word, 'the *Christ-Anna*. It's an awfu' name.'

I made him my salutations, and complimented him upon his look of health; for I feared he had perhaps been ill.

'I'm in the body,' he replied, ungraciously enough; 'aye in the body and the sins of the body, like yoursel'. Denner,' he said abruptly to Mary, and then ran on to me: 'They're grand braws,[15] thir that we hae gotten, are they no? Yon's a bonny knock,[16] but it'll no gang; and the napery's by ordnar. Bonny, bairnly braws; it's for the like o' them folk sells the peace of God that passeth understanding;[17] it's for the like o' them, an' maybe no even sae muckle worth, folk daunton God to His face and burn in muckle hell; and it's for that reason the Scripture ca's them, as I read the passage, the accursed thing. Mary, ye girzie,' he interrupted himself to cry with some asperity, 'what for hae ye no put out the twa candlesticks?'

'Why should we need them at high noon?' she asked.

But my uncle was not to be turned from his idea. 'We'll bruik[18] them while we may,' he said; and so two massive candlesticks of wrought silver were added to the table equipage, already so unsuited to that rough sea-side farm.

'She cam' ashore Februar' 10, about ten at nicht,' he went on to me. 'There was nae wind, and a sair run o'sea; and she was in the sook[19] o' the Roost, as I jaloose.[20] We had seen her a' day, Rorie, and me, beating to the wind. She wasnae a handy craft, I'm thinking, that *Christ-Anna*; for she would neither steer nor stey wi' them. A sair day they had of it; their hands was never aff the sheets, and it perishin' cauld—ower cauld to snaw;

---

[15] Beautiful, good things.
[16] A clock.
[17] The reference is to Philippians 4:7, which reads, "The peace of God, which passeth all understanding." In Anglican rite & Scottish reformed rite, the peace is passed in church by the minister: "The peace of God, which passeth all understanding, keep your hearts and minds in the love of God and of His son, Jesus Christ. . . ." and then the people are blessed.
[18] Enjoy.
[19] Suck.
[20] Surmise or suspect.

and aye they would get a bit nip o' wind, and awa' again, to pit the emp'y hope into them. Eh, man! but they had a sair day for the last o't! He would have had a prood, prood heart that won ashore upon the back o' that.'

'And were all lost?' I cried. 'God help them!'

'Wheesht!'[21] he said sternly. 'Nane shall pray for the deid on my hearth-stane.'

I disclaimed a Popish sense for my ejaculation; and he seemed to accept my disclaimer with unusual facility, and ran on once more upon what had evidently become a favourite subject.

'We fand her in Sandag Bay, Rorie an' me, and a' thae braws in the inside of her. There's a kittle[22] bit, ye see, about Sandag; whiles the sook rins strong for the Merry Men; an' whiles again, when the tide's makin' hard an' ye can hear the Roost blawin' at the far-end of Aros, there comes a back-spang[23] of current straucht into Sandag Bay. Weel, there's the thing that got the grip on the *Christ-Anna*. She but to have come in ram-stam[24] an' stern forrit; for the bows of her are aften under, and the back-side of her is clear at hie-water o' neaps. But, man! the dunt that she cam' doon wi' when she struck! Lord save us a'! but it's an unco[25] life to be a sailor— a cauld, wanchancy[26] life. Mony's the gliff[27] I got mysel' in the great deep; and why the Lord should hae made yon unco water is mair than ever I could win to understand. He made the vales and the pastures, the bonny green yaird, the halesome, canty[28] land—

> And now they shout and sing to Thee,
> For Thou hast made them glad,

as the Psalms say in the metrical version. No that I would preen my faith to that clink neither; but it's bonny, and easier to mind. "Who go to sea in ships,"[29] they hae't again—

---

[21] Hush.
[22] A ticklish matter. A difficult thing.
[23] A sudden, violent movement.
[24] Headstrong, rash, heedless.
[25] Strange.
[26] Ill-fated.
[27] A sudden scare.
[28] Lively.
[29] Psalm 107:23 reads, "They that go down to the sea in ships, that do business in great waters."

and in

> Great waters trading be,
> Within the deep these men God's works
> And His great wonders see.

Weel, it's easy sayin' sea. Maybe Dauvit[30] wasnae very weel acquant wi' the sea. But, troth, if it wasnae prentit in the Bible, I wad whiles be temp'it to think it wasnae the Lord, but the muckle, black deil that made the sea. There's naething good comes oot o't but the fish; an' the spentacle o' God riding on the tempest, to be shüre, whilk would be what Dauvit was likely ettling[31] at. But, man, they were sair wonders that God showed to the *Christ-Anna*—wonders, do I ca' them? Judgments, rather: judgments in the mirk nicht among the draygons o' the deep. And their souls—to think o' that—their souls, man, maybe no prepared! The sea—a muckle yett[32] to hell!'

I observed, as my uncle spoke, that his voice was unnaturally moved and his manner unwontedly demonstrative. He leaned forward at these last words, for example, and touched me on the knee with his spread fingers, looking up into my face with a certain pallor, and I could see that his eyes shone with a deep-seated fire, and that the lines about his mouth were drawn and tremulous.

Even the entrance of Rorie, and the beginning of our meal, did not detach him from his train of thought beyond a moment. He condescended, indeed, to ask me some questions as to my success at College, but I thought it was with half his mind; and even in his extempore grace, which was, as usual, long and wandering, I could find the trace of his preoccupation, praying, as he did, that God would 'remember in mercy fower puir, feckless, fiddling, sinful creatures here by their lee-lane beside the great and dowie[33] waters.'

Soon there came an interchange of speeches between him and Rorie.

'Was it there?' asked my uncle.

'Ou, ay!' said Rorie.

I observed that they both spoke in a manner of aside, and with some show of embarrassment, and that Mary herself appeared to colour, and

---

[30] King David, the attributed author of the Psalms.
[31] Aiming.
[32] A large gate.
[33] Doleful.

looked down on her plate. Partly to show my knowledge, and so relieve the party from an awkward strain, partly because I was curious, I pursued the subject.

'You mean the fish?' I asked.

'Whatten fish?' cried my uncle. 'Fish, quo! he! Fish! Your een are fu' o' fatness, man; your heid dozened[34] wi' carnal leir. Fish! it's a bogle!'

He spoke with great vehemence, as though angry; and perhaps I was not very willing to be put down so shortly, for young men are disputatious. At least I remember I retorted hotly, crying out upon childish superstitions.

'And ye come frae the College!' sneered Uncle Gordon. 'Gude kens what they learn folk there; it's no muckle service onyway. Do ye think, man, that there's naething in a' yon saut wilderness o' a world oot wast there, wi' the sea-grasses growin', an' the sea-beasts fechtin', an' the sun glintin' down into it, day by day? Na; the sea's like the land, but fearsomer. If there's folk ashore, there's folk in the sea—deid they may be, but they're folk whatever; and as for deils, there's nane that's like the sea-deils. There's no sea muckle harm in the land-deils, when a's said and done. Lang syne, when I was a callant[35] in the south country, I mind there was an auld, bald bogle in the Peewie Moss. I got a glisk[36] o' him mysel' sittin' on his hunkers in a hag,[37] as grey's a tombstane. An', troth, he was a fearsome-like taed.[38] But he steered naebody. Nea doobt, if ane that was a reprobate, ane the Lord hated, had gane by there wi' his sin still upon his stamach, nae doobt the creature would hae lowped upo' the likes o' him. But there's deils in the deep sea would yoke[39] on a communicant! Eh, sirs, if ye had gane doon wi' the puir lads in the *Christ-Anna*, ye would ken by now the mercy o' the seas. If ye had sailed it for as lang as me, ye would hate the thocht o' it as I do. If ye had but used the een God gave ye, ye would hae learned the wickedness o' that fause, saut, cauld, bullering[40] creature, and of a' that's in it by the Lord's permission: labsters an' partans,[41] an' sic like, howking[42] in the deid; muckle, gutsy, blawing whales; an' fish—the hale clan o' them—cauld-wamed,[43] blind-ee'd uncanny ferlies.[44] O, sirs,' he cried, 'the horror—the horror o' the sea!'

---

[34] Stupefied.
[35] Lad, youth.
[36] Glimpse.
[37] Here, it probably means a hollow of marshy bog.
[38] Toad.
[39] Bring into bondage.
[40] Bellowing.
[41] Crabs.
[42] Digging.

We were all somewhat staggered by this outburst; and the speaker himself, after that last hoarse apostrophe, appeared to sink gloomily into his own thoughts. But Rorie, who was greedy of superstitious lore, recalled him to the subject by a question.

'You will not ever have seen a teevil of the sea?' he asked.

'No clearly,' replied the other. 'I misdoobt if a mere man could see ane clearly and conteenue in the body. I hae sailed w' a lad—they ca'd him Sandy Gabart; he saw ane, shüre eneuch, an' shüre eneuch it was the end of him. We were seeven days oot frae the Clyde—a sair wark we had had—gaun north wi' seeds an' braws an' things for the Macleod. We had got in ower near under the Cutchull'ns, an' had just gane about by Soa, an' were off on a lang tack, we thocht would maybe hauld as far's Copnahow. I mind the nicht weel; a mune smoored[45] wi' mist; a fine gaun breeze upon the water, but no steady; an'—what nane o' us likit to hear—anither wund gurlin' owerheid, amang thae fearsome, auld stane craigs o' the Cutchull'ns. Weel, Sandy was forrit wi' the jib sheet; we couldnae see him for the mains'l, that had just begude to draw, when a' at ance he gied a skirl. I luffed for my life, for I thocht we were ower near Soa; but na, it wasnae that, it was puir Sandy Gabart's deid skreigh,[46] or near-hand, for he was deid in half an hour. A't he could tell was that a sea-deil, or sea-bogle, or sea-spenster, or sic-like, had clum up by the bowsprit, an' gi'en him ae cauld, uncanny look. An', or the life was oot o' Sandy's body, we kent weel what the thing betokened, and why the wund gurled in the taps[47] o' the Cutchull'ns; for doon it cam'—a wund do I ca' it! it was the wund o' the Lord's anger—an' a' that nicht we foucht like men dementit, and the neist that we kenned we were ashore in Loch Uskevagh, an' the cocks were crawing in Benbecula.'

'It will have been a merman,' Rorie said.

'A merman!' screamed my uncle with immeasurable scorn. 'Auld wives' clavers![48] There's nae sic things are mermen.'

'But what was the creature like?' I asked.

'What like was it? Gude forbid that we suld ken what like it was! It had a kind of a heid upon it—man could say nae mair.'

Then Rorie, smarting under the affront, told several tales of mermen,

---

[43] Cold-bellied.
[44] Strange sights.
[45] In context, covered by.
[46] Screech.
[47] Wind snarled in the tops.
[48] Gossip.

mermaids, and sea-horses that had come ashore upon the islands and attacked the crews of boats upon the sea; and my uncle, in spite of his incredulity, listened with uneasy interest.

'Aweel, aweel,' he said, 'it may be sae; I may be wrang; but I find nae word o' mermen in the Scriptures.'

'And you will find nae word of Aros Roost, maybe,' objected Rorie, and his argument appeared to carry weight.

When dinner was over, my uncle carried me forth with him to a bank behind the house. It was a very hot and quiet afternoon; scarce a ripple anywhere upon the sea, nor any voice but the familiar voice of sheep and gulls; and perhaps in consequence of this repose in nature, my kinsman showed himself more rational and tranquil than before. He spoke evenly and almost cheerfully of my career, with every now and then a reference to the lost ship or the treasures it had brought to Aros. For my part, I listened to him in a sort of trance, gazing with all my heart on that remembered scene, and drinking gladly the sea-air and the smoke of peats that had been lit by Mary.

Perhaps an hour had passed when my uncle, who had all the while been covertly gazing on the surface of the little bay, rose to his feet and bade me follow his example. Now I should say that the great run of tide at the south-west end of Aros exercises a perturbing influence round all the coast. In Sandag Bay, to the south, a strong current runs at certain periods of the flood and ebb respectively; but in this nothern bay—Aros Bay, as it is called—where the house stands and on which my uncle was now gazing, the only sign of disturbance is towards the end of the ebb, and even then it is too slight to be remarkable. When there is any swell, nothing can be seen at all; but when it is calm, as it often is, there appear certain strange, undecipherable marks—sea-runes, as we may name them—on the glassy surface of the bay. The like is common in a thousand places on the coast; and many a boy must have amused himself as I did, seeking to read in them some reference to himself or those he loved. It was to these marks that my uncle now directed my attention, struggling, as he did so, with an evident reluctance.

'Do ye see yon scart[49] upo' the water?' he inquired; 'yon ane wast the grey stane? Ay? Weel, it'll no be like a letter, wull it?'

'Certainly is it,' I replied. 'I have often remarked it. It is like a C.'

---

[49] Scribble or scratched mark.

He heaved a sigh as if heavily disappointed with my answer, and then added below his breath: 'Ay, for the *Christ-Anna*.'

'I used to suppose, sir, it was for myself,' and I; 'for my name is Charles.'

'And so ye saw't afore?' he ran on, not heeding my remark. 'Weel, weel, but that's unco strange. Maybe, it's been there waitin', as a man wad say, through a' the weary ages. Man, but that's awfu'.' And then, breaking off: 'Ye'll no see anither, will ye?' he asked.

'Yes,' said I. 'I see another very plainly, near the Ross side, where the road comes down—an M.'

'An M,' he repeated, very low; and then, again after another pause: 'An' what wad ye make o' that?' he inquired.

'I had always thought it to mean Mary, sir,' I answered, growing somewhat red, convinced as I was in my own mind that I was on the threshold of a decisive explanation.

But we were each following his own train of thought to the exclusion of the other's. My uncle once more paid no attention to my words; only hung his head and held his peace; and I might have been led to fancy that he had not heard me, if his next speech had not contained a kind of echo from my own.

'I would say naething o' thae clavers to Mary,' he observed, and began to walk forward.

There is a belt of turf along the side of Aros Bay where walking is easy; and it was along this that I silently followed my silent kinsman. I was perhaps a little disappointed at having lost so good an opportunity to declare my love; but I was at the same time far more deeply exercised at the change that had befallen my uncle. He was never an ordinary, never, in the strict sense, an amiable, man; but there was nothing in even the worst that I had known of him before, to prepare me for so strange a transformation. It was impossible to close the eyes against one fact; that he had, as the saying goes, something on his mind; and as I mentally ran over the different words which might be represented by the letter M—misery, mercy, marriage, money, and the like—I was arrested with a sort of start by the word murder. I was still considering the ugly sound and fatal meaning of the word, when the direction of our walk brought us to a point from which a view was to be had to either side, back towards Aros Bay and homestead, and forward on the ocean, dotted to the north with isles, and lying to the southward blue and open to the sky. There my guide came to a halt, and stood staring for a while on that expanse. Then he turned to me and laid a hand on my arm.

'Ye think there's naething there?' he said, pointing with his pipe; and then cried out aloud, with a kind of exultation: 'I'll tell ye, man! The deid are down there—thick like rattons!'[50]

He turned at once, and, without another word, we retraced our steps to the house of Aros.

I was eager to be alone with Mary; yet it was not till after supper, and then but for a short while, that I could have a word with her. I lost no time beating about the bush, but spoke out plainly what was on my mind.

'Mary,' I said, 'I have not come to Aros without a hope. If that should prove well founded, we may all leave and go somewhere else, secure of daily bread and comfort; secure, perhaps, of something far beyond that, which it would seem extravagant in me to promise. But there's a hope that lies nearer to my heart than money.' And at that I paused. 'You can guess fine what that is, Mary,' I said. She looked away from me in silence, and that was small encouragement, but I was not to be put off. 'All my days I have thought the world of you,' I continued; 'the time goes on and I think always the more of you; I could not think to be happy or hearty in my life without you: you are the apple of my eye.' Still she looked away, and said never a word; but I thought I saw that her hands shook. 'Mary,' I cried in fear, 'do ye no like me?'

'O, Charlie man,' she said, 'is this a time to speak of it? Let me be, a while; let me be the way I am; it'll not be you that loses by the waiting!'

I made out by her voice that she was nearly weeping, and this put me out of any thought but to compose her. 'Mary Ellen,' I said, 'say no more: I did not come to trouble you: your way shall be mine, and your time too; and you have told me all I wanted. Only just this one thing more: what ails you?'

She owned it was her father, but would enter into no particulars, only shook her head, and said he was not well and not like himself, and it was a great pity. She knew nothing of the wreck. 'I havenae been near it,' said she. 'What for would I go near it, Charlie lad? The poor souls are gone to their account long syne; and I would just have wished they had ta'en their gear with them—poor souls!'

This was scarcely any great encouragement for me to tell her of the

---

[50] Rats.

210

Espirito Santo; yet I did so, and at the very first word she cried out in surprise. 'There was a man at Grisapol,' she said, 'in the month of May— a little, yellow, black-avised body, they tell me, with gold rings upon his fingers, and a beard; and he was speiring[51] high and low for that same ship.'

It was towards the end of April that I had been given these papers to sort out by Dr Robertson: and it came suddenly back upon my mind that they were thus prepared for a Spanish historian, or a man calling himself such, who had come with high recommendations to the Principal, on a mission of inquiry as to the dispersion of the great Armada. Putting one thing with another, I fancied that the visitor 'with the gold rings upon his finger' might be the same with Dr Robertson's historian from Madrid. If that were so, he would be more likely after treasure for himself than information for a learned society. I made up my mind I should lose no time over my undertaking; and if the ship lay sunk in Sandag Bay, as perhaps both he and I supposed, it should not be for the advantage of this ringed adventurer, but for Mary and myself, and for the good, old, honest, kindly family of the Darnaways.

Chapter III
LAND AND SEA IN SANDAG BAY

I was early afoot next morning; and as soon as I had a bite to eat, set forth upon a tour of exploration. Something in my heart distinctly told me that I should find the ship of the Armada; and although I did not give way entirely to such hopeful thoughts, I was still very light in spirits and walked upon air. Aros is a very rough islet, its surface strewn with great rocks and shaggy with fern and heather; and my way lay almost north and south across the highest knoll; and though the whole distance was inside of two miles, it took more time and exertion than four upon a level road. Upon the summit, I paused. Although not very high—not three hundred feet, as I think—it yet outtops all the neighbouring lowlands of the Ross, and commands a great view of sea and islands. The sun, which had been up some time, was already hot upon my neck; the air was listless and thundery, although purely clear; away over the north-west, where the isles lie thickliest congregated, some half a dozen small and ragged clouds hung

---

[51] Seeking.

together in a covey; and the head of Ben Kyaw wore, not merely a few streamers, but a solid hood of vapour. There was a threat in the weather. The sea, it is true, was smooth like glass: even the Roost was but a seam on that wide mirror, and the Merry Men no more than caps of foam; but to my eye and ear, so long familiar with these places, the sea also seemed to lie uneasily; a sound of it, like a long sigh, mounted to me where I stood; and, quiet as it was, the Roost itself appeared to be revolving mischief. For I ought to say that all we dwellers in these parts attributed, if not prescience, at least a quality of warning, to that strange and dangerous creature of the tides.

I hurried on, then, with the greater speed, and had soon descended the slope of Aros to the part that we call Sandag Bay. It was a pretty large piece of water compared with the size of the isle; well sheltered from all but the prevailing wind; sandy and shoal and bounded by low sand-hills to the west, but to the eastward lying several fathoms deep along a ledge of rocks. It is upon that side that, at a certain time each flood, the current mentioned by my uncle sets so strong into the bay; a little later, when the Roost begins to work higher, an undertow runs still more strongly in the reverse direction; and it is the action of this last, as I suppose, that has scoured that part so deep. Nothing is to be seen out of Sandag Bay but one small segment of the horizon and, in heavy weather, the breakers flying high over a deep sea reef.

From halfway-down the hill, I had perceived the wreck of February last, a brig of considerable tonnage, lying, with her back broken, high and dry on the east corner of the sands; and I was making directly towards it, and already almost on the margin of the turf, when my eyes were suddenly arrested by a spot, cleared of fern and heather, and marked by one of those long, low, and almost human-looking mounds that we see so commonly in graveyards. I stopped like a man shot. Nothing had been said to me of any dead man or interment on the island; Rorie, Mary, and my uncle had all equally held their peace; of her at least, I was certain that she must be ignorant; and yet here, before my eyes, was proof indubitable of the fact. Here was a grave; and I had to ask myself, with a chill, what manner of man lay there in his last sleep, awaiting the signal of the Lord in that solitary, sea-beat resting-place? My mind supplied no answer but what I feared to entertain. Shipwrecked, at least, he must have been; perhaps, like the old Armada mariners, from some far and rich land oversea; or perhaps one of my own race, perishing within eyesight of the smoke of home. I stood a while uncovered by his side, and I could have desired that it had lain in our religion to put up some prayer for that unhappy stranger, or, in the old classic way, outwardly to honour his misfortune. I knew, although his bones lay there, a part of Aros, till the trumpet sounded, his imperishable soul was forth and far away, among the raptures of the everlasting Sabbath or the pangs of hell; and yet my mind misgave me even with a fear, that perhaps he was near me where I stood, guarding his sepulchre, and lingering on the scene of his unhappy fate.

Certainly it was with a spirit somewhat overshadowed that I turned away from the grave to the hardly less melancholy spectacle of the wreck. Her stem was above the first arc of the flood; she was broken in two a little abaft the foremast—though indeed she had none, both masts having broken short in her disaster; and as the pitch of the beach was very sharp and sudden, and the bows lay many feet below the stern, the fracture gaped widely open, and you could see right through her poor hull upon the farther side. Her name was much defaced, and I could not make out clearly whether she was called *Christiania*, after the Norweigian city, or *Christiana*, after the good woman, Christian's wife, in that old book the *Pilgrim's Progress*. By her build she was a foreign ship, but I was not certain of her nationality. She had been painted green, but the colour was faded and weathered, and the paint peeling off in strips. The wreck of the mainmast lay alongside, half buried in the sand. She was a forlorn sight, indeed, and I could not look without emotion at the bits of rope that still hung about her, so often handled of yore by shouting seamen; or the little scuttle where they had passed up and down to their affairs; or that poor noseless angel of a figurehead that had dipped into so many running billows.

I do not know whether it came most from the ship or from the grave, but I fell into some melancholy scruples, as I stood there, leaning with one hand against the battered timbers. The homelessness of men and even of inanimate vessels, cast away upon strange shores, came strongly in upon my mind. To make a profit of such pitiful misadventures seemed an unmanly and a sordid act; and I began to think of my then quest as of something sacrilegious in its nature. But when I remembered Mary, I took heart again. My uncle would never consent to an imprudent marriage, nor would she, as I was persuaded, wed without his full approval. It behoved me, then, to be up and doing for my wife; and I thought with a laugh how long it was since that great sea-castle, the *Espirito Santo*, had left her bones in Sandag Bay, and how weak it would be to consider rights so long extinguished and misfortunes so long forgotten in the process of time.

I had my theory of where to seek for her remains. The set of the

213

current and the soundings both pointed to the east side of the bay under the ledge of rocks. If she had been lost in Sandag Bay, and if, after these centuries, any portion of her held together, it was there that I should find it. The water deepens, as I have said, with great rapidity, and even close alongside the rocks several fathoms may be found. As I walked upon the edge I could see far and wide over the sandy bottom of the bay; the sun shone clear and green and steady in the deeps; the bay seemed rather like a great transparent crystal, as one sees them in a lapidary's shop; there was naught to show that it was water but an internal trembling, a hovering within of sun-glints and netted shadows, and now and then a faint lap and a dying bubble round the edge. The shadows of the rocks lay out for some distance at their feet, so that my own shadow, moving, pausing, and stooping on the top of that, reached sometimes half across the bay. It was above all in this belt of shadows that I hunted for the *Espirito Santo*; since it was there the undertow ran strongest, whether in or out. Cool as the whole water seemed this broiling day, it looked, in that part, yet cooler, and had a mysterious invitation for the eyes. Peer as I pleased, however, I could see nothing but a few fishes or a bush of sea-tangle, and here and there a lump of rock that had fallen from above and now lay separate on the sandy floor. Twice did I pass from one end to the other of the rocks, and in the whole distance I could see nothing of the wreck, nor any place but one where it was possible for it to be. This was a large terrace in five fathoms of water, raised off the surface of the sand to a considerable height, and looking from above like a mere outgrowth of the rocks on which I walked. It was one mass of great sea-tangles like a grove, which prevented me judging of its nature, but in shape and size it bore some likeness to a vessel's hull. At least it was my best chance. If the *Espirito Santo* lay not there under the tangles, it lay nowhere at all in Sandag Bay; and I prepared to put the question to the proof, once and for all, and either go back to Aros a rich man or cured for ever of my dreams of wealth.

I stripped to the skin, and stood on the extreme margin with my hands clasped, irresolute. The bay at that time was utterly quiet; there was no sound but from a school of porpoises somewhere out of sight behind the point; yet a certain feat withheld me on the threshold of my venture. Sad sea-feelings, scraps of my uncle's superstitions, thoughts of the dead, of the grave, of the old broken ships, drifted through my mind. But the strong sun upon my shoulders warmed me to the heart, and I stooped forward and plunged into the sea.

It was all that I could do to catch a trail of the sea-tangle that grew

214

so thickly on the terrace; but once so far anchored I secured myself by grasping a whole armful of these thick and slimy stalks, and, planting my feet against the edge, I looked around me. On all sides the clear sand stretched forth unbroken; it came to the foot of the rocks, scoured into the likeness of an alley in a garden by the action of the tides; and before me, for as far as I could see, nothing was visible but the same many-folded sand upon the sun-bright bottom of the bay. Yet the terrace to which I was then holding was as thick with strong sea-growths as a tuft of heather, and the cliff from which it bulged hung draped below the water-line with brown lianas. In this complexity of forms, all swaying together in the current, things were hard to be distinguished; and I was still uncertain whether my feet were pressed upon the natural rock or upon the timbers of the Armada treasure-ship, when the whole tuft of tangle came away in my hand, and in an instant I was on the surface, and the shores of the bay and the bright water swam before my eyes in a glory of crimson.

I clambered back upon the rocks, and threw the plant of tangle at my feet. Something at the same moment rang sharply, like a falling coin. I stooped, and there, sure enough, crusted with the red rust, there lay an iron shoe-buckle. The sight of this poor human relic thrilled me to the heart, but not with hope nor fear, only with a desolate melancholy. I held it in my hand, and the thought of its owner appeared before me like the presence of an actual man. His weather-beaten face, his sailor's hands, his sea-voice hoarse with singing at the capstan, the very foot that had once worn that buckle and trod so much along the swerving decks—the whole human fact of him, as a creature like myself, with hair and blood and seeing eyes, haunted me in that sunny, solitary place, not like a spectre, but like some friend whom I had basely injured. Was the great treasure-ship indeed below there, with her guns and chain and treasure, as she had sailed from Spain; her decks a garden for the seaweed, her cabin a breeding-place for fish, soundless but for the dredging water, motionless but for the waving of the tangle upon her battlements—that old, populous, sea-riding castle, now a reef in Sandag Bay? Or, as I thought it likelier, was this a waif from the disaster of the foreign brig—was this shoe-buckle bought but the other day and worn by a man of my own period in the world's history, hearing the same news from day to day, thinking the same thoughts, praying, perhaps, in the same temple with myself? However it was, I was assailed with dreary thoughts; my uncle's words, 'the dead are down there,' echoed in my ears; and though I determined to dive once more, it was with a strong repugnance that I stepped forward to the margin of the rocks.

A great change passed at that moment over the appearance of the bay. It was no more that clear, visible interior, like a house roofed with glass, where the green, submarine sunshine slept so stilly. A breeze, I suppose, had flawed the surface, and a sort of trouble and blackness filled its bosom, where flashes of light and clouds of shadow tossed confusedly together. Even the terrace below obscurely rocked and quivered. It seemed a graver thing to venture on this place of ambushes; and when I leaped into the sea the second time it was with a quaking in my soul.

I secured myself as at first, and groped among the waving tangle. All that met my touch was cold and soft and gluey. The thicket was alive with crabs and lobsters, trundling to and fro lopsidedly, and I had to harden my heart against the horror of their carrion neighbourhood. On all sides I could feel the grain and the clefts of hard, living stone; no planks, no iron, not a sign of any wreck; the *Espirito Santo* was not there. I remember I had almost a sense of relief in my disappointment, and I was about ready to leave go, when something happened that sent me to the surface with my heart in my mouth. I had already stayed somewhat late over my explorations; the current was freshening with the change of the tide, and Sandag Bay was no longer a safe place for a single swimmer. Well, just at the last moment there came a sudden flush of current, dredging through the tangles like a wave. I lost one hold, was flung sprawling on my side, and, instinctively grasping for a fresh support, my fingers closed on something hard and cold. I think I knew at that moment what it was. At least I instantly left hold of the tangle, leaped for the surface, and clambered out next moment on the friendly rocks with the bone of a man's leg in my grasp.

Mankind is a material creature, slow to think and dull to perceive connections. The grave, the wreck of the brig, and the rusty shoe-buckle were surely plain advertisements. A child might have read their dismal story, and yet it was not until I touched that actual piece of mankind that the full horror of the charnel ocean burst upon my spirit. I laid the bone beside the buckle, picked up my clothes, and ran as I was along the rocks towards the human shore. I could not be far enough from the spot; no fortune was vast enough to tempt me back again. The bones of the drowned dead should henceforth roll undisturbed by me, whether on tangle or minted gold. But as soon as I trod the good earth again, and had covered my nakedness against the sun, I knelt down over against the ruins of the brig, and out of the fulness of my heart prayed long and passionately for all poor souls upon the sea. A generous prayer is never presented in vain; the petition may be refused, but the petitioner is always, I believe, rewarded by some gracious visitation. The horror, at least, was lifted from my mind; I could look with calm of spirit on that great bright creature, God's ocean; and as I set off homeward up the rough sides of Aros, nothing remained of my concern beyond a deep determination to meddle no more with the spoils of wrecked vessels or the treasures of the dead.

I was already some way up the hill before I paused to breathe and look behind me. The sight that met my eyes was doubly strange.

For, first, the storm that I had foreseen was now advancing with almost tropical rapidity. The whole surface of the sea had been dulled from its conspicuous brightness to an ugly hue of corrugated lead; already in the distance the white waves, the 'skipper's daughters,' had begun to flee before a breeze that was still insensible on Aros; and already along the curve of Sandag Bay there was a splashing run of sea that I could hear from where I stood. The change upon the sky was even more remarkable. There had begun to arise out of the south-west a huge and solid continent of scowling cloud; here and there, through rents in its contexture, the sun still poured a sheaf of spreading rays; and here and there, from all its edges, vast inky streamers lay forth along the yet unclouded sky. The menace was express and imminent. Even as I gazed, the sun was blotted out. At any moment the tempest might fall upon Aros in its might.

The suddenness of this change of weather so fixed my eyes on heaven that it was some seconds before they alighted on the bay, mapped out below my feet, and robbed a moment later of the sun. The knoll which I had just surmounted overflanked a little amphitheatre of lower hillocks sloping towards the sea, and beyond that the yellow arc of beach and the whole extent of Sandag Bay. It was a scene on which I had often looked down, but where I had never before beheld a human figure. I had but just turned my back upon it and left it empty, and my wonder may be fancied when I saw a boat and several men in that deserted spot. The boat was lying by the rocks. A pair of fellows, bare-headed, with their sleeves rolled up, and one with a boat-hook, kept her with difficulty to her moorings, for the current was growing brisker every moment. A little way off upon the ledge two men in black clothes, whom I judged to be superior in rank, laid their heads together over some task which at first I did not understand, but a second after I had made it out—they were taking bearings with the compass; and just then I saw one of them unroll a sheet of paper and lay his finger down, as though identifying features in a map. Meanwhile a third was walking to and fro, poking among the rocks and peering over the edge into the water. While I was still watching them with the stupefaction of surprise, my mind hardly yet able to work on what my eyes reported, this third person suddenly stooped and summoned his companions with a cry so loud that it reached my ears upon the hill. The others ran to him, even dropping the compass in their hurry, and I could see the bone and the shoe-buckle going from hand to hand, causing the most unusual gesticulations of surprise and interest. Just then I could hear the seamen crying from the boat, and saw them point westward to that cloud continent which was ever the more rapidly unfurling its blackness over heaven. The others seemed to consult; but the danger was too pressing to be braved, and they bundled into the boat carrying my relics with them, and set forth out of the bay with all speed of oars.

I made no more ado about the matter, but turned and ran for the house. Whoever these men were, it was fit my uncle should be instantly informed. It was not then altogether too late in the day for a descent of the Jacobites; and maybe Prince Charlie, whom I knew my uncle to detest, was one of the three superiors whom I had seen upon the rock. Yet as I ran, leaping from rock to rock, and turned the matter loosely in my mind, this theory grew ever the longer the less welcome to my reason. The compass, the map, the interest awakened by the buckle, and the conduct of that one among the strangers who had looked so often below him in the water, all seemed to point to a different explanation of their presence on that outlying, obscure islet of the western sea. The Madrid historian, the search instituted by Dr Robertson, the bearded stranger with the rings, my own fruitless search that very morning in the deep water of Sandag Bay, ran together, piece by piece, in my memory, and I made sure that these strangers must be Spaniards in quest of ancient treasure and the lost ship of the Armada. But the people living in outlying islands, such as Aros, are answerable for their own security; there is none near by to protect or even to help them; and the presence in such a spot of a crew of foreign adventurers—poor, greedy, and most likely lawless—filled me with apprehensions for my uncle's money, and even for the safety of his daughter. I was still wondering how we were to get rid of them when I came, all breathless, to the top of Aros. The whole world was shadowed over; only in the extreme east, on a hill of the mainland, one last gleam of sunshine lingered like a jewel; rain had begun to fall, not heavily, but in great drops; the sea was rising with each moment, and already a band of white encircled Aros and the nearer coasts of Grisapol. The boat was still pulling seaward, but I now became aware of what had been hidden from me lower down—a large, heavily sparred, handsome schooner, lying to at the south end of

Aros. Since I had not seen her in the morning when I had looked around so closely at the signs of the weather, and upon these lone waters where a sail was rarely visible, it was clear she must have lain last night behind the uninhabited Eilean Gour, and this proved conclusively that she was manned by strangers to our coast, for that anchorage, though good enough to look at, is little better than a trap for ships. With such ignorant sailors upon so wild a coast, the coming gale was not unlikely to bring death upon its wings.

Chapter IV
THE GALE

I found my uncle at the gable-end, watching the signs of the weather, with a pipe in his fingers.

'Uncle,' said I, 'there were men ashore at Sandag Bay—'

I had no time to go further; indeed, I not only forgot my words, but even my weariness, so strange was the effect on Uncle Gordon. He dropped his pipe and fell back against the end of the house with his jaw fallen, his eyes staring, and his long face as white as paper. We must have looked at one another silently for a quarter of a minute, before he made answer to this extraordinary fashion: 'Had he a hair kep on?'

I knew as well as if I had been there that the man who now lay buried at Sandag had worn a hairy cap, and that he had come ashore alive. For the first and only time I lost toleration for the man who was my benefactor and the father of the woman I hoped to call my wife.

'These were living men,' said I, 'perhaps Jacobites, perhaps the French, perhaps pirates, perhaps adventurers come here to seek the Spanish treasure ship; but, whatever they may be, dangerous at least to your daughter and my cousin. As for your own guilty terrors, man, the dead sleeps well where you have laid him. I stood this morning by his grave; he will not wake before the trump of doom.'

My kinsman looked upon me, blinking, while I spoke; then he fixed his eyes for a little on the ground, and pulled his fingers foolishly; but it was plain that he was past the power of speech.

'Come,' said I. 'You must think for others. You must come up the hill with me, and see this ship.'

He obeyed without a word or a look, following slowly after my impatient strides. The spring seemed to have gone out of his body, and he scrambled heavily up and down the rocks, instead of leaping, as he was wont, from one to another. Nor could I, for all my cries, induce him to make better haste. Only once he replied to me complainingly, and like one in bodily pain: 'Ay, ay, man, I'm coming.' Long before we had reached the top, I had no other thought for him but pity. If the crime had ben monstrous, the punishment was in proportion.

At last we emerged above the sky-line of the hill, and could see around us. All was black and stormy to the eye; the last gleam of sun had vanished; a wind had sprung up, not yet high, but gusty and unsteady to the point; the rain, on the other hand, had ceased. Short as was the interval, the sea already ran vastly higher than when I had stood there last; already it had begun to break over some of the outward reefs, and already it moaned aloud in the sea-caves of Aros. I looked, at first, in vain for the schooner.

'There she is,' I said at last. But her new position, and the course she was now lying, puzzled me. 'They cannot mean to beat to sea,' I cried.

'That's what they mean,' said my uncle, with something like joy; and just then the schooner went about and stood upon another tack, which put the question beyond the reach of doubt. These strangers, seeing a gale on hand, had thought first of sea-room. With the wind that threatened, in these reef-sown waters and contending against so violent a stream of tide, their course was certain death.

'Good God!' said I, 'they are all lost.'

'Ay,' returned my uncle, 'a'—a' lost. They hadnae a chance but to rin for Kyle Dona. The gate they're gaun the noo, they couldnae win through an the muckle deil were there to pilot them.[52] Eh, man,' he continued, touching me on the sleeve, 'it's a braw nicht for a shipwreck! Twa in ae twalmonth! Eh, but the Merry Men 'll dance bonny!'

I looked at him, and it was then that I began to fancy him no longer in his right mind. He was peering up to me, as if for sympathy, a timid joy in his eyes. All that had passed between us was already forgotten in the prospect of this fresh disaster.

'If it were not too late,' I cried with indignation, 'I would take the coble and go out to warn them.'

'Na, na,' he protested, 'ye maunnae interfere; ye maunnae meddle wi' the like o' that. It's His'—doffing his bonnet—'His wull. And, eh, man! but it's a braw nicht for't!'

---

[52] The way they are going now, they could not get through even if the very devil were there to pilot them.

Something like fear began to creep into my soul; and, reminding him that I had not yet dined, I proposed we should return to the house. But no; nothing would tear him from his place of outlook.

'I maun see the hail thing, man, Cherlie,' he explained; and then as the schooner went about a second time, 'Eh, but they han'le her bonny!' he cried. 'The *Christ-Anna* was naething to this.'

Already the men on board the schooner must have begun to realise some part, but not yet the twentieth, of the dangers that environed their doomed ship. At every lull of the capricious wind they must have seen how fast the current swept them back. Each tack was made shorter, as they saw how little it prevailed. Every moment the rising swell began to boom and foam upon another sunken reef; and ever and again a breaker would fall in sounding ruin under the very bows of her, and the brown reef and streaming tangle appear in the hollow of the wave. I tell you, they had to stand to their tackle: there was no idle man aboard that ship, God knows. It was upon the progress of a scene so horrible to any human-hearted man that my misguided uncle now pored and gloated like a connoisseur. As I turned to go down the hill, he was lying on his belly on the summit, with his hands stretched forth and clutching in the heather. He seemed rejuvenated, mind and body.

When I got back to the house already dismally affected, I was still more sadly downcast at the sight of Mary. She had her sleeves rolled up over her strong arms, and was quietly making bread. I got a bannock[53] from the dresser and sat down to eat it in silence.

'Are ye wearied, lad?' she asked after a while.

'I am not so much wearied, Mary,' I replied, getting on my feet, 'as I am weary of delay, and perhaps of Aros too. You know me well enough to judge me fairly, say what I like. Well, Mary, you may be sure of this: you had better be anywhere but here.'

'I'll be sure of one thing,' she returned: 'I'll be where my duty is.'

'You forget, you have a duty to yourself,' I said.

'Ay, man?' she replied, pounding at the dough; 'will you have found that in the Bible, now?'

'Mary,' I said solemnly, 'you must not laugh at me just now. God knows I am in no heart for laughing. If we could get your father with us, it would be best; but with him or without him, I want you far away from here, my girl; for your own sake, and for mine, ay, and for your father's

---

[53] An unleavened oat or barley cake.

too, I want you far—far away from here. I came with other thoughts; I came here as a man comes home; now it is all changed, and I have no desire nor hope but to flee—for that's the word—flee, like a bird out of the fowler's snare, from this accursed island.'

She had stopped her work by this time.

'And do you think, now,' said she, 'do you think, now, I have neither eyes nor ears? Do ye think I havenae broken my heart to have these braws (as he calls them, God forgive him!) thrown into the sea? Do ye think I have lived with him, day in, day out, and not seen what you saw in an hour or two? No,' she said, 'I know there's wrong in it; what wrong, I neither know nor want to know. There was never an ill thing made better by meddling, that I could hear of. But, my lad, you must never ask me to leave my father. While the breath is in his body, I'll be with him. And he's not long for here, either: that I can tell you, Charlie—he's not long for here. The mark is on his brow; and better so—maybe better so.'

I was a while silent, not knowing what to say; and when I roused my head at last to speak, she got before me.

'Charlie,' she said, 'what's right for me, neednae be right for you. There's sin upon this house and trouble; you are a stranger; take your things upon your back and go your ways to better places and to better folk, and if you were ever minded to come back, though it were twenty years syne, you would find me aye waiting.'

'Mary Ellen,' I said, 'I asked you to be my wife, and you said as good as yes. That's done for good. Wherever you are, I am; as I shall answer to my God.'

As I said the words, the wind suddenly burst out raving, and then seemed to stand still and shudder round the house of Aros. It was the first squall, or prologue, of the coming tempest, and as we started and looked about us, we found that a gloom, like the approach of evening, had settled round the house.

'God pity all poor folks at sea!' she said. 'We'll see no more of my father till the morrow's morning.'

And then she told me, as we sat by the fire and hearkened to the rising gusts, of how this change had fallen upon my uncle. All last winter he had been dark and fitful in his mind. Whenever the Roost ran high, or, as Mary said, whenever the Merry Men were dancing, he would lie out for hours together on the Head, if it were at night, or on the top of Aros by day, watching the tumult of the sea, and sweeping the horizon for a sail. After February the tenth, when the wealth-bringing wreck was cast ashore at

Sandag, he had been at first unnaturally gay, and his excitement had never fallen in degree, but only changed in kind from dark to darker. He neglected his work, and kept Rorie idle. They two would speak together by the hour at the gable-end, in guarded tones and with an air of secrecy and almost of guilt; and if she questioned either, as at first she sometimes did, her inquiries were put aside with confusion. Since Rorie had first remarked the fish that hung about the ferry, his master had never set foot but once upon the mainland of the Ross. That once—it was in the height of the springs— he had passed dryshod while the tide was out; but, having lingered overlong on the far side, found himself cut off from Aros by the returning waters. It was with a shriek of agony that he had leaped across the gut,[54] and he had reached home thereafter in a fever-fit of fear. A fear of the sea, a constant haunting thought of the sea, appeared in his talk and devotions, and even in his looks when he was silent.

Rorie alone came in to supper; but a little later my uncle appeared, took a bottle under his arm, put some bread in his pocket, and set forth again in his outlook, followed this time by Rorie. I heard that the schooner was losing ground, but the crew were still fighting every inch with hopeless ingenuity and courage; and the news filled my mind with blackness.

A little after sundown the full fury of the gale broke forth, such a gale as I have never seen in summer, nor, seeing how swiftly it had come, even in winter. Mary and I sat in silence, the house quaking overhead, the tempest howling without, the fire between us sputtering with raindrops. Our thoughts were far away with the poor fellows on the schooner, or my not less unhappy uncle, houseless on the promontory; and yet ever and again we were startled back to ourselves, when the wind would rise and strike the gable like a solid body, or suddenly fall and draw away, so that the fire leaped into flame and our hearts bounded in our sides. Now the storm in its might would seize and shake the four corners of the roof, roaring like Leviathan[55] in anger. Anon, in a lull, cold eddies of tempest moved shudderingly in the room, lifting the hair upon our heads and passing between us as we sat. And again the wind would break forth in a chorus of melancholy sounds, hooting low in the chimney, wailing with flute-like softness round the house.

It was perhaps eight o'clock when Rorie came in and pulled me mysteri-

---

[54] A narrow, rocky inlet.

[55] Any monstrous sea creature. Chapter 41 of the Book of Job begins, "Canst thou draw out Leviathan with an hook? or his tongue with a cord which thou lettest down?" The rest of Chapter 41 is richly descriptive of this mythological creature.

ously to the door. My uncle, it appeared, had frightened even his constant comrade; and Rorie, uneasy at his extravagance, prayed me to come out and share the watch. I hastened to do as I was asked; the more readily as, what with fear and horror, and the electrical tension of the night, I was myself restless and disposed for action. I told Mary to be under no alarm, for I should be a safeguard on her father; and wrapping myself warmly in a plaid, I followed Rorie into the open air.

The night, though we were so little past midsummer, was as dark as January. Intervals of a groping twilight alternated with spells of utter blackness; and it was impossible to trace the reason of these changes in the flying horror of the sky. The wind blew the breath out of a man's nostrils; all heaven seemed to thunder overhead like one huge sail; and when there fell a momentary lull on Aros, we could hear the gusts dismally sweeping in the distance. Over all the lowlands of the Ross, the wind must have blown as fierce as on the open sea; and God only knows the uproar that was raging around the head of Ben Kyaw. Sheets of mingled spray and rain were driven in our faces. All round the isle of Aros the surf, with an incessant, hammering thunder, beat upon the reefs and beaches. Now louder in one place, now lower in another, like the combinations of orchestral music, the constant mass of sound was hardly varied for a moment. And loud above all this hurly-burly I could hear the changeful voices of the Roost and the intermittent roaring of the Merry Men. At that hour, there flashed into my mind the reason of the name that they were called. For the noise of them seemed almost mirthful, as it out-topped the other noises of the night; or if not mirthful, yet instinct with a portentous joviality. Nay, and it seemed even human. As when savage men have drunk away their reason, and, discarding speech, bawl together in their madness by the hour; so, to my ears, these deadly breakers shouted by Aros in the night.

Arm in arm, and staggering against the wind, Rorie and I won every yard of ground with conscious effort. We slipped on the wet sod, we fell together sprawling on the rocks. Bruised, drenched, beaten, and breathless, it must have taken us near half an hour to get from the house down to the Head that overlooks the Roost. There, it seemed, was my uncle's favourite observatory. Right in the face of it, where the cliff is highest and most sheer, a hump of earth, like a parapet, makes a place of shelter from the common winds where a man may sit in quiet and see the tide and the mad billows contending at his feet. As he might look down from the window of a house upon some street disturbance, so, from this post, he looks down upon

224

the tumbling of the Merry Men. On such a night, of course, he peers upon a world of blackness, where the waters wheel and boil, where the waves joust together with the noise of an explosion, and the foam towers and vanishes in the twinkling of an eye. Never before had I seen the Merry Men thus violent. The fury, height, and transiency of their spoutings was a thing to be seen and not recounted. High over our heads on the cliff rose their white columns in the darkness; and the same instant, like phantoms, they were gone. Sometimes three at a time would thus aspire and vanish; sometimes a gust took them, and the spray would fall about us, heavy as a wave. And yet the spectacle was rather maddening in its levity than impressive by its force. Thought was beaten down by the confounding uproar; a gleeful vacancy possessed the brains of men, a state akin to madness; and I found myself at times following the dance of the Merry Men as it were a tune upon a jigging instrument.

I first caught sight of my uncle when we were still some yards away in one of the flying glimpses of twilight that chequered the pitch darkness of the night. He was standing up behind the parapet, his head thrown back and the bottle to his mouth. As he put it down, he saw and recognised us with a toss of one hand fleeringly above his head.

'Has he been drinking?' shouted I to Rorie.

'He will aye be drunk when the wind blaws,' returned Rorie in the same high key, and it was all that I could do to hear him.

'Then—was he so—in February?' I inquired.

Rorie's 'Ay' was a cause of joy to me. The murder, then, had not sprung in cold blood from calculation; it was an act of madness no more to be condemned than to be pardoned. My uncle was a dangerous madman, if you will, but he was not cruel and base as I had feared. Yet what a scene for a carouse, what an incredible vice, was this that the poor man had chosen! I have always thought drunkenness a wild and almost fearful pleasure, rather demoniacal than human; but drunkenness, out here in the roaring blackness, on the edge of a cliff above that hell of waters, the man's head spinning like the Roost, his foot tottering on the edge of death, his ear watching for the signs of shipwreck, surely that, if it were credible in anyone, was morally impossible in a man like my uncle, whose mind was set upon a damnatory creed and haunted by the darkest superstitions. Yet so it was; and, as we reached the bight of shelter and could breathe again, I saw the man's eyes shining in the night with an unholy glimmer.

'Eh, Charlie, man, it's grand!' he cried. 'See to them!' he continued, dragging me to the edge of the abyss from whence arose that deafening clamour and those clouds of spray; 'see to them dancin,' man! Is that no wicked?'

He pronounced the word with gusto, and I thought it suited with the scene.

'They're yowlin' for thon schooner,' he went on, his thin, insane voice clearly audible in the shelter of the bank, 'an' she's comin' aye nearer, aye nearer, aye nearer an' nearer an' nearer; an' they ken't the folk kens it, they ken weel it's by wi' them. Charlie, lad, they're a' drunk in yon schooner, a' dozened wi' drink. They were a' drunk in the *Christ-Anna*, at the hinder end. There's nane could droon at sea wantin' the brandy. Hoot awa, what do you ken?' with a sudden blast of anger. 'I tell ye, it cannae be; they daurnae droon without it. Hae,' holding out the bottle, 'tak' a sowp.'

I was about to refuse, but Rorie touched me as if in warning; and indeed I had already thought better of the movement. I took the bottle, therefore, and not only drank freely myself, but contrived to spill even more as I was doing so. It was pure spirit, and almost strangled me to swallow. My kinsman did not observe the loss, but, once more throwing back his head, drained the remainder to the dregs. Then, with a loud laugh, he cast the bottle forth among the Merry Men, who seemed to leap up, shouting to receive it.

'Hae, bairns!' he cried, 'there's your hansel.[56] Ye'll get bonnier nor that or morning.'

Suddenly, out in the black night before us, and not two hundred yards away, we heard, at a moment when the wind was silent, the clear note of a human voice. Instantly the wind swept howling down upon the Head, and the Roost bellowed, and churned, and danced with a new fury. But we had heard the sound, and we knew, with agony, that this was the doomed ship now close on ruin, and that what we had heard was the voice of her master issuing his last command. Crouching together on the edge, we waited, straining every sense, for the inevitable end. It was long, however, and to us it seemed like ages, ere the schooner suddenly appeared for one brief instant, relieved against a tower of glimmering foam. I still see her reefed mainsail flapping loose, as the boom fell heavily across the deck; I still see the black outline of the hull, and still think I can distinguish

---

[56]   Payment.

226

the figure of a man stretched upon the tiller. Yet the whole sight we had of her passed swifter than lightning; the very wave that disclosed her fell burying her for ever; the mingled cry of many voices at the point of death rose and was quenched in the roaring of the Merry Men. And with that the tragedy was at an end. The strong ship, with all her gear, and the lamp perhaps still burning in the cabin, the lives of so many men, precious surely to others, dear, at least, as heaven to themselves, had all, in that one moment, gone down into the surging waters. They were gone like a dream. And the wind still ran and shouted, and the senseless waters in the Roost still leaped and tumbled as before.

How long we lay there together, we three, speechless and motionless, is more than I can tell, but it must have been for long. At length, one by one, and almost mechanically, we crawled back into the shelter of the bank. As I lay against the parapet, wholly wretched and not entirely master of my mind, I could hear my kinsman maundering to himself in an altered and melancholy mood. Now he would repeat to himself with maudlin iteration, 'Sic a fecht as they had—sic a sair fecht as they had, puir lads, puir lads!' and anon he would bewail that 'a' the gear was as gude's tint',[57] because the ship had gone down among the Merry Men instead of stranding on the shore; and throughout, the name—the *Christ-Anna*—would come and go in his divagations, pronounced with shuddering awe. The storm all this time was rapidly abating. In half-an-hour the wind had fallen to a breeze, and the change was accompanied or caused by a heavy, cold, and plumping rain. I must then have fallen asleep, and when I came to myself, drenched, stiff, and unrefreshed, day had already broken, grey, wet, discomfortable day; the wind blew in faint and shifting capfuls, the tide was out, the Roost was at its lowest, and only the strong beating surf round all the coasts of Aros remained to witness of the furies of the night.

Chapter V
A MAN OUT OF THE SEA

Rorie set out for the house in search of warmth and breakfast; but my uncle was bent upon examining the shores of Aros, and I felt it a part of duty to accompany him throughout. He was now docile and quiet, but

---

[57] Lost.

tremulous and weak in mind and body; and it was with the eagerness of a child that he pursued his exploration. He climbed far down upon the rocks; on the beaches, he pursued the retreating breakers. The merest broken plank or rag or cordage was a treasure in his eyes to be secured at the peril of his life. To see him, with weak and stumbling footsteps, expose himself to the pursuit of the surf, or the snares and pitfalls of the weedy rock, kept me in a perpetual terror. My arm was ready to support him, my hand clutched him by the skirt, I helped him to draw his pitiful discoveries beyond the reach of the returning wave; a nurse accompanying a child of seven would have had no different experience.

Yet, weakened as he was by the reaction from his madness of the night before, the passions that smouldered in his nature were those of a strong man. His terror of the sea, although conquered for the moment, was still undiminished; had the sea been a lake of living flames, he could not have shrunk more panically from its touch; and once, when his foot slipped and he plunged to the midleg into a pool of water, the shriek that came up out of his soul was like the cry of death. He sat still for a while, panting like a dog, after that; but his desire for the spoils of shipwreck triumphed once more over his fears; once more he tottered among the curded foam; once more he crawled upon the rocks among the bursting bubbles; once more his whole heart seemed to be set on driftwood, fit, if it was fit for anything, to throw upon the fire. Pleased as he was with what he found, he still incessantly grumbled at his ill-fortune.

'Aros,' he said, 'is no place for wrecks ava'—no ava'. A' the years I've dwalt here, this ane maks the second; and the best o' the gear tint!'

'Uncle,' said I, for we were now on a stretch of open sand, where there was nothing to divert his mind, 'I saw you last night, as I never thought to see you—you were drunk.'

'Na, na,' he said, 'no as bad as that. I had been drinking, though. And to tell ye the God's truth, it's a thing I cannae mend. There's nae soberer man than me in my ordnar; but when I hear the wind blaw in my lug, it's my belief that I gang gyte.'[58]

'You are a religious man,' I replied, 'and this is sin.'

'Ou,' he returned, 'if it wasnae sin, I dinnae ken that I would care for't. Ye see, man, it's defiance. There's a sair spang[59] o' the auld sin o' the warld in yon sea; it's an unchristian business at the best o't; an' whiles when it gets up, an' the wind skreighs—the wind an' her are a kind of

---

[58] Go mad.
[59] A bound or leap.

228

sib, I'm thinkin'—an' thae Merry Men, the daft callants, blawin' and laun-
chin',[60] and puir souls in the deid-thraws warstlin' the leelang nicht wi'
their bit ships—weel, it comes ower me like a glamour.[61] I'm a deil, I
ken't. But I think naething o' the puir sailor lads; I'm wi' the sea, I'm just
like ane o' her ain Merry Men.'

I thought I should touch him in a joint of his harness. I turned me
towards the sea; the surf was running gaily, wave after wave, with their
manes blowing behind them, riding one after another up the beach, tower-
ing, curving, falling one upon another on the trampled sand. Without, the
salt air, the scared gulls, the widespread army of the sea-chargers, neighing
to each other, as they gathered together to the assault of Aros; and close
before us, that line on the flat sands that, with all their number and their
fury, they might never pass.

'Thus far shalt thou go,' said I, 'and no farther.' And then I quoted as
solemnly as I was able a verse that I had often before fitted to the chorus
of the breakers:

> But yet the Lord that is on high,
> Is more of might by far,
> Than noise of many waters is,
> Or great sea-billows are.[62]

'Ay,' said my kinsman, 'at the hinder end the Lord will triumph; I
dinnae misdoobt that. But here on earth, even silly men-folk daur Him to
His face. It is nae wise; I am nae sayin' that it's wise; but it's the pride
of the eye, and it's the lust o' life, an' it's the wale o'[63] pleesures.'

I said no more, for we had now begun to cross a neck of land that lay
between us and Sandag; and I withheld my last appeal to the man's better
reason till we should stand upon the spot associated with his crime. Nor
did he pursue the subject; but he walked beside me with a firmer step.
The call that I had made upon his mind acted like a stimulant, and I could
see that he had forgotten his search for worthless jetsam, in a profound,
gloomy, and yet stirring train of thought. In three or four minutes we had
topped the brae and begun to go down upon Sandag. The wreck had been
roughly handled by the sea; the stem had been spun round and dragged a

---

[60] Plunging.
[61] Spell, deceiving enchantment, illusion.
[62] This is a metrical and rhymed version of verse four of Psalm 93, which reads: "The Lord on high
is mightier than the noise of many waters, yea, than the mighty waves of the sea."
[63] The best of.

229

little lower down; and perhaps the stern had been forced a little higher, for the two parts now lay entirely separate on the beach. When we came to the grave I stopped, uncovered my head in the thick rain, and, looking my kinsman in the face, addressed him.

'A man,' I said, 'was in God's providence suffered to escape from mortal dangers; he was poor, he was naked, he was wet, he was weary, he was a stranger; he had every claim upon the bowels of your compassion; it may be that he was the salt of the earth, holy, helpful, and kind; it may be he was a man laden with iniquities to whom death was the beginning of torment. I ask you in the sight of heaven: Gordon Darnaway, where is the man for whom Christ died?'

He started visibly at the last words; but there came no answer, and his face expressed no feeling but a vague alarm.

'You were my father's brother,' I continued; 'you have taught me to count your house as if it were my father's house; and we are both sinful men walking before the Lord among the sins and dangers of this life. It is by our evil that God leads us into good; we sin, I dare not say by His temptation, but I must say with His consent; and to any but the brutish man his sins are the beginning of wisdom. God has warned you by this crime; He warns you still by the bloody grave between our feet; and if there shall follow no repentance, no improvement, no return to Him, what can we look for but the following of some memorable judgment?'

Even as I spoke the words, the eyes of my uncle wandered from my face. A change fell upon his looks that cannot be described; his features seemed to dwindle in size, the colour faded from his cheeks, one hand rose waveringly and pointed over my shoulder into the distance, and the oft-repeated name fell once more from his lips: 'The *Christ-Anna!*'

I turned; and if I was not appalled to the same degree, as I return thanks to Heaven that I had not the cause, I was still startled by the sight that met my eyes. The form of a man stood upright on the cabin-hutch of the wrecked ship; his back was towards us; he appeared to be scanning the offing with shaded eyes, and his figure was relieved to its full height, which was plainly very great, against the sea and sky. I have said a thousand times that I am not superstitious; but at that moment, with my mind running upon death and sin, the unexplained appearance of a stranger on that sea-girt, solitary island filled me with a surprise that bordered close on terror. It seemed scarce possible that any human soul should have come ashore alive in such a sea as had raged last night along the coasts of Aros; and the only vessel within miles had gone down before our eyes among the Merry

Men. I was assailed with doubts that made suspense unbearable, and, to put the matter to the touch at once, stepped forward and hailed the figure like a ship.

He turned about, and I thought he started to behold us. At this my courage instantly revived, and I called and signed to him to draw near, and he, on his part, dropped immediately to the sands, and began slowly to approach, with many stops and hesitations. At each repeated mark of the man's uneasiness I grew the more confident myself; and I advanced another step, encouraging him as I did so with my head and hand. It was plain the castaway had hard indifferent accounts of our island hospitality; and indeed, about this time, the people farther north had a sorry reputation.

'Why,' I said, 'the man is black!'[64]

And just at that moment, in a voice that I could scarce have recognised, my kinsman began swearing and praying in a mingled stream. I looked at him; he had fallen on his knees, his face was agonised; at each step of the castaway's the pitch of his voice rose, the volubility of his utterance and the fervour of his language redoubled. I call it prayer, for it was addressed to God; but surely no such ranting incongruities were ever before addressed to the Creator by a creature: surely if prayer can be a sin, this mad harangue was sinful. I ran to my kinsman, I seized him by the shoulders, I dragged him to his feet.

'Silence, man,' said I, 'respect your God in words, if not in action. Here, on the very scene of your transgressions, He sends you an occasion of atonement. Forward and embrace it; welcome like a father yon creature who comes trembling to your mercy.'

With that, I tried to force him towards the black; but he felled me to the ground, burst from my grasp, leaving the shoulder of his jacket, and fled up the hillside towards the top of Aros like a deer. I staggered to my feet again, bruised and somewhat stunned; the negro had paused in surprise, perhaps in terror, some half-way between me and the wreck; my uncle was already far away, bounding from rock to rock; and I thus found myself torn for a time between two duties. But I judged, and I pray Heaven that I judged rightly, in favour of the poor wretch upon the sands; his misfortune was at least not plainly of his own creation; it was one, besides, that I could certainly relieve; and I had begun by that time to regard my uncle as an incurable and dismal lunatic. I advanced accordingly towards the black,

---

[64] See ''Thrawn Janet,'' note 65, page 155. Though here, the black man is clearly mortal and admirable, the folk superstition about the blackness of Satan clearly serves Stevenson's fiction. Gordon Darnaway's guilt, we will shortly see, makes him believe that Satan has come for him.

who now awaited my approach with folded arms, like one prepared for either destiny. As I came nearer, he reached forth his hand with a great gesture, such as I had seen from the pulpit, and spoke to me in something of a pulpit voice, but not a word was comprehensible. I tried him first in English, then in Gaelic, both in vain; so that it was clear we must rely upon the tongue of looks and gestures. Thereupon I signed to him to follow me, which he did readily and with a grave obeisance like a fallen king; all the while there had come no shade of alteration in his face, neither of anxiety while he was still waiting, nor of relief now that he was reassured; if he were a slave, as I supposed, I could not but judge he must have fallen from some high place in his own country, and fallen as he was, I could not but admire his bearing. As we passed the grave, I paused and raised my hands and eyes to haven in token of respect and sorrow for the dead; and he, as if in answer, bowed low and spread his hands abroad; it was a strange motion, but done like a thing of common custom; and I supposed it was ceremonial in the land from which he came. At the same time he pointed to my uncle, whom we could just see perched upon a knoll, and touched his head to indicate that he was mad.

We took the long way round the shore, for I feared to excite my uncle if we struck across the island; and as we walked, I had time enough to mature the little dramatic exhibition by which I hoped to satisfy my doubts. Accordingly, pausing on a rock, I proceeded to imitate before the negro the action of the man whom I had seen the day before taking bearings with the compass at Sandag. He understood me at once, and, taking the imitation out of my hands, showed me where the boat was, pointed out seaward as if to indicate the position of the schooner, and then down along the edge of the rock with the words 'Espirito Santo,' strangely pronounced, but clear enough for recognition. I had thus been right in my conjecture; the pretended historical inquiry had been but a cloak for treasure-hunting; the man who had played on Dr Robertson was the same as the foreigner who visited Grisapol in spring, and now, with many others, lay dead under the Roost of Aros: there had their greed brought them, there should their bones be tossed for evermore. In the meantime the black continued his imitation of the scene, now looking up skyward as though watching the approach of the storm; now, in the character of a seaman, waving the rest to come aboard; now as an officer, running along the rock and entering the boat; and anon bending over imaginary oars with the air of a hurried boatman; but all with the same solemnity of manner, so that I was never even moved to smile. Lastly, he indicated to me, by a pantomime not to be described in words, how he himself had gone up to examine the stranded wreck, and, to his grief and indignation, had been deserted by his comrades; and thereupon folded his arms once more, and stooped his head, like one accepting fate.

The mystery of his presence being thus solved for me, I explained to him by means of a sketch the fate of the vessel and of all aboard her. He showed no surprise nor sorrow, and, with a sudden lifting of his open hand, seemed to dismiss his former friends or masters (whichever they had been) into God's pleasure. Respect came upon me and grew stronger, the more I observed him; I saw he had a powerful mind and a sober and severe character, such as I loved to commune with; and before we reached the house of Aros I had almost forgotten, and wholly forgiven him, his uncanny colour.

To Mary I told all that had passed without suppression, though I own my heart failed me; but I did wrong to doubt her sense of justice.

'You did the right,' she said. 'God's will be done.' And she set out meat for us at once.

As soon as I was satisfied, I bade Rorie keep an eye upon the castaway, who was still eating, and set forth again myself to find my uncle. I had not gone far before I saw him sitting in the same place, upon the very topmost knoll, and seemingly in the same attitude as when I had last observed him. From that point, as I have said, the most of Aros and the neighbouring Ross would be spread below him like a map; and it was plain that he kept a bright look-out in all directions, for my head had scarcely risen above the summit of the first ascent before he had leaped to his feet and turned as if to face me. I hailed him at once, as well as I was able, in the same tones and words as I had often used before, when I had come to summon him to dinner. He made not so much as a movement in reply. I passed on a little farther, and again tried parley, with the same result. But when I began a second time to advance, his insane fears blazed up again, and still in dead silence, but with incredible speed, he began to flee from before me along the rocky summit of the hill. An hour before, he had been dead weary, and I had been comparatively active. But now his strength was recruited by the fervour of insanity, and it would have been vain for me to dream of pursuit. Nay, the very attempt, I thought, might have inflamed his terrors, and thus increased the miseries of our position. And I had nothing left but to turn homeward and make my sad report to Mary.

She heard it, as she had heard the first, with a concerned composure, and, bidding me lie down and take that rest of which I stood so much in need, set forth herself in quest of her misguided father. At that age it would have been a strange thing that put me from either meat or sleep; I slept long and deep; and it was already long past noon before I awoke and came downstairs into the kitchen. Mary, Rorie, and the black castaway were seated about the fire in silence; and I could see that Mary had been weeping. There was cause enough, as I soon learned, for tears. First she, and then Rorie, had been forth to seek my uncle; each in turn had found him perched upon the hilltop, and from each in turn he had silently and swiftly fled. Rorie had tried to chase him, but in vain; madness lent a new vigour to his bounds; he sprang from rock to rock over the wildest gullies; he scoured like the wind along the hilltops; he doubled and twisted like a hare before the dogs; and Rorie at length gave in; and the last that he saw, my uncle was seated as before upon the crest of Aros. Even during the hottest excitement of the chase, even when the fleet-footed servant had come, for a moment, very near to capture him, the poor lunatic had uttered not a sound. He fled, and he was silent, like a beast; and this silence had terrified his pursuer.

There was something heart-breaking in the situation. How to capture the madman, how to feed him in the meanwhile, and what to do with him when he was captured, were the three difficulties that we had to solve.

'The black,' said I, 'is the cause of this attack. It may even be his presence in the house that keeps my uncle on the hill. We have done the fair thing; he has been fed and warmed under this roof; now I propose that Rorie put him across the bay in the coble, and take him through the Ross as far as Grisapol.'

In this proposal Mary heartily concurred; and bidding the black follow us, we all three descended to the pier. Certainly, Heaven's will was declared against Gordon Darnaway; a thing had happened, never paralleled before in Aros; during the storm, the coble had broken loose, and, striking on the rough splinters of the pier, now lay in four feet of water with one side stove in. Three days of work at least would be required to make her float. But I was not to be beaten. I led the whole party round to where the gut was narrowest, swam to the other side, and called to the black to follow me. He signed, with the same clearness and quiet as before, that he knew not the art; and there was truth apparent in his signals, it would have occurred to none of us to doubt his truth; and that hope being over, we must all go back even as we came to the house of Aros, the negro walking in our midst without embarrassment.

234

All we could do that day was to make one more attempt to communicate with the unhappy madman. Again he was visible on his perch; again he fled in silence. But food and a great cloak were at least left for his comfort; the rain, besides, had cleared away, and the night promised to be even warm. We might compose ourselves, we thought, until the morrow; rest was the chief requisite, that we might be strengthened for unusual exertions; and as none cared to talk, we separated at an early hour.

I lay long awake, planning a campaign for the morrow, I was to place the black on the side of Sandag, whence he should head my uncle towards the house; Rorie in the west, I on the east, were to complete the cordon, as best we might. It seemed to me, the more I recalled the configuration of the island, that it should be possible, though hard, to force him down upon the low ground along Aros Bay; and once there, even with the strength of his madness, ultimate escape was hardly to be feared. It was on his terror of the black that I relied; for I made sure, however he might run, it would not be in the direction of the man whom he supposed to have returned from the dead, and thus one point of the compass at least would be secure.

When at length I fell asleep, it was to be awakened shortly after by a dream of wrecks, black men, and submarine adventure; and I found myself so shaken and fevered that I arose, descended the stair, and stepped out before the house. Within, Rorie and the black were asleep together in the kitchen; outside was a wonderful clear night of stars, with here and there a cloud still hanging, last stragglers of the tempest. It was near the top of the flood, and the Merry Men were roaring in the windless quiet of the night. Never, not even in the height of the tempest, had I heard their song with greater awe. Now, when the winds were gathered home, when the deep was dandling itself back into its summer slumber, and when the stars rained their gentle light over land and sea, the voice of these tide-breakers was still raised for havoc. They seemed, indeed, to be a part of the world's evil and the tragic side of life. Nor were their meaningless vociferations the only sounds that broke the silence of the night. For I could hear, now shrill and thrilling and now almost drowned, the note of a human voice that accompanied the uproar of the Roost. I knew it for my kinsman's; and a great fear fell upon me of God's judgments, and the evil in the world. I went back again into the darkness of the house as into a place of shelter, and lay long upon my bed, pondering these mysteries.

It was late when I again woke, and I leaped into my clothes and hurried to the kitchen. No one was there; Rorie and the black had both stealthily departed long before; and my heart stood still at the discovery. I could rely on Rorie's heart, but I placed no trust in his discretion. If he had thus set out without a word, he was plainly bent upon some service to my uncle. But what service could he hope to render even alone, far less in the company of the man in whom my uncle found his fears incarnated? Even if I were not already too late to prevent some deadly mischief, it was plain I must delay no longer. With the thought I was out of the house; and often as I have run on the rough sides of Aros, I never ran as I did that fatal morning. I do not believe I put twelve minutes to the whole ascent.

My uncle was gone from his perch. The basket had indeed been torn open and the meat scattered on the turf; but, as we found afterwards, no mouthful had been tasted; and there was not another trace of human existence in that wide field of view. Day had already filled the clear heavens; the sun already lighted in a rosy bloom upon the crest of Ben Kyaw; but all below me the rude knolls of Aros and the shield of sea lay steeped in the clear darkling twilight of the dawn.

'Rorie!' I cried; and again, 'Rorie!' My voice died in the silence, but there came no answer back. If there were indeed an enterprise afoot to catch my uncle, it was plainly not in fleetness of foot, but in dexterity of stalking, that the hunters placed their trust. I ran on farther, keeping the higher spurs, and looking right and left, nor did I pause again till I was on the mount above Sandag. I could see the wreck, the uncovered belt of sand, the waves idly beating, the long ledge of rocks, and on either hand the tumbled knolls, boulders, and gullies of the island. But still no human thing.

At a stride the sunshine fell on Aros, and the shadows and colours leaped into being. Not half a moment later, below me to the west, sheep began to scatter as in a panic. There came a cry. I saw my uncle running. I saw the black jump up in hot pursuit; and before I had time to understand, Rorie also had appeared, calling directions in Gaelic as to a dog herding sheep.

I took to my heels to interfere, and perhaps I had done better to have waited where I was, for I was the means of cutting off the madman's last escape. There was nothing before him from that moment but the grave, the wreck, and the sea in Sandag Bay. And yet Heaven knows that what I did was for the best.

My uncle Gordon saw in what direction, horrible to him, the chase was driving him. He doubled, darting to the right and left; but high as the fever ran in his veins, the black was still the swifter. Turn where he would, he was still forestalled, still driven toward the scene of his crime. Suddenly

he began to shriek aloud, so that the coast re-echoed; and now both I and
Rorie were calling on the black to stop. But all was vain, for it was written
otherwise. The pursuer still ran, the chase still sped before him screaming;
they avoided the grave, and skimmed close past the timbers of the wreck;
in a breath they had cleared the sand; and still my kinsman did not pause,
but dashed straight into the surf; and the black, now almost within reach,
still followed swiftly behind him. Rorie and I both stopped, for the thing
was now beyond the hands of men, and these were the decrees of God
that came to pass before our eyes. There was never a sharper ending. On
that steep beach they were beyond their depth at a bound; neither could
swim; the black rose once for a moment with a throttling cry; but the
current had them, racing seaward; and if ever they came up again, which
God alone can tell, it would be ten minutes after, at the far end of Aros
Roost, where the sea-birds hover fishing.

Appendix B
Le Chevalier Double
by Théophile Gautier

>≥€

Translated from the French by Leonard Wolf

What is it that makes the blonde Edwige so sad? What is she doing sitting there withdrawn, her chin in her hand, her elbow on her knee, more sorrowful than despair, paler than an alabaster statue weeping over a tomb?

Out of the corner of an eye, a large tear rolls moistening her downy cheek. Only one, but its flow does not cease. Just as a drop of water that seeps over a massive rock wears down the grantite in the course of time, so that single tear flowing without interruption from her eye to her heart has pierced it through and through.

Edwige, my blonde Edwige, do you no longer believe in the sweet savior, Jesus Christ? Have you no faith in the compassion of the most holy Virgin Mary? Why, like an elf or a wraith do you hold your frail, translucent hands continually at your sides? You're going to be a mother; it was your dearest wish: if you give your noble husband, Count Lodbrog, a son, he has promised to give the church of St. Euthbert a massive silver altar and a fine-gold ciborium.

Alas, alas. Poor Edwige's heart has been pierced with seven swordblades of sorrow; a terrible secret weighs on her soul. Some months ago, a stranger came to the castle; the weather was dreadful that night; the timbers of the castle tower trembled; the weathercocks whimpered, the fire groveled in the fireplace and the wind banged at the window like someone who wanted urgently to come in.

The stranger was as fair as an angel—a fallen angel. His smile was gentle; his gaze was gentle. That smile and that gaze made you shiver with fear; chilled you with the horror one feels leaning over an abyss. When he moved it was with a wicked grace—with the perfidious languor of a tiger stalking his prey. He fascinated the way a serpent fascinates a bird.

This stranger was a great bard: his dark complexion was proof that he was a far wanderer. He said that he came from the heart of Bohemia and asked only for a night's hospitality.

He stayed that night, and still other days and other nights because the storm would not subside, and the old castle shook on its foundations as if the blast wished to uproot it, to topple its crenellated crown into the torrent's foaming waters.

To while away the hours, he recited strange poems that troubled the heart and roused passionate thoughts: throughout his recitation a sleek black raven, gleaming like jet, perched on his shoulder, keeping time to the cadence of the verse with its ebony beak and flapping its wings as if applauding. Edwige turned as pale as lilies in moonlight; Edwige blushed, as red as the roses at dawn. She leaned back in her large armchair, intoxicated, languishing, half-dead, as if she had inhaled the fumes of death-dealing flowers.

At last, the bard could leave. A small blue smile had just smoothed the sky's face. From that time on, Edwige, the blonde Edwige could do nothing but weep in her window corner.

Edwige became a mother. She gave birth to a beautiful son, all red and white. The old Count Lodbrog commissioned the smelter to make a massive silver altar and he gave the goldsmith a reindeer-hide purse containing a thousand pieces of gold with which to make the ciborium: it would be large and heavy and able to hold a generous measure of wine. The priest who could empty it could claim he was a great drinker.

The child was red and white, but it had the dark gaze of the stranger: his mother could not help seeing it. Ah, poor Edwige, why did you gaze so long at the stranger with his harp and his raven?

The chaplain baptized the child: he was named Oluf, a truly fine name. The astrologer climbed to the highest tower to cast his horoscope.

It was a clear, cold day: cold, sharp and white as the jaw of a lynx. Sawtoothed, snow-covered mountains frayed the sky's hem. Large pale stars gleamed in the crude blue of the sky like silver suns.

The astrologer calculated the elevation, noted the year, the day and the minute. He made extensive calculations in red ink on a long parchment studded with cabalistic symbols; he returned to his study and mounted the platform again. No, he had not been mistaken in his conclusions; his measurements regarding the nativity were as accurate as the balance scale a jeweler uses. Still, he did them once more; but he had not been mistaken.

The infant Count Oluf had a double star, one green and the other red. Green as hope; red as hell. One star was favorable, the other, disastrous. Had he ever before known a child to have a double star?

His manner grave and measured, the astrologer returned to the newly delivered mother and, passing his bony hand through the ripples of his long beard, said, "Countess Edwige, and you, Count Lodbrog, two influences have presided over the birth of your precious son; one is good, the other evil: which is why there is a green star and a red one. He is under the influence of a double ascendant: he will be very happy or very unhappy, I don't know which. Perhaps both at once."

To the astrologer, Count Lodbrog said, "The green star will triumph." But Edwige, in her maternal heart, feared that it would be the red one. Once again she rested her chin on her hand and renewed her weeping in the window corner. After she had nursed the child, her only occupation was to gaze through the window at the snow falling in thick flakes, as if someone on high had plucked the feathers from the wings of all the angels and all the cherubim.

From time to time a croaking raven flew past the window, shedding a silver-tinged dust. This made Edwige think of the remarkable raven which was always perched on the shoulder of the stranger with the gentle gaze of the tiger and the charming smile of a serpent.

And the tears flowed more quickly from her eyes to her heart, to a heart that was pierced through and through.

Young Oluf was a very strange child. One might have said that beneath his pale and rosy complexion there were two quite different children. One day, he was as good as an angel; on another as wicked as the devil. He bit his mother's breast and scratched his nurse's face with his nails.

The old Count Lodbrog, smiling behind his gray mustache, said that

Oluf because of his warlike temper would be a good soldier. The truth is, Oluf was an intolerably bizarre little fellow. Sometimes he wept, sometimes he laughed. He was capricious as the moon, as fanciful as a woman; he came and went; stopped abruptly without any apparent reason; abandoned what he undertook. One of his periods of absolute immobility might be followed by one that was disturbingly turbulent. When he was alone, he seemed to be talking to an invisible companion. When asked what agitated him, he would say that it was the red star tormenting him.

Soon, he would be in his fifteenth year. His character was becoming inexplicable; his features, though perfectly handsome, bore a perplexing expression. He was as blond as his mother, with all the characteristics of her Nordic race. But beneath that forehead that was as white as snow— beneath that forehead that belonged to the ancient race of the Lodbrogs, there glowed a pair of long-lashed eyes made bright by the primitive ardors of Italian passion, a velvet gaze as soft and cruel and sweet as that of the Bohemian bard.

And how the months flew by, and the years even more quickly. Edwige now lay beneath the shadowy arches of the Lodbrog tomb beside the old count who, in his casket, smiled at the knowledge that his line would not perish. Edwige had been so pale that death had not changed her much. Above her tomb there lay a beautiful statue, its hands folded, its feet touching a marble greyhound, a faithful companion of the dead. No one knew what Edwige said in her final hour, but the priest who heard her confession turned paler than the dying woman.

Oluf, the dark and fair son of the grieving Edwige, was twenty years old. He was very skillful in all manner of arms. No one could handle a bow better than he; he could split an arrow trembling in the bull's-eye; he could tame the wildest horses using neither bit nor spurs.

He never cast his eye on a woman or a young girl in vain, but none of those who loved him was ever happy. The unsteadiness of his character stood in the way of any happiness between himself and a woman. One of his halves might feel passion; the other, hatred. Sometimes the green star triumphed; sometimes the red. One day he might say, "O white virgin of the North, sparkling and pure as polar ice; with pupils like moonlight; with cheeks cooled by the freshness of the aurora borealis." On another day he might cry, "O daughters of Italy, orange blonde and gilded by the sun; hearts of flame in bosoms of bronze." What was saddest of all was that he was sincere expressing both those feelings.

Alas, poor grievers, unhappy plaintive shadows. You don't even accuse him because you know he is more unhappy than you; his heart is a battleground trampled incessantly by the feet of two unknown foes each of them seeking, as in the fight between Jacob and the angel, each seeking to wither the knee of his adversary.

If one went to the cemetery, one would find under the large velvety leaves of deeply cut mullein, under the green boughs of the unhealthful asphodel, among the rank growth of the stinging nettle—one would find more than one abandoned stone on which only the morning dew spreads its tears. Mina, Dora, Thecla! Is the earth heavy as it presses on your delicate breasts; on your delightful bodies?

One day, Oluf called Dietrich, his faithful stableman, and told him to saddle his horse.

"Master, see how the snow is falling, how the wind blows and bows the tops of the pines to the very ground; don't you hear the distant howling of the famished wolves like souls in pain and the death-cry of the reindeer?"

"Dietrich, my faithful stableman, I will shake off the snow the way one shakes off a burr that attaches itself to one's coat; bending the crest of my helmet a little, I will pass under the arch made by the pines. As for the wolves, their claws will be blunted against my fine armor, and I will move the ice aside with the tip of my sword to uncover the fresh flourishing moss that the poor weeping, whimpering reindeer cannot reach."

The Count Oluf de Lodbrog—because that was his title since the death of the old count—departed on his good horse accompanied by his giant dogs Murg and Fenris, because the young lord with the bronzed eyelids had a rendezvous; and it may be that despite the cold there already leaned from the sculptured balcony of the little pointed tower shaped like a peppermill a worried young woman trying to distinguish in the whiteness of the plain the knight's plume.

Oluf on his massive horse, whose sides he had lacerated with his spurs, advanced across the plain; he crossed the lake which had been turned by the cold into a single block of ice in which the fish were encased, their fins extended like the veins in a block of marble; the horses's four iron shoes, studded with hooks, bit deeply into the hard surface; a fog, made of sweat and exhalations, enveloped and trailed after him; one would have said that he was galloping through a cloud; on both sides of their master, the two dogs, Murg and Fenris, like mythological animals, snorted long jets of steam through their bloody nostrils.

Here is the pine forest; like ghosts, the trees spread their heavily draped white arms. The weight of the snow bent those that were the youngest and most flexible. One would have thought that they formed a line of silver longbows. Dark terror lived in this forest where the rocks assumed the shapes of monsters, and in which each tree with its roots seemed to be hatching a nest of sluggish dragons at its feet. But Oluf knew no fear.

The path got narrower and narrower; the pines twined their grieving branches together inextricably; only rarely, a flash of lightning permitted one to see the chain of snowy hills which extended in white waves against the black and sorrowful sky.

Fortunately, Mopse was a vigorous steed who could have carried the gigantic Odin without sagging; no obstacle could stop him; he leaped over rocks and strode over ditches. From time to time his hooves striking the rocks under the snow sent up plumes of sparks that were immediately extinguished.

"Let's go, Mopse. There's a brave fellow. You've only to cross the small plain and then the birch forest. A pretty hand will caress your satin throat, and there, in a warm stable, you will eat blanched barely and a full measure of oats."

What a charming sight, that birch forest! All the branches seemed to be sheathed in icy white plush. The smallest twigs seemed to be sketched in white against the darkness. One might think they were an enormous filigree basket; or a coral made of silver; or a grotto with all of its stalactites; the network of designs and bizarre flowers with which the cold frosts windows could not be more complicated or more various.

"Lord Oluf, why are you so late? I was afraid that you might have been stopped on your way by a mountain bear. Or that the elves had invited you to dance," said the castelan's young daughter as she seated Oluf in the oak easy chair beside the fireplace. "But why have you brought a companion with you on a rendezvous of love? Were you then afraid of passing through the forest alone?"

"What companion are you talking about, flower of my soul?" said Oluf, surprised by what she had said.

"The knight of the red star whom you always bring with you. The one who was born with the look of the Bohemian bard. The baleful spirit who possesses you. Rid yourself of the knight with the red star or I will never listen to another of your words of love. I cannot be the wife of two men at the same time."

Nothing Oluf could say or do was any help. All he could accomplish was to kiss the rosy little finger of Brenda's hand. He went away very discontented, resolved to fight with the knight of the red star if he could but meet with him.

The next morning, despite the severe reception he had had from Brenda, Oluf took the road to the castle whose tower was shaped liked a pepper-mill. Those who are in love are not easily rebuffed.

As he rode on his way, he said to himself, "No doubt Brenda is mad. What does she mean by her 'knight of the red star'?"

The storm was one of the most violent kind. The whirling snow made it hard to distinguish the earth from the sky. Despite the barking of Fenris and Murg, who leaped into the air to seize them, a flock of ravens made a sinister spiral above the plume on Oluf's helmet. Leading the flock was the gleaming, jet black raven that had perched on the Bohemian bard's shoulder beating time.

Suddenly Fenris and Murg came to a stop. Their sensitive nostrils sniffed the air fearfully. They smelled the presence of an enemy. It was neither a wolf nor a fox. A wolf or a fox would have been no more than a mouthful to these brave dogs.

The sound of a footstep was heard and soon, in a bend in the road, there appeared a knight mounted on a huge horse. He was followed by two enormous dogs.

You would have taken him to be Oluf. He was armed in exactly the same way, with the same coat-of-arms emblazoned on his cuirasse. The only difference was that he wore a red plume on his helmet instead of a green one. The trail was so narrow that one of the two knights would have to back up.

"Lord Oluf, move back so I can pass," said the knight, who had his visor down. "I've been on a long voyage and am waited for. It's time I got there."

"By my father's mustache, it's you who will have to move back. I'm on my way to a lovers' meeting, and lovers are in a hurry," said Oluf, putting his hand to the hilt of his sword.

The unknown knight drew his sword and the battle began. The swords striking the chain mail sent up a shower of sparks. Though the swords were of high-tempered steel, it was not long before they were both as jagged as saws. The two combatants, seen through the steam made by their horses and by their own panting exhalations, might have seemed to be a couple of soot-covered blacksmiths laboring over the same forge. The horses, animated by the same frenzy as their masters, gnashed their teeth at the veins in each other's throats and slashed strands of hair from their chests. They made furious leaps, reared up on their hind legs and, using their hooves like clenched fists, they exchanged dreadful blows while their masters hammered frightfully at each other's heads. The dogs were transformed into a single bite; into a single howl.

Lukewarm drops of blood seeped across the overlapping scales of the armor and fell to the snow, where they made small pink holes. At the end of a very short while, the drops of blood fell so frequently that one thought of a sieve. The two knights had been wounded.

Strangely enough, Oluf had felt the blows he gave the unknown knight. He experienced those wounds as well as those he received. He felt a sharp cold in his chest like steel that had entered it searching for his heart, and yet his armor above his heart was undented. The only wound he received had been a cut on the flesh of his right arm. Strange duel in which the victor had suffered as much as the vanquished! In which there had been no difference between giving and receiving blows!

With a surge of strength, Oluf knocked his adversary's dreadful helmet off. Horrors! What was it that the son of Edwige and Lodbrog saw? It was himself he saw. A mirror could not have been more precise. He had been battling with his own apparition—with the knight of the red star. The apparition uttered a great cry and disappeared.

The spiral of ravens ascended to the sky and the brave Oluf continued on his way. When he returned to his castle that evening, he bore on the crupper of his saddle the young daughter of the manor who, this time, had been willing to hear what he had to say. Now that the knight of the red star was gone, she had allowed to let fall from her rosy lips and into Oluf's heart the confession that had cost her so many blushes. The night had been clear and blue. Meaning to show his fiancée to the double star, Oluf had looked up to find it, but there was only the green star there. The red one had disappeared.

As she came in, Brenda, overjoyed by that marvel—which she attributed to love—called young Oluf's attention to the fact that his eyes, which had been jet black, were now changed to blue, a sign of celestial reconciliation. At that, old Lodbrog, deep in his tomb, smiled a relieved smile under his white mustache because, to tell the truth, though he had never given any hint of it, Oluf's eyes had occasionally given him pause. Edwige's shade was very happy because the son of the noble Lord Lodbrog had finally overcome the malign influence of the bard with the bronze eyelids, of the black raven and the red star. The man had overthrown the incubus.

246

This story shows how a moment of forgetfulness, or a glance, however innocent, can be influential.

Young women, never cast your eyes on Bohemian bards who recite intoxicating and diabolical verses. You, young maidens, have faith in no star but the green one. And you, whose misfortune it is to be double, fight bravely though with your own sword you may have to strike at and wound yourself, the interior enemy, the wicked knight.

If you ask who brought us this legend from Norway, it was a swan: a lovely bird with a yellow beak that, half swimming, half flying, crossed the fjord.

Appendix C
Architectural Renderings of the Jekyll/Hyde House
by Glen Montag

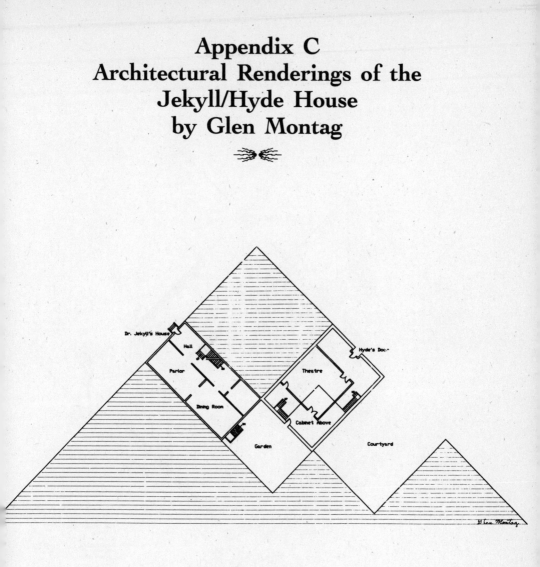

First Floor Plan

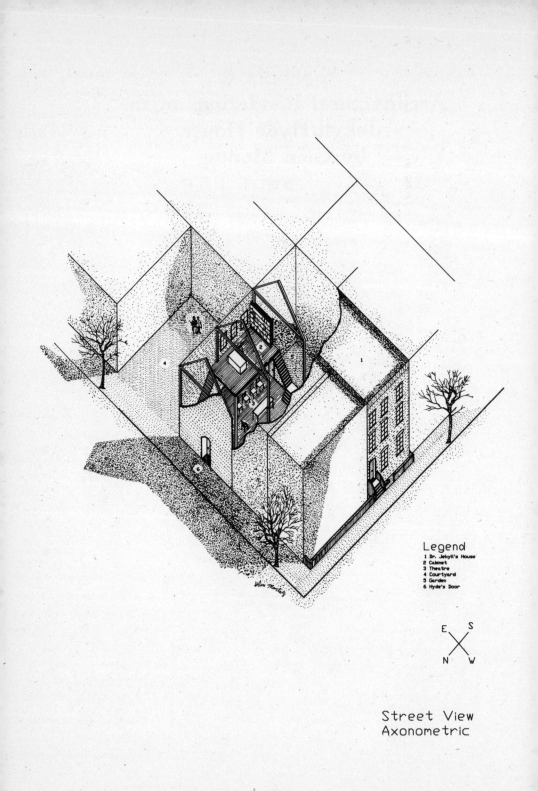

Legend
1 Dr. Jekyll's House
2 Cabinet
3 Theatre
4 Courtyard
5 Garden
6 Hyde's Door

Street View
Axonometric

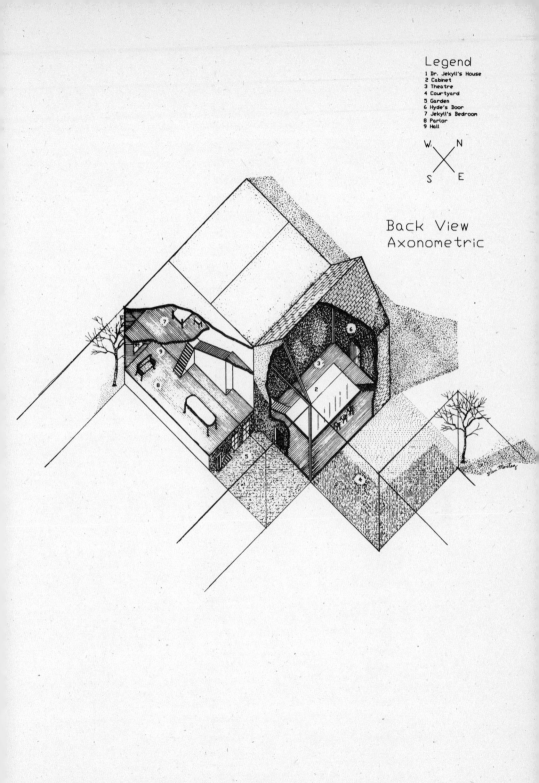

Legend
1 Dr. Jekyll's House
2 Cabinet
3 Theatre
4 Courtyard
5 Garden
6 Hyde's Door
7 Jekyll's Bedroom
8 Parlor
9 Hall

W   N
S   E

Back View
Axonometric

Appendix D
Calendar of Events

≫€

Note: X stands for the year when the story begins.

−10X		Lanyon and Jekyll part company over differences in their scientific points of view. Jekyll, presumably, is already pursuing his researches.
−1X		Jekyll's research is successful. Hyde is born. Notebook entries stop, p. 108. Hyde, then, is one year old at the time he stomps the little girl on a winter's night preceding the October in which the story begins.
X	October.	The story begins on a Sunday. Enfield tells his tale. That evening, Utterson reviews Jekyll's will, then goes to Lanyon's house (p. 44).
	October.	Some time later (frost in the air, p. 48). Utterson meets Hyde (p. 48–49).
	October.	That same night, Utterson talks to Poole, Jekyll's butler (p. 51–52).
	October.	Two weeks later, Jekyll gives a dinner. Utterson stays behind and discusses will with Jekyll (p. 56–57)
X + 10 months	August.	The last date, before the Carew murder, when Hyde's landlady has seen him (p. 66). It is on this day that Jekyll finds himself inadvertently transformed to Hyde in his own house on the square (p. 124–125).

	August to October.	Jekyll is "good" (p. 121). But he does not give up the Soho rooms and still keeps Hyde's clothes in his cabinet in the house on the square (p. 127).
X+1 year	October.	Jekyll takes the draft again (p. 127). His "devil came out roaring" (p. 128).
	October.	Sir Danvers Crew is murdered, 11 P.M. (p. 61–62). The maid servant witness faints and is unconscious for three hours. Hyde flees to the house in Soho (p. 63 and p. 128) where his landlady sees him briefly "very late" (p. 66).
	October.	Later that night. Hyde, having burned his papers in the Soho house, goes to the Jekyll house where, still exulting in the murder he has committed, he "pledged the dead man" as he drinks the transforming draft (p. 128). Transformed to Jekyll, he is instantly penitential and vows never to be Hyde again, and grinds the key to the side door underfoot (p. 129).
	October.	Early in the morning after the Carew murder, Carew's letter is brought to Utterson (p. 64). About nine in the morning, Utterson is taken to the police station, where he identifies Carew's body (p. 64).
	October.	Still the morning after the murder. Utterson and policeman visit Hyde's Soho rooms, find charred checkbook and half of murder weapon, and then visit Hyde's bank (p. 67).
	October.	Late that same afternoon. Utterson visits a pale and disordered Jekyll (p. 72).
	October.	That same evening. Utterson has wine with Guest, his chief clerk (p. 74). The signature on Jekyll's will is discussed. Utterson receives an invitation to dinner at Jekyll's (p. 75).
	October to January.	Jekyll is "good" (p. 129).
X + 1 year and 2 months	January, early.	The second month during which Jekyll has again been "good" comes to a close.
	January 8.	Jekyll gives a dinner party that includes Lanyon and Utterson (p. 80).
	January 9.	Hypocrite Jekyll, without recourse to the potion, feels the itch to a sin a little. "And it was as an ordinary secret sinner, that I at last fell before the assaults of

temptation." What sin or vice he committed, we do not know (p. 130). We do not know what sin or crime he committed that day, but as he is sitting in Regent's Park, as Jekyll, savoring its memory, he becomes, against his will, Hyde again (p. 131).

January 9. Terrified, Jekyll sends out letters from his hotel in Portland Street (p. 132).

January 9. Lanyon receives Jekyll's letter (misdated as December 10, p. 105–106). Lanyon does all he is told to do on that date.

January 9. Midnight. Hyde appears at Lanyon's house, drinks the potion and becomes Jekyll. Lanyon hears the story of Jekyll's transformation for the next hour, until:

January 10, Partly in a dream, Jekyll finds his way home (p. 133).
1:00 A.M.

January 10, After a good night's sleep, Jekyll after breakfast is without
morning. his will transformed to Hyde again. He takes a double dose to become Jekyll. Six hours later, the Hyde pangs begin again "and the drug had to be re-administered (p. 133).

January 10. From late that afternoon of January 10, the two characters are in constant flux (p. 133)

January 12. Utterson is turned away from Jekyll's door (p. 80). The number of the refusals is specified, but not their corresponding dates. To bring things into alignment, one has to assume that there was a refusal also on January 13. In which case, this is what we get:

Night one: January 12
Night two: January 13, the date also of "Doctor Lanyon's Narrative" (p. 105)
Night three: January 14
Night four: January 15
Night five: January 16, when Utterson had Guest in to dine (p. 80).
Night six: January 17, when Utterson "betook himself to Lanyon's" (p. 80).

January 17. Utterson goes to Lanyon and finds him ready to die (p. 80–81). Utterson writes complaining letter to Jekyll (p. 81).

January 18. Utterson gets Jekyll's reply begging Utterson to forgive him but asking him to stay away (p. 81).

January 25. "A week afterwards" (p. 82). Lanyon takes to his bed, and two weeks later, on or about February 6, he is dead (p. 82).

February 7.   The night after the funeral, we see Utterson holding, but
               not reading, Lanyon's papers (p. 82).

February to   Time goes by. Utterson does not visit Jekyll (p. 83).

March, early   Utterson and Enfield take a Sunday walk and talk with
               Jekyll from the courtyard. Jekyll has a Hyde seizure (p.
               86).

March, the   Poole shows up at Utterson's to say: "I've been afraid
middle of   for about a week," that is, from about the time of the
the month.   Utterson-Enfield conversation with Jekyll. Utterson and
               Poole go to Jekyll's house. They break into Jekyll's cabi-
               net and find the still twitching body of Edward Hyde.
               "Utterson knew that he was looking on the body of a
               self-destroyer" (p. 99). They find a large envelope ad-
               dressed to Utterson which contains "Henry Jekyll's Full
               Statement of the Case" (p. 102).

Appendix E
Contemporary Reviews

Andrew Lang, An Unsigned Review, *Saturday Review*

January 9, 1886

Mr. Stevenson's 'Prince Otto' was, no doubt, somewhat disappointing to many of his readers. They will be hard to please if they are disappointed in his 'Strange Case of Dr. Jekyll and Mr. Hyde.' To adopt a recent definition of some of Mr. Stevenson's tales, this little shilling work is like 'Poe with the addition of a moral sense.' Or perhaps to say that would be to ignore the fact that Poe was extremely fond of one kind of moral, of allegories in which embodied Conscience plays its part with terrible efficacy. The tale of William Wilson, and perhaps that of the Tell-Tale Hearts, are examples of Poe in this humour. Now Mr. Stevenson's narrative is not, of course, absolutely original in idea. Probably we shall never see a story that in germ is absolutely original. The very rare possible germinal conceptions of romance appear to have been picked up and appropriated by the very earliest masters of fiction. But the possible combinations and possible methods of treatment are infinite, and all depends on how the ideas are treated and combined.

Mr. Stevenson's idea, his secret (but a very open secret) is that of the double personality in every man. The mere conception is familiar enough.

257

Poe used it in William Wilson and Gautier in Le Chevalier Double. Yet Mr. Stevenson's originality of treatment remains none the less striking and astonishing. The double personality does not in his romance take the form of a personified conscience, the *doppel ganger* of the sinner, a 'double' like his own double which Goethe is fabled to have seen. No; the 'separable self' in this 'strange case' is all unlike that in William Wilson, and, with its unlikeness to its master, with its hideous caprices, and appalling vitality, and terrible power of growth and increase, is, to our thinking, a notion as novel as it is terrific. We would welcome a spectre, a ghoul, or even a vampire gladly, rather than meet Mr. Edward Hyde. Without telling the whole story, and to some extent spoiling the effect, we cannot explain the exact nature of the relations between Jekyll and Hyde, nor reveal the mode (itself, we think, original, though it depends on resources of pseudo-science) in which they were developed. Let it suffice to say that Jekyll's emotions when, as he sits wearily in the park, he finds that his hand is not his own hand, but another's; and that other moment when Utterson, the lawyer, is brought to Jekyll's door, and learns that his locked room is haunted by somewhat which moans and weeps; and, again, the process beheld by Dr. Lanyon, are all of them as terrible as anything ever dreamed of by Poe. They lack, too, that quality of merely earthly horror or of physical corruption and decay which Poe was apt to introduce so frequently and with such unpleasant and unholy enjoyment.

It is a proof of Mr. Stevenson's skill that he has chosen the scene for his wild 'Tragedy of a Body and a Soul,' as it might have been called, in the most ordinary and respectable quarters of London. His heroes (surely *this* is original) are all successful middle-aged professional men. No woman appears in the tale (as in 'Treasure Island', and we incline to think that Mr. Stevenson always does himself most justice in novels without a heroine. It may be regarded by some critics as a drawback to the tale that it inevitably disengages a powerful lesson in conduct. It is not a moral allegory, of course; but you cannot help reading the moral into it, and recognizing that, just as every one of us, according to Mr. Stevenson, travels through life with a donkey (as he himself did in the Cévennes), so every Jekyll among us is haunted by his own Hyde. But it would be most unfair to insist on this, as there is nothing a novel-reader hates more than to be done good to unawares. Nor has Mr. Stevenson, obviously, any didactic purpose. The moral of the tale is its natural soul, and no more separable from it than, in ordinary life, Hyde is separable from Jekyll.

While one is thrilled and possessed by the horror of the central fancy, one may fail, at first reading, to recognize the delicate and restrained skill of the treatment of accessories, details, and character. Mr. Utterson, for example, Jekyll's friend, is an admirable portrait, and might occupy a place unchallenged among pictures by the best masters of sober fiction.

At friendly meetings, and when the wine was to his taste, something eminently human beaconed from his eye; something indeed which never found its way into his talk; but which spoke not only in these silent symbols of the after-dinner face, but more often and loudly in the acts of his life. He was austere with himself, but tolerant to others, sometimes wondering, almost with envy, at the high pressure of spirits involved in their misdeeds.

It is fair to add that, while the style of the new romance is usually as plain as any style so full of compressed thought and incident can be, there is at least one passage in the threshold of the book where Mr. Stevenson yields to his old Tempter, 'preciousness.' Nay, we cannot restrain the fancy that, if the good and less good of Mr. Stevenson's literary personality could be divided like Dr. Jekyll's moral and physical personality, his literary Mr. Hyde would greatly resemble—the reader may fill in the blank at his own will. The idea is capable of development. Perhaps Canon McColl is Mr. Gladstone's Edward Hyde, a solution of historical problems which may be applauded by future generations. This is wandering from the topic in hand. It is pleasant to acknowledge that the half-page of 'preciousness' stands almost alone in this excellent and horrific and captivating romance, where Mr. Stevenson gives us of his very best and increases that debt of gratitude which we all owe him for so many and such rare pleasures.

There should be a limited edition of the 'Strange Case' on Large Paper. It looks lost in a shilling edition—the only 'bob'svorth,' as the cabman said when he took up Mr. Pickwick, which has real permanent literary merit.

E. T. Cook, Unsigned Notice, *Athenaeum*

January 16, 1886

Mr. R. L. Stevenson's proved ability in the invention of exciting stories is by no means at fault in his 'Strange Case of Dr. Jekyll and Mr. Hyde.' It is certainly a very strange case, and one which would be extremely difficult to see through from the beginning. It has also the first requisite of such a story—it is extremely clearly narrated, and it holds one's interest. It overshoots the mark, however, by being not merely strange, but impossible, and even absurd when the explanation is given. So good an artist in fanciful mysteries as Mr. Stevenson should have avoided the mistake of a lengthy rationalization at all. In the effective part of the story two points strike the reader as weak: the first incident which is meant to show the diabolical character of Mr. Hyde is inadequate, and the terms of Dr. Jekyll's will would have been inoperative. Mr. Stevenson has overlooked the fact that a man's will does not come into force until he is dead, and that the fact that he has not been heard of for three months would not enable his executor to carry out his testamentary directions.

James Ashcroft Noble, from a Review, *Academy*

January 23, 1886

'The Strange Case of Dr. Jekyll and Mr. Hyde' is not an orthodox three-volume novel; it is not even a one-volume novel of the ordinary type; it is simply a paper-covered shilling story, belonging, so far as external appearance goes, to a class of literature familiarity with which has bred in the minds of most readers a certain measure of contempt. Appearances, it has been once or twice remarked, are deceitful; and in this case they are very deceitful indeed, for, in spite of the paper cover and the popular price, Mr. Stevenson's story distances so unmistakably its three-volume and one-volume competitors, that its only fitting place is the place of honour. It is, indeed, many years since English fiction has been enriched by any work at once so weirdly imaginative in conception and so faultlessly ingenious in construction as this little tale, which can be read with ease in a couple of hours. Dr. Henry Jekyll is a medical man of high reputation, not only as regards his professional skill, but his general moral and social character; and this reputation is, in the main, well-deserved, for he has honourable instincts and high aspirations with which the greater part of his life of conduct is in harmony. He has also, however, 'a certain impatient gaiety of disposition,' which at times impels him to indulge in pleasures of a kind which, while they would bring to many men no sense of shame, and therefore no prompting to concealment, do bring to him such sense and such prompting, in virtue of their felt inconsistency with the visible tenor of his existence. The divorce between the two lives becomes so complete that he is haunted and tortured by the consciousness of a double identity which deprives each separate life of its full measure of satisfaction. It is at this point that he makes a wonderful discovery, which seems to cut triumphantly the knot of his perplexity. The discovery is of certain chemical

agents, the application of which can give the needed wholeness and homoge-
neity of individuality by destroying for a time all consciousness of one set
of conflicting impulses, so that when the experimenter pleases his lower
instincts can absorb his whole being, and, knowing nothing of restraint from
anything above them, manifest themselves in new and quite diabolical activi-
ties. But this is not all. The fateful drug acts with its strange transforming
power upon the body as well as the mind; for when the first dose has been
taken the unhappy victim finds that 'soul is form and doth the body make,'
and that his new nature, of evil all compact, has found for itself a corresponding environment, the shrunken shape and loathsome expression of
which bear no resemblance to the shape and expression of Dr. Jekyll. It is
this monster who appears in the world as Mr. Hyde, a monster whose play
is outrage and murder; but who, though known, can never be captured,
because when he is apparently tracked to the doctor's house, no one is
found there but the benevolent and highly honoured doctor himself. The
re-transformation has, of course, been effected by another dose of the drug;
but as time goes by Dr. Jekyll notices a curious and fateful change in its
operation. At first the dethronement of the higher nature has been difficult;
sometimes a double portion of the chemical agent has been found necessary
to bring about the result; but the lower nature gains a vitality of its own,
and at times the transformation from Jekyll to Hyde takes place without
any preceding act of volition. How the story ends I must not say. Too
much of it has already been told; but without something of such telling it
would have been impossible to write an intelligible review. And, indeed,
the story has a much larger and deeper interest than that belonging to a
mere skillful narrative. It is a marvellous exploration into the recesses of
human nature; and though it is more than possible that Mr. Stevenson
wrote with no ethical intent, its impressiveness as a parable is equal to its
fascination as a work of art. I do not ignore the many differences between
the genius of the author of 'The Scarlet Letter' and that of the author of
'Dr. Jekyll and Mr. Hyde' when I say that the latter story is worthy
of Hawthorne.

An Unsigned Review, *The Times*

January 25, 1886

Nothing Mr. Stevenson has written as yet has so strongly impressed us
with the versatility of his very original genius as this sparsely-printed little
shilling volume. From the business point of view we can only marvel in

these practical days at the lavish waste of admirable material, and what strikes us as a disproportionate expenditure on brain-power, in relation to the tangible results. Of two things, one. Either the story was a flash of intuitive psychological research, dashed off in a burst of inspiration; or else it is the product of the most elaborate forethought, fitting together all the parts of an intricate and inscrutable puzzle. The proof is, that every connoisseur who reads the story once, must certainly read it twice. He will read it the first time, passing from surprise to surprise, in a curiosity that keeps growing, because it is never satisfied. For the life of us, we cannot make out how such and such an incident can possibly be explained on grounds that are intelligible or in any way plausible. Yet all the time the seriousness of the tone assures us that explanations are forthcoming. In our impatience we are hurried towards the denouement, which accounts for everything upon strictly scientific grounds, though the science be the science of problematical futurity. Then, having drawn a sigh of relief at having found even a fantastically speculative issue from our embarrassments, we begin reflectively to call to mind how systematically the writer has been working towards it. Never for a moment, in the most startling situations, has he lost his grasp of the grand ground-facts of a wonderful and supernatural problem. Each apparently incredible or insignificant detail has been thoughtfully subordinated to his purpose. And if we say, after all, on a calm retrospect, that the strange case is absurdly and insanely improbable, Mr. Stevenson might answer in the words of Hamlet, that there are more things in heaven and in earth than are dreamed of in our philosophy. For we are still groping by doubtful lights on the dim limits of boundless investigation; and it is always possible that we may be on the brink of a new revelation as to the unforeseen resources of the medical art. And, at all events, the answer should suffice for the purposes of Mr. Stevenson's sensational *tour d'esprit.*

The 'Strange Case of Dr. Jekyll' is sensational enough in all conscience, and yet we do not promise it the wide popularity of 'Called Back.' The *brochure* that brought fame and profit to the late Mr. Fargus was pitched in a more commonplace key, and consequently appealed to more vulgar circles. But, for ourselves, we should many times sooner have the credit of 'Dr. Jekyll,' which appeals irresistibly to the most cultivated minds, and must be appreciated by the most competent critics. Naturally, we compare it with the sombre masterpieces of Poe, and we may say at once that Mr. Stevenson has gone far deeper. Poe embroidered richly in the gloomy grandeur of his imagination upon themes that were but too material, and not very novel—on the sinister destiny overshadowing a doomed family, on a living and breathing man kept prisoner in a coffin or vault, on the wild whirling of a human waif in the boiling eddies of the Maelstrom— while Mr. Stevenson evolves the ideas of his story from the world that is unseen, enveloping everything in weird mystery, till at last it pleases him to give us the password. We are not going to tell his strange story, though we might well do so, and only excite the curiosity of our readers. We shall only say that we are shown the shrewdest of lawyers hopelessly puzzled by the inexplicable conduct of a familiar friend. All the antecedents of a life of virtue and honour seem to be belied by the discreditable intimacy that has been formed with one of the most callous and atrocious of criminals. A crime committed under the eyes of a witness goes unavenged, though the notorious criminal has been identified, for he disappears as absolutely as if the earth had swallowed him. He reappears in due time where we should least expect to see him, and for some miserable days he leads a charmed life, while he excites the superstitious terrors of all about him. Indeed, the strongest nerves are shaken by stress of sinister circumstances, as well they may be, for the worthy Dr. Jekyll—the benevolent physician—has likewise vanished amid events that are enveloped in impalpable mysteries; nor can any one surmise what has become of him. So with overwrought feelings and conflicting anticipations we are brought to the end, where all is ac- counted for, more or less credibly.

Nor is it the mere charm of the story, strange as it is, which fascinates and thrills us. Mr. Stevenson is known for a master of style, and never has he shown his resources more remarkably than on this occasion. We do not mean that the book is written in excellent English—that must be a matter of course; but he has weighed his words and turned his sentences so as to sustain and excite throughout the sense of mystery and of horror. The mere artful use of an 'it' for a 'he' may go far in that respect, and Mr. Stevenson has carefully chosen his language and missed no opportunity. And if his style is good, his motive is better, and shows a higher order of genius. Slight as is the story, and supremely sensational, we remember nothing better since George Eliot's 'Romola' than this delineation of a feeble but kindly nature steadily and inevitably succumbing to the sinister influences of besetting weaknesses. With no formal preaching and without a touch of Pharisaism, he works out the essential power of Evil, which, with its malig- nant patience and unwearying perseverance, gains ground with each casual yielding to temptation, till the once well-meaning man may actually become a fiend, or at least wear the reflection of the fiend's image. But we have said enough to show our opinion of the book, which should be read as a finished study in the art of fantastic literature.

A Parody of *Dr. Jekyll and Mr. Hyde, Punch*

February 6, 1886

THE STRANGE CASE OF DR. T. AND MR. H.
Or Two Single Gentlemen rolled into one.

CHAPTER I.——*Story of the Bore.*

Mr. STUTTERSON, the lawyer, was a man of a rugged countenance, that was never lighted by a smile, not even when he saw a little old creature in clothes much too large for him, come round the corner of a street and trample a small boy nearly to death. The little old creature would have rushed away, when an angry crowd surrounded him, and tried to kill him. But he suddenly disappeared into a house that did not belong to him, and gave the crowd a cheque with a name upon it that cannot be divulged until the very last chapter of this interesting narrative. Then the crowd allowed the little old creature to go away.

'Let us never refer to the subject again,' said Mr. STUTTERSON.

'With all my heart,' replied the entire human race, escaping from his button-holding propensities.

CHAPTER II.——*Mr. Hidanseek is found in the Vague Murder Case.*

Mr. STUTTERSON thought he would look up his medical friends. He was not only a bore, but a stingy one. He called upon the Surgeons when they were dining, and generally managed to obtain an entrance with the soup. 'You here!' cried Dr. ONION, chuckling. 'Don't speak to me about TREKYL——he is a fool, an ass, a dolt, a humbug, and my oldest friend.'

'You think he is too scientific, and makes very many extraordinary experiments,' said STUTTERSON, disposing of the fish, two *entrées* and the joint.

'Precisely,' replied ONION, chuckling more than ever——'as you will find out in the last Chapter. And now, as you have cleared the table, hadn't you better go?'

'Certainly,' returned the Lawyer, departing (by the way, *not* returning), and he went to visit Mr. HIDANSEEK. He found that individual, and asked to see his face.

'Why not?' answered the little old creature in the baggy clothes, defiantly. 'Don't you recognise me?'

'Mr. R. L. STEVENSON says I mustn't,' was the wary response; 'for, if I did, I should spoil the last chapter.'

Shortly after this Mr. HIDANSEEK, being asked the way by a Baronet out for a midnight stroll, immediately hacked his interrogator to pieces with a heavy umbrella. Mr. STUTTERSON therefore called upon Dr. TREKYL, to ask for an explanation.

'Wait a moment,' said that eminent physician, retiring to an inner apartment, where he wrote the following note:—

'Please, Sir, I didn't do it.'

'TREKYL forge for a murderer!' exclaimed STUTTERSON; and his blood ran cold in his veins.

CHAPTER III.—*And any quantity of Chapters to make your flesh creep.*

And so it turned out that TREKYL made a will, which contained a strange provision that, if he disappeared, HIDANSEEK was to have all his property. Then Dr. ONION went mad with terror, because, after some whiskey-and-water, he fancied that his old friend TREKYL had turned into the tracked and hunted murderer, HIDANSEEK.

'Was it the whiskey?' asked STUTTERSON.

'Wait until the end!' cried the poor medical man, and, with a loud shriek, he slipped out of his coat, leaving the button-hole in the bore's hand, and died!

CHAPTER THE LAST.—*The Wind-up.*

I am writing this—I, TREKYL, the man who signed the cheque for HIDANSEEK in Chapter I., and wrote the forged letter a little later on. I hope you are all puzzled. I had no fixed idea how it would end when I began, and I trust you will see your way clearer through the mystery than I do, when you have come to the imprint.

As you may have gathered from ONION's calling me 'a humbug, & c., &c.,' I was very fond of scientific experiments. I was. And I found one day, that I, TREKYL, had a great deal of sugar in my composition. By using powdered acidulated drops I discovered that I could change myself into somebody else. It was very sweet!

So I divided myself into two, and thought of a number of things. I thought how pleasant it would be to have no conscience, and be a regular bad one, or, as the vulgar call it, bad 'un. I swallowed the acidulated drops, and in a moment I became a little old creature, with an acquired taste for trampling out children's brains, and hacking to death (with an umbrella) midnight Baronets who had lost their way. I had a grand time of it! It was all the grander, because I found that by substituting sugar for the drops I could again become the famous doctor, whose chief employment was to give Mr. STUTTERSON all my dinner. So much bad had been divided into the acidulated HIDANSEEK that I hadn't enough left in the sugary TREKYL to protest against the bore's importunities.

Well, that acidulated fool HIDANSEEK got into serious trouble, and I wanted to cut him. But I couldn't; when I had divided myself into him one day, I found it impossible to get the right sort of sugar to bring me back again. For the right sort of sugar was adulterated, and adulterated sugar cannot be obtained in London!

And now, after piecing all this together, if you can't see the whole thing at a glance, I am very sorry for you, and can help you no further. The fact is, I have got to the end of my '141 pages for a shilling.' I might have made myself into four or five people instead of two,—who are quite enough for the money.

F. W. H. Myers, Criticism and Proposed Revisions of *Jekyll and Hyde*, from Letters to Stevenson

Myers to Stevenson, from a letter dated February 21, 1886

My dear Sir,

We have a common friend in Mr. J. A. Symonds, who has often spoke of you to me—and I have often wished that I might have the pleasure of meeting you. The present letter is called forth by the extreme admiration with which I have read and reread your 'Strange Case of Dr. Jekyll and Mr. Hyde.' I should be afraid to say how high this story seems to me to stand among imaginative productions; and I cannot but hope that it may take a place in our literature as permanent as 'Robinson Crusoe'.

But, owing part to the brevity which forms one of the book's merits, partly perhaps to a certain speed in its composition which also reflects itself—especially in the style, there are certain points which I think that you might expand or alter with advantage; and which are well worth the slight trouble involved. These are specially on pages [1st edition]

37 Nature of crime.

52 Handwriting.

56 Change in Dr. Lanyon.

83 Condition of room.

103 Metamorphosis in Dr. L's presence.

111 Nature of Metamorphosis.

127 Same as p. 37.

131 Omission of precaution.

137 Relationship of consciousness; reason for fear of apprehension.

I think that I would select pp. 121, 138 as instances of a mastery of language and imagination which it would be hard to parallel in fiction.

I do not know whether you will care to receive any of these suggestions which have occurred to me. But I venture to say that [it] is primarily as the author of this work that you will be known to posterity, and that pains spent on perfecting it will be well repaid. If pushed, I will explain the suggestions which I have thought of. . . .

Yours sincerely,
Frederick W. H. Myers

Pages (dated February 27, 1886) enclosed in a letter from Myers to Stevenson dated February 28, 1886

NOTES ON 'DR. JEKYLL AND MR. HYDE'
[*pages from 1st edition*]

p.6 Quite admirable. Some foolish review (I believe) missed this altogether and saw his act as not sufficiently criminal.

9 After 'in my chambers' are not a few words like '—a grisly time—' needed? One has rather too vague an idea of the group. A word or two as to Hyde's demeanour would be valuable.

19 Admirable!

22–26 Admirable!

33 *Admirable!*

35–38 This is the weakest point, to my mind. The cruelty developed from *lust* surely never becomes of just the same quality as the cruelty developed from mere madness and savagery. Hyde would, I think, have simply brushed the baronet aside with a curse, and run on to some long-planned crime. The ground is ticklish, but could you not hint at a projected outrage (not on the baronet) hurried into dangerous haste by his having been long away from Soho and not made the usual preparations? Page 6 is the key-note. If you think it needful to avoid a female victim it might be a policeman or some relation of a tacitly-understood victim. No real temptation to make body of baronet jump on roadway (p. 37). Jekyll was thoroughly civilized, and his degeneration must needs take certain lines only. Have you not sometimes thought of incarnate *evil* rather too vaguely? Hyde is really not a generalized but a specialized fiend. Minor objections. 1) Ambiguity as to house where maid was. Was it in Westminster? How did Baronet need to ask way to post close to Parliament or to his own house? If house is meant to be in a low district how did Baronet come there? 2) Why did Hyde leave the stick? Excitement too *maniacal* to make us thoroughly enter into Hyde.

39–40 Admirable!

42 One would like to hear more of this house. Would Jekyll have sent a picture there? Would he not have concealed the house from his servants? If picture wanted you might try one or two small Jan Steens which he could have taken in a cab.

43 'Other half of stick' Why not thrown away?

45 No obvious reason why Jekyll receives Utterson in *theatre*. (Not important, as he *must* be made to do so, and *need not* give explicit reason.)

52 Here I think you miss a point for want of familiarity with recent psycho-physical discussions. Handwriting in cases of double personality (spontaneous . . . or induced, as in hypnotic cases) *is not* and *cannot be* the same in the two personalities. Hyde's writing might look like Jekyll's done *with the left hand*, or done when partly drunk, or ill that is the kind of resemblance there might be. Your imagination can make a good point of this.

56 The effect of shock in Dr. Lanyon might be more specified. At present it seems rather *unreal*. It *might* induce diabetes, if there were previous kidney weakness. Could some slight allusion be made to this on p. 57?

62–65 *Admirable!*

74 Admirable!

83 Surely not a true point—tidiness of room. When had the housemaid been in? Who had removed cinders from under grate? Surely coals were left at door and only the empty coal scuttle put out. Who washed cups? Sugar in tea-cup p. 86 seems to me a false point. Neither J. nor H. would prepare in that minute way for comfort.

99–100 Excellent.

102 Objections to this page stated later: on page 131.

103 Two objections. (1) Style too elevated for Hyde. (Of this further on p. 138.) These are not remarks that fit the husky broken voice of Hyde—they are Jekyllian. Surely Hyde's admirable style (p. 24) should be retained for him. (2) He would have been more unwilling to show the transformation. Lanyon should show, I think, more resolve (hint at pistol?) to make him do it.

106–110 Excellent.

111 I suppose the agent must be a drug. But the description of the process surely needs more substance and novelty. For one thing, there must have been a loss of consciousness. (This point admirable when we come to the spontaneous reversions into Hyde during sleep.) The first time the loss of consciousness might last for some hours.

112 *Admirable*—but I think there should be more physical exhaustion the first time. Then he might revive himself by wine placed nearby: his new body would be specially sensitive to stimulants. You perhaps purposely make *few* (but admirable) points as to the new body.

114 Excellent! excellent!

115 The return to Jekyll should surely be more insisted on—the doubt whether possible, and doubt whether taking drug again might not be *fatal*. A little more too about subsequent shrinkings from the pain etc.—overcome by restless impulse. I don't understand the phrase 'kept awake by ambition.' I thought the stimulus was a different one.

116 We should understand already that he hadn't yet conquered his aversion. Surely the motive for the change was this. And, by the way, I think that it might somewhere be hinted that Jekyll was a good deal more licentious in early life than he avows. I don't want him to be prematurely aged but might there not be something more of flabbiness in his portliness? And some hint of his desiring *variety*? And a word or two more of Utterson's? Or a *thought* of Utterson's? How had Jekyll come across the housekeeper whom he placed in Soho? (What led you to specify Greek street?)

118 Excellent, but needs expansion. 'They soon began to turn towards the monstrous' is almost the only hint in the book of the process by which the thoroughly sympathetic and gently apolaustic Jekyll becomes the ruffianly Hyde. This is one of the great moral nodes of the book, and while I thoroughly admire your rapidity of manner and absence of didactic preoccupation, I nevertheless feel that this is a point on which Jekyll's memory would have dwelt: which he would have insisted on. He would not have liked that his friends should think that he had *fiendish* qualities in him at all to begin with: he would rather have laid all that on the continually expanding desires and insatiable enterprise of Hyde— 'That insatiability which is attached to inordinate desires as their bitterest punishment.'

120 'Sloping my own hand backward': see on p. 52. (Note that Hyde would have to make great effort to simulate Jekyll's signature—be long about it—signature would look odd, but unmistakably Jekyll's.)

121 *This is genius.*

123 Excellent! But correspondinly Jekyll's body should have got flabbier. See also p. 55 where Jekyll, I think, regains vigour and cheerfulness far too rapidly. There should be something deprecative rather than complacent about him after the murder.

124 An admirable page but 'begun to pamper' might be stronger and we here also begin to note a slight uncertainty in the psychical relationship of the two personalities. Here Hyde is (bandit simile) hardly at all Jekyll; later on (and on p. 120) he is much more Jekyll and see p. 103.

127 Here I again feel a false note. See on p. 36, 'mauled the unresisting body'—no, not an elderly MP's!

129 'the hands of all men would be raised:' Surely the one servant maid and his few acquaintances were not so dangerous. Hyde might have escaped from England easily enough. Why does Jekyll not think of a trip to Brussels?

131 An admirable page! But here one asks why, after the metamorphosis in bed, take the risk of separation from the drug? At any time even before the spontaneous metamorphosis it might have been extremely desirable to change back into Jekyll. If the drug was portable and manageable anywhere he would likely have taken it with him:—and after the murder certainly. Can you suppose that a Bunsen burner or some means of producing intense heat was necessary to effect a chemical combination? Or an electrical machine (which Lanyon also might possess) to assist change of body?

136–138 Genius!

138 But Hyde was in very little danger. Who could identify him? Probably almost any acquaintance that he had could have been bought off. And what chance of their seeing him if he went to an unfamiliar quarter of London? Or why does he not think of Paris or New York? For he is now so psychically separate from Jekyll (and I think something should be said as to growing psychical separation, if you determine to take that line)—he would surely have thought 'I will give up the Jekyll life, which can't really be retained, and will start fresh in New York.' (Even Liverpool would have tempted him, if you say that he was not enough for New York.)

141 How would it be if Jekyll committed suicide and we were left to infer, from the finding of Hyde's body, that the death-agony had so transformed him?

My dear Sir,—I know not how to thank you: this is as handsome as it is clever. With almost every word I agree—much of it I even knew before— much of it, I must confess, would never have been, if I had been able to do what I like, and lay the thing by for the matter of a year. But the wheels of Byles the Butcher drive exceeding swiftly, and 'Jekyll' was con- ceived, written, re-written, re-re-written, and printed inside ten weeks. Nothing but this white-hot haste would explain the gross error of Hyde's speech at Lanyon's. Your point about the specialised fiend is more subtle, but not less just: I had not seen it.—About the picture, I rather meant that Hyde had brought it himself; and Utterson's hypothesis of the gift (p. 42) an error.—The tidiness of the room, I thought, but I dare say my psychology is here too ingenious to be sound, was due to the dread weariness and horror of the imprisonment. Something has to be done: he would tidy the room. But I dare say it is false.

I shall keep your paper; and if ever my works come to be collected, I will put my back into these suggestions. In the meanwhile, I do truly lack words in which to express my sense of gratitude for the trouble you have taken. The receipt of such a paper is more than a reward for my labours. I have read it with pleasure, and as I say, I hope to use it with profit.— Believe me, your most obliged,

Robert Louis Stevenson.

Additional notes from Myers to Stevenson, dated March 17, 1886

FURTHER MEDITATIONS ON THE CHARACTER
OF THE LATE MR. HYDE

'We could have better spared a better man'
I. Would Hyde have brought a picture? I think—and friends of weight support my view—that such an act would have been altogether unworthy of him. What are the motives which would prompt a person in his situation to that act?
1. There are jaded voluptuaries who seek in a special class of art a substitute or reinforcement for the default of primary stimuli. Mr. Hyde's whole career forbids us to insult him by classing him with these men.
2. There are those who wish for elegant surroundings to allure or overawe the minds of certain persons unaccustomed to luxury or splendour. But

does not all that we know of Mr. Hyde teach us that he disdained these modes of adventitious attractions? When he is first presented to us as 'stumping along eastward at a good walk' (I have mislaid my copy and must quote from memory) does not this imply the gait of one who aimed at energy but not at grace? And when we read that he was 'very plainly dressed,' don't we know that his means were such that he might have permitted himself without extravagance an elegant costume,—does not this show us the man aiming only at simple convenience, direct sufficiency? not anxious to present himself as personally attractive to others, but relying frankly on a cash nexus, and on that decision of character which would startle—almost terrify into compliance in cases where the blandishments of the irresolute might have been lavished in vain?

3. There are those, again, who surround their more concentrated enjoyments with a halo of mixed estheticism; who even if blameably adventurous in action are gently artistic in repose. Such, no doubt, was Dr. Jekyll: such, no doubt, he *expected* that Mr. Hyde would be. But was he not deceived? Was there not something unlooked for, something Napoleonic, in Hyde's way of pushing aside the aesthetic as well as the moral superfluities of life? Between the conception of some lawless design and its execution do we suppose that Jekyll himself could look at his pictures with tranquil pleasure? Did not his inward state 'suffer with the likeness of an insurrection'? And was not Hyde's permanent state this stabler and intenser reproduction of such absorbed and critical moments in Jekyll's inward history? We do not imagine the young Napoleon as going to concerts or taking a walk in a garden. We imagine him as now plunged in gloomy torpor, now warmly planning crimes to be. I cannot fancy Hyde looking in at picture shops. I cannot think that he ever even left his rooms, except on business. And in these rooms I fancy that there would be a certain look as of lower tenancy supervening on a high-class outfit; a certain admixture of ill-chosen with handsome things; an unhomelike bareness along with provision for ready ease.

II. I have thought of how you could alter the murder with least trouble. Perhaps it might do if the servant maid looked out of the window when the murderous assault had just begun and mentions that there was no one else in the street except 'a shabbily dressed johnny just a-scampering around the street corner.' The girl need never appear again; but Jekyll might speak of the Baronet as having interfered to baulk what (in his way of speaking of Hyde) he would probably call 'an enterprise too hastily conceived.'

III. A very small point. I think that the housekeeper says 'What's he been doing?' If 'now' were added, it might imply that in her view he had already been fortunate in escaping the interference of the Law.

IV. A criticism of Mr. Gladstone's (to whom my sister-in-law took the book while he was forming a ministry which is now, I hope, splitting up more irretrievably than Dr. Jekyll's personality) may introduce my next suggestion. He said that while he much admired and enjoyed the book, he felt that the ethical retransference of Hyde into Jekyll was made too easy a thing;—that he could not fancy so profound and sudden a *backward* change. This, as you perceive, bears out what I ventured to hint as to the progressive effect which the repeated changes must needs operate on the Jekyllian phase. And it suggests, I think, the need of dealing with the subject of community of memory. At first I think such community would be very imperfect; gradually the two memories would fuse into one; and in the last stage you might make an effective contrast of the increasing *fusion* of the two personalities in all except ethical temper, joined with the increasing revulsion in all except ethical temper, joined with the increasing revulsion of Jekyll against the ethical temper of Hyde; a revulsion maintained, no doubt, at great cost of nervous exhaustion—like the prolonged attention needed down an ice-slope which gets steeper and steeper; till the suicide (of Jekyll in my view, not of Hyde) would represent the kind of despairing spring with which the thoroughly exhausted climber leaps to a point where he could not in his right senses have expected to find foothold, misses and falls.

F. W. Myers.

Myers to Stevenson, letter dated April 17, 1887

My dear Sir,

I do not want to be importunate, but I cannot but help reminding you that time is going on, and your masterpiece remains (so far as I know) without that final revision, the possible lack of which would be a real misfortune to English literature. The works, even of the most fertile and brilliant authors, which can hope for *permanent* preservation must needs be few. Is it not well worth while to make them as perfect as possible? I have heard the views of many other persons on 'Dr. Jekyll and Mr. Hyde' since I last wrote. I have not found any competent person who does not think it your best work, or who did not also feel it contained obvious, and removable, blots.

I will not trouble you with further words; but may I add how perfectly I admire the story called The Merry Men,

I remain, etc.

F. W. H. Myers.

Julia Wedgwood, Notice, *Contemporary Review*

April 1886

By far the most remarkable work we have to notice this time is 'The Strange Case of Dr. Jekyll and Mr. Hyde,' a shilling story, which the reader devours in an hour, but to which he may return again and again, to study a profound allegory and admire a model of style. It is a perfectly original production; it recalls, indeed, the work of Hawthorne, but this is by kindred power, not by imitative workmanship. We will not do so much injustice to any possible reader of this weird tale as to describe its *motif*, but we blunt no curiosity in saying that its motto might have been the sentence of a Latin father—'Omnis anima et rea et testis est.' Mr. Stevenson has set before himself the psychical problem of Hawthorne's 'Transformation,' viewed from a different and perhaps an opposite point of view, and has dealt with it with more vigour if with less grace. Here it is not the child of Nature who becomes manly by experience of sin, but a fully-developed man who goes through a different form of the process, and if the delineation is less associated with beautiful imagery, the parable is deeper, and, we would venture to add, truer. Mr. Stevenson represents the individualizing influence of modern democracy in its more concentrated from. Whereas most fiction deals with the relation between man and woman (and the very fact that its scope is so much narrowed is a sign of the atomic character of our modern thought), the author of this strange tale takes an even narrower range, and sets himself to investigate the meaning of the word *self*. No woman's name occurs in the book, no romance is even suggested in it; it depends on the interest of an idea; but so powerfully is this interest worked out that the reader feels that the same material might have been spun out to cover double the space, and still have struck him as condensed and close-knit workmanship. It is one of those rare fictions which make one understand the value of temperance in art. If this tribute appears exaggerated, it is at least the estimate of one who began Mr. Stevenson's story with a prejudice against it, arising from a recent perusal of its predecessor, his strangely dull and tasteless 'Prince Otto.' It is a psychological curiosity that the same man should have written both, and if they were bound up together, the volume would form the most striking illustration of a warning necessary for others besides the critic—the warning to judge no man by any single utterance, how complete soever.

From an Unsigned Review, "Secret Sin," *Rock*

April 2, 1886

A very remarkable book has lately been published, which has already passed through a second edition, called 'Strange Case of Dr. Jekyll and Mr. Hyde'. . . . It is an allegory based on the two-fold nature of man, a truth taught us by the Apostle PAUL in Romans vii., 'I find then a law that, when I would do good, evil is present with me.' We have for some time wanted to review this little book, but we have refrained from so doing till the season of Lent had come, as the whole question of temptation is so much more appropriately considered at this period of the Christian year, when the thoughts of so many are directed to the temptations of our Lord.

Our readers, however, must not understand us to mean that this is a religious book. The name of CHRIST we do not remember to have seen, and the name of GOD, we think, only appears once. As for texts, or quotations from the Word of GOD, such are conspicuous by their absence. Nevertheless, the book is calculated to do a great deal of good, not only to those who profess and call themselves Christians, but to those who are, in every sense of the word, true believers. Though there is nothing distinctively Christian about it, we hope none will suppose that we mean to imply that there is anything antagonistic to Christianity. The truth taught us by the Apostle, to which we have referred above, is one recognised by those outside Christian Churches. Every thoughtful Hindoo, Mahommedan, Buddhist, or Parsee recognises the fact of the dual nature of his composition— the higher and the lower. Among the heathen in all ages have ever been found some who, like one well-known classical writer, confessed that he approved of that which is good, though he followed that which was evil.

In the allegory with which we are dealing we are introduced to a Dr. JEKYLL, who was a well-to-do medical man of a very respectable type, pleasant and genial, but somewhat weak and yielding. Of the best of men it can always be said that there is about them an element of evil, whereas with the worst of men there is, if we can only discover it, an element of good—doubtless a relic of primitive man 'made in the image of God' before the fall of our ancestors. Dr. JEKYLL is no exception to the general rule, and he finds that mixed up with much that was good there was in his character a certain amount of evil. He discovers a medicine which is capable of separating his two natures into two distinct identities. By taking one dose he completely throws off all traces of his better self, and his lower nature asserts itself without any of the constraining influences of his higher nature being left. Not only was this the case with regard to his moral nature, but even his very appearance became so changed that no one could possibly recognise him. Consequently he assumes another name when the evil nature predominated, and called himself Mr. HYDE. Even the worst of men have something good in them, and consequently they do not appear to us so repulsive as Mr. HYDE, who had not a single trace of the better nature.

The allegory is good. How many men live out two distinct characters? To the outer world they are the honourable, upright men, with a good professional name, holding a respectable position in society, looked up to and spoken well of by all their neighbours. Within, however, the inner sanctum of their own hearts they are conscious of another self, a very different character. So far this is more or less common to all. It is a result of the Fall of Man that we have ever present a lower nature struggling to get the mastery. So conscious was the Apostle of this second self that he cried out, 'O wretched man that I am! Who shall deliver me from the body of this death?' The metaphor here, is, doubtless, borrowed from an ancient cruel custom of binding together a living captive with a corpse. The dead body must of necessity be repugnant to the living man, and to the living Christian the very existence of the lower nature must be abhorrent. Unfortunately, however some act the part played by Dr. JEKYLL. They live the respectable life 'to be seen of men,' and then, when away from the public gaze, they give way to the lower nature. Our SAVIOUR says of them, 'For every one that doeth evil hateth the light, neither cometh to the light, lest his deeds should be reproved.'

There are two strange scenes brought before us in the allegory. The first is, Mr. HYDE trampling over the body of a child in the street, treading down, as it were, innocence. In the second scene, Mr. HYDE commits a murder. Both scenes take place at night, both bring a penalty. The first one was comparatively easily atoned for, as the child, no thanks to Mr. HYDE, was not permanently injured. The second scene, however, results in a price being set on the head of the murderer, which finally leads to his committing suicide. Immediately after the crime of murder, however, Mr. HYDE takes his dose of chemicals, and he becomes again Dr. JEKYLL, the respectable member of a scientific profession, about the last man in town to be suspected of such a crime. We need hardly say that, though no one could recognise in Dr. JEKYLL the foul villain who had trampled down innocence and committed a murder, his memory was keenly alive and his sorrow was intense. In the words of the author 'the pangs of transformation' had not done tearing him, before HENRY JEKYLL, with streaming tears of gratitude and remorse, had fallen upon his knees and lifted his clasped hands to GOD. The veil of self-indulgence was rent from head to foot, 'I saw my life as a whole; I followed it up from the days of childhood, when I walked with my father's hand, and through the self-denying toils of my professional life, to arrive again and again, with the same sense of unreality, at the damned horrors of the evening. I could have screamed aloud; I sought with tears and prayers to smother down the crowd of hideous images and sounds with which my memory swarmed against me; and still, into my soul. . . . But I was still cursed with my duality of purpose, and, as the first edge of my penitence wore off, the lower side of me, so long indulged, so recently chained down, began to growl for licence. Not that I dreamt of resuscitating HYDE, the bare idea of that would startle me to frenzy; no, it was in my own person that I was once more tempted to trifle with my conscience, and it was as an *ordinary secret sinner* that I at last fell before the assults of temptation.

We regret that our limited space prevents us going more into the details of the book which we are considering. The most thrilling part is that in which Dr. JEKYLL, to his horror, discovers that from having so frequently assumed the form of Mr. HYDE, that nature gradually begins to assert itself in him. To such an extent is this the case that, though he retires to rest at night as Dr. JEKYLL, he finds that when he wakes up in the morning he is Mr. HYDE. At first this discovery does not trouble him so much, as a dose of his chemicals effects a transformation back again. But, by degrees, he finds that from frequent interchange of character the chemicals lose their power. He doubles the strength of the ingredients, but all to no avail. The better man has gone, the lower and the viler nature gains the ascendancy. Mr. HYDE is the murderer—he, if discovered, will be hanged—so that the conviction grows on his mind that the day of reckoning is coming, the penalty will, sooner or later, have to be paid. After a very graphic description of the appalling horrors of his position, we find Dr. JEKYLL has disappeared, but that Mr. HYDE has taken his place and, with a view to escape his impending fate, dies by his own hand.

How many there may be who will read this book, and, if they rightly understand it, will recall the words of NATHAN the prophet to DAVID the King, 'Thou art the man.' At first they trifle with their lower nature, always conscious that they can, at any time, reassume their better self. By degrees, however, the unfortunate victim finds that he is losing his better self, and that the lower nature acquires more and more power. The jovial man does not mean to become a drunkard, though he yields now and then in secret. The man whose passions are strong has no intentions of becoming a sensualist, though he, too, gives way to the fascinating power of temptation. The fashionable lady of the world does not mean to become insincere, though she, too, with a view of pleasing those around her, does not always strictly adhere to the path of truth. We might enumerate many other different forms of sin. But enough: *ex une omne discit*. The appalling truth bursts on the victim that the will, which once was so powerful, has lost its strength, and that the lower nature, which every one should seek to bring into subjection, has gained the ascendancy. That which has hitherto been done in secret is at last proclaimed upon the house-tops; all restraints are thrown aside. May GOD grant that this book may be a warning to many who are trifling with sin, unconscious of its awful power to drag them down to the lowest depths of hell. We need hardly say even to the most guilty, even to those who have sunk lowest, that we believe that there is a Divine power in CHRIST to enable us to become more than conquerors through Him that loved us, and washed us in His own most precious blood.

Gerard Manley Hopkins in Defense of *Treasure Island* and *Jekyll and Hyde*, from a Letter to Robert Bridges

October 28, 1886

. . . I have at much length remonstrated with Canon Dixon for slighting Wordsworth's Ode on the Intimations, at which he might have taken offence but on the contrary he took it with his usual sweetness; and I beg you will with my remonstrances with you about Barnes and Stephenson; of both of whom, but especially S., you speak with a sourness which tinges your judgment. . . .

I have not read 'Treasure Island'. When I do, as I hope to, I will bear your criticisms in mind. . . . Nevertheless I mean to deal with two of these criticisms now, for it is easy to do so on the face of them.

One is that a boy capable of a brave deed would be incapable of writing it down—well *that* boy. Granting this, still to make him tell it is no fault or a trifling one. And the criticism, which ignores a common convention of romance or literature in general, is surely then some 'αγροικία [boorishness] on your part. Autobiography in fiction is commonly held a hazardous thing and few are thought to have succeeded in it on any great scale: Thackeray in 'Esmond' is I believe held for one of the exceptions. It is one of the things which 'O Lord, sir, we must connive at.' The reader is somehow to be informed of the facts. And in any case the fault is removable without convulsing the structure of the whole: like a bellglass or glass frame over cucumbers or flowers it may be taken off, cleansed, and replaced without touching them. So this criticism I look on as trifling.

The other criticism is the discovery of a fault of plot about the whereabouts of some schooner: I take your word for it. One blot is no great matter, I mean not a damning matter. One blot may be found in the works of very learned clerks indeed. 'Measure for Measure' is a lovely piece of work, but it was a blot, as Swinburne raving was overheard for hours to say, to make Isabella marry the old Duke. 'Volpone' is one of the richest and most powerful plays ever written, but a writer in a late 'Academy' points out a fault of construction (want of motive, I think, for Bonario's being at Volpone's house when Celia was brought there); it will stand that one fault. True you will say that in Stevenson's book there are many such: but I do not altogether believe there are.

This sour severity blinds you to his great genius. 'Jekyll and Hyde' I have read. You speak of the 'gross absurdity' of the interchange. Enough that it is impossible and might perhaps have been a little better masked: it must be connived at, and it gives rise to a fine situation. It is not more impossible than fairies, giants, heathen gods, and lots of things that literature teems with—and none more than yours. You are certainly wrong about Hyde being overdrawn: my Hyde is worse. The trampling scene is perhaps a convention: he was thinking of something unsuitable for fiction.

I can by no means grant that the characters are not characterised, though how deep the springs of their surface action are I am not yet clear. But the superficial touches of character are admirable: how can you be so blind as not to see them? e.g. Utterson frowning, biting the end of his finger, and saying to the butler 'This is a strange tale you tell me, my man, a very strange tale.' And Dr. Lanyon: 'I used to like it, sir [life];

280

yes, sir, I liked it. Sometimes I think if we knew all' etc. These are worthy of Shakespeare. Have you read the Pavilion on the Links in the volume of 'Arabian Nights' (not one of them)? The absconding banker is admirably characterised, the horror is nature itself, and the whole piece is genius from beginning to end.

In my judgment the amount of gift and genius which goes into novels in the English literature of this generation is perhaps not much inferior to what made the Elizabethan drama, and unhappily it is in great part wasted. How admirable are Blackmore and Hardy! Their merits are much eclipsed by the overdone reputations of the Evans—Eliot—Lewis—Cross woman (poor creature! one ought not to speak slightingly, I know), half real power, half imposition. Do you know the bonfire scenes in the 'Return of the Native' and still better the sword-exercise scene in the 'Madding Crowd,' breathing of epic? or the wife-sale in the 'Mayor of Casterbridge' (read by chance)? But these writers only rise to their great strokes; they do not write continuously well: now Stevenson is master of a consummate style, and each phrase is finished as in poetry. It will not do at all, your treatment of him.

Appendix F
Filmography and Theatrical Listings
of *Dr. Jekyll and Mr. Hyde*
compiled by Nancy C. Hanger

⋙⋘

    This film and television compilation reflects films that either are based firmly on the Stevenson Jekyll and Hyde story or have their main storyline from Stevenson's imagery. If we had listed all films with a Jekyll and Hyde-like nature, our list here would be endless: we have limited our scope here to horror (and, in one case, a comedy), which not only has a "split nature" theme, but owes its story in some part to Stevenson's original. Although we have tried to be thorough in our compilation here, we apologize for any omissions, however inadvertent.

    [Based on information from Magill's survey of Cinema (online edition from Dialog); *Timeout Film Guide*, 2nd ed. (Tom Milne, ed., Penguin Books, 1991); and the kind folks on the SFRT on GEnie and the ShowBiz Forum on the CompuServe Information Service.]

Scene from *Dr. Jekyll & Mr. Hyde* (1920).

1920
Dr. Jekyll & Mr. Hyde
b&w film, 7 reels (USA)
Starring John Barrymore
Produced by Famous Players-Lasky
Screenplay by Clara Beranger (based on Stevenson)
Directed by John S. Robertson

1932
Dr. Jekyll & Mr. Hyde
b&w film, 90 min., Paramount (USA)
Starring Fredric March [Oscar winner]
Screenplay by Samuel Hoffman & Percy Heath (based on Stevenson)
Produced and directed by Rouben Mamoulian

1941
Dr. Jekyll & Mr. Hyde
b&w film, 127 min., MGM (USA)
Starring Spencer Tracy

Produced by Victor Saville
Screenplay by John Lee Mahin (based on Stevenson)
Directed by Victor Fleming

1953
Abbott & Costello Meet Dr. Jekyll & Mr. Hyde
b&w film, 76 min., Universal (USA)
Starring Bud Abbott, Lou Costello, and Boris Karloff
Produced by Howard Christie
Screenplay by Lee Loeb & John Grant, based on stories by Sidney Fields &
Grant Garrett
Directed by Charles Lamont

1955
Climax!
b&w TV series (USA)
Starring Michael Rennie

Publicity still from *Dr. Jekyll & Mr. Hyde* (1932).

1957
Dr. Jekyll & Mr. Hyde
Matinee Theater TV show (USA)
Starring Douglas Montgomery

1958
Grip of the Strangler (or, *The Haunted Strangler*)
b&w film, 79 min., (UK)
Starring Boris Karloff
Screenplay uncredited (based on Stevenson)
Directed by Robert Day

1960
The Two Faces of Dr. Jekyll
color film, 88 min., Columbia (UK)
Starring Paul Massie
Produced by Michael Carreras
Screenplay by Wolf Mankowitz (based on Stevenson)
Directed by Terence Fisher

1961
House of Fright
color film, 80 min., American International Pictures (USA)
American release of *The Two Faces of Dr. Jekyll*

1963
The Nutty Professor
color film, 107 min., Paramount (USA)
Starring and directed by Jerry Lewis
Produced by Ernest D. Glucksman
Written by Jerry Lewis & Bill Richmond

1968
The Strange Case of Dr. Jekyll & Mr. Hyde
TV movie (Canada)
Starring Jack Palance
Directed by Dan Curtis

Publicity still from *Dr. Jekyll & Sister Hyde* (1970)

1970
I, Monster
color film, 75 min., Cannon Films (USA)
[produced in 3D but released in 2D]
Starring Christopher Lee
Produced by Max J. Rosenburg & Milton Subotsky
Written by Milton Subotsky
Directed by Stephen Weeks

Dr. Jekyll & Sister Hyde
color film, 97 min., Hammer Films (U.K.)
Starring Ralph Bates and Martine Beswick
Produced by Albert Fennell & Brian Clemens
Written by Brian Clemens
Directed by Roy Ward Baker

1971
Dr. Jekyll y el Hombre Lobo (or *Dr. Jekyll and the Wolfman*)
b&w film, International Cinema Films (Spain)
Starring Paul Naschy

Produced by José Frade
Directed by Leon Limovsky

1972
Dr. Jekyll & Mr. Blood (or the Man with Two Heads)
color film, 80 min., Mishkin Films (UK)
Starring Denis de Marne
Produced by William Mishkin
Written and directed by Andy Milligan

1973
Dr. Jekyll & Mr. Hyde
color TV movie musical (USA)
Starring Kirk Douglas

1976
Dr. Black & Mr. Hyde (or The Watts Monster; originally *Dr. Black & Mr. White)*
color film, Dimension (USA)
Starring Bernie Casey
Produced by Charles Walker
Directed by William Crain

1980
Dr. Heckyll and Mr. Hype
color film, 99 min., Cannon Films (USA)
Starring Oliver Reed
Produced by Menahem Golan & Yorma Globus
Written and directed by Charles B. Griffith

1981
Docteur Jekyll et les Femmes (or The Blood of Dr. Jekyll, or Doctor Jekyll and Miss Osbourne)
color film, 92 min. (France)
Starring Udo Kier
Directed by Walerian Borowczyk

1982
Dr. Jekyll's Dungeon of Death
color film, New American (USA)

Starring and written by James Mathers
Produced and directed by James Woods

Jekyll & Hyde . . . Together Again
color film, 87 min. (USA)
Starring Mark Blankfield
Directed by Jerry Belson

1989
Dr. Jekyll & Mr. Hyde
color TV movie (USA)
Starring Anthony Andrews
Written by J. Michael Straczynski

Edge of Sanity
color film, 90 min., Millimeter Films (UK/Hungary)
Starring Anthony Perkins
Produced by Edward Simons & Harry Alan Towers
Screenplay by J. P. Felix & Ron Raley (based on Stevenson)
Directed by Gerard Kikoine

1990
Jekyll & Hyde
color TV movie, 100 min. (USA/UK)
Starring Michael Caine
Written and directed by David Wickes

Appendix G
Bibliography

෩෪

Abbot, Richard. *Dr. Jekyll and Mr. Hyde: A Play in Three Acts.* New York: n.p., 1941.

Adcock, A. St. J., ed. *Robert Louis Stevenson—His Work and His Personality.* London: Hodder & Stoughton, 1924.

Aldington, Richard. *Portrait of a Rebel: Robert Louis Stevenson.* London: Evans, 1957.

Anobile, Richard J., ed. *Rouben Mamoulian's "Dr. Jekyll and Mr. Hyde."* New York: Universe Books, 1975.

Baildon, H. B. *Robert Louis Stevenson.* London: Chatto & Windus, 1901.

Balfour, Graham. *The Life of Robert Louis Stevenson.* 2 vols. London: Methuen, 1901.

Beer, Thomas. *The Mauve Decade: American Life at the End of the Nineteenth Century.* New York: Alfred A. Knopf, 1926.

Bell, Ian. *Dreams of Exile: Robert Louis Stevenson; a Biography.* New York: Henry Holt, 1991.

Bell, Ian, ed. *Robert Louis Stevenson: The Complete Short Stories,* 2 vols. New York: Henry Holt and Company, 1994.

Berman, Barbara L. "The Strange Case of Dr. Jekyll & Mr. Hyde." In *Survey of Modern Literature,* ed. Frank N. Magill, 4:1834–39. Englewood Cliffs, N.J.: Salem Press, 1983.

Berman, Richard A. *Home from the Sea.* New York: Bobbs-Merrill, 1939.

Brewer, E. Cobham, *The Dictionary of Phrase and Fable*, Classic Edition. New York: Avenel, 1978.

Buckley, Jerome Hamilton. *William Ernest Henley.* Princeton: Princeton University Press, 1945.

Calder, Jenni. *Robert L. Stevenson: A Critical Celebration.* Totowa, N.J.: Barnes and Noble, 1980.

————. *R. L. S.: A Life Study.* New York: Oxford University Press, 1980.

Chesterton, G. K. *Robert Louis Stevenson.* London: Hodder and Stoughton, 1927; New York: Dodd, Mead, 1928.

Colvin, Sir Sidney. *Memories and Notes of Persons and Places, 1852–1912.* London: Arnold, 1921.

————. *The Works of Robert Louis Stevenson.* New York: Charles Scribner's Sons, 1925.

Connell, John. *W. E. Henley.* London: Constable, 1949.

Daiches, David. *Robert Louis Stevenson.* Norwalk, Conn.: New Directions, 1947.

————. *Robert Louis Stevenson and His World.* London: Thames & Hudson, 1973.

Eigner, Edwin M. "The Double in the Fiction of Robert Louis Stevenson." Unpublished doctoral dissertation, State University of Iowa, 1963.

————. *Robert Louis Stevenson and the Romantic Tradition.* Princeton, N.J.: Princeton University Press, 1966.

Ellison, Joseph W. *Tusitala of the South Seas: The Story of Robert Louis Stevenson's Life in the South Pacific.* New York: Hastings House, 1953.

Ferguson, Delancey, and Marshall Waingrow, eds. *RLS: Stevenson's Letters to Charles Baxter.* New Haven: Yale University Press, 1956.

Field, Isobel Osbourne Strong. *This Life I've Loved.* London: Michael Joseph, 1937.

Fraustino, Daniel V. "Dr. Jekyll and Mr. Hyde: Anatomy of Misperception." *Arizona Quarterly* 38 (1982): 235–40.

Furnas, J. C. *Anatomy of Paradise.* London: Gollancz, 1950.

————. *Voyage to Windward: The Life of Robert Louis Stevenson.* New York: William Sloane Associates, 1952.

Geduld, Harry M., ed. *The Definitive Dr. Jekyll and Mr. Hyde Companion.* New York: Garland Publishing, 1983.

Gilbert, W. S. *Plays and Poems of W. S. Gilbert.* New York: Random House, 1932.

Good, Graham. "Rereading Robert Louis Stevenson." *Dalhousie Review* 62 (1982): 44–59.

Gosse, Edmund. *Robert Louis Stevenson, His Work and Personality*. London: Hodder & Stoughton, 1924.

Guerard, Albert J. "Concepts of the Double." In *Stories of the Double*, ed. by Albert J. Guerard. Philadelphia: J. B. Lippincott, 1967.

Hart, James D., ed. *From Scotland to Silverado, Robert Louis Stevenson*. Cambridge: Harvard University Press, 1966.

Harvie, Christopher. "The Politics of Stevenson." In *Stevenson and Victorian Scotland*, edited by Jenny Calder. Edinburgh: Edinburgh University Press, 1981.

Heath, Stephen. "Psychopathia Sexualis: Stevenson's Strange Case." *Critical Quarterly* 28 (1986): 93–108.

Hellman, George S. "R.L.S. and the Streetwalker." *American Mercury*, July, 1936.

Herdman, John. *The Double in Nineteenth-century Fiction*. Basingstoke, Hampshire: Macmillan Press, 1990.

———. "Stevenson and Henry James." *Century*, December 1992.

Hinkley, Laura L. *The Stevensons:* Louis and Fanny. New York: Hastings House, 1950.

Henessy, John–Pope. *Robert Louis Stevenson*. Simon and Schuster, 1974.

James, Henry. *Partial Portraits*. London: Macmillan, 1888.

———. "Robert Louis Stevenson." *In Maixner,* 290–311.

Kiely, Robert. *Robert Louis Stevenson and the Fiction of Adventure*. Cambridge, Mass.: Harvard University Press, 1964.

Limedorfer, Eugene. "The Manuscript of Dr. Jekyll and Mr. Hyde." *Bookman* 12 (1900): 52–58; reprinted in Geduld, 99–102.

Low, Will H. *A Chronicle of Friendships, 1873–1900*. London: Hodder & Stoughton, 1908.

Mackay, Margaret. *The Violent Friend*. Garden City, N.Y.: Doubleday, 1969.

Maixner, Paul, ed. *Robert Louis Stevenson: The Critical Heritage*. London: Routledge and Kegan Paul, 1981.

Miller, Karl. *Doubles: Studies in Literary History*. New York: Oxford University Press, 1985.

Nabokov, Vladimir. "The Strange Case of Dr. Jekyll and Mr. Hyde (1885)." In *Lectures on Literature*, edited by Fredson Bowers, 179–205. New York: Harcourt Brace Jovanovich, 1980.

Noble, Andrew. *Robert Louis Stevenson*. London: Vision Press and Barnes and Noble, 1983.

Osbourne, Katherine Durham. *Robert Louis Stevenson in California*. Chicago: A. C. McClurge, 1911.

Osbourne, Lloyd. *An Intimate Portrait of R.L.S.* New York: Charles Scribner's Sons, 1924.

Pope-Hennessy, James. *Robert Louis Stevenson*. New York: Simon and Schuster, 1974.

Prawer, S. S. "Book into Film: *Dr. Jekyll and Mr. Hyde.*" *Times Literary Supplement*. December 21, 1979, 161–64.

Sanchez, Nellie Van de Grift. *The Life of Mrs. Robert Louis Stevenson*. London: Chatto & Windus, 1920.

Saposnik, Irving S. *Robert Louis Stevenson*. New York: Twayne, 1974.

Simpson, Eve Blantyre. *Robert Louis Stevenson's Edinburgh Days*. London: Hodder & Stoughton, 1914.

Smith, Ralph. "Jekyll and Hyde and Victorian Science Fiction." *Sphinx* 4 (1975): 62–70.

Stevenson, Fanny Van de Grift. *Cruise of the Janet Nichol among the South Sea Islands, A Diary*. London: Chatto & Windus, 1915.

———. *Letters to Charles Baxter*. London: Oxford University Press, 1956.

Stevenson, Robert Louis. *The Castaways of Soledad*. Buffalo, N.Y.: Privately printed, 1928.

———. *Dr. Jekyll and Mr. Hyde; Island Night's Entertainment; The Merry Men; and Other Stories*. London: Collins, 1958.

———. *The Strange Case of Dr. Jekyll and Mr. Hyde*. Lincoln: University of Nebraska Press, 1990.

———. *The Complete Short Stories, "The Centenary Edition."* New York: Henry Holt and Company, 1994.

Stone, Donald David. *Novelists in a Changing World*. Cambridge: Harvard University Press, 1972.

Swearingen, Roger C. *The Prose Writings of Robert Louis Stevenson*. Hamden, Connecticut: Archon Books, 1980.

Swinnerton, Frank. *Robert Louis Stevenson*. New York: George H. Doran, n.d.

Trent, William P., ed. *Stevenson's Workshop*. Boston: Bibliophile Society, 1921.

Twitchell, James B. *Dreadful Pleasures*. New York: Oxford University Press, 1985.

Tymms, Ralph. *Doubles in Literary Psychology*. Cambridge: Bowes and Bowes, 1949.

Veeder, William, and Gordon Hirsch. *Dr. Jekyll and Mr. Hyde after One Hundred Years*. Chicago: University of Chicago Press, 1988.

Welsch, Jamice R. "The Horrific and the Tragic." In *The English Novel and the Movies*, edited and introduced by Micheal Klein and Gillian Parker, 165–79. New York: Ungar, 1981.

Wolf, Leonard, ed. *The Essential Frankenstein: The Complete Annotated Edition of Mary Shelley's Classic Novel*. New York: Plume, 1993.

Zaic, Franz. "Robert Louis Stevenson: The Strange Case of Dr. Jekyll and Mr. Hyde." In *Der Englische Roman im 19 Jahrhundert: Interpretationen. Zu Ehren von Horst Oppel,* eds., Paul Goetsch, Heinz Kosok, and Kurt Otten, eds., 243–52. Berlin: E. Schmidt, 1973.

ABOUT LEONARD WOLF

Leonard Wolf's works on terror literature and film include *A Dream of Dracula* (1972), *The Annotated Dracula* (1974), *The Annotated Frankenstein* (1976), *Monsters* (for children, 1974), *Wolf's Complete Book of Terror* (1979), and *Horror: A Connoisseur's Guide to Literature and Film* (1989). His most recent books in the genre are *The Essential Dracula* and *The Essential Frankenstein* (both Plume, 1993). Wolf served as historical and critical consultant to Francis Ford Coppola's film *Bram Stoker's Dracula* and Kenneth Branagh's movie *Mary Shelley's Frankenstein*.

Wolf has spent most of his adult life as a writer of poetry, fiction, social history and biography, and as a professor of English, teaching Chaucer and Creative Writing. His poetry and fiction have appeared in *The Kenyon Review*, *The Atlantic*, *Harper's*, *The New York Yorker*, *The Yale Review* and other magazines. He has been an O. Henry Fiction Award winner and, for his work in the horror genre, has twice received the Ann Radcliffe Award for Literature.

He is the author of a wide range of books. The *New York Times* said of his *Voices of the Love Generation* (1968), a social history of the hippy movement, that it "humanizes the subject. His observations . . . constitute some of the clearest and most level-headed commentary currently available." His book *The Passion of Israel* (1970) is a graphic account of a euphoric and tragic year in Israel's history. His *Bluebeard: The Life and Crimes of Gilles de Rais* (1980), a biography of perhaps the worst serial killer in history, has been called "the most important contribution to the problem of evil since Hannah Arendt's *Eichmann in Jerusalem*." *The False Messiah* (1984), a historical novel about Shabbatai Tsvi, a messianic figure of the seventeenth century whose brief career shook and nearly shattered the Jewish communities in Europe and the Turkish Empire in the middle of the seventeenth century, was praised by the *New York Times* for its "graphic recreation of Shabbatai's world."

Wolf is, according to Irving Howe, the finest translator of Yiddish literature in America. He has published translations from the work of most of this century's greatest Yiddish poets. The publishers of Isaac Bashevis Singer have chosen Leonard Wolf to write the Nobel Prize-winning author's biography.

The National Foundation for Jewish Culture commissioned Wolf's verse play, *Queen Esther*. Two scary plays for children, *Dracula's School for Vampires* and *Frankenstein the Thirteenth*, were commissioned by The San Francisco Children's Theatre (1986 and 1987) and were performed in San Francisco, New York, and Providence. Frank Langella has called *Dracula's School for Vampires* "marvelous entertainment for children and grown-ups alike."

Leonard Wolf's most recent novel is *The Glass Mountain* (1993). Forthcoming from Plume Books is Wolf's *The Essential Phantom of the Opera*.